CARDINAL WHISPERS

A DARK, BULLY, REVERSE HAREM ROMANCE

LISA CULLEN

© Copyright 2024, by Author Lisa Cullen .

All Rights Reserved.

No part of this publication may be reproduced, distributed or transmitted in any form or by any means including photocopying, recording, or other electronic or mechanical methods except in the case of brief quotations embodied in critical reviews and certain other non commercial uses permitted by copyright law. Unauthorised reproduction or distribution of this work is illegal.

This book is a work of fiction. Names, characters, businesses, places, events, and incidents are either the products of author's imagination or used in a fictitious manner. Any resemblance to actual persons, living or dead, is purely coincidental.

This book is intended for adult readers only. Any sexual activity portrayed in these pages occurs between consenting adults over the age of 18 who are not related by blood.

ALSO BY LISA CULLEN

Check out my entire catalogue available on KindleUnlimited.

The Forbidden Reverse Harem Collection

Boss Daddies | Good Girl | A Nanny for Christmas | Brother's Best Friends for Christmas | Christmas with Daddy's Best Friends | Lie No More | Thin Ice | Cardinal Whispers | Stepping Up

The Bratva

Season of Malice | Season of Desire | Season of Wrath

Sinister Alliances

Unlikely Protector | Unlikely Avenger

DESCRIPTION

Their terms are simple: become their toy, or else...

What do you do when the Crimson Blades come after you? Not agree to be their plaything, that's for sure.

But it's the only way to live under their cruel rule. I'm here to change this town, and if I have to play along with the three brothers to make a change in Caspian Springs, I will.

Even if it costs me my sanity.

Bastian Ravenwood is the leader of the Crimson Blades. Not only does he rule Caspian Springs with an iron fist, he's determined to rule me as well.

Dominic, the oldest of the three brothers, is the enforcer of the trio. His quiet demeanor could be mistaken for coldness, but I know just how heated he gets when I'm around...

Caleb may be the youngest, but he's sharp as hell and always comforts me. Except now I'm wishing I'd get more than a kiss on the cheek and a warm hug.

CARDINAL WHISPERS is a full-length, dark romance with a why choose theme.
Trigger warnings include dubious consent, violence and mentions of suicide.

1

SIENNA

"**G**ood afternoon!" I call out, waving to a man standing on the corner, a smile on my face. "May I have a moment of your time?"

"Fuck off," he drawls, taking a deep hit of his vape before ambling off.

I puff my cheeks, letting out a slow breath. I guess I should have expected that.

Walking down the street, I spot another potential participant. A lanky man is standing outside of the local Quik-Mart and I stop, smoothing my hands down my skirt. "Hello! Do you think I could have just a moment of your time?" I ask.

"What the hell you want?" the man asks. He's got a buzz cut and a scorpion tattoo around his neck, and his eyes narrow as I step closer. "You some kind of religious freak?"

He scans me up and down and my smile falls under the scrutiny. I can see how he might think that. My outfit probably doesn't help his impression—I've got on a white turtleneck under a plaid jumper and tights, and I'm holding a clipboard.

"Actually, I'm here to do some research for a study that's being conducted on this community!" I say, my mouth curving back up into a smile. "Would you mind if I interviewed you? It would only take five minutes."

He rolls his eyes before shaking his head. "Sorry. I ain't got time to help you with your school project, kid."

"It's not a school project," I protest, my voice carrying a hint of frustration. "It's important research into urban health."

The man ignores me before taking off, getting into a low-rider that pulls up to the curb in front of us.

I stare down at my clipboard, biting my lip. Why won't anyone talk to me? If I could just get one person to agree to an interview, I know I can get the ball rolling from there.

Stepping into the fluorescent-lit corner store, I approach the worn-out cash register where a woman with greasy black hair and dark circles is manning the counter with a dead look in her eyes.

"Hello," I say, mustering up the courage to speak to her. "My name is Sienna Bennett. I'm a researcher working on a project about urban resilience. Do you have a few minutes for a short interview?"

The woman stares at me, almost as though staring right through me. "I'm from Beaumont Falls," I say, referring to a small town a few hours' drive away. "I know what it's like to grow up in a neighborhood like this. I just want to help make things better. If I could just get five minutes of your time …"

"I ain't interested," the woman says, finally looking at me. Her cheeks are sunken and she looks as though she hasn't had a hot shower in days. "Besides, you don't got permission from the Blades."

I blink, trying to understand her. "I'm sorry. Who?"

"The Blades, girly. Crimson Blades? They run this place. Nothing happens without their say-so. You want anyone round here to help you, you gotta get their go-ahead first."

My brain tries to catch up. "Are they like … a gang or something?"

"You deaf or some shit? The Crimson Blades aren't a gang. Told you, they're the leaders of this town."

"Well, who are they? Can you point them out? If I could just talk to them, maybe they can help me get my research going," I plead.

She shakes her head, glancing out the window from the corner of her eye. "Sorry, can't help you."

I knew going into this project that I was going to face some resistance. Growing up in a town similar to Caspian Springs, I realize that community members can be a little fearful of, or hostile to outsiders, but I didn't realize that it would take so much work to get even one person to agree.

"I'm just going to grab a soda then," I tell her. She shrugs and I head to the cooler in the back, spotting a curly-haired little boy playing in the chip aisle. I smile at him before grabbing a Coke and heading back to the front to pay.

As I'm walking outside with my soda, a little boy follows me. "Hey!" he calls out. "Hey, Miss!"

I turn, the boy giving me a gap-toothed grin. "Can you buy me a bag of Takis?" he asks.

That gets a laugh out of me. "How about this? You give me a little bit of your time, answer a couple of questions for my research project, and I'll buy you the chips," I offer.

"Deal," he holds his hand out and I take it, shaking it firmly. Turning around, I head back inside as he trails behind me and picks out the bag of chips.

We head outside once again, into the afternoon sun and he walks me down the street to a small lot with a couple of picnic tables and a rusty jungle gym. It would be generous to call this place a park.

We sit down at one of the picnic tables together.

"So what do you wanna ask me then, Miss?" the boy asks, pulling the bag open and stuffing a chip into his mouth.

"Can you tell me your name?" I ask, flipping the first page over on my clipboard to jot it down.

"I'm Beau Brant. I'm eight years old and I go to Caspian Springs Elementary," he recites, around his mouthful of food.

"Thank you, Beau."

He shrugs and licks salty seasoning off his fingers.

"My name is Sienna Bennett," I tell him. "I was hired to work for Dr. Richard Thornton. He's a psychologist and researcher over at

Watford University. Dr. Thornton is trying to study people who live in towns like these, to understand what it's like for them. He does it by interviewing them and getting their stories."

"Are you a doctor too?" he asks, tilting his head.

I chuckle. "No, not yet. I'm just a lowly research assistant. He has a bunch of people like me going around to some of the towns nearby, to talk to people. You're the first person today who's let me talk to them for more than five minutes."

"Probably cuz the Crimson Blades don't like outsiders," he says.

"I see. Who are the Crimson Blades?" I ask, trying to get more info out of him. "Can they help me with my project?"

"They're like, the bosses," Beau informs me. "They tell people what to do and stuff."

"And what happens if someone doesn't do what they say?"

Beau shrugs. "I don't know."

I refrain from rolling my eyes. "Well, they aren't here and you can see that they aren't saying that you can't talk to me, right?"

His eyes dart around for a moment before nodding slowly. "Okay. What are the questions?"

I scan down the list. These are just pre-qualifiers—questions to see if people fit the parameters of our study. "What grade are you in?" I ask, choosing from the second column of questions.

Beau starts answering the questions I have and I write down what he says, checking off the criteria that he fits.

"Thank you so much for your help," I tell him as soon as we're done. "If you'd be interested in participating, and your parent or guardian will allow it, I can pay you if you are willing to sit down for a longer interview." I start reading off our disclaimer. "Your participation is not mandatory. Your name will be anonymous, along with identifying information you give me."

"What's anonymous?" Beau asks.

"Means we'll keep your identity private," I tell him, looking up at him again with a smile. "If people read Dr. Thornton's book that he's going to write with the information, they won't be able to find you."

He pouts. "So I won't be famous?"

That gets a laugh out of me. "Nope, sorry," I apologize. "But you'll help other doctors like Dr. Thornton, who can show his research to politicians and lawmakers and use it to make improvements to communities like this one."

His eyes light up. "What kind of improvements?"

"Better education, maybe, and better community help. Lots of things. And maybe one day I'll be one of those doctors," I add. "I don't get to work directly with Dr. Thornton yet, but I hope that if I do a good job I'll get to study under him."

Beau nods. "You're still gonna have to get permission from the Blades," he tells me. "But yeah, if they're okay with it, I'll do another interview."

"Great!" I grab my bag and pull out my wallet. "Here's my card. If you have any questions or anything, that's my phone number. You or your parents can reach out any time."

He pockets it. "See ya." Slipping off the picnic bench, he takes off down the road and I glance back over the info he'd given me.

At least this was a step in the right direction. I'd spent all day here and Beau was the only interview I'd gotten. The sun was starting to dip below the horizon and I figured that was my cue to head back to my crappy motel room and work on compiling these notes.

The only cars in the parking lot when I return are a rusty pickup and a Charger. I double-check to make sure no one has been following me before unlocking my room and heading inside.

Just as I get my laptop set up though, my stomach gives a rumble. I haven't eaten since breakfast and walked around the neighborhood all day. There's a diner on the far side of the motel, so I figure I can grab a quick bite before returning to work.

The diner, bathed in a warm glow, hums with the low murmur of conversation between a few truckers and the clinking of cutlery against ceramic plates. A cranky, old waitress approaches, silently ushering me over to a slightly sticky table.

"Can I just get the burger," I ask. She rolls her eyes before leaving to put in my order.

There's a commotion at the door and I glance over, spotting three men walking inside. Their gazes sweep the place before landing on me.

My eyes widen and I watch them stride towards me. The one in front has striking blue eyes and a steely look that makes my stomach flip. The two flanking him look as though they could be his brothers, with the same sharp, chiseled jawlines and the same sloping nose.

They walk with confidence, taking up all the space around them as they move.

The three men stop at my table, standing over me. The one in front, ostensibly their leader, leans in. "I don't know what you think you're doing here, *Princess*," he drawls. "But this is our neighborhood."

These must be the Crimson Blades everyone was talking about. "I'm here to do work," I tell them. "That's all."

His eyes bore into mine. "We don't know who you are, or what you want," he growls, his voice laced with warning. "But if you know what's good for you, you'll leave."

A nervous gulp catches in my throat as their imposing figures loom over me, thick tension in the air.

2

CALEB

"The Serpents are getting restless again," Dominic says as he knocks the cue into the balls on the table. "Heard from Hutch that they approached him yesterday."

The back room of Dave's Bar is glowing under neon signs, the quiet hum of conversation from the other room blending with the clink of the billiard balls. The scent of stale cigarette smoke lingers in the air as my brothers stand around the worn table.

I keep an eye on them from my seat at a nearby booth. I'm an observer tonight, content to sit on the sidelines as I work on a new logo for our bike shop.

A flicker of concern creeps into my mind. Serpents sniffing around is never a good thing but sightings of them have increased lately. My mind races, wondering if there's more going on than we know about.

"What did they say?" Bastian demands, echoing my own thoughts. "What were they after?"

"Hutch said they asked him a bunch of questions," Dom replies, not taking his eyes off the balls as they bounce around. "Asked if he was interested in making some easy money, if there were any complaints with how we run things, that sort of shit."

"Don't understand why they're suddenly everywhere lately." Bastian grumbles as he leans against his cue to wait for his turn. "We haven't had to deal with their shit in years."

"We can deal with it," Dominic reassures him, sinking the three-ball into the corner pocket. "They're trying to intimidate us though. I wouldn't worry. They know we run this place."

Dominic's easy dismissal of the Serpent Syndicate does little to quell the unease inside me. It's only when I see a few mentions of vague incidents on Nextdoor that I relax. "There's not much chatter online," I tell my brothers. "A few complaints about harassing people here and there but not much else."

"I'm not worried," Bastian says, leaning over the table. "But if they don't stop trying to make trouble, they're going to learn why the Crimson Blades run this place."

Bastian always worries easily. After everything we've been through, I don't blame him. He tries to look out for us, even taking up the mantle of leader of the Blades.

"The bike shop's new logo is done," I say, trying to change the subject. "What do you guys think?" I turn my laptop around and the two of them saunter over, leaning in to see.

"That looks weird," Dominic frowns. "What's that supposed to be?"

Bastian rolls his eyes, pointing at the screen. "It's vintage, you dumbass." He turns to me "I like it," he adds, ruffling my hair.

I shove his hand away. There's only two years between each of us, but they treat me like I'm much younger sometimes. "Quit it. And yes, it's supposed to look vintage. Like those old ads from the 50s and 60s."

"Do you really think a new logo is going to help the shop?" Dominic asks. "I mean, we're barely scraping by already."

"I think the new logo can't hurt," Bastian says, reaching out to grab his beer and taking a swig. "We need to do something to stand out."

"It's because no one is riding bikes anymore," Dominic points out, plucking his own beer from the table. "I still think we ought to go into auto repair. Money is probably better in that."

"We don't need money," Bastian snaps. A flash of something crosses his features and he schools them. "We have plenty of money. I thought this bike shop was your dream."

Dominic grips the neck of his beer so tight I worry he might snap it off. "This wasn't my dream. You know what my dream was."

"It doesn't matter now." Bastian waves his hand. "We're running the bike shop. Don't worry about the money."

"You know the benefits won't last forever," Dominic argues. "We need a plan."

"Guys, can we just decide if we're okay with the logo?" I point to the screen. "I gotta get it to the sign-maker guy today."

"It's fine with me," Bastian shrugs. "Dom?"

Before Dominic can respond, Beau slips in through the back, carrying a huge bag of candy and humming to himself. He grins when he spots us and comes up, dropping into the seat across from me in the booth.

"Where'd you get that, squirt?" Bastian asks.

"Got info for you," Beau says, ignoring the question. Knowing Beau, he'd probably conned it out of some poor innocent sap.

"Yeah?" Bastian asks, reaching for his wallet. "What have you got for me?"

"A lady was nosing around today, asking questions," Beau tells us. "She says she's doing research."

"Yeah, I heard about that from Hutch," Dominic says with a chuckle, taking another swallow of his beer. "Says she approached him outside of the Quik-Mart earlier."

"What did she want?" I ask. "Did she say what kind of research she was doing?"

"Yeah," Beau says, popping a gummy worm into his mouth. "Urban ... re-still-ents."

"Urban resilience?" I ask, furrowing my brow. "Wasn't that the stuff..."

Bastian shoots me a look and I stop talking. He heads back over to the pool table. "Did you help her out?"

"After she bought me Takis," Beau grins, his missing front teeth on display.

Dominic gives him a fist bump. "Good boy."

"She was pretty," Beau adds. "She has long red hair and she's big and soft like my mom." I chuckle at his description. "And she told me she was working for this guy. Dr. Thorn. No, wait, Dr. Thornton."

The room goes quiet. The only noise is the soft whirr of the fan blades from above. My shoulders tense and I grip the table under my hands.

Glancing over at Dominic, I notice he looks pale like he's just seen a ghost. On the other hand, when I risk a look at Bastian, his blue eyes have darkened, gaze hardening.

"I'll get rid of her," he promises. "Don't worry about it."

He tosses his stick on the table, but Dominic seems to come back to himself because he reaches out and pulls Bastian back.

"You can't do that," I say, half out of my seat. "Just because she's working with ... with him doesn't mean ..."

"I don't care. She can fuck right off for all I care. Let me go run her off, dammit," Bastian says, jerking his arm out of Dominic's grip.

"You're acting like a crazy person," Dominic protests. "Calm the fuck down, dude. We don't know why she's here, maybe it's innocent."

"Did she say anything else?" I ask Beau, hoping that she dropped more info.

He shakes his head and eats another gummy candy. "No, but I get money if I do a longer interview with her. I told her no one was gonna help her if you guys said no."

"Good," Dominic says. "She ought to know that no one does shit around here unless we let them."

"I think we should just tell her to get lost." Bastian curls a lip. "She doesn't belong here. She's an outsider. We don't want outsiders around here, do we?"

"Yeah," Dominic echoes. "We could just tell her to leave, then we won't have a problem."

"Aren't you guys curious though?" I ask. "Why is he suddenly so interested in this place again? Two years with no contact? Maybe if we talk to her, we can find out more, see if he's sent her out here to spy on us."

"Who gives a rat's ass?" Dominic spits out. "We don't need outsiders trying to study and dissect us. It doesn't matter why."

"It just seems strange," I continue. "What does Dr. Thornton want, exactly?"

"Shut up," Bastian turns to me, balling his hands into fists. "Stop talking about him. I don't want to hear his name."

"You can't even hear his name?" I ask, gaze fixed on my older brother. The raw intensity of his reaction leaves me bewildered. "It's been two years, Bastian. Besides, he said he was never trying to hurt us ..."

"Shut *up!*" Bastian yells, lunging at me. "I said stop talking about it! We don't talk about her, ever!"

Dominic curses loudly. "Now look what you've done." He grabs for Bastian, trying to keep him from hitting me. "You got him all riled up because you wouldn't stop."

"Hey, don't blame me!" I snap back. "I'm just saying that there's something weird about this, okay? I say we go confront this girl and find out what's going on, that's all."

Bastian glowers and narrows his eyes but relaxes in Dominic's grip, enough for Dom to let him go.

"Fine. We'll do it your way, Caleb," Bastian says. "We'll just tell her that her presence is unwanted and she should take off. If that bastard comes around, then we can deal with whatever he wants at that point."

At least Bastian had calmed a little on the murderous rage. He wasn't usually like this but hearing that name after so long must have completely rattled him.

I have to admit that it had me a little spooked as well. Confronting this chick seems like the obvious next step, but it means facing demons I thought were long dead and buried.

"Maybe it's nothing," I say, laying a hand on Bastian's shoulder. "But if we find out, maybe we can get some closure."

"Fine," Bastian gives a jerking nod. "Let's go then. Before I change my mind."

I breathe out a sigh of relief and shut my laptop. "Beau, go home. Bastian will give you the money tomorrow," Dominic says.

Beau scampers off and we step out of the bar and into the cool night air. The restored '75 Firebird, a relic from our late grandfather, gleams under flickering streetlights. Its engine roars to life, resonating through the quiet alley as we prepare to embark on our mission.

"Get in," Bastian says. "Let's go … have a chat."

3

BASTIAN

"Why can't the past stay in the past?" I mutter as we walk into the brightly lit diner. It didn't take long for us to glean her location, not when this chick practically wore a neon sign that screamed "outsider."

"Let's just confront her and get this over with," Dominic says in a low voice.

She's sitting in a booth near the middle of the diner, looking like even more of an outsider than I expected. The girl is pudgy, wearing a stupid-looking beret on her red hair and what looks like kindergarten clothes—a jumper and a turtleneck with black leather shoes.

"She belongs on Sesame Street, not here in Caspian Springs," I whisper to my brothers. Dom snorts; Caleb's lips quirk into a smile.

As we walk up to her, her eyes scan us over and I smirk, seeing the fear in them. "I don't know what you think you're doing here, *Princess*," I tell her, leaning into her space. "But this is our neighborhood."

"I'm here to do work," she protests, hands in her lap. "That's all." This close I notice her vivid green eyes and her oval face, covered in a smattering of freckles. She bites her bottom lip and scrunches her brows before sitting up higher in the booth.

"We don't know who you are, or what you want," I threaten. "But if you know what's good for you, you'll leave." The place goes silent, tension thickening as the silence hangs in the air for a beat before she finally responds.

"I have every right to be here."

"You're not from around here, so you don't know us," I say, indicating the three of us with my hand. "I'm Bastian Ravenwood, these are my brothers. That right there is Dominic, and that's Caleb. We aren't just your friendly, local bike shop owners. We're the ones in charge around here. So if we want you to leave, you leave."

"I'm not here to make enemies," she says, staring at the table in front of her. "I'm just here to do some research."

I scoff. "Research. Right. You're an outsider. You're here to examine and analyze us like we're little ants in your ant farm."

"That's not true!" she insists, her green eyes moving to meet mine. "I work for an important professor, a doctor who is trying to help impoverished communities like yours, to make them better."

"Newsflash, Princess. We don't need you or the professor. This town can manage by itself."

She squares her shoulders, meeting my gaze. "You need to understand. Dr. Thornton genuinely wants to help towns like yours. I took this job because I've seen firsthand how his research can help communities and I want that for Caspian Springs too!"

"You aren't going to get anywhere. Caspian Springs was fine before the *professor* waltzed in and will be fine long after he's lost interest in us," I tell her, annoyance rising.

The girl's face twists. "I doubt it," she says, standing up from the table. "You're just a group of thugs. You couldn't possibly understand the research that someone as brilliant as Dr. Richard Thornton is doing. You're trying to intimidate me and it's not going to work. I know how bullies like you act!"

My jaw drops and I step back, holding my hands up. "Wow."

Dominic whistles and Caleb lets out a low, nervous laugh. The unexpected defiance from the girl catches me off guard, and for a moment, I can't find the words to respond. I stare at her for a beat before finding my voice and leaning in closer.

"You think you've got it all figured out, huh Princess?"

"Don't call me that," she says, pointing a finger at me and jabbing me in the chest. "My name is Sienna, not Princess."

"Well, *Princess*," I drawl. "You'll find that unless we let you, you're not going to get anything done around here."

"I don't need your help," she sneers. "I'm sure there are people who are tired of your tyranny around here. They'll talk to me even if you think they won't. I met a boy today who was willing to be interviewed."

"Beau?" I ask with a smirk. "He's kind of our little messenger boy. He's the one who came straight over to give us the news of your presence."

Sienna's eyes widen for a fraction of a moment before narrowing again. "I'm sure there will be people around here who want to help me out, who don't care for the way you and your little 'gang' have been running things," she says, using finger quotes around the word gang. "Or maybe you could you know, let me do my own thing and I'd be out of your hair," she adds.

Under normal circumstances, I might not have cared what she was doing. But ever since I found out who she's working for, I've been invested in getting rid of her. On top of that, she can't waltz in here and defy me and think she can get away with it.

"You're not getting it," I tell her. Shaking my head, I turn to my brothers. "Let's go."

We head out to the parking lot, tires screeching as we peel away. "You and Caleb spread the word. The little princess won't get anything done here. She'll have to go crying back to her boss that she can't do it, and she'll be forced to leave."

"I can't believe she called us thugs," Caleb mutters. "Jesus."

"Yeah, me neither," I say, my mind still buzzing with the encounter. "She has no idea who we are. We're nothing like those Serpent gangbangers."

As soon as we get home, the two of them head out again to spread the word through town—don't engage with the outsider.

Once alone, I head up to my room, each step heavier than the last. My head is still reeling from everything that's happened. I can't believe he's back in our lives so casually like this. Two years of nothing, and then he sends some rando out here to "do research."

I scoff. As if the good doctor isn't using the little princess to spy on us.

I pace my room, the creaking floorboards beneath my steps mirroring the unrest in my mind. My hands open and close rhythmically, as if trying to grasp hold of the past and rip it out of me.

I need to do something to fight the unsettled feelings that threaten to spill out and consume me. It's not until I'm halfway out the door, keys in hand that I realize I'm leaving the house. I stop and stare at the keys, wondering what I hope to accomplish with this. Am I trying to confront him? That won't help anything. He knows what he did. He knows how it felt for us.

Nothing good could come of me going over there to break his door down in the middle of the night.

I force myself to take deep breaths and fight the instinct to break something. Instead, I head back up to my room and crouch down to pull out a box from under my bed, leaning against it to look through it.

The box hasn't been touched in over two years, and a layer of dust covers the top. Blowing it off, I open the lid and stare. There's a photo sitting on the top, one of us with her—with Emily. Her smiling face beams back at me and I grasp the edges, ready to tear it apart but something stops me. I can't bring myself to tear up this last memory of her.

Under the photo is a ticket stub, a matchbox, and a napkin with a doodle—each item holding a piece of our shared history. My fingers linger over the napkin, a portal to a time when life was simpler, before the incident.

I feel the surge of anger inside again looking at these items before shoving them back in the box and stuffing it all back under the bed.

Too restless to stay still, I decide to go for a run. After throwing on some joggers and a tank, I stuff my feet into my worn sneakers and head out the door into the cool night air.

Each step echoes with the weight of old memories. The flickering streetlights cast shadows and Dr. Thornton rises in my mind. I clench my fists. Deep wounds lay beneath the surface, wounds I thought I fixed but this outsider's arrival had ripped the bandage off.

The rhythm of my feet against the cracked pavement is melodic as I pass rusty old cars, boarded-up shops, and an overflowing scrapyard. This place isn't what it once was. It was never a suburban paradise but once upon a time, it was a much better place to grow up.

But that changed after the center closed. I close my eyes briefly, remembering the days the three of us spent at the Haven Center, running around on the playground out back, going on field trips to fun and interesting places like museums and water parks, and learning from some of the most amazing teachers and staff.

Why can't we go back to those times? I wish we could turn back the clock to when the three of us were kids and we didn't have to worry about things like neighborhood gang brawls, keeping up with bills, running businesses, or watching old dreams get further and further from sight.

My run takes me down a dark alley and I stop by a dumpster to catch my breath, leaning against the brick wall for support. A light suddenly spills out from a nearby building and I look up to see the silhouette of two figures facing each other in the dark.

"Yeah, I heard from the Syndicate," one says to the other. "I mean, they made some good arguments."

I duck behind the dumpster, trying to stay out of sight at the mention of the Serpents.

"Did they offer you money?" the other voice asks.

"Yeah, they promised good money if I joined up. But I'm more afraid of the Ravenwood brothers than I am of the Serpents. They went so wild after that girl died."

"Yeah. I heard she was …"

Not wanting to hear anymore, I take off running again, in the opposite direction.

Once I return home, I collapse on my bed just as Dominic and Caleb get back.

"We're home!" Dom calls up the steps.

I sit up and poke my head through my door. "Is it done?"

"The little princess won't have anyone to talk to tomorrow," Dominic promises. Caleb nods, a grin on his face.

"She won't be a problem anymore."

I head down and the three of us grab beers, toasting to running her out of the community. Little does she know that this is simply the calm before the storm for her.

4

SIENNA

"Can I just take my order to go?" I ask the waitress when the boys leave. I'm a little shaken up about going toe-to-toe with a local gang, so I just want to go back to my motel room and eat in peace.

As soon as it's all boxed up, I take my stuff to the register and pay before walking briskly through the dark parking lot to my car.

My heart is still racing after my confrontation with the Ravenwood brothers. Did I do the right thing by confronting them or am I just making things more complicated for myself?

Maybe I should have figured out a less confrontational approach to the situation. I can't shake the feeling that I had crossed a line.

I hesitate, hand on my car door as my mind wrestles with what I've done. I can't change it now though, I can only move forward.

Back at the motel, I eat quickly and once I'm done eating, I strip down and take a shower in the water-stained tub before climbing into bed.

The motel room is enveloped in silence, broken only by the hum of distant traffic. I lie under scratchy covers, staring up at the ceiling. Despite how tiring the day was, sleep seems to be eluding me. I try to shake off the unease, reminding myself that this place is a small town like any other, but the weight of uncertainty still claws at me.

My supervisor—a grad student named Owen Hardy—is supposed to go with me on these community visits but he texted this morning that he was sick, and to go on without him.

Maybe I should have waited for Owen to be over his cold before starting the interviews again.

I'd considered canceling earlier before I realized that this was my chance to impress Dr. Thornton. If I could get the interviews without my supervisor, Dr. Thornton might be impressed, giving me an "in" for a meeting with him, and possibly securing a TA position.

But for now, I need to get some sleep so I can get up and do more interviews tomorrow. Deciding to try again, I shut my laptop and slid under the covers once more.

This time, I'm asleep within minutes.

When I wake, I get dressed in a cream blouse, with watercolor flowers printed on it, a rust-colored corduroy skirt with black buttons, and a lightweight, gray wool jacket with red trim sleeves.

I feel like I look a little more professional today, maybe just what people need to see to take me seriously around here.

Stepping out the door, I make my way down to my car and drive over to the Quik-Mart for a breakfast bar and a bottle of coffee.

The same woman is manning the register today but when I smile at her, she frowns and turns away.

Shaking my head, I take my stuff to the register and she silently scans my items before shoving them back across the counter at me, crossing her arms and glaring until I leave.

I blink a few times as I walk out of the convenience store, wondering what that was about. I shrug and open the coffee, taking a sip of the bittersweet brew.

With a clipboard in hand, I start walking through the nearest neighborhood, intent on door-knocking today.

Stepping up to the first door, I raise my hand and knock but someone yells from the window to get off their property. I'm used to that sort of thing and it doesn't phase me as I head to the next home on the block.

But it's the same there, and then I get a door slammed in my face. People yell at me to leave them alone, or I get blank stares even after I explain I'm not soliciting money.

Feeling defeated after an hour of this, I head back to my car only to find my tires have been slashed.

My hands fly to my mouth and I stare, tears filling my eyes. Is this in retaliation for last night? Because I dared to stand up for myself against the Crimson Blades, suddenly the whole town has turned against me?

I feel frozen, my eyes fixated on the now-deflated tires. A sinking realization of the situation settles over me. My initial shock turns to frustration and anger. Taking a deep breath, I close my eyes, attempting to steady my racing thoughts.

"Why would they do this?" I mumble to myself. My hands tremble as I reach out to touch the damaged tires, fingers running over the punctured rubber. A knot forms in my stomach.

I take another deep breath, determined to shake this off. I can't let this setback derail my mission. With a resolute look, I glance around, trying to figure out if I can make it on foot to a service station.

As I make my way along the main road, noisy yells catch my attention. I turn, seeing a car passing by. The group inside is yelling taunts, telling me to go back home, and calling me names. As they catch up, they fling plastic bottles at me from the car window.

The bottles are mostly empty thankfully, but one has soda inside, which explodes all over me as soon it hits the ground.

I jump back, the sticky substance drenching my skirt and part of my blouse. I let out a curse and start running, but the car is too far away now to catch up.

Feeling defeated, I trudge along until I spot a service station inside a tiny strip mall.

"Hi, can you help me?" I ask, walking into the lobby, which seemed to have frozen in time sometime around the 90s.

Fluorescent lights hum overhead as I walk on cracked linoleum floors up to the desk. The guy manning it looks up, giving me a once-over.

"I seem to have found myself with four flat tires. How much would it be to tow it here to get them replaced?"

"Be a hundred bucks to tow it here." The man scratches his belly. "But I can't do it, sorry."

"What? Why?" There's a note of panic in my voice.

"Sorry," he shrugs. "Blades' orders."

I let out a stifled scream and take a few deep breaths, trying to calm down. "Please? Can't you at least get the car towed here? I don't want to leave it where I've got it parked. I can pay you extra if that's what this is about."

The man scrunches his weathered face and shrugs again. "I'm not going to go against their orders."

"What did they tell you?" I step closer to the counter. "Whatever it is, they've got it all wrong. I'm not here trying to study you guys like bugs under a microscope or whatever it is they've told you. I'm just doing a research project, I don't want any trouble."

"Ma'am, you made trouble for yourself the moment you mouthed off to Bastian Ravenwood. I can't help you, now you'll have to leave my shop."

I deflate, turning to head back outside. It seems like I'm losing the battle here, but if he doesn't want my business, someone else probably will.

Walking further down the street, I spot a group of kids playing with a soccer ball near an alleyway. I perk up and watch them for a moment.

Kids are usually pretty easygoing. It can't hurt to ask them if there's anyone who can help me, right?

Approaching them, the kids catch sight of me and as a group, turn their backs on me. I gape. How could word have spread so fast in this town? I only talked to the Blades last night!

"Guys, please. I know that the Blades told you not to talk to me, but I need help. Do any of you know where I can get my car fixed? Because the guy at that shop down the road won't do it."

One of the kids, a girl with curly pigtails, turns to face me. She looks sympathetic and glances at her friends, who are all holding themselves stiffly. "We're not supposed to talk to the lady with the red hair," she says, voice quiet. "We could get in trouble. But my dad has a car shop."

"Really?" I ask. "Can you take me there? I'll give you money for your trouble!"

She nods and I pull out my wallet, intending to give her the twenty I have stored for emergencies, but she grins before snatching my wallet, running away with it.

I close my eyes, frustration and hurt building inside me. Stealing my wallet feels like a cruel punctuation to the events of the day. I can't shake the feeling of isolation, as though the entire town has turned its back on me overnight.

I fumble with my phone, contemplating whether to call Owen. Maybe this mess is beyond repair, and it's time to admit defeat.

I dial his number, my hand trembling as I hold the phone to my ear. The ringing feels like an eternity until Owen's groggy voice answers. "Hullo?"

"Sorry if I woke you up," I murmur, my voice betraying the turmoil within. "This is Sienna. Things ... aren't going well. I can't seem to get the community members to talk to me at all."

Owen's voice crackles through the phone, each word laced with frustration and disappointment. "Are you kidding? You alienated the community we're supposed to be helping? You screwed this up, didn't you? Now Rich can't get the info he needs, Sienna!"

My throat tightens, a lump forming as I try to find words. "I didn't screw it up. We can fix it, right? Rich won't be upset with me if I fix it?"

A bitter laugh escapes him, his irritation palpable. "I'm supposed to be recovering from being sick, and now I have to worry I'm going to lose my job over this. And my TA position. Great job, Bennett. Maybe you aren't cut out for academia if you can't handle a simple task like qualitative interviews."

Tears well up in my eyes as I see my dreams crumbling around me. "I can do this. I'll fix it," I stammer, my voice small.

"Don't bother. I'll have to do damage control myself. If you've alienated the community somehow, they won't be willing to work with the both of us, would they?" Owen's tone is cold.

I don't have an answer for him so he sighs. "I'll call you back tomorrow after I've figured out a way to fix this."

Owen hangs up and I stare down at my phone. The dream I've worked so hard for seems to be slipping away, replaced by the stark reality of my inadequacies.

Just as doubt begins to settle in, my eyes catch a glimmer of hope across the street. A small sign, almost hidden away, reads "Morgan's Auto Repair—Quality Service You Can Trust."

A determined spark ignites within me. I might have hit rock bottom, but there's a chance, a slim one, that this shop could be the key to turning things around. With a newfound resolve, I head towards the shop.

5

DOMINIC

I watch the little redhead for a moment, her lip quivering as she ends her phone call. She looks down at it, but then something catches her eye. Instead of breaking down, she smiles. It's a fragile, fleeting thing, but it tells me we haven't gotten to her yet.

Reaching for my phone, I hit the button to call my brother, listening to it ring twice before he picks up.

"Caleb," I say, voice low. "We have a problem."

As I brief Caleb over the phone, I watch the girl, trying to figure her out. Hands shaking at her sides, she seems on edge. What's going on in her mind? Is she unraveling, or is this the calm before the storm?

Caleb and I agree to meet up and discuss the situation further, and I hang up, getting back onto my bike.

Caleb is already waiting for me when I arrive at the diner.

"What's going on?" he asks, flipping up his sunglasses.

"I was watching the newbie, keeping an eye to make sure everyone was following our orders when I heard her on the phone with some guy."

"Yeah?" Caleb quirks a brow. "And?"

"She was talking about him," I say, hands shaking at my sides. "She called him Rich."

"Damn." Caleb whistles low. "She's got to be close to him to call him that. Maybe she's sleeping with him, just like—"

"Don't finish that thought," I warn him. "Let's not even go there. That's not the only reason I called you here. She doesn't seem to be getting the hint we want her gone."

"What do you want to do?" Caleb asks.

"We need to step up our game," I say. "It's not enough for the community to be on her, because it's just making Polly Sunshine more determined than ever to 'help' us with her experiments."

Caleb stares off into the distance, a thoughtful expression on his face. "Bastian would probably say that the best way to get something done is to do it ourselves."

My lips curl into a smirk. "Yes, that's what we need to do. We need to go after her ourselves, make sure she knows that she isn't wanted here and that she can't defy us and get away with it."

"She might be cute but she's dangerous," Caleb agrees. I nod. The princess has the cute innocent look down, but it's a front. She's a snake in the grass, just like they all are.

My eyes flit to Caleb and I recognize the same flicker of intensity in his eyes. There's more at stake than just keeping the town in check here. It's about ensuring history doesn't repeat itself. I can't let someone like her disrupt what we've built after everything we've been through.

"Time for plan B," I say. "You follow her everywhere she goes. I'm going to talk to Bastian about this and come up with something else to do, something big."

Caleb grins and sticks his hands in his pockets. "Can do."

We part ways and Caleb takes off for Morgan's Auto and I call Bastian, agreeing to get him to meet me at the park near the Quik-Mart.

He shows up within a half hour, carrying a bag and wearing a wide smirk. "Got it," he says, showing me the contents.

I grin. "That's perfect."

We execute our plan quickly, stepping back to admire our handiwork. It doesn't take long for Sienna to approach, Caleb trailing her a few paces back. She stops, seeing the newest addition to her car.

She stares, a flurry of emotions crossing her face before she starts to shake, hands balled into fists.

If she wants to sleep with Rich, she can face the consequences. I watch in delight as her eyes fill with tears at the word now spray-painted on her car, in large letters.

"Slut?" she whispers. "Why?"

"You know why," I say, shrugging. "Now everyone else knows too."

A tear falls down her cheek, and for a moment, I feel a twinge of guilt. But this is the game we're in, and sentimentality won't cut it.

"You're not welcome here," Bastian says simply. "Get the hint yet?"

"I'm not giving in to you," she says, one hand on her hip, wiping her tears away with the other. "You're a bunch of bullies and thugs, and I'm not backing down."

Sienna's defiance grates on my nerves, a tightening in my jaw betraying the frustration simmering beneath the surface.

"Have it your way," I say, stepping closer to her, close enough to see her tremble minutely under my gaze. "But we're not backing down either. This is just a taste of what we have for you if you don't get out of town."

She sets her mouth into a thin line, staring at the three of us. "I'm not going anywhere."

"Then we aren't either," Bastian tells her. "Dominic here will spend the rest of today with you, making sure you don't get a chance to talk to anyone and then we'll take turns with you, keeping you company until you get sick of us and finally decide to do the right thing and leave."

"Fine," she says, turning her head away to hide the pink on her cheeks. "You can bully me, you can try to intimidate me, you can harass me but I'm going to see this project through."

She ignores me as I follow her, heading for the auto shop once more. "Tow the car here," she tells Mr. Morgan. "And charge it to the

Ravenwood boys," she adds. "They're going to help take care of my car today."

I can't help the smirk that crosses my features. She may be stubborn, but she plays just as dirty as us.

"Go ahead," I tell Mr. Morgan. "Take care of it, just like she said."

Mr. Morgan looks between us for a moment before shaking his head and shrugging.

The girl flounces over to the hard plastic seats of the lobby and sits down.

"What are you doing?" I ask.

"Waiting for my car to be repaired," she answers, grabbing a magazine.

"Nah, you're coming with me," I tell her. "Come on."

She stares at me, green eyes widening. "What?"

"I've got stuff to do and I need to keep an eye on you. Let's go."

"No."

"You want to do this the easy way or the hard way?" I ask, stepping closer to her. A thrill shoots down my spine as I see the fear in her eyes. I'm over a foot taller than her and could easily lift her over my shoulder if I wanted, even with her plus-size frame.

Sienna doesn't answer, instead standing up and following me as we walk out of the garage. "Good girl," I say over my shoulder.

She lets out a little squeak and I smirk to myself.

We approach my bike and she stares at it. "How are we both going to fit?" she asks, uncertainty in her tone. "I'm not exactly lithe, and you're ... very broad," she says, waving her hands at me.

"We'll fit," I tell her, thrusting a helmet towards her. She takes it and starts buckling it on while I climb onto the bike.

Once I'm seated, I wait for Sienna to throw her leg over the back before revving the engine. She shrieks and clings to me, making me grin wider under my helmet.

"Hold on Princess," I call out, wrapping her arms around my waist more securely. We take off and I drive us through town to the local hardware store.

Once we arrive, Sienna seems in a hurry to get off the bike, shoving the helmet on the seat before tagging along behind me as I walk into the hardware store.

"Hey Joe," I call. "Need to pick up that part I ordered."

Joe nods at me and his eyes slide over to Sienna, who is looking around the shop with curious eyes.

"That the girl you said not to help?" he asks.

Sienna makes a face at that and I grin. "Yep. She's hanging out with me today. She can't be a nuisance if she's being supervised."

"Come on," she whines. "I'm just trying to do my job!"

"Your job is to scrutinize our town like it's a bug under a microscope," I say, reaching for the plumbing part that Joe ordered for me. "And we don't need that."

Joe pauses when he starts ringing me up, "By the way, one of the Serpents was lurking around last night. I chased him off but he threatened to come back with some friends."

"I'll look into it," I promise him.

"We ran that Serpent slime out of town two decades ago," Joe complains. "What are they doing back?"

"That's what I want to know," I say, taking the bag from his offered hand. "The Blades will find out, don't worry."

I exchange a nod with him, a silent acknowledgment that the Blades always protect what's ours.

Sienna follows me out as I leave and I tuck the bag into the back of the bike before getting back on. She taps me on the arm and I turn so I can hear her.

"What are the Serpents?"

I grimace. "Serpent Syndicate. Local gang that terrorized the area when I was a kid. They were driven off by some of the older folks, but they've started showing back up."

Sienna nods, absorbing my explanation. Her curiosity is evident, and I can't help but wonder what she thinks. The town's history is tangled, and I've only scratched the surface with my explanation.

We head for my next errand, and I try not to think too hard about how Sienna's body feels clinging to mine. She's the enemy here and I have no desire to get involved.

Just because she's cute and kind of sexy in a buttoned-up way doesn't mean anything. I'm only having her stay with me so I can keep an eye on her and make sure she can't get her work done.

Besides, she's probably already sleeping with the good doctor anyway.

We pick up a few more items around town before heading back to Morgan's Auto.

"Well, it's been real, it's been fun, but it ain't been real fun," I tell her. "Lucky for you, I've got to go snake hunting tonight so I can't stick around."

Sienna rolls her eyes. "Good. Maybe I can actually get some work done."

"Uh-uh," I shake my finger at her. "You aren't getting off so easily. Caleb will be taking over for me, spending all his time with you tonight."

"I can't believe this!" Sienna says, throwing her hands in the air. "You and your brothers think you can just harass me into leaving but I know you'll get tired of it eventually. I'll just have to outlast you."

"Even if we don't stick to you twenty-four-seven, it doesn't mean that the town is going to welcome your presence with open arms," I remind her. "You made your bed; lie in it."

Sienna glowers but I grin and wave, just as Caleb strolls into the shop.

"Have fun with her," I tell Caleb. "She's getting restless."

"I'll see how far I can push her," Caleb promises. "She'll be fun to break."

"Be a good little princess for Caleb," I tell her and take off on my bike.

6

BASTIAN

I start seeing the cracks in the princess's armor after a couple more days of our campaign. Currently, I'm the one on babysitting duty, and I've been keeping an eye on her while she attempts to persuade some of the local children to take part in her study by offering them candy.

"Don't fall for it," I tell the boys who crowd around to check out her goods. "She's off-limits. The candy is a bribe."

She ignores me and gives them a big smile, like some kind of storybook princess. "You guys just have to answer a couple quick questions about yourselves and you can have this goody bag full of candy," she says, shaking it in front of them. The bag has an assortment of fun-size candy bars as well as some fruit chews and some chocolates.

As I watch her try to sway them, unease grows. What are her intentions here? Is she merely trying to get them to help her or is this a ploy to exploit them?

"Stop treating my town like your personal pet project," I spit out. Sienna's eyes meet mine and she narrows them.

"Your town *is* my project," she says, irritation rolling off of her in waves. "I have an actual, real job to do here, one that I could get fired from if I don't do it."

"Sure, Princess," I say, idly tapping my pocketknife against the wooden picnic bench, the metallic clicking noise echoing with every tap. "But I don't give a rat's ass about your job. I care about this town and protecting it from people like you and the good doctor over at his shiny university."

"What do you have against Dr. Thornton anyway?" Sienna asks, turning to face me. She tucks a lock of red curls behind her ear and tilts her head.

The mention of Dr. Thornton strikes a nerve. My jaw tightens and I silently curse him for getting involved again.

"It's between us and him," I tell her. "Nothing to worry your pretty little head about."

"I feel like I have a right to know since you made this personal for me too," she says. Her face twists and she bites her lower lip. "If you tell me, maybe I can figure out a way we can both get what we want."

I smile. "Nice try, Princess. It's none of your business and you've almost run out of time to solicit today," I add, pointing to the sun which is sinking over the horizon. "If you'd just run along, I can do the stuff I need to take care of now."

"What could you *possibly* have to do that's so important?" she asks, rolling her eyes.

I snort. "Seeing as I'm in charge around here, plenty." We're patrolling the edges of the town tonight, trying to keep an eye out for Serpent run-ins, but it's none of Sienna's business.

She shakes her head and frowns. "Maybe I'll just go over to the local church then. I'm sure the people there are the kind who might be interested in a project to improve the community."

"Good luck with that," I say, grinning as I flick the knife blade open and shut. "The pastor there is a regular at our pool nights at the bar. He owes us enough money that he'd probably turn you away from the church himself."

Sienna throws her hands up. "I don't get you. I don't get any of you guys. What do you have against Dr. Thornton? He's a brilliant researcher, and his research has revitalized several small communities in our area. Don't you understand that Caspian Springs could start to prosper and thrive?"

"This place is doing fine," I say, my voice taking on an edge as my frustration rises. "Sure, we may not be as flashy as some of the bigger cities, but we're not some pit either."

Sienna sighs and shakes her head. "I'm not going to give up."

I shrug. "You'll have to give up eventually. Now hurry up and get in the car because I'm done with you for today."

"Yeah, well I'm done with you too," she says, sticking out her tongue.

"Want me to show you where you can put that, sweetheart?" I offer, but she doesn't back down, meeting my gaze.

"No," she says, her voice steady despite how she's trembling. "Just drop me off at the diner."

"Your wish is my command, Princess," I say, waving my arms at the car like a footman in front of a carriage. "Climb inside."

She nods, her posture straightening, though she makes a point not to hurry.

Despite having no car and being rejected at every turn, Sienna still makes us drive her around Caspian Springs every day, trying to find people who will participate in her study. It would almost be kind of adorable, if not for the fact that she's working for the good doctor, and probably sleeping with him too.

Remembering that sends a cold chill down my spine, so I ignore her when she attempts to make small talk and drop her in front of the diner without another word. I'm not interested in getting to know anything more about the girl.

After dropping her off, I take a second to clear my mind before heading to the bike shop to meet up with Caleb and Dominic.

"How was business?" I ask.

"Slow," Caleb snaps. "Like always."

"It was fine," Dominic interjects, giving Caleb a look. "We had a couple of people come in for some custom stuff and one guy needed us to look at his combustion chamber."

I blow out a breath, considering our options. "Maybe we can host some kind of event to drum up business," I suggest. "Like a charity ride."

"Let's just figure out how we're going to keep the lights on," Caleb says, shoulders tense. "I can't keep redesigning our gear over and over, hoping it might sell."

"Shouldn't we focus on—" Dominic starts, but I cut him off.

"We'll figure it out," I say. "For now, let's focus on patrolling tonight."

Once everything is cleaned up, we head out for patrol, starting from the north side of town. It's quiet, but tension from earlier still lingers.

Fortunately, there aren't any sightings of Serpent slime, so we're able to call it a night early and head home.

The next day, Caleb is supposed to be on babysitting duty, but he backs out when Joe asks for his help with the computer at the hardware store.

"I'll go," I tell Dominic. "You run the shop today. I think Caleb needs to get out anyway."

He gives me a quick nod. "I've got it."

Taking off, I make my way over to see what the princess is up to today. She's standing outside the diner when I arrive and I amble over, enjoying the flush on her cheeks that rises when she sees me.

"Sorry, Princess," I say, crowding her against the wall of the building. "You're stuck with me today. I know you were looking forward to spending more one-on-one time with Caleb but it's you and me."

"God. What would it take for you guys to back off?" she asks, reaching out to push me away from her. "I'm sick of this. I don't need to be watched like a hawk. Stop breathing down my neck!"

"No can do." I shrug. "There's nothing you can do to stop us."

"You're ruining my life," she says, her gaze defiant despite the tears welling up in her eyes. "I'm getting heat from my boss over this. If I don't get something done soon, I'm going to lose out on something I've spent half my life working towards."

"What can I say? Your dreams aren't on my list of priorities."

Sienna's jaw tightens and her gaze drops to the ground. She takes a sharp breath, her fingers clenching and unclenching at her sides.

"I hate you," she hisses through gritted teeth, lower lip quivering. "I hate you so much. Please, just leave me alone. I'll do anything you want if you just leave me the hell alone and let me do this work!"

"Anything?" I ask, a half-smile forming on my lips as Sienna's offer hangs in the air.

Her blotchy face turns up to meet my gaze and I see the desperation in her eyes. Something about it tugs at me. A tantalizing itch of curiosity blooms under my skin, the desire to see just how far she's willing to go catching fire inside.

"Anything," she repeats. "I need this opportunity. I cannot lose this job."

"Interesting." I give her a sidelong glance. "Your car is done. Let's go pick it up and if you promise to behave yourself for the rest of the day and stay out of the way, I'll come up with something you can do in exchange, so you can do this work you're so desperate to get done." I quirk my eyebrow. "Have we got a deal?"

She stares at me for a moment, worrying her lower lip with her teeth. With a heavy sigh, she nods, her eyes betraying the end of an internal struggle. "Fine, if that's what it takes. I just need some space to complete my project. I can't risk losing everything."

"Wait until you hear the offer," I tell her, chuckling. "You might not want to agree. Meet me here, tomorrow morning, first thing."

She nods and I walk over to my car, opening the passenger door for her. "Get in." Sienna slinks over and slips inside, quietly watching me as I take her to Morgan's Auto.

Once I've paid for the repairs, Sienna speeds away, unable to look me in the eye after putting her offer on the table.

Heading for the bike shop, the curiosity of what "anything" could mean still lingers in her wake. I mull it over as I walk inside, spotting Dominic under a bike as he finishes a repair.

"Hey," Caleb waves. "Just got back from Joe's. How was the princess?"

"She offered to do anything we wanted if we let her do her

project," I say, forgoing a greeting. "And she was desperate. She meant it."

"Anything?" Caleb asks, raising an eyebrow. "Interesting."

"Maybe we ought to use it to our advantage," Dominic says, getting out from under the bike. "It could be a way to get back at the good doctor, and maybe we can use her to take out some frustrations as well."

"Sounds like a plan to me," Caleb agrees. "Let's see just how desperate she really is."

I grin. "Looks like we've figured out what she can do for us," I say.

The next day, as agreed, Sienna shows up in front of the diner.

"We have a proposition for you," I say, stepping towards her.

7

SIENNA

I set my jaw, trying not to let the fear show as I tilt my chin up at the boys and square my shoulders. "What is it you want from me?" I ask.

Bastian's smile grows, as does the unease in my belly.

"It's pretty simple. We want you to completely surrender yourself to us. You become ours, our dirty little mistress, our slave. Bow to our every whim, let us use you however we want, and not only will we no longer keep you from completing your research, we'll help you get it done."

My gaze flits between each of the brothers. As Bastian lays out the proposal, a chilling smile etches across his face. The hunger in his eyes is unsettling, intense, and focused as though something lurks beneath the surface.

My jaw drops. "What?" I ask, voice cracking. "Is this real? Am I being pranked?"

"Dead serious," Dominic says, his voice measured but holding an undercurrent of possessiveness. I catch a glimpse of a shared bond in their eyes, an interest in me that stretches beyond my mere presence in Caspian Springs.

Their words echo around inside my head. Become theirs. Their slave, their mistress.

Glancing over at Caleb, I see something hinting towards longing written on his face.

I'd be lying to myself if I didn't say I found them attractive, but it's one thing to drool over some good-looking guys, it's another to surrender myself completely to them.

"Are you crazy?" I say, finally finding my voice. "That's what you want? Sexual favors?"

"Not just sexual favors," Dominic says, biting his lip as he tilts his head to study me. "You'd be ours, completely." His gaze burns and I shift, reflexively wrapping my arms around myself.

"Can you step back please?" I ask Bastian. "I can't think when you're so close."

"Am I making you nervous?" he asks, the dark grin sending chills down my spine. The dim lights of the garage cast long shadows, partially obscuring his face as he steps even closer.

He reaches out and brushes my cheek with a thumb, an instant buzz of electricity crackling over my skin. "How about a taste of what we can offer?"

Before I can protest, he's leaning in and capturing my mouth with his, sending a million volts racing through me. I feel drugged, my mind almost completely wiped as our mouths fuse together.

A noise escapes me as his tongue probes the seam of my lips, and before I can take a moment to think about what I'm doing, I'm granting him access and his tongue fills my mouth.

His hands wrap around my arms as we kiss, my toes curling inside my Mary-Janes. Heat coils inside of me and I feel like my skin is on fire.

Breaking away, he smirks as he wipes his mouth with the back of his hand. His blue eyes are dark like a stormy ocean as they take me in. My mind races, the lingering taste of him a heavy reminder of what this decision could mean.

Am I strong enough to resist temptation like this at my fingertips?

"That was just a taste of what we can give you," Bastian intones. "There's three of us and one of you. Imagine the possibilities."

My mind nearly short-circuits as it rushes to fill in the blanks with a million ideas. "How ... I mean, what ... I mean ... you're okay with sharing?"

"We share everything," Bastian explains. "The three of us are a team, always have been."

My brain still feels fuzzy from the kiss we shared and I reach up to touch my lips, the sensation still lingering. "Why me?" I ask, suddenly feeling shy. "I'm ... big."

Men don't usually look at me this way. I'm the friend that men shove their other friends at, so they can get with the slim, pretty girls.

"You're still sexy," Caleb insists, making me blush from head to toe. "Size doesn't matter to us."

Emotions are warring inside me and I feel torn. On the one hand, the boys have proven they're fiercely loyal to whatever they consider "theirs," so they would keep their word about helping me.

On the other, they're complete brats, doing whatever they want, whenever they want. Saying yes would guarantee that I'm all but walking into the mouth of the dragon on this.

I bite my lip, trying to think. It's hard when they're so close, their presence clouding my judgment.

Taking a deep breath, I ask, "Can I get back to you?"

Bastian's expression remains hard, but he steps back slightly. "Of course, Princess. You can have twelve hours to think over our little proposition. But time is ticking, sweetheart. If you don't give us an answer soon, you'll find that we can make your life even harder than we have been."

His fingers reach out once more, trailing along my jaw as he leaves. The three of them walk away and I immediately feel a weight lift from my chest, finally able to breathe.

Never in my wildest dreams did I expect them to come out with an offer like that? My mind is still spinning over it.

Could I really do it? Could I really surrender myself to them, all for the sake of a job?

I take my time heading back to my car, trying to calm myself down after that encounter. My skin is still buzzing, lips still tingling from the kiss.

Once I'm back at my motel room, I open my laptop and try to work on an article I'm writing for the *Journal of Urban Studies,* but my mind keeps circling back to the kiss and to their offer.

As brain-melting as the kiss was, it's definitely not worth throwing myself into the snake pit over. Not even their offer of helping me with my work could sway me away from my goals here.

Could it?

It would be nice to have the Blades help with getting the residents of Caspian Springs to cooperate with me on my research project. I could complete my research much faster with their help.

"No," I say out loud, shaking my head. That isn't worth sacrificing my integrity. They already labeled me a slut, I'm not about to become one just to secure a spot studying under the prestigious Dr. Richard Thornton. I could get there on my own merit.

But could you ... ? a nagging voice in the back of my head asks.

If you're out of a job, you don't have enough money to stay here in Caspian Springs. You'll have to move home, you'll have to get another job. You won't have another opportunity like this ever again.

Shutting my eyes, I press the heel of my palm against them as the threat of tears emerges, hot and heavy against my closed eyelids. I realize I'm not in the mindset to make a decision right now, I need to clear my head.

Stepping outside, I lock the door behind me and head down to the main road, breathing in and out slowly as I try to let go of the racing thoughts swirling around in my head.

Needing to take my mind off things, I pull out my camera. Even if I don't have narrative research, I can still document my time here.

Some kids are hanging around outside the Quik-Mart playing a marble game, and I stop to snap a photo. The expression on their faces, determination and joy, buoy me. This is why I'm doing this job —for kids like this.

The weight of the Blades' proposition hangs over me, and I

wonder about their sudden interest. The three of them have gone out of their way to harass and bully me ever since I showed up, just to try to do some research. Why are they suddenly so interested in me now?

Maybe they only see me as a challenge. I've refused to bow to their tyranny so far, and since I'm an outsider, they see it as a threat to their rule. Once they figure out what makes me tick, they'll probably get bored of me and leave me alone.

I pause to capture another shot—a tiny wooden bridge spanning a small creek. Caspian Springs is a living narrative of what it's like to be a human being in the modern day; with each ripple in the creek whispering the stories of resilience, and every weathered plank of the bridge bearing the weight of shared existence.

Dr. Thornton's fascination with this place makes sense now. The town has a charm unlike any other, especially the way its residents work together when faced with the pursuit of a singular goal.

It feels as though I'd not only be letting myself down, but I'd be personally letting Dr. Thornton down if I couldn't complete the research for his study.

I turn, looking for more moments to capture on film but my phone chimes, alerting me of an incoming text. I stick my camera back in my bag and pull the phone out, half expecting it to be the Blades, having somehow gotten my number and texting me to demand an answer.

I'm relieved when I see it's from Owen. But when I open it, my relief turns to anxiety.

Get something to us within two days or we will have to let you go from this project.

I feel my heart in my throat seeing those words. I can't breathe. Panic grips me and I feel dizzy, light-headed, and nauseous. I knew this was a possibility, but I think I was trying to assure myself that this wouldn't happen.

Everything I've done to get to this moment is now hanging in the balance. I can't let it slip between my fingers.

Before I can stop to question myself, I find myself racing to my car, revving out of the parking lot, and rushing for the Blades' bike shop.

Arriving at the shop, I jump out and spot the three of them bent over, working on a bike together.

I walk forward on shaky legs and try to keep myself together. "I … have an answer for you," I tell them. They look up at me and I step forward.

"I'll do it," I say, the words hanging in the air. The room falls silent as their eyes lock onto mine and I hold my breath, waiting for their response.

Bastian's grin is instant. "Great choice, Princess."

I release a sharp exhale. Even though I'm terrified of what I've just agreed to do, relief still floods me from knowing that I will be able to keep my job and get my boss off my back.

"Where are you staying?" Caleb asks.

"The motel on Dumond," I tell them, gesturing towards the road.

"That rat trap?" Dominic scoffs. "Nah, you're moving in with us."

My eyes widen. Oh God. What are they going to do with me now?

8

CALEB

Sienna stares at us, a mixture of fear and uncertainty in her eyes, hands clenching by her side. "I'm sorry, I'm not moving in with you. There's no way that I'm—"

"You agreed to do whatever we asked," Bastian snaps. "Which means we get to keep an eye on you twenty-four-seven. Are you in or was that all just talk?"

She casts a glance around. "But ..."

Something in her eyes has me speaking up.

"You belong to us," I say, moving closer to her. Her eyes track my movements, as though hypnotized. "You're ours, and we can make it so good for you. Or we can make things much harder than we've already done."

As I speak, I can't ignore the subtle shivers coursing through her. She forces a nod, not quite able to hide the turmoil lurking under the surface.

Bastian reaches out to pet her hair. "Good girl." There's a subtle change to her expression and I notice the way her body seems to straighten under the praise.

She climbs into the backseat of the Firebird, next to me and I lean over and stroke her cheek. "We're gonna have fun, Princess. Don't worry."

She stays silent, looking down at her hands in her lap. I pull her close to me as we drive away, enjoying the warmth of her body pressed close to mine. She's a sweet girl, but she's in for a rough time if she thinks we're going to go easy on her.

I get the feeling she wouldn't want it to be easy anyway. She seems like someone who enjoys a good challenge and she won't back down easily.

Arriving at her motel room, Dom and I march her upstairs to get her stuff. We watch as she gathers her things silently, with shaky hands. She picks up a brush and it falls from her hands; Dominic crosses the floor in two strides to grab it before it can hit the ground.

"Here," he says, watching with an amused smirk as she takes it, cheeks red.

Once everything is packed up, we head back down to the car. As soon as she gets in, I pull her onto my lap.

She freezes, trying to shy away but I wrap my arms around her and place a hand on her thigh, just above the knee. She stares at it for a moment before moving her head up to look at me, lower lip caught in her teeth.

I smile back at her, a wolfish grin that does nothing to soothe her.

Once we arrive, Sienna studies the home as she gets out of the car, taking in the peeling paint and the missing roof shingles. It's not much, this place, but it's what we could afford and it's home.

The place is two stories, with three bedrooms and two bathrooms. Each of us has our own room, with mine being the first at the top of the stairs. Guiding Sienna there now, the three of us crowd around her.

"This is where you'll be storing your stuff." Bastian points to the floor. "But you'll take turns sleeping in each of our beds," he adds.

Sienna glances at me and I wink at her. She looks away and wraps her arms around herself.

Dominic speaks up. "For now, you'll stay in here until we come back."

"Where are you going?" Sienna asks, eyes wide.

"The princess needs the right kind of attire for her stay in the castle," Bastian says, mocking her voice. "You'll be locked in here, and we're taking your phone. If you try to run, you'll be punished. Prove your loyalty by staying here like a good girl."

She stares at us without moving. "Phone," Bastian snaps. "Now."

She still doesn't move so I walk up, running my hand along her curves and dipping it into her pocket. She snaps out of her trance, staring as my fingers lightly brush the space between her thighs before curling around the phone in her pocket and pulling it back out.

"Be a good girl for us while we're gone," Bastian orders.

She opens her mouth, probably to argue, but we exit the room before she can speak and I lock the door from the outside.

"Hopefully she behaves," Dominic says as we head back downstairs. "Or not, it'll be fun to break her if she misbehaves."

Once we leave, the three of us head for Target first. We weren't kidding about getting her new clothes. Sienna deserves to look like a grown woman. After picking out some clothing, we tool around, running a few more errands just to stretch the time we're gone. Bastian wants to see how far we can push her before she breaks.

As soon as we get back though, I bound up the stairs to check on her. She's lying on my bed, back facing the door but she sits up when I enter.

"You were gone a while," she says, voice small.

"Sorry Princess. We had a lot of errands to get done," I say, holding up a bag for her. "We got you some things to wear."

She takes the bag, curiosity in her eyes. As she pulls out the items though, she scoffs.

"Really? Do you want me to dress in these skimpy things? There's no way I'm doing that!"

"Thought you might say that," I tell her, bringing a hand up to trace a finger over her cheek. "But if you don't, you can wear nothing when we go out to the bar tonight if that makes you more comfortable."

Sienna's eyes widen. "You wouldn't!"

"Try me," I offer. "You can wear these clothes or you can go naked."

"I'm not wearing it," she says, jutting out her chin defiantly.

"Excellent. Naked it is then," I say. "Dom, Bastian, come on in."

The two of them step into the room, identical grins on their faces. "Seems the princess doesn't want to obey our orders already."

"We should rectify that then," Dominic offers. They haul Sienna to her feet and roughly begin to strip her down, helpfully removing her clothes for her, and tossing them to the side in a heap.

Sienna tries to fight back but Dom and Bastian are too strong for her, overpowering her and pushing her wrists down by her sides.

Standing before us, stark naked and trembling, her eyes meet mine briefly, and I catch a glimpse of vulnerability there. I can't help but notice her undeniable beauty, but as she casts her eyes downward, something like shame colors her features.

I wonder how she's been shaped by the judging eyes of others, telling her she's ugly because of her size. It brings a pang of sympathy to my heart, along with a burst of anger. Her body is perfect; generous curves and a pudgy belly, with soft skin and full breasts. She reminds me of one of those Venus of Willendorf sculptures or a Rubens painting.

"Please, don't look at me," she begs, unable to meet our eyes. "I'm not …"

"Not what?" Dominic prompts.

"Not pretty," she whispers. "I'm fat."

"You're gorgeous," Bastian says, stepping forward. "You have a beautiful body, you're like a goddess, Princess."

Sienna blushes from head to toe and I smile, though a nagging feeling of doubt lingers, wondering if we're doing the right thing here, or if we're tangling ourselves up in something we won't be able to untangle.

"Ready to go?" Bastian asks, pulling her along. Sienna digs in her heels.

"Wait, what?" she says, the panic evident in her eyes. "Are you really going to force me to go out with you like this?"

"You need to learn that we're always serious when we make promises," Dominic says. "You should know that by now."

"But ... but ..." she sputters.

"You wanna wear the clothes now?" I offer. The more she gives in, the easier it will be for her. Bastian can be cruel when he's being challenged. I purse my lips, holding them out, silently pleading with her to obey.

Sienna breathes hard, in and out for a beat, trying to gather herself before she nods, though she maintains the defiant look in her eyes. I think I like that she's not going to make this easy on us.

Bastian hands her the bag and she digs through it. We selected a range of clothing, stuff that we know will push her to her limits.

"Pick something out for tonight, Princess," I tell her. "We're going to show you off at the bar."

She selects a lacy, mesh, black and pink bra and matching thong, along with a tight-fitting bodycon dress.

"Can you turn around?" she asks, shifting uncomfortably.

None of us move, so she starts putting the clothes on. She looks damn sexy when she's done, a vast improvement to those bulky cardigans and shapeless dresses.

"I know you like to wear kindergarten clothing, but tonight you're our queen," I tell her. "And we want to show you off."

She blushes again and catches a glimpse of herself in the mirror, eyes widening. Her hair has been mussed from being taken out of its clip, so it's framing her face now. And the dress hugs her in all the right places, showing off her assets like it was made to do. It's backless, with a high halter neckline and thin straps that twist around her neck.

"You look amazing," Dominic says in a low voice.

Sienna squirms under our praise. It's so damn fun to watch her as she tries to hide the way our praise makes her light up.

I sling my arm around her, pulling her to me before leaning down to kiss her neck, the three of us leading her down the stairs.

"I can barely keep myself from ripping this dress off you right now," I whisper into her ear.

Bastian steps closer as well. "You're nothing but a slut, aren't you?" He moves his hand so he can bring her face up to look him in the eyes. "A good little slut, just for our enjoyment."

Sienna's eyes fill with tears at our words and something primal stirs inside me.

"We should see how willing the slut is to behave herself now," I say to my brothers. "Get on your knees."

Sienna looks up, seeking mercy from us but we don't budge. Slowly, she sinks to her knees, which pulls a smile from Bastian.

9

SIENNA

The air feels more chilly in the skimpy clothes I'm forced to wear. The living room is dim with only a couple of lamps turned on, and I'm on my knees on the laminate wood floor. Bastian is seated on their worn couch, the other two hovering near him, flanking me on either side.

There's a challenge in Bastian's eyes, as though daring me to protest. I want to fight back, to tell him that I take orders from no one, but the competitive part of me wants to show him that I'm not afraid.

Fear and desire wage war inside me as I lick my lips and stare at the bulge in his jeans. I reach out my hands and pull down the zipper, opening it enough to slip his thick, heavy cock out and wrap my hand around it. It smells musky, with a hint of spice.

Leaning forward, I'm about to wrap my lips around the tip when my hair is yanked back unceremoniously.

"You didn't think we were gonna make it easy on ya, did you?" he asks. I try to move forward again but his grip tightens.

"Two taps means stop," Caleb says, far too calm for this entire situation. "Open your mouth and stick your tongue out. Yes, just like that. Good girl."

Bastian lays his cock on my tongue and I slowly inch forward, trying to take it down while his hand is still fisted in my hair.

"You're doing so well, little girl," Caleb croons.

I'd never been praised like this before, and most definitely not by men as attractive as the three in front of me. Caleb's words go straight to my core and fill my mouth with saliva. I realize the stupid thong has gone damp and horror washes over me—being bossed around is getting me off.

"Move your head slow, like this," Bastian says, demonstrating with his hands. I try to copy him and take him further down, nearly gagging. It's too big, too much and some saliva drips out the side of my mouth.

"Slow down," Dominic orders. "Breathe through your nose. Have you ever done this before?"

I half shrug, mouth still wrapped around Bastian's cock.

"You're a quick learner," Bastian groans as my tongue flicks the underside of his shaft, rubbing along the vein there.

My eyes water as I try to push down further, but Bastian's large hand strokes across my forehead, encouraging me to keep going. It's cold but I feel as though my entire body is on fire with how warm I feel, as though someone cranked the heat in the house on high.

"That's it, keep going," Bastian says, his voice husky as he reaches around the neck of my dress to yank the ties open.

In seconds, Dominic is there, pulling the top of the dress down, plunging his hand into the lacy material of my bra. A moan escapes me as his fingers tug at my nipple, the peak stiffening with the rough contact.

Oh God. I'm getting turned on by this. My thong sticks to me as I shift around, trying to relieve some of the pressure on my knees while I keep moving my head at a steady pace. Dominic's fingers tease my nipple, rolling it between his thumb and forefinger as I continue to move on Bastian's cock. Another noise escapes me and I want to move my hand down to relieve the incessant throbbing between my thighs.

Bastian's hand in my hair loosens for a moment, his hand stroking through the strands. "Stop," he orders. His cock slips out of my mouth and I stare up at him, wondering if I'm doing something wrong.

"Take her panties off," he tells Caleb, who comes over and pushes me backward, spreading my legs. My cheeks grow hotter, the thought of them seeing my chubby pussy sending me into a momentary spiral. I'm not cute, I'm not petite like other girls. They'll think I'm disgusting and they'll push me away.

Panic has me gripped by the throat, but suddenly, Caleb yanks my thong down, spreading my legs wider. His grin surprises me enough to quell the racing thoughts.

Bastian whistles. "Look at how wet the little slut is," he says. "You want this, don't you? You want to be teased and humiliated and used by us."

It's too much and I hide my face in my hands, unable to look them in the eye. How could I let them touch me like this? How could I just let them use me?

"Look at you," he reaches out and pulls my hands away from my face, the smirk on his face glinting in the dim light. "You're such a little tease, flaunting yourself in those clothes. I bet you're dying to get off, aren't you?"

When I don't respond, his hands are back in my hair, yanking my head backward once more. "Answer me, slut," he growls out.

"Yes!" I cry out, tears in my eyes. "Yes, please!"

"Then do it." He releases his grip. "I want you to lower that pussy onto this boot right here," He says, holding out his leather-clad foot. "And rub yourself off on it while you suck me off."

My mouth goes dry as I look down at his shoe. It's thick-soled leather, with stiff laces and sleek metal straps. I feel my cheeks burn as I stare, debating how badly I want this release.

With slow movements, I maneuver my body so I'm hovering just over it, but Caleb pushes my shoulders down, forcing me into direct contact. A squeak escapes me, which turns into a whimper as I grind down, the contact sending sparks through my core.

Bastian's hands move my head back into position at the same time. "You have one minute, or you're not getting off the rest of the night," he warns me. My eyes widen before I start rocking my hips experimentally, trying to find the right rhythm.

The thrum of my body increases as I move, the volume of slick leaking out of me making my movements erratic. My head bobs back and forth on Bastian's cock, speed increasing as I try to find my own release.

"Tick-tock," Dominic whispers in my ear. "Thirty seconds to go."

I whine high in my throat and grind down harder, desperation bubbling up. Dominic finds the clasp at the back of the bra and releases it with a quick motion, letting my breasts spill out as he reaches for them.

Kneading the soft flesh under his fingers, he toys with me again, pinching and pulling the nipples hard enough to leave marks.

I feel the orgasm building low in my belly, movements growing more frantic as Caleb joins in, sucking dark bruises into my neck with his tongue and biting into the skin with his teeth. The sensations are too much and a trickle of sweat rolls down my back.

"Ten, nine, eight," Dominic whispers into my ear. "Seven, six, five, four …"

Bastian shoves my head down on his cock, hard and the salty, bitter taste of his orgasm explodes on my tongue and I swallow it down, trying not to let any spill.

At that same moment, the timer on Dominic's watch starts beeping but my orgasm hits and I let out a yell, hips stuttering to a stop as the tension seeps from my body. "God," I groan, feeling boneless.

Dominic hauls me to my feet and tosses me on the couch, yanking my legs apart as he drives himself home into my dripping core in one smooth motion. He's so big that it's bordering on painful as he begins to work his hips, thrusting himself in and out.

"Take it," he grunts. "Just like that, Princess. Take it."

Caleb leans over me, stroking the hair away from my face. "Open up," he says, tapping my cheek. Obediently, my mouth falls open and he slips his own cock inside, pressing forward as far as I can take it.

I start sucking, eager for the taste of him on my tongue. I hollow my cheeks and use one hand to keep him steady as he rolls his hips back and forth.

"That's a good girl," Bastian says, stroking his own shaft idly as he watches us. "You'd really do anything for us, wouldn't you? What a perfect little whore; made just for us."

Everything is happening so fast now, and I can barely keep up as Dominic roughly takes me over and over, thrusting deep inside while Caleb uses my mouth for his own pleasure.

My brain is floating, a high I'd never experienced before. I'm wetter and more turned on than I've ever been in my entire life.

"Fuck!" Dominic curses, hips slamming into me once more as he releases inside me. Caleb's cock slips into my throat and I nearly gag on it before forcing myself to breathe through my nose like they taught me.

I'm sobbing as Caleb finishes, unsure why. "Shhh," he says, pulling me up and sitting me in his lap.

He strokes my back as he turns me around, my legs dangling over his thighs. Bastian kneels in front of me, stroking warm fingers over my inner thighs before they slip inside, his thumb going straight for the bud. He rubs circles into it as my body writhes under him, but it's too much, I'm too sensitive.

"I can't," I whine, thrashing around. "I can't!"

"Yes you can," he says, voice low. "Come for me, Princess."

As if his words have a direct line to my brain, my body obeys, legs shaking as I come undone. I slump backward and Caleb wraps his arms around me.

"Knew you'd be good for us, good to us," Caleb murmurs, kissing my cheek. He holds me against his chest, letting my breathing slow to a few ragged gasps.

Bastian's fingers tangle in my hair again, moving it out of my face. "Get her cleaned up," he says to his brothers. "Then lock her up again. We'll go out without her tonight."

I want to protest, to yell and plead with them, but all the energy for a fight has been wrung out of my body and I can't even give a feeble protest as Dominic lifts me in his arms and carries me up the stairs, Caleb following behind.

They deposit me on Caleb's bed again and I sit there, head spinning.

I shiver as Caleb uses a wet cloth to wipe me down gently, then dresses me in an oversized shirt and tucks me under the covers.

"Be good, Princess," Caleb says. They leave and lock the door and I feel a wave of emotions crash over me, a sob escaping me.

Why did I let them use me like this? And worse, why did it feel so good?

10

DOMINIC

"Ready to go, Princess?" I ask, leaning against the door jamb. After we cleaned her up last night and tucked her into bed, we went out to the bar for a few hours but my mind was on Sienna the whole time. I think it was the same for Caleb and Bastian because we left earlier than normal and headed straight back home.

Caleb stayed with her last night but tonight it's my turn, and I'm spending the day with her too. Bastian is going to work at the shop and Caleb is planning on looking into whatever is going on with the Serpents lately, so I've been assigned babysitting duty.

"Yeah, hang on a moment," Sienna says, moving slowly, a wince escaping her. She must still be sore after last night. A smirk paints itself on my face as I watch her pull on a sweater.

"Hurry up," I snap, enjoying the way she trembles. It's kind of hot how nervous she still is around us, despite what we did to her last night.

She's back to wearing the same kindergarten clothing since we're allowing her to do her work today and it wouldn't be appropriate to let her parade around the neighborhood in crop tops and miniskirts.

"Let's go," she mumbles, clutching her clipboard to her chest. "I've got to get something turned in by today or I'm sunk. No thanks to you," she whispers.

"What's that, Princess?" I ask, enjoying the way she squirms as her eyes meet mine.

She goes pink. "Nothing."

"Thought so. Let's go."

I herd her down the stairs and out the back door as we climb into the Firebird. "So where do you want to go today?" I ask. "We spread the word last night that everyone can give you any info you want from now on."

"I guess let's go to the park near the Quik-Mart on Main," she says, studying something on her clipboard. "There's always plenty of people hanging around so I'm sure I'll get some interviews there."

"We could try the old community center later," I offer. "People still hang around there even though it's closed down."

She nods, tucking a strand of red hair behind her ear. She's still wearing it down today, a change I find I like.

"You look gorgeous," I comment, picking up her hand and bringing it to my lips to kiss it. She pulls it away and her cheeks turn red.

"No I don't," she protests. "I know you're just saying that to get to me."

"Shit, Princess, you're crazy if you think I do anything I don't want to do," I tell her. "I ain't that kind of guy. That's why I'm not in charge. Bastian is better at doing the hard stuff. I'm too stubborn." I chuckle and she gives me a sidelong glance.

"Really?"

"Yep. What's so hard about the fact that we find you attractive?"

"Because I'm not!" she says, toying with the seatbelt. Her eyes are on the road and she doesn't look at me. "I'm chubby and short, and I have frizzy hair and freckles."

"Don't you know that they say Aphrodite was a redhead?" I tell her, reaching over to put a hand on her thigh. "And she's always been depicted as curvy. So you're basically calling a goddess ugly."

"I am not," she says, refusing to look at me. But I see how she peeks at me from the corner of her eye. "I didn't know that about Aphrodite," she adds.

"It's true. One of my favorite subjects in school was history," I say as we pull onto the main drag. "I was obsessed with Greek myths."

"Really? I loved history too!" Sienna exclaims, turning to face me. "My favorite was Tudor history."

"Yeah, that was a crazy era," I agree. "Henry was kind of a dick."

She giggles and I watch as the tension leaves her. "You're not wrong," she says. "Have you ever—" but at that moment, we pull into the tiny park and Sienna gasps.

There are at least fifty people hanging out and milling around when we get out of the car.

"Hey!" Davis, one of the older residents of the neighborhood comes trotting over, waving us down. "I put out the word like you said. Told everyone to show up here first thing in the morning."

"Thanks, Davis," I say, slipping him a ten for his troubles. I turn to Sienna. "Told you we'd help you out."

Her eyes are wide as she takes in the sight of all these people waiting to be interviewed for her research study.

"You guys really did this?" she asks. Her voice is soft, eyes wide.

"Yup. I'll be over there," I say, pointing to a picnic table a few feet away. "Gonna keep an eye out while you do your thing."

Sienna beams at me, her smile hitting me right in the chest. I watch for a moment as she scrambles for her bag, pulling out her clipboard.

"Right," she says, more to herself than me. Raising her voice, she calls out to the people standing around. "Form an orderly line, please! You'll all be asked a series of short questions. If you qualify for the study, there will be a longer interview that we can schedule for later. Anyone who participates in the study will receive compensation."

People start lining up as instructed and I hang out on the picnic bench, watching with an amused smirk as she gets down to business. She sits on one side of a table, taking down information from each person in turn.

It's a few hours before she's done and she comes back over to me in a daze, leafing through the stack of paperwork she's collected on everyone.

"I can't wait to make Owen eat his words," she says, a giggle escaping her. "Owen is my boss on the project. He's been riding me hard about this."

"Looks like you've got what you need for today, right?" I ask. "Do you still want to go to the old community center?"

"I should get back and compile this data," she says, shaking her head. "Let's go back."

Hiding a grin, I escort her back to the car and we head for the house. Bastian and Caleb are still gone when we arrive.

"You know," Sienna says, her voice tinged with a hint of vulnerability, "I just wonder sometimes if all this research I'm doing will actually make a difference. I feel like I'm constantly fighting to prove myself against my boss."

"You did good today," I tell her. "Don't let your boss get you down."

Sienna's eyes light up at that and it tugs at my heart to know that she's had so few compliments in her life that a few crumbs of praise have her glowing like the sun.

"I'm going to reward you for your good behavior," I say, stepping up to her to lean down and kiss her. "Lie down on the couch."

She hesitates a moment, searching my eyes with her own, then obeys, climbing onto the couch. I tug her tights, plaid skirt, and panties down in one go before spreading her pussy lips and fusing my mouth with her wet cunt.

A shudder escapes her, body writhing as I lick and suck her clit, moving fingers down to slip inside her. She's already wet, making the slide easy. I peek up and she's got a blush going from head to toe.

"You like that?" I ask, moving back down to nose at her bud. "You've never been eaten out before, have you, Princess?"

"No," she stutters out, hands moving down to grip my hair. She tastes sweet and a little salty as I curl my tongue around her entrance, thrusting inside.

It's not long before she's rocking against me, slick spilling out as she comes under my ministrations. "Good girl," I say, before cleaning her up with my tongue. "Can you grab my laptop, it's over near the recliner."

Sienna takes a moment to put herself back together as I head into the bathroom to wash my face and hands.

Once I'm done, I come back to find she's got my laptop with her on the couch.

"Do you mind if we watch some YouTube?" I ask, lifting the top. "There's this cooking show I always watch. The guy replicates food from movies and TV shows."

"Oh, yeah I've heard of that," Sienna says, moving so I can place the laptop on the TV tray. "Sure, I can wait to input this data until later."

We sit back on the couch and I pull it up, pressing play. "I used to try to do some of his recipes but they're hard," I tell her. "He makes every single thing from scratch."

"Do you cook?" she asks, turning her head to face me.

I nod "Yeah. I do most of the cooking between the three of us. I was the oldest, so I had to make sure we got fed."

She looks down at her hands. "What happened to your parents, if I can ask?"

"They died when Caleb was little," I tell her. "We were raised by our grandfather, but he worked a lot, so I learned how to cook early on."

"I'm sorry," she murmurs, reaching out to place her hand on mine. "I was raised by my mom. No dad in the picture, and my mom worked two jobs until I was a teenager. Then she decided she was tired of missing out on her youth, so I kind of had to fend for myself."

It makes sense why Sienna is so passionate about helping the economically underprivileged. I sling an arm around her shoulder and pull her close to me. "Life is rough," I tell her. "But you make it work."

"Sounds like we both had to make it work," she says. We watch the video in silence, my heart beating hard in my chest.

Was I too quick to judge Sienna? I glance at her from the corner of my eye as she fidgets with her sleeve. Maybe we were too hard on her at first. Is she more innocent than we thought?

I don't have any answers, so I turn my attention back to the video, trying to ignore the ache in my chest.

11

SIENNA

"C'mon, Princess," Bastian calls. "Get over here. I'm on babysitting duty today."

I walk down the stairs, tugging on the skirt that Bastian picked out for me today. I have no idea why but he got a wild hare this morning and decided that I needed to start wearing the clothes they picked out for me more often.

"I don't like this skirt," I grumble as I step into the kitchen.

"Relax, Princess. You look hot," Bastian says, leaning in to give me a quick kiss that leaves me feeling dizzy, nipping at my bottom lip with his teeth. "And you know we wouldn't let any creeps come near you," he adds, his tone belying a lingering hint of protectiveness.

"I guess I just didn't realize I was going to be dressed like a dime-store hooker," I complain as we climb into the car. "I should have never agreed to this stupid charade."

Bastian's eyes lock on me from across the console, the intensity of his gaze making the hairs on the back of my neck stand on end. He leans over, crowding my space. "You're free to leave any time," he says, his voice low. "But you agreed to our terms," he adds. "So you don't get to start bitching now."

I roll my eyes, but Bastian's hand is suddenly on my thigh,

pushing my knees apart. Before I can protest, he's pushing my panties to the side and rubbing a finger inside my wet folds.

"Seems like you're not as mad about our arrangement as you act," he says, the smug smile on his face making me want to smack him. Just as I'm ready to reach out and push his hand away, he twists his fingers along my clit, pulling a ragged moan from my lips.

"God," I whisper, knees falling limply to either side as Bastian continues to work a finger down and into me, using two more to continue teasing the spot that has me moaning and rocking my hips up into his hand.

"But I suppose if you want, we could always stop this arrangement," Bastian says, moving his hand slowly away from me. I whimper as my hips follow his hand.

"Dammit, just keep touching me," I say in a growl.

"Beg for it," Bastian orders. I shut my mouth and his hand moves further away.

"Please?" I ask, squeezing my eyes shut.

"What's that?"

"Please, please finger me," I beg, hating how desperate I sound. "Please fuck me, I need it."

Bastian smiles. "Good girl."

My pulse jumps when he slides his fingers into me once more, slipping deeper into me. His other fingers continue their relentless teasing dance along my clit and it seems like mere seconds before I'm arching upward with a cry.

"Feeling better?" Bastian asks as he pulls his hand away. I give him a half-hearted glare but he sticks his hand in my face and pushes his fingers into my mouth. "Suck them clean."

Tongue darting out, I swipe over the offered digits, lapping up the taste of myself from his hand. As I clean him up, I catch a glimpse of a tattoo along the inside of his wrist. I'd seen it before, the other night.

"What is that?" I ask, pulling his fingers from my mouth and turning the wrist to examine it. There are some spindly lines there, branching upward into his sleeve.

He takes his hand back, wiping it carelessly over his jeans, before unbuttoning the cuff of his flannel shirt and rolling it up to his elbow, turning his arm to show me.

I reach out and grab his arm, looking at it more closely. The spindly lines go upward and turn into thicker roots, which join together into an intricately twisting trunk and then continue upward towards his elbow where it splits off into more intricate branches.

"It's so good," I say. "The line work on this is amazing. What made you get it?"

"It's the Tree of Life," he says, twisting his arm a little. "Got it when I turned eighteen. The roots are supposed to represent the past, keeping me grounded. The branches symbolize the future and opportunity for growth."

I nod, removing my hand when I realize I've been tracing the lines absentmindedly with my finger. There's a softness in his eyes as we share in this quiet moment alone. His usual stoicism seems to momentarily melt away, revealing hidden layers that I'd never expected from someone like him.

"Anyway, let's get going so you can get your shit done. You've got me worked up and all I can think about is bending you over in that skirt," he says, rolling his sleeve back down.

Then again, maybe not, I think as I buckle the seatbelt with a frown.

While out, I watch as he hovers nearby, a scowl on his face. He seems stiff, almost uncomfortable, and I wonder if it might be his protective side coming out. What made him like this?

As soon as we're done, he drags me back to the car. "Let's go home so I can keep my promise and bend you over," he whispers in my ear. I blush and follow him to the car.

As soon as we get home though, Bastian gets a call. Caleb is lounging in the living room and pats the spot next to him. I fall onto the couch next to him and watch as Bastian starts to argue with whoever is on the other end of the line, sounding more agitated as the call continues.

I turn to Caleb. "What's going on?"

"Nothing," he shakes his head. "Don't worry about it."

"Oh, come on. You can't even give me a hint?" I ask, turning to face him and batting my lashes. "You guys never tell me anything."

"It's nothing for you to worry about," Caleb says again. "Do you want to come up to the bedroom with me? I'm in the mood to play *The Sims*."

"You play *The Sims*?" I exclaim. "I love that game!"

"You can help me with my current build challenge," he offers. "I can't seem to get the roofing right on this one."

He takes my hand in his and I follow him up the stairs, practically bouncing in excitement.

Within a few minutes of us sitting down though, Bastian trudges up the stairs and sticks his head into Caleb's room, a grim look on his face. "We need to go," he says.

I stand up but he shakes his head. "Not you."

"What's going on?" I ask, raising an eyebrow. "Are you okay?"

"We're fine. Just sit tight," he says. "We'll be back soon."

"Can't I just come, just this once?"

"I said no," Bastian's voice grows firm. "We've got some business to take care of."

"What kind of business?" I press. "I already know you guys are street criminals. I'm sure I can hang out in the car while you shake down some poor snot for his money."

Bastian's eyes betray a flicker of hurt. "We're not like that," he grits out.

"You've got the wrong idea," Caleb adds.

"Whatever. Fine. I'll just stay here," I say, flouncing over to the bed. "Have fun with whatever it is you do."

Bastian's gaze lingers on me for a moment longer than usual, betraying a hint of uncertainty before he turns, preparing to leave with Caleb.

"Fine, leave me behind like I'm just some brainless bimbo," I say, my voice tinged in frustration. "But don't be surprised if I decide that I'm done with this arrangement when you leave. I'm sick of being treated like a pawn."

"Don't even think about it," Bastian warns me. "Sit your ass down and behave yourself, dammit. Now let's go." He ushers Caleb away.

I wait until they're gone and test the door. It's locked, like usual.

A sob of frustration escapes my throat and I ball my hands into fists. This isn't fair. I'm not stupid and I'm not a bimbo. I can handle whatever it is that they get up to.

"It's not worth it," I tell myself, squeezing my eyes shut tightly. "This entire stupid situation isn't worth it. I can figure out the rest of this project on my own now. I'm not staying here like their little slave forever."

But I can't get out of the room, either. I'm stuck inside here, locked away like a misbehaving animal.

My eyes sweep the room, trying to find a solution. Caleb's window faces the side of the house, so there's no way for me to climb down.

I try shoving my shoulder into the door but I bounce off it, realizing that they're steel on the inside. "Ow, fuck," I curse, rubbing my shoulder.

There's a case by Caleb's desk, with some computer stuff inside. A quick rifle through shows that he's got a few tiny screwdrivers and I grin, brandishing one of them.

It takes me forever to unscrew all the screws in the door, and I'm sweating by the time I'm done but I take the door off its hinges and I beam.

Who said I'm not handy?

Just as I step into the hall, I hear voices downstairs. In my panic, I try to put the door back but it falls over and bangs against the wooden floor.

"Shit!" My eyes widen and I scramble to pick it up again but it's heavy. All three of them rush up the stairs and catch me red-handed.

"You seriously tried to escape, even though I warned you?" Bastian asks, raising one eyebrow. "I told you what would happen, didn't I?"

"I'm not afraid of you," I say, standing up to him with defiance in my eyes. Bastian shakes his head. "Nice try, but you're not getting out of this. Take her clothes off."

Dominic and Caleb step on either side of me, making short work of my clothes before I can even blink.

"How does …ten spankings sound?" Bastian offers as he sits on the edge of the bed.

"You're going to spank me like I'm some naughty child?" I ask, unable to believe what I'm hearing.

"Do you want to make it twenty?" Bastian's eyebrows raise and I scowl, shaking my head. "Get over here," he orders.

I shuffle forward and he yanks me down over his lap, no warning before his hand connects with my backside. I cry out, the sting immediate and unrelenting.

"Stop! Please!" I yell as Bastian spanks me again. I feel exposed and humiliated but when I squirm, I realize I'm getting wetter with every smack against my ass. I press my head against the comforter, squirming to hide my face.

With the next strike, my body tingles in a mixture of pain and pleasure and I feel myself getting too close to the edge for comfort.

Thwack! Thwack!

No, please, I beg silently. But my body betrays me, sending me over the edge as soon as Bastian's hand connects with my ass once more.

Fuck.

12

BASTIAN

The tension of last night still lingers in the air, casting a heavy pall over the morning. Sienna's escape attempt caught me off guard and left a bitter taste in my mouth. Her disobedience had added fuel to the fire of my frustration—we missed a chance at confronting some wayward Serpents yesterday and it still has me on edge.

Standing in the dim living room, Caleb's voice breaks through my swirling thoughts.

"We can't afford any more slip-ups," Caleb says, tone laced with urgency. "The Serpents aren't going to wait around for us to catch them. They're going after our weak links, targeting businesses we haven't visited in a while."

I nod, feeling the weight of the responsibility that rests on my shoulders. Despite our best efforts, the Serpent threat still looms large, reminding me that if we don't take care of things soon, we're putting our community in danger.

Dominic jogs down the stairs, a look of steely resolve on his face. "She's sleeping," he says, mouth set in a grim line. "And the door is finally back on its hinges."

Despite the gravity of the situation, I can't help the chuckle that escapes me. "She's pretty smart, I have to admit."

"I can't believe she managed to use those computer tools to take the door off," Caleb agrees. "Good thing we installed those reinforced doors when we moved in."

Dominic heads into the kitchen to start making breakfast. We've got a full day at the shop today, but Caleb will stay with Sienna to keep an eye on her. She's not going anywhere, not with the Serpents lurking around.

I can't shake the feeling of unease that gnaws at the edges of my mind. It's there, lurking—telling me that something big is coming down the pipe.

The smell of bacon pulls me out of my head and I sniff the air, a smile curling up on my mouth. "Smells good, Dom," I call out.

"Thanks. I'm trying something new," Dom calls back.

A buzz from my pocket has me pulling out my phone and I glance down, a sense of foreboding creeping over me. "Neil just texted me," I say, frowning at the message. "Some Serpents are lurking around his music shop and scaring away customers. He says that they're asking to talk to him but he's refusing."

Caleb and Dominic are immediately at attention, Dominic flipping the switch on the stove. "Let's go," Dominic says, grabbing his coat from the hook.

Caleb snatches his jacket from the back of the couch and the three of us head for the door. Sienna is still locked up in Caleb's room, so we aren't worried about another escape attempt. She knows the consequences now.

Tension crackles in the air as we slip into the Firebird. No one speaks, too busy preparing for the confrontation we know is coming.

The Serpents have been doing the same thing at several businesses in the area. When they hit up the Quik-Mart yesterday, we went to confront them but they cleared out before we could get there.

Arriving at Neil's music shop, we immediately spot the greasy-haired meatheads hanging around the entrance, leering at passers-by.

"Yo, what's up?" I say as we roll up, stepping out of the car as soon as Dom kills the engine. "We got a problem, fuckfaces?"

"Nah," a bug-eyed Serpent with a flaming skull tattoo on his neck steps forward. "We were here first so clear out, Blade bitches."

Bug Eyes waves a hand and I step forward, getting into his space. "In case you missed it, this entire place is our territory. So *we* were here first, or are you as stupid as that tattoo on your neck?"

"You wanna step?" Bug Eyes asks. Three more of his buddies move forward as well, four Serpents against the three of us.

"We'd take you down before you could even take your thumb out of your ass long enough to fight," I warn him. "Slither back to the hole you crawled out of or you'll find out firsthand what we do to snakes around here."

"We ain't going anywhere, pretty boy," Bug Eyes says, flicking open the knife in his hand. "If it's a turf war you want, we're more than happy to oblige. But we have the numbers on our side, sunshine. You take us out and there's a hundred more Serpents waiting to cut you down."

As he speaks, half a dozen more Serpents come around the corner, facing us with knives and clubs.

"Bastian," Caleb says, holding a hand out to keep me from attacking the cretin in front of me. "He's right. We can't afford to start something right now."

"Take it easy, pretty boy," Bug Eyes says, a smug grin on his face that's begging to be knocked off. "How about you mind your own business and move along?"

"We're coming for you assholes," I warn him. "We may not have the numbers but you haven't seen the last of us. Watch your back!"

Dom and Caleb flank me as we head back to the car and I slam the door, fuming inside. I'm not going to let those snake assholes crawl back into Caspian Springs—not when so much work was put into clearing their nest all those years ago.

"We need a plan," I tell them as we head back home. "We can't afford to get shown up again like that."

"The man who fights and runs away lives to fight another day," Caleb quotes. "You remember who taught us that."

"Don't bring him up," I warn Caleb. Even if he's right, I don't want to hear the bastard's name right now.

"Let's just all head back to the house and cool down over breakfast," Dominic says. I glare at the dashboard but give a half-hearted shrug.

"Fine."

Once we arrive, I head upstairs to check on Sienna. The spanking was supposed to teach her a lesson, but it turns out we learned a lot more from her than she did from us when I realized how much she gets off on being spanked.

"Hey," I say, slipping inside Caleb's room. Sienna is sitting up, staring out the window. "We had some business to take care of. You're free to leave the bedroom now."

"Great," Sienna says, voice dull. "Are you going to hit me if I don't act perfectly from now on?"

Lingering anger at her disobedience battles inside me, along with a strange sense of attraction, leaving me torn between reprimanding her and giving in to the desire that simmers beneath my frustration.

I reach out to run a hand up her arm. "You know the rules, Sienna," I say, my voice rough with emotion. I feel the pull to give into temptation whenever I'm around her. "And second of all Princess, don't try to pretend like you didn't enjoy yourself last night. I know you did—you came all over me."

Sienna's cheeks flush and she lowers her gaze. "So what? You were mean."

"I think you like it when I'm mean," I tell her, leaning in to kiss a trail up her jaw. "I think you like it when I'm rough. I think it scares you."

She's trembling, but she isn't trying to pull away so, buoyed by this, I give a nip to her ear and she lets out a breathy moan.

"Do you want to try things a little more rough?" I ask, reaching up to toy with her puckering nipples over the threadbare cotton of her shirt.

"What do you mean?" Sienna asks.

"Biting, scratching, more spanking, that sort of thing," I offer. The desire to take back control and show her who's in charge surges inside as I describe her options. "You can use a safe word if you don't like it."

"Safe word?"

"Yeah, something that tells me to stop. How about rutabaga?"

Sienna chuckles. "Sure."

"Alright, I'm going to touch you and ignore it if you say stop, but if you don't want something, use the safe word. What is it?" I ask, prompting her.

"Rutabaga," she repeats.

"Good girl." I stand up and start stripping Sienna down, having her get on the bed on all fours. "I've got something I want to try," I tell her, reaching under the bed for the box I know Caleb keeps in here.

Taking out the flogger, I let it fall onto Sienna's ass, lightly at first. She jumps but relaxes when she realizes it doesn't hurt as much as anticipated. Bringing it down on her again, I test to see if she can handle a little more pain.

She gasps but doesn't say anything, so I rain down a few more blows, enjoying the way her ass turns redder with every strike.

Sienna is shivering now, body tense but I reach down to touch her and she's dripping wet. Pulling my finger back, I stick it in my mouth and suck, relishing the taste of her juices.

I squeeze her ass roughly, kneading it under my palms. "That's right, little girl. Take it," I tell her, raising a hand and smacking her ass again and again. She cries out and I feel myself harden at the noise.

"Take it, you little slut," I tell her, grabbing her hair and yanking her backward roughly. "Take this like the whore you are."

Sienna's eyes widen for a moment, but she lays down on the bed obediently, while I straddle her, undoing my belt and pulling my cock out. "Open," I tell her.

She opens her mouth and takes me down, letting me roughly fuck her face while tears leak out of the corners of her eyes. "Fucking slut, take it!" I yell, shoving myself deeper down her throat and holding her down by her wrists. "Take it!"

Sienna starts to gag and I pull out for a moment. "You can take it, you dirty whore." She shakes her head, coughing and pushing me away.

"Rutabaga!" Sienna calls out.

Before I can react, Caleb and Dominic burst into the room. Dominic scoops Sienna up in his arms, while Caleb shoves me backward, hard.

"What the fuck?" I yell. "What's your problem?"

"We could hear her use the safe word," Caleb says, glaring at me. "You know we're supposed to be responsible, we never let it get that far."

"She's fine,' I argue, crossing my arms.

"She's covered in bruises," Dominic says, holding Sienna close to him. "And she's terrified. You should have been checking in long before things got to this point, you asshole."

"What were you thinking?" Caleb jabs a finger into my chest.

"I don't need this shit. I'm sick of everyone questioning me!" I tell him, pushing him away before running a hand through my hair.

"Fine!" Caleb yells. "Then leave. Don't come back until your head's been screwed on straight."

I feel the weight of his order pressing down on me, a realization dawning that I've spiraled out of control. For a moment, defiance flares inside, but it dissipates, replaced by burning shame.

Without another word, I turn on my heel and storm out, the echo of Caleb's rebuke ringing in my ears.

Everything is just so screwed up right now.

13

CALEB

As soon as we're sure Bastian is gone, Dominic bundles Sienna up and takes her into the bathroom. I follow behind, taking note of the fact that Dom looks like he needs a minute.

"Hey, I've got her," I tell him. "I can clean her up." I wave him off. He deposits Sienna on the counter and takes off, storming downstairs.

Stepping into the bathroom, the air feels thick with tension, the weight of what happened hanging heavy over us in the confined space. Despite the warmth emanating from the heating vent, there's a distinct chill in the air.

Sienna is still shaking as I look her over, taking inventory of her bruises. Shit. Bastian did a number on her.

"Are you alright?" I ask. "That was rough."

"I feel like shit," she admits, a shaky sigh escaping her.

"Next time knee him in the balls."

This brings a weak laugh from her.

"Why is he like this?" Sienna asks. "He's so hot and cold with me."

I shrug and gently wipe her off with a damp cloth. "That's just

Bastian for you. Prince Charming was never his style. He's always been a bit rough around the edges."

Sienna looks down as I open the drawer between her knees. "I'm going to put some ointment on you now," I tell her.

Twisting off the cap of the tube, I dab some onto my fingers before spreading it across the bruises on her thighs. She winces but doesn't make a peep.

As I work, my thoughts drift back to when we were kids and the three of us roamed around without a care in the world. Bastian had always been the more impulsive one of the three of us, quick to anger and even quicker to lash out. And I'd always been there to diffuse the situation, and smooth things over.

I can't help wondering how I failed this time. I should never have let him go upstairs when I knew he was still reeling over the situation with the Serpents earlier.

"What happened in there?" I ask.

"He seemed fine at first, I guess," Sienna tells me. "He asked if we could try some more rough stuff. But he told me that he would stop if I used a safe word."

I sigh. "When we're into rough stuff, we use a system," I explain. "I prefer something like a traffic light system. Green means all good, yellow for caution, and red for stop."

"Do you guys always go after the same girl?" Sienna asks.

"No," I shake my head. "There was only one other time ..." I trail off, a lump rising in my throat. Taking a deep breath, I continue "Someone from our past. They hurt us, but Bastian took it the hardest."

"I'm sorry," Sienna says, voice soft. "Being hurt like that sucks."

"He probably sees some of her in you, when he looks at you. He's always been sensitive, feels things deeply. It makes it tough for him to let people in, so sometimes he pushes them away before they get too close.'"

"Then why does he want to be involved with me at all?" Sienna questions, a note of frustration in her voice. "Why does he want to keep me here under lock and key if he's so hell-bent on never getting close to another person."

"That's something you'd have to ask him," I tell her as I dab more ointment on the bruises on her wrists. "He probably just wants to keep you safe."

"I can take care of myself," Sienna says, giving me a measured look. "I grew up in a place just like this. I might seem naive and innocent, but I'm not. It's because of what happened to me that I try so hard to be kind and upbeat. I guess I just don't understand Bastian. One minute he's treating me like I'm nothing, the next he's ... like this."

"I know. But he's ... complicated," I tell her. "Turn around. I want to look at your ass."

She stands up, wincing again as her feet make contact with the ground. Her ass is red, marked up from the flogger and his hands. It's slowly turning to purple bruises and I start to gently rub ointment into the irritated skin.

"Complicated? He's downright confusing," Sienna says, snorting. "One minute, he's rough with me, and then he's apologizing like he's two different people."

I shake my head. "That's just how he is. He doesn't know how to handle ... well, any of this."

"But why keep me here if he's just going to hurt me?"

"I don't think he sees it like that," I tell her. "Bastian is an ass but he's trying to protect you, in his own messed-up way."

"Protect me?" Sienna scoffs. "By locking me up like some kind of prisoner?"

"You're not a prisoner," I say. She makes a noise. "I promise. You're free to leave but there are dangers out there that you don't know about. Stuff that could get you seriously hurt around here. And Bastian's been through so much, he's just afraid of losing control."

She rolls her eyes. "What about you and Dominic? Are you just following his lead?"

I hesitate, trying to find the words. "We have our reasons, Sienna. It's complicated."

"Complicated. Right. That seems to be the word of the day. I just wish I knew how to figure you guys out."

I don't have an answer for her, so I stay silent.

"You didn't have to help me, you know," Sienna breaks the silence. "I could have cleaned myself up."

"It's my job to look after you," I say. "The Blades protect what's ours."

"What if that's not what I want?" Sienna asks. "What if I want to take care of myself?"

I chuckle. "Now you're just being stubborn, dumbass. You don't always need to look after yourself."

"No one ever looked after me before," Sienna snaps. "And things were fine until you came along."

"Then let us help you anyway. You don't always have to be so strong."

"I'm not that strong," she mumbles.

"You're stronger than you look," I say. "Did you at least enjoy any of it?"

"Some of it, yeah," Sienna admits. "It was kind of hot when he was ordering me around. I've never done anything like that before. It felt good to give up control like that."

"We can try similar, but less intense stuff another time," I offer. "Take it slow and do a lot of checking in. We can figure out what you like."

"Maybe," Sienna turns her head and gives me a tight-lipped smile.

"Not anytime soon," I say, rushing to correct myself. "For tonight, you should take it easy."

I wonder if Bastian even knows how bruised up she is. He can be a bastard sometimes, but I don't doubt he's kicking himself right now for how much he hurt her. If he wasn't a good person, I wouldn't follow him around like I do. He's always had our backs, being the one to make the tough decisions, even when we were young.

And he's good about owning up to his mistakes. I know he'll come back and apologize, once he's cleared his head.

"Is Dominic okay?" Sienna asks. "He looked like he was about to yell."

"He's fine," I tell her. "He's more pissed at Bastian than anything. Dom is the oldest, so sometimes he starts feeling like he should be better at taking care of things."

Sienna frowns. "He's a lot better at that sort of thing than he thinks."

I nod. "Dom's tough on himself. We all can be," I remark, finishing up.

"We can be our own worst critics," Sienna agrees. I help her stand and check her once more, trying to make sure I didn't miss anything.

"How do you feel now?"

"Still shitty, but better," she admits.

"Good. Are you still wanting to go out canvassing tomorrow?"

She shakes her head. "I have to turn in some work. I need to go to the campus and see Dr. Thornton."

I can't help the frown that etches itself on my face at that.

"What? Why do you hate him so much?"

"We go way back," I mutter. "So just trust me, you don't want to be alone with him."

"How do you know him?" Sienna asks, tilting her head as she studies me. I step back instinctively.

"We knew him a long time ago," I mutter. "It doesn't matter. You're not allowed to be around him without one of us going with you."

"If you won't tell me, I'll just assume you're biased against him," Sienna retorts, her eyes narrowing.

"It's complicated. Trust me on this one," I say, a hint of tension in my voice.

"You guys haven't given me much reason to trust you yet," Sienna says, narrowing her eyes. "You keep asking me to trust you, but you won't extend that courtesy to me."

"Come on, you know it's not that simple. Trust goes both ways," I tell her, trying to ease the tension.

"Exactly," Sienna says, eyes issuing a challenge.

I take a deep breath. "What do you want to do now?" I ask instead. "Do you want to go watch a movie or anything?"

"I want some space," she says. "Can I at least have that?"

I look down at the floor for a moment. "Yeah. You can have space."

"I'm going to my room," she says, exiting the bathroom.

"You mean my room?"

Silence hangs in the air as she slips inside my room, shutting the door behind her and locking it with a soft click.

I scrub my face with my hands, wondering how everything got so ... complicated all of a sudden.

14

SIENNA

Despite Caleb's comfort, I still feel so lost, so alone in this place. I frown, mind swirling with conflicting thoughts. Why am I here, why am I subjecting myself to this?

At first, it was fun, maybe a little sexy. But I can't help wondering —was it worth sacrificing my dignity for my career? Can I live with myself knowing I've compromised my values for the sake of a job?

A knot tightens in my chest and I fight to keep the tears from spilling out again. I don't know if I can even cry anymore—I've already spent so long crying over this whole thing.

"Princess?" There's a knock at the door and I scramble to sit up, wiping my eyes furiously to hide the evidence that I'd been crying all afternoon.

It's Bastian, and I don't know if I'm ready to face him yet, but he knocks again.

"Can I come in?" His voice is gruff and he pauses momentarily before adding a soft "Please?"

With shaky legs, I cross the room and push the door open a crack, his blue eyes meeting mine through the gap.

"Can I come in?" he asks again. "I need to talk to you."

I let go of the door and walk back to the bed, allowing Bastian to slip in behind me, and he shuts the door before standing in front of the bed, crossing his arms while he stares at the floor for a moment.

There's tension in his shoulders and a guarded look in his eyes, making me wonder what demons are lurking under the surface.

"What did you want to talk about?" I ask, slipping back into the bed and pulling the covers up to my chin.

"I ... I'm sorry," he grits out. "I was an ass. You didn't deserve that, all that shit I did. I shouldn't have done that with you when I was in such a messed-up headspace."

My heart hammers in my chest, his words softening my heart. "And?"

Bastian takes a deep breath. "And yeah, you're ours to do with as we want but that doesn't mean that we can treat you like you're nothing. You're not nothing."

Despite the apology, it still felt as though there was a wall between us, one that I had no idea how to break down.

"But hear me out," Bastian went on, running a hand through his unruly hair. "I'm not gonna promise we won't do the rough stuff like that again. I swear, next time, I'll check in with you. Make sure you're okay with it."

My defenses soften slightly at his words, though I still feel a twinge of skepticism. I'm just not sure if I can trust him to keep his promise.

Bastian sighs, his shoulders slumping with defeat. "Look, I'm not good with this mushy shit," he admits, his voice gruff. "But I'm trying here, okay? I don't want things to be fucked up between us."

He takes a deep breath. "I'm going to hug you now." He hesitates a moment, hands hovering uncertainly before his arms finally wrap around me and pull me into his chest.

I stiffen on contact, his spicy, woodsy smell filling my senses. My mind races, wondering if this hug is sincere or another attempt at manipulating me. But despite my reservations, I find myself melting into the embrace, craving the comfort and closeness he's offering.

I want to trust him but I'm wary of letting my guard down

completely around him. Every time I think I've got him figured out, he shows me another side that I've never seen before.

Bastian pulls away after a few moments and stares at me, my cheeks heating up under his gaze. "You have no idea what you do to me," he mutters. "Don't look at me like that, Princess. I'm going to want to do bad things to you again if you do."

"What?" I cover my face with my hands. "I'm not looking at you like anything."

"You know, you're the one who agreed to this," Bastian tells me. "It's not my fault that you can't seem to wrap your head around the fact that we want you."

I pick at the comforter, unsure how to respond to his words. "Why did I agree to this again?" I mutter. Is it even worth it? I could back out of the arrangement at this point. I probably have enough material to get things done at this point and I wouldn't need to rely on the guys for help.

"I guess I agreed because I felt like I had no other choice," I admit to him.

Bastian leans in, voice low. "You always have a choice, Princess. But you chose us. Remember that."

"I just don't know what you want from me," I tell him. "I'm ... I'm struggling here."

He smirks, but his eyes betray a flicker of vulnerability. "You'll figure it out, you're a smart girl."

Despite how much time we've spent together over the past few days, I still feel like I barely know these guys. I feel like an outsider, like I don't belong in their world. And they've got something going on that they won't talk about. Am I just a pawn in some larger scheme?

Bastian's voice cuts through the tension in the air, "Let's play cards."

"What?" I glance up, caught off guard by the sudden change of subject.

"I'm bored of fighting with you. Let's play cards." He produces a pack of playing cards from his pocket and opens it, shuffling the cards a few times. I shake my head and rearrange myself to make room for the two of us to face each other so we can play.

"Do you know how to play gin?" Bastian asks. I nod and he deals out ten cards to each of us before flipping the top card of the deck over.

"My great uncle used to play this with me when I was little," I tell him. "He died when I was a kid, but I still remember how much fun it was to play with him."

"Grandpa taught us," Bastian says. "He passed when I was fifteen."

"I'm sorry. Do you miss him?"

"Yeah. He was a good guy," Bastian says. "Taught us a lot, including how to repair bikes. That's why we opened the shop."

"Was that your dream?" I ask, drawing a card from the pile.

Bastian goes silent for a moment, clenching his cards tighter in his fist. "Not at first. Our dream when we were teenagers was to get into the police academy. But things changed and we thought maybe it would be better to do some good in the world in a different way."

"How so?"

"We wanted to reopen the Haven Center. That place was a refuge for us as kids and we thought it would be good for the community to have it opened again. But it just didn't work out."

I feel my heart clench as he speaks. Bastian is so different from the image I had of him in my head. I feel guilty for judging the Ravenwoods now.

What if you tried again, Bastian? It's not too late." I lay down a card.

Bastian picks it up and shuffles his hand around. "Nah. Some dreams just aren't meant to be."

I chew the inside of my cheek for a moment. "You know, when I was a kid, I wanted to be a midwife. But my mom and one of my middle school teachers told me that I didn't have the aptitude for it. I was mad at the time but in a way, it helped push me to where I am now."

Bastian discards one of his cards. "You can still do something great with your life, even if it's not being a midwife."

"Then the same goes for you," I tell him. "Dreams might change, but it doesn't mean the new dream can't be just as big."

"That's some Hallmark shit right there," Bastian says, snorting as he lays out his hand, showing me that he's got gin.

"Damn," I flash my hand. "I was so close." Scooping up the cards, I start shuffling the deck again.

"What's the plan for tomorrow?" Bastian asks.

"I gotta take these notes to campus, to go over the results with my supervisor. He's been saying that if I don't show him proof, he's pulling me from the study. I've emailed him some of the results but he wants to see them in person."

"He sounds like a dick," Bastian says. I chuckle as I deal out our hands.

"Yeah, a little," I agree. "Academia can make people like that though. I don't know what it is about being an academic, but it attracts toxic people left and right."

"When do you need to go over there?"

"Probably around ten," I tell him. "I think that's when my boss is on campus doing his work."

"You know one of us will have to go with you, right?" Bastian asks. I roll my eyes internally.

"I figured. I don't know what's got you guys so paranoid but I'm not about to run off."

"I know you can take care of yourself," Bastian says, cutting me off before I can start ranting. "There's just shit going on right now and it's better if one of us comes with."

I hope Caleb can come. He's been the nicest to me so far. Dominic is kind of intimidating sometimes and Bastian can be a dick sometimes.

"Fine, whatever. Do you think Caleb will let me go to the library on campus for a while then?"

Bastian chuckles. "Sorry to dash your dreams, Princess. Caleb can't go with you tomorrow. He's working on a project for me. I'm going to be the one to go with you."

I feel a sense of dread in the pit of my stomach. Fuck. Bastian is going with me? Why?

I cross my arms, feeling defensive. "I don't know if I want you to go with me. I don't know if I can trust you."

Bastian reaches out to touch my shoulder, then pulls back, hand hovering uncertainly. "I'm not asking you to trust me blindly. Just … give me a chance."

I sigh, squeezing my eyes shut. "Okay."

15

SIENNA

"Climb on, Princess," Bastian pats the motorcycle and I take a few deep breaths, wishing we were taking the car instead.

"I hate motorcycles," I grumble as I buckle the helmet he hands me. "Why can't we just take the car?"

"Faster this way," Bastian says. "Now stop bitching. I thought you wanted to get to campus?"

I grit my teeth and wrap my arms around his waist, still salty about the fact that I couldn't go with Caleb.

There might be an uneasy truce between us now, but that doesn't mean things are fine. Whenever I'm around him, my heart feels like it's going to beat out of my chest. His gaze sends shivers down my spine and I feel like a mouse being stalked by a cat.

The bike's engine roars, drowning out my thoughts as we speed towards Watford. I keep my eyes closed the whole time and cling tightly to Bastian, not wanting to see it happen if we die.

Once we arrive, I get off, grateful that we arrived in one piece. Owen has an office near Dr. Thornton's, and he's usually on campus at this time so I head straight there. Bastian follows me like a guard dog the entire way.

"Stay here," I tell him as I walk to the stairs of the Psychology building. "I don't need you breathing down my neck while I'm talking to my boss."

"Yes ma'am," Bastian says, giving me a mocking salute. "I'll be a good boy."

I glare at him, rolling my eyes. "Be back soon."

Walking up the steps, I turn left to head down the first hallway to knock on Owen's door, but there's a sign on it that reads "Out sick, will be back tomorrow."

Dang it. Now what?

Dr. Thornton's office door is open and I wonder if I can give him my research. I haven't spoken to him in person much, just the one time during the interview and another time in passing after a meeting with Owen.

Approaching his door, I softly knock.

"Come in," he calls out.

"Hello," I step inside and wave. Large bookcases line the wall, the spines of the books cracked from years of use. Stacks of papers are scattered across his desk, bathed in the flickering light of a dimly lit lamp that casts long shadows in the room.

"I'm Sienna Bennett. I'm one of the research assistants working on your Urban Resilience study. I wanted to turn in some of my work but my supervisor isn't in. Can I give it to you?"

"Sienna, yes!" Dr. Thornton rises and reaches out to shake my hand. "I remember you. You made quite the impression with your interview. How are things going out in Caspian Springs?"

He's tall, with dark blue eyes, neatly trimmed stubble, and carefully manicured eyebrows. His blond hair is slicked back and he's got on a tweed, three-piece suit. He gives off the look of a typical professor.

"Good," I tell him. "I'm making great progress with the residents. They've really opened up to me about their experiences."

"Wonderful." Dr. Thornton leans against his desk, giving me a wide smile. The corners of his deep, blue eyes crinkle as he smiles.

"It's quite a task to get all this done. You and Owen have been going out together?"

"Owen's been busy," I say, trying to be vague. I'm not petty enough to throw him under the bus, as frustrating as he's been to deal with. "So I took over getting the initial screenings done."

"Impressive," he says, leaning in as he listens to me speak. "You know there's not many people who can get an entire community to trust an outsider like this. We're lucky to have you on the project."

Lips quirking upward into a smile, I reach into my bag and pull out the folder of data I have. "Here's the preliminary results of our research," I say, handing it over.

"Would you mind if I took a quick look?"

"Sure," I say as he opens it up. He scans the pages and I watch his eyebrows draw upward, then back down as he reads it. I can't figure out how he feels. Is he unimpressed? Is he happy with the results?

"This is good stuff, Sienna," Dr. Thornton says, looking back up at me with a smile. "You're doing great work. You're right on track. I look forward to seeing what else you come up with during the study."

"Thank you," I say, my heart suddenly light as a feather. "I appreciate the feedback."

My eye catches something out the window of his office and I turn my head, clenching my fists at my side when I realize that it's Bastian hanging around by a large maple tree, smoking his vape.

Dr. Thornton's eyes follow mine and he spots Bastian as well. His face falls and he looks pale and withdrawn suddenly.

"Are you okay?" I ask.

Dr. Thornton nods, his gaze distant. "I'm fine. Thought I saw someone I used to know."

"You mean Bastian Ravenwood?" I ask, suddenly curious. "He came with me, he and his brothers have been kind of helping me on the project. Do you know them?"

"Ah, the Ravenwoods," he said, his voice tight with restraint. "Yes, I'm aware of them. Caspian Springs is a small town, after all."

His eyes avoid mine as he busies himself with shuffling some papers around on his desk. There's a stiffness in his posture, as though retreating inside himself. "Have they been bothering you?"

I shake my head. "No. They rallied the community behind my project and have been helping me with my interviews."

"That's wonderful," Dr. Thornton says, though his smile doesn't reach his eyes. "I just wish …" he trails off. "Never mind, don't worry about it." He waves a hand, but I can't shake the feeling that there is more to their relationship than they've all been letting on.

I need to tread carefully here. "Can I ask, what happened between you guys? I know there was some kind of bad blood, but why do they seem to dislike you?"

He goes quiet for a moment, sitting back down at his desk and steepling his hands. There's a sad sort of tension in the air when he speaks again.

"Did you know that I knew them growing up?" he asks. I shake my head, eyes widening.

"I fancied myself like a father figure to those boys," he admits, a sigh escaping him. "I started my work in psychology as an undergrad, working at the community center in Caspian Springs. That's where I met them. They were just kids back then. When I did my graduate studies, I stayed there because I wanted to be close to the boys, to help them grow."

My eyes widen. "What happened?"

"When the boys became young men, they … well there was a girl," he explains. "She was a sweet girl, very good for them. But one day she confessed that she had feelings for me, that she was in love with me."

I inhale sharply, hand flying up to my mouth.

"Don't judge them too harshly, my dear," Dr. Thornton adds. "She tried to kiss me and I didn't handle it well. I rejected her advances and told her that I was going to tell the boys what had transpired. But a few days later, it was found that she had taken her own life in her grief over my rejection."

I stare, the pieces finally falling into place. This explains so much—why they were so hostile when they found out who I was working with, why they assumed my relationship with him, and why, when offering their bargain, they demanded complete obedience.

My head spins, and I consider sitting down.

"My dear, you look like you're about to faint. Come," he says, leading me gently by the arm over to one of the armchairs. "Breathe."

"Sorry." I shake my head, trying to clear away the dizziness. "Sorry about that. It was just ... surprising, that's all."

"I understand," Dr. Thornton gives me a tight smile. "It's difficult to talk about, but I thought maybe it would help you understand them and the community better. It's why I can't bring myself to go back in person to handle the research there myself. I feel connected to Caspian Springs but after what I did, I don't blame the boys for needing space."

"I'm sorry about what happened," I say. "You didn't do anything wrong. You tried to protect them."

"I don't know if they see it that way," he says quietly. "Grief is a strange thing, you and I know that as psychology researchers. The way it can manifest varies from person to person and in this instance, it's easier to blame me."

"Thank you for sharing," I tell him. A million emotions flood my brain, warring for the top spot. Anger, grief, frustration, overwhelming sadness, it's all so much at once.

"Please try not to dwell on it too much," Dr. Thornton says. "It was a long time ago now. Whatever happened, it's in the past. The wounds will heal eventually."

"It just sucks that they threw away all those years because they blame you for their girlfriend's actions," I say, squeezing my fingers into my palms. "They had to know that it wasn't your fault. You tried to help."

"Maybe one day they will find a way to forgive me but for now, I understand how their trauma has led them down this path. You're a kind-hearted person, Sienna. Don't let anyone take that away from you."

"I should get going," I tell him, glancing out the window again at the figure lurking under the tree. "I'm sure Bastian wants to get out of here and he's my ride."

"Understandable," Dr. Thornton agrees. "Keep up the good work, and don't let my mistakes cause you any issues in your research. You can handle this."

I pause, my hand on the door handle. "Who was the girl?" I ask.

"Her name was Emily," he says. "Emily Newberry."

I nod, turning to leave. Each step feels heavy with the weight of our conversation. What am I going to do now that I know the truth?

16

DOMINIC

"We're back!" Bastian calls, the screen door smacking shut as he and Sienna come into the house. "Hope lunch is ready cuz I'm starving."

"I made meatballs," I tell him, stirring the bubbling pot on the cracked stovetop. "It's almost done."

Sienna enters the kitchen, Bastian hot on her heels. She gives me a quick look but then turns away, heading for the living room.

She seems subdued and I almost reach out, but she brushes past me and I turn back to my brother instead.

"How was it?" I ask him, watching as he opens the cupboard doors to find a mug.

He shrugs. "Fine. Whatever," he says, attention already shifting. "I didn't have to see him if that's what you're asking."

I nod, turning my focus back to the sauce. "Taste this sauce for me."

He opens his mouth and takes the spoon, testing it out. "Needs more pepper," he declares, handing it back. Bastian clears his throat. "Any news?" he asks, voice tense.

I reach for the grinder to adjust the seasoning. "Caleb delivered the message. Made sure it was loud and clear. Any Serpents in our territory from here on out will be dealt with immediately and without mercy."

Bastian's frustration bubbles to the surface. "I'm not dealing with their bullshit anymore," he growls.

I shoot him a warning look before telling him, "The Serpent Syndicate are like vultures. They've been circling for years, just waiting for an opportunity to scavenge. They saw a weakness and exploited it."

"Do you think it's because we've spent so much time in the bike shop?" Bastian asks. "We should have been expanding when we had the chance."

"We said it wasn't going to be like that," I counter, hackles rising. "Remember? We vowed it wouldn't be like the old days."

"The Crimson Blades drove the Serpents out of town before, and they can do it again," Bastian argues. "But they have the numbers we don't."

"It's not about the numbers." I glance at the living room to ensure Sienna isn't listening in. "The three of us promised that we wouldn't handle things like they did in the old days anymore. But we've gone back on that, haven't we? We're no better than the Serpents and we're the thugs that Sienna painted us out to be."

"We're not like those slimy Serpents," Bastian hisses. "We're *nothing* like them."

There's a heavy tension in the air between us now, the two of us too stubborn to back down. I know Bastian is in charge, but as the oldest, I still have a responsibility to rein him in when he's going off.

"Hey," Caleb swings into the kitchen and opens the old fridge, creaking noises filling the room. "I'm starving. Can we eat yet?"

"Yeah." I step back, suddenly aware of how close Bastian and I are to each other. "It's all ready. Go get Sienna, we'll eat in here."

Bastian turns and begins setting the table, a farmhouse-style piece that we found online for super cheap. The table is long and rectangular with a heavy piece of glass to protect the surface from scratches. Around it, sit six mismatched chairs from the local thrift store.

Sienna and Caleb slip into the kitchen, sitting down just as I bring the food over to dish it out. "I got some bread in the oven," I tell them.

Sienna's quiet, eyes downcast.

"Everything okay?" Caleb nudges her.

Sienna glances up at him. "Oh, yeah, it's fine. Just a long day."

"It's only noon," I point out. "Was your boss a giant buzzkill?"

"Owen wasn't in today," she says, folding her hands together.

"Did you turn your work in still?" I ask, putting a few meatballs on her plate.

"Yeah, I went and saw Dr. Thornton."

My stomach knots up at the mention of his name, the room feeling colder all of a sudden.

"Oh," I nod, trying to hide my anxiety. On the other side of the table, Caleb turns pale, and Bastian's hand curls into a fist in his lap as he drinks his water.

"Why didn't you guys tell me about Emily?"

Ice floods my veins. The room goes silent, and when Caleb accidentally drops his fork, the clattering noise makes us all jump.

"How do you know about her?" I ask, turning to look at Sienna. She still can't meet my eyes, but her jaw is set, and she holds onto her cup with a death grip.

"It doesn't matter," Sienna says, clenching her hands tightly. "Why didn't you guys tell me about her?"

Bastian's fist slams down on the table and Sienna's eyes fly up to stare at him.

"Sienna, don't," I warn her. "Please, just drop it."

She pushes back from the table and stands up. "Dr. Thornton told me about her," she says, jutting her chin out. "He told me everything, and he feels awful for what happened. I don't understand why you guys blame him!"

Bastian stands up as well. "How dare you fucking say that!" He advances towards Sienna, hands outstretched. I'm not sure if he's going to attack her, so I jump up to grab him and hold him back. Hearing her name has me shaken up too, but I don't want things to escalate beyond our control either.

Taking a deep breath, I try to diffuse things. "It's more complicated than you think," I tell her. "I don't know what he said, but there are some things you just can't forgive."

Sienna's hands fly up to her mouth, her eyes widening. "You guys are willing to throw away your relationship with him over what happened? It was a mistake, one that he tried to tell you about to protect you but because she took her life, you can't forgive him?"

"Are you kidding me with this shit? Get out!" Bastian roars, breaking free. "Get the fuck out! Leave! Get out before I throw you out!"

Sienna's eyes fill with tears and she lurches forward, grabbing her purse from the hook. "Fine! I'm leaving!" she says, and with one last look, she slams the back door and races out onto the gravel driveway.

Her car is parked next to the Firebird, at the edge, near a tall oak tree. Skirting the tree, she climbs into her car and revs the engine, taking off under a rapidly darkening sky, the distant sound of thunder rumbling in the background.

As we watch her depart, leaving behind a series of unanswered questions, my heart clenches in my chest. I turn my attention back to my brother, rounding on him.

"Fuck!" I yell, grabbing for him again. "Fucking hell, what the fuck man! You can't do this to her. She's got nowhere to go!"

"She can go anywhere as long as it isn't here," Bastian says, features contorted with barely controlled rage.

The muscles in Bastian's jaw clench and unclench, his hands balling into fists at his sides. I can see the storm brewing behind his eyes, a tempest of emotions that threaten to consume him whole.

"Bastian, calm down," I urge, voice laced with concern.

He ignores me, fury radiating off him in waves. His chest heaves with each breath, his body practically vibrating with pent-up aggression.

We all just need to calm down," I try again, moving closer to my brother in a feeble attempt to defuse the situation.

But Bastian's gaze remains fixed on the spot Sienna stood moments before. His fists clench tighter, the knuckles turning white with the force of his grip. "Fuck!" Bastian bursts out, his voice a raw, guttural roar of frustration. Tears well up as anger gives way to helplessness.

I reach out tentatively, my hand hovering in the air, not sure if I should comfort him or try to hold him back. Before I can decide, Bastian tears himself away, pacing the length of the kitchen like a caged animal.

"There's a storm coming," Caleb says, staring out the window at the last spot where we saw Sienna. "I know we're all on edge but sending her away was a bad idea. She's got nowhere to go."

He turns back to face us, shoulders shaking. "I'm angry too, but you shouldn't have made her leave, Bastian," he says, pointing an accusing finger at him. "You fucked up."

"We all just need to calm down," I tell them, releasing Bastian. "There's a lot of shit she stirred up. We don't need to go off half-cocked right now, not until we've figured out what we want to do."

"I'll tell you what I want," Bastian snarls. "I want you to box her shit up, get it out of here. Throw it out on the lawn for all I care. Don't let her back in this house. I never want to see her prissy little face ever again."

It's as though Sienna kicked a metaphorical hornet's nest, stirring shit up like this. Bastian isn't handling it well, but it's not her fault either. We probably should have told her about this sooner. It doesn't feel fair that it was sprung on her, and in a way that we couldn't control.

As I watch Bastian pace, I feel torn. Am I doing the right thing by standing by his side, or should I go look for Sienna? How much of the true story does she know about Rich's involvement with Emily anyway? She says he told her the truth but what does that mean?

Sienna doesn't deserve to be thrown out for wanting to get some answers. Now we have no way of contacting her since her phone is still on the coffee table where she left it.

"I wish we'd dealt with all this shit a long time ago," I say, thinking back to Emily's funeral and how, after lowering her into the ground, it was like we buried her in our minds too. We haven't talked about her since that day. "Don't you think it would have been better than this?"

"No," Bastian snaps. "It's in the past, it needs to stay there where it belongs. I'm not interested in 'dealing with my unresolved trauma,'" he says, using air quotes. "Or any of that shit he used to feed us. Right now, I want to fucking eat my food."

"But don't you think …" Caleb says, but Bastian interrupts him.

"Sit the fuck down," he orders. "You too Dom. Eat before this shit gets cold."

The two of us share a look before we sit back down at the table and start eating, the silence speaking volumes.

I don't know what's going to happen next but maybe when everyone cools down a little, we can figure it out.

For now, I eat the lunch I made and try to ignore the ache in my chest and the lump in my throat.

17

SIENNA

"Fine! I'm leaving!" I scream, slamming the door behind me. A burst of adrenaline fills me as I run to my car, jamming my keys into the ignition and taking off as fast as I can, weaving through the streets like a madman in my quest to get away.

How dare they! The image of their faces, so nonchalant and deceitful, burns in my mind. I opened up to them, like when I told Dominic about my mother's alcoholism. I told Caleb about how I felt like an outsider. I guess it meant *nothing*.

Anger pulses through my veins, mixing with the raw ache of betrayal. But beneath the rage, there's a nagging doubt that I can't shake.

My mind drifts back to a few days ago, hanging out in the garage while Bastian worked. We were chatting about something dumb—something funny about banana milkshakes. When I asked him what his favorite dessert was as a kid, he'd locked up, jaw clenched tight. He shut down any further attempts at conversing, leaving me bewildered.

Then there were the fleeting glances that Caleb and Dominic exchanged whenever I asked about their secret phone calls and middle-of-the-night rendezvous—silent communication that left me feeling like an outsider, excluded from their pack.

At now, I realize I've been so consumed with being with them, that I've let myself ignore the red flags lurking under the surface.

My stomach starts knotting up and it feels like a heavy weight is sitting on my chest. I can't get enough air and I yank the wheel, pulling into a nearby parking lot to try to calm my racing thoughts.

But the tightness in my chest still won't go away. I shove open my door and stumble out, leaning against the hood as I take several ragged breaths. Bile rises in my throat and I swallow hard, trying to keep it together.

"Son of a bitch!" I curse, knuckles turning white as I clench my hands into fists against the hood. Burning hatred boils up, and I yank the door open to reach inside. My hands close around my spare sunglasses and I pull them out and throw them across the parking lot as hard as I can, then let out a ragged sob.

Scrubbing a hand over my face, I try to calm myself down, but I feel several drops of water splash over my skin. Glancing up, I realize dark, ominous-looking clouds have gathered across the sky, so I jump back inside just as the sky opens up around me.

Torrential rain begins pouring down, the realization washing over me that I've got nowhere to go. As I sit there in the rain, I think back to how kind Dr. Thornton had been to me this morning. Maybe I can hang out in his office, just until the rain subsides.

By the time I park and run to his office, my clothes are plastered to my skin, my hair is stuck to my forehead and there's a chill running down my spine.

When I knock on the door to his office, Dr. Thornton appears, eyes widening as he takes in my disheveled state.

"Sorry! Didn't know where else to go," I say, practically breathless. "Don't know anyone else around here and …"

"Oh jeez, come in." Dr. Thornton urges me into his office, taking off his jacket and wrapping it around my shoulders. "You look like a drowned cat, take some tissues."

As I wipe my face, I struggle to resist the tears that threaten to leak out. "I'm sorry," I say again, voice soft. "You were the only person I could think of."

Dr. Thornton guides me to his couch. "It's fine. Can you tell me what happened?"

Sinking onto the worn, plaid couch, I shake, feeling the tears come finally. "I was ... kicked out of where I was staying. I didn't know where to go, so I came here."

"You poor thing." Dr. Thornton shakes his head. "Do you have anywhere to go?"

I shake my head and he frowns. "That's terrible. My house is nearby, if you need somewhere to go."

My eyes widen. "I can't put you out like that," I tell him, waving my hands.

"Nonsense. You won't be putting me out. I inherited a large manor home some years ago, it's so large that it feels like I'm rattling around in there sometimes."

"Are you sure?" I ask, twisting my fingers together, hope blooming in my chest.

"I often have visiting students or faculty stay at the manor," he explains. "There's six bedrooms, so there's plenty of space. You may not even see me when you're there," he adds, winking.

My eyes sting. "Thank you so much. I just need a few days to sort things out, then I can find somewhere else to go."

Besides, after what happened, things are probably over between me and the Ravenwoods anyway.

"Stay as long as you need," Dr. Thornton insists. "You'd be doing me a favor because then I'd get quicker updates on our research."

He chuckles and I crack a smile, the first one all day. "I have a little more paperwork to do for today, but here's a spare key," he says, opening a drawer. "Go ahead and go over there now. You can let yourself in and clean up and I'll be there as soon as I'm done."

"Thank you so much, Dr. Thornton," I tell him. "Thank you."

"Call me Rich," he insists.

"Rich," I repeat his name. "Thank you."

"See you soon, Sienna."

I leave, plugging his address into my GPS—surprised that he lives just a few minutes from campus.

When I arrive, I gasp, taken aback by the size of the place. It really is a manor house, complete with ivy growing on the walls and a driveway the Crawley family would be jealous of.

Heading inside, I take the stairs up to the third floor, where the guest rooms are. Selecting one near the end of the hall, I step inside, grateful the room has an en suite. I need a shower after being soaked by the rain.

It feels good to get out of my wet clothes and get warm again, though I realize I've got nothing to wear once I'm done. Bastian kicked me out with nothing but the clothes on my back.

I groan, sitting on the edge of the bed in my towel. Just then a text message comes in.

Hey Sienna, I just realized you may not have anything to change into. I keep spare clothes in the dresser so feel free to grab something. I'll be heading out in the next fifteen minutes.

Once I'm dressed, and I've blow-dried my hair with a borrowed dryer, I head back down the grand staircase just as Dr. Thornton walks through the tall, double doors of the entryway, shaking rain off his black umbrella.

"Oh, good, you found some clothes. You can throw your stuff in the wash if you want. It's behind the kitchen, just that way," he says, pointing to the left. "Let me take you on a tour actually, so you know where everything is."

I follow him as he starts showing off the well-curated manor home, then leads me back downstairs, bringing me into a cozy-looking living room with overstuffed armchairs, deep couches, and a stone fireplace.

"So, how are you?" he asks, perching on the edge of one of the armchairs. "You looked terribly upset when you came to my office."

"I'm alright, I guess," I say, sinking into a nearby couch. "I told you the other day that the Ravenwoods were helping me with my project but there's more to it than that," I admit.

"I see," he says, smoothing his hands over his thighs.

"We're sort of ... involved. It's complicated. But we had a fight today and I kind of left in a hurry."

Rich sighs. "Look, I don't mean to overstep, but I should be honest with you. Getting mixed up with the Ravenwoods is risky business, Sienna. They've changed so much since I knew them. Back in the day, they were softer, but they've hardened."

I frown, absorbing his words. "I appreciate the concern. I can handle myself." But curiosity grows so I lean forward. "What were they like, you know, back before everything happened?"

Rich leans back, a glint in his eyes as he thinks. "Back then, they were just so different," he muses, voice carrying a hint of wistfulness. "They had a fire inside, passion, and dreams for the future. Bastian especially—he was their ringleader. Always rallied the other kids to make sure homework got done and the center was cleaned before the end of the day."

He paints a stark contrast between the boy of his past and the man I know now. Bastian seems to have transformed into a colder, more distant version of himself. "What about Caleb and Dominic?"

Rich's smile softens at the mention of Dominic. "Oh, Dominic was quite the prankster back then, always eager to lighten the mood with harmless jokes. One time he hid behind the door of the elementary classroom and yelled 'boo' as everyone entered. And Caleb was the sweetest child. He held the door open for everyone after play time and always had a valentine for every classmate."

As I listen to him talk, I feel a pang inside. The boys he's describing—the jovial prankster, the sweetheart, the kind leader—those boys feel like strangers.

"I find it hard to reconcile the boys you're describing with the ones I know," I confess, curling my bare feet up onto the couch, seeking comfort in their warmth.

Rich nods, eyes dimming. "People change, sometimes in ways we least expect. Especially after losing Emily like they did. Death can alter us all."

I stare at the coffee table, gathering my thoughts. It's a dark wood, with carved legs and a glass piece in the center. "You spent a lot of time with them, back before?"

"I did," he says. "I spent so much time with the boys that I think maybe it went beyond a mentor relationship," he confesses. "It felt more like I was a father figure or an older brother. They would come to me to ask for advice or confide their problems. I wanted to study how boys like them could be so optimistic and strong, despite everything being against them."

I don't know what made them change, and I can't help but ache for the boys they once were.

"Thanks for sharing with me, Rich," I say. "I appreciate you letting me stay here as well. I only hope I can find a way to repay you."

"As long as you continue producing excellent work, that's payment enough," Rich says, holding a hand up. "You have a promising future in community health."

I smile, though my heart still aches inside. Why have the Ravenwoods changed so much? Is there any way to bring that light back into their lives? Do I even want to try?

18

CALEB

I have no appetite for the food in front of me. I still can't believe Bastian threw Sienna out like this. He's always been the most temperamental of the three of us, but he never let it out like this before.

Sienna has done every single thing we've asked of her, with minimal pushback. She's proven her loyalty to us. My hands clench under the table, angry that Bastian is still treating her like an outsider.

I've always followed Bastian's decisions without question. I trusted him to lead the way for us. Now I'm starting to wonder if that was a mistake. I should have stood up for Sienna. I should have stopped him.

We let things fester after Emily died, and now Sienna is paying the consequences.

"Pass the bread," Bastian says, voice gruff.

I stare down at the basket by my elbow, then look over at him. Something breaks inside me and I shove the basket of bread towards him so hard it flies off the table.

"Fucking dick!" I yell. "You seriously threw her out? She has nowhere to go! And we're just sitting here. We should be going out to find her!"

"The storm is getting really bad," Dominic points out. "If we go out now, it's going to be harder to find her. It's better to wait until it passes."

I lean back against the chair, crossing my arms. "This is stupid. We could track her, maybe I can hack into her car's computer and find her that way."

"I think everyone just needs to calm down first," Dominic says, giving me a pointed look. "Just give her some time."

He's always been the most level-headed of the three of us, but right now I don't want level-headed. I want him to fight for Sienna. I want him to care like I do, dammit!

With a withering glare, I push my plate away from me. "It's your fault, Bas," I mutter. "You never moved on from Emily, so you're taking all your pissed-off, pent-up rage out on Sienna. Do I need to spell it out for you, bro? Sienna is *not* Emily."

"Shut the fuck up," Bastian growls, standing up so fast his chair falls over. "You don't know anything. Just shut up."

"Emily is gone," I say through clenched teeth. "Whatever happened, it's over. You can't get your head around that fact, so you want to make it Sienna's problem. You were the one who brought her into our lives in the first place. You were the one who suggested the arrangement. If it wasn't for you, she'd still be here!"

"Shut up!" Bastian bellows. Dominic snaps his head around to stare at him, his eyes wide with shock.

I shake my head, a sneer on my face. I'm sick of Bastian making all the decisions around here and trying to act like he speaks for all of us.

"Sienna never should have gotten tangled up with us in the first place. She's too naive, too innocent, and soft. She doesn't need delinquents like us hanging around corrupting her," I tell him.

"Fucking shut up!" Bastian lunges for me and I throw up my hands, ready to defend myself. He lashes out and I block his arm, pushing it away with my own.

Before the situation can escalate into a full-blown fight, Dominic seems to come back to himself, stepping in between us and holding out his hand to keep us apart.

"Calm the hell down! Both of you!" His eyes have grown hard, his usual calm demeanor replaced by a trace of bitterness.

I stumble backward, trying to catch my breath. Bastian turns away from us, crossing his arms and staring at the ceiling.

"You're both in time-out," Dominic snaps at us. "Bas, you really fucked up and you've hurt more than just Sienna today. Caleb, you need to check yourself. Screaming at Bastian isn't going to change anything."

"You're right." I let out a breath and shake my head. "Yelling at each other won't do shit about finding Sienna. So I'm going to look for her."

I grab the keys to the Firebird and head out the back door, ignoring the yells behind me. Dominic stands on the back steps and calls my name, but I flip him the bird and slide into the car, starting the engine.

The rain is pouring now and I can barely see as I turn out of the driveway, but I can't stay home. I've never been able to sit still, even as a kid.

Right now, I'm too angry at my brothers to speak to them. I want to get out and do something instead of waiting for things to calm down like Dominic or writing the situation off like Bastian always does.

The windshield wipers are working overtime as the rain streams down, my stomach in my throat as I realize she's out in this storm, all alone.

She's only been in our lives a short time, but she's already made a huge impact on us. Being with her has made me feel more alive than I have in years. Waking up next to her every day has started to thaw my icy heart.

Turning onto the main road, I'm faced with a dilemma. Right or left? The choice seems simple on the surface but the implications weigh heavily on my mind.

Turning left means heading towards the familiar hustle and bustle of the town center, where the three of us played as kids. The shops that line the town center beckon me, inviting me to slip inside to get out of the rain and indulge in the same carefree, childish activities that occupied us as kids.

On the other hand, going right leads out of town, towards the outskirts, the place where we once grew up. It still holds memories—of how isolated we felt and how much like outsiders we were back then.

The sound of the downpour against the car roof triggers a vivid memory, transporting me back to those summer days when Rich taught me how to drive by having me take him back and forth from the university.

The two of us would cruise down this very road, radio tuned to classic country songs. One afternoon, "Thunder Rolls" came on, filling the car with a haunting melody. As we sang along, the dark sky opened up and a storm rolled in.

Pulling up to this intersection, the song reached its crescendo just as a brilliant flash of lightning illuminated the sky, followed by a deafening clap of thunder. I remember how I nearly jumped out of my skin, my heart racing with a mix of fear and exhilaration.

But Rich, he just laughed—a hearty, genuine laugh that echoed through the car. Before long, I found myself joining in, the tension melting away as we continued onward.

Now, as I sit here facing the same intersection, that memory comes flooding back. I'm reminded of a time when the only thing that seemed to matter was the open road ahead and the bond between us.

Taking a deep breath, I make my decision.

Turning right, I head out of town, some part of me instinctively feeling she'd be seeking solace from the same person I used to seek out.

As I navigate the rain-slicked streets, I feel another memory stir in the back of my mind. When I was a kid, still in elementary school, and Dominic and Bastian were in middle school, we took a field trip with the Haven Center to the local zoo.

Rich held my hand as we walked through the exhibits, letting me cling to him like a baby elephant next to its mother.

"Look, guys! Look!" *I called, excitedly pointing to the Komodo dragons.* "They have dragons! I thought they weren't real but there's dragons! It says so right on the sign!"

"That isn't a dragon," *Dominic said, a grin on his face as he came over to stand next to me.* "It's a lizard."

"But it says dragon on it," *I said, my face falling.*

"Komodo dragons are called that because they have long, forked tongues and some people thought they looked like the dragons of myth," *Rich explained to me.* "So, you're both right."

Dominic nudged me. "Maybe they fly and breathe fire at night when no one is looking."

"Yeah!" *Bastian called out, coming over to join us.* "They transform at nighttime and they fly around the zoo, looking at the other animals."

I stared at the Komodos, certain my brothers were right, or why would they be called dragons if they were just lizards like the salamander I'd found on the playground the other day?

Back then, it seemed like my brothers had all the answers, and when I didn't know something, I could trust them to tell me the truth, or at least give me hope that the truth was out there.

Now I'm not so sure anymore. It seems like the older we get, the more cynical I feel about everything. I know now that Komodo dragons don't transform into giant, winged, fire-breathing lizards at night and I know that Bastian and Dominic don't always have the answers.

I wish I was still young, still hopeful enough to believe that anything was possible if you just believed hard enough.

Shifting focus to my present situation, I merge onto the interstate and set my mouth in a firm line. If I'm right and Sienna is with Rich, I'm going to have to face him again.

My stomach feels like it's being flipped around in a tumble dryer as I try to think about what I might say after two years.

How can I face him after everything that passed between us? I tell myself I need to let it go, just like I told Bastian to do. I need to be the bigger person and reach out.

Still, I can't seem to shake the anxiety that crawls down my spine as I turn into the campus crossing. It's been just over two years but the thought of seeing him again still has my mouth going dry, and my stomach in knots.

Squaring my shoulders, I head into the building where his office is located, stopping in front of his door.

Reaching out a hand, I knock but there's no answer.

If Sienna was here, she's gone and so is Rich.

What now?

19

DOMINIC

After Caleb takes off, the tension in the air still lingers. He returns a while later, looking defeated, and heads up to his room without another word.

Meanwhile, Bastian has been slamming things around in the kitchen the whole time, getting on my last nerve. I can't take the dreary mood, so I leave to clear my head at the gym.

As I pound the punching bag, I feel the anger rise up—anger at Bastian for running Sienna off, anger at Caleb for pushing things to the boiling point between them—but I think maybe I'm the most angry at myself.

Punching the bag over and over isn't doing it for me, so I head over to the leg press machine.

I should have stepped in sooner. Sienna doesn't deserve our messed-up crap. If I'd just stepped in to de-escalate the situation, things wouldn't have gone so far.

I close my eyes, a memory floating back into my head, of a sun-drenched afternoon watching *Encanto* with Emily.

"You know, you don't always have to be the strong one," she whispered, leaning into me.

"Hmm?" I turned to face her, unsure of what she was saying.

"I was just thinking that sometimes you're like Luisa in the movie. You hold so much weight on your shoulders. Sometimes it's okay to let other people be the strong ones."

I took her hands in mine and leaned in, giving her a soft kiss. "You're right. Maybe sometimes I'll try to let you help me."

As I finish my workout, the realization sinks in that I'm still carrying the weight of the world on my shoulders. With a sigh, I know I need to address the situation with Bastian.

I need to figure out where he wants to go from here. He says he doesn't want to see Sienna ever again, but I doubt he means it. Once I finish my workout, I head back home and check his room, hoping to talk to him.

He's not there, or anywhere else in the house. I wonder if he went over to the garage. He usually goes there when he needs space. I head over there now to check.

"Hey," I call out, walking through the front. Bastian grunts in response, tinkering with a Royal Enfield Continental GT.

I come over and sit on a stool near his workbench. "I know you're upset but you can't just pretend like everything is fine."

"Ain't nothing to talk about," Bastian says, voice curt. "You gonna stand around or hand me a torque wrench?"

I reach out and grab a wrench from his workbench and stand up, passing it over to him. "Quit the act. We both know what's going on. You and Sienna, the blow-up at lunch."

"Doesn't ring a bell," Bastian says while tightening a lug nut. I can see the way his jaw flexes when he grits his teeth to tighten it and I know he's trying to avoid the topic. He doesn't want to admit that he fucked up.

"Stop playing," I tell him. "You threw her out with nowhere to go. You let your ego get in the way of common decency and what's worse, you've pissed off Caleb. He's not talking to you right now."

"Don't care," Bastian says, the sound of the wrench emphasizing his words. "I told you that I never want to see her face again."

I roll my eyes. "Bastian. Be for real. You're not serious, you're just mad."

"She doesn't belong here, not in our world," he says, sitting up. His eyes are downcast, shoulders tensed. "She's an outsider. She doesn't belong."

"You brought her into this world!" I throw my hands up and start walking away.

"And I kicked her back out," Bastian calls. I ignore him and head for my bike, needing to get away from him for now. If he's going to refuse to acknowledge how he messed up and drove Sienna away, then I'm not willing to be the mediator this time.

As the days crawl by, Sienna remains conspicuously absent from Caspian Springs, her stuff remaining untouched. Even her research is being neglected. No one's seen her around the town.

Caleb has barricaded himself in his room, his silence palpable. Bastian, on the other hand, wears his sullenness like a cloak, though he feigns indifference.

Sienna's absence hangs heavy over us all. Even if I could find her, which I can't—there's no way I could bring her back without pissing off Bastian.

I feel like there's nothing I can do to fix things except to try to keep moving forward. Despite my best efforts at maintaining a sense of normalcy at the bike shop, Bastian's bad mood is getting us in trouble left and right with the customers.

Fed up, I approach him one morning. "Go home," I say. "Until you can be less of an asshole, I don't want you around here."

Bastian leaves in a huff and I spend the rest of the day trying to play nice with some of the regulars, so they won't leave and take their business elsewhere.

"Thanks for the discount," Billy says as I ring him up. "If it weren't for you, I probably would have gone elsewhere after Bas was such a dick to me earlier."

"No probs. Bastian wasn't feeling good, but we value your business and I wanted to make it up to you."

"Sorry he's sick," Billy says. "Hope he feels better soon."

"Me too," I mutter as Billy leaves.

Flipping the sign to Closed, I decide to take my lunch break and maybe try again to talk some sense into my pig-headed brother.

Just as I'm locking up though, I spot Flynn, one of the local teens who sometimes helps out in the bike shop. He's rushing up to me, a worried look on his face.

"What's up, Flynn?" I ask.

"Serpents," he tells me, bending over to catch his breath. "There's a Serpent over at Delilah's sign store, and he's harassing her."

I swear and twist the key in the lock. "I'll take care of it," I tell him. "No stress."

He watches as I pull out my phone and call Bastian up. "Hey," I say. "We got a problem."

"Who and where?" Bastian asks.

"Serpents. Delilah's sign shop. Meet me there."

We hang up and I wave Flynn off as I get on my bike. "Go home," I call out. "We're going to handle it."

Once I arrive, I step out to see the slimy bastard from the window of the shop. It looks like he's yelling at Delilah, waving his arms, and getting into her space.

Just as he reaches out to shove her, I find myself flying into the shop, grabbing him by the neck, and yanking him outside.

"Fucking hell!" the weasel yells. He catches sight of me and his face changes into a smirk.

"You think you can take me on?" he asks as I dump him on the ground. He gets to his feet and squares off. "You interrupted my sales pitch, and I'm not happy about that."

"Looks to me like you were trying to shake her down," I growl. "You best step off before you find out what happens next."

He laughs at me, whipping out a knife. "I'm not scared of some stupid Blood Crips."

"Jesus Christ, you can't even get our name right?" Bastian asks, walking around the corner to join us. "We're the Crimson Blades, you dumbass."

Relief floods me. "Glad you're here," I say.

"I always got your back," Bastian responds, his eyes never leaving the Serpent.

The Serpent rolls his eyes, lunging for me, but I grab him by the arm and bend it down so the knife clatters to the ground.

He turns, eyes meeting mine. "You wanna do this then?" he sneers, landing a sucker punch directly in my gut. I double over, the wind knocked out of me.

Bastian immediately jumps forward, grabbing the man's head, and slamming him into the ground. He holds the Serpent down, but the weasel manages to throw his head back and connect with Bastian's nose, making him release his grip as his hands fly up to his face.

With Bastian occupied, the worm gets back up, spits out a mouthful of blood, and wipes his face with the back of his hand; giving us a deranged smile before kicking a heavy-soled boot into Bastian's knee.

Bastian lets out a grunt of pain but I'm on the man immediately, shoving him backward into the concrete wall of the shop. "You don't get to mess with my brother like that," I say, rising to my full height and towering over him. I reach back and my fist connects with his jaw and he's knocked backward.

"Shit!" I hear Delilah yell from inside the shop. "Do I need to call the cops?"

"We can handle it," I call back. "Just get in the back. Don't hang around out here."

"Yeah, that's right. Run off like a little bitch," the man calls, taunting her. "Don't worry, I'll be back for you," he adds.

I reach out and grab him by the collar, shoving him into the wall again, holding him up there. "What the fuck are you even doing here?" I demand. "What's your endgame? Why target Caspian Springs?"

"We want what was once ours," he sneers. "You petty little Blades think you run things but you're weak and defenseless out here. This place is ripe for the picking and we're ready to take it back. I mean, did you think that it wasn't going to happen?"

I can't believe this guy thinks the Serpents can just stroll in and take over, acting like they won't get pushback on it. They're terrors, they roamed the neighborhood when we were kids harassing shopkeepers, and demanding money in exchange for leaving them alone. When people didn't pay, they'd beat them up or ransack the shops.

The Serpent Syndicate also started buying up available properties and charging triple the market rate, driving long-time residents out of the community.

No one wants a repeat of that shit, so we have to make sure they don't get a foothold again.

"You make a move and you'll regret it," I snap. "You guys had nothing when you were run out of town years back. The Blades of old dismantled your entire syndicate, from the top down. How could you possibly have gotten things off the ground since then?"

He smirks. "Wouldn't you like to know?"

I shake my head, done with the conversation, and drop him before leaning down by the shoulder and tackling him into the wall again, slamming his head back.

He howls, clutching his head, dropping down to his knees. But I'm caught off guard when he looks up, a wretched smile on his face, and says something that has me freezing.

"You fight like that asshole we did a few years back ... just kept going till we finished him," he hisses. My blood runs cold. The only person the Serpents managed to kill in the last few years was Beau's dad. White hot rage fills me.

"You fucking bastard!" I yell, but he jumps to his feet and staggers forward, ready to continue our fight. I'm more prepared this time, so when he swings out his fist, I catch it and twist, hearing a satisfying *crack*.

"Holy hell ..."

The three of us turn at the same time, caught off guard by whoever just showed up in the middle of this fight.

My eyes widen upon realizing it's Sienna standing there, a hand over her mouth. Startled, I back away from the man and he takes the opportunity to get away, clutching his arm and cursing up a storm.

Bastian and I turn to look at each other at the same time, the expressions on our faces revealing our inner thoughts—*What do we do now?*

20

BASTIAN

"Holy hell..."

Whipping around, I catch sight of the last person I thought I'd be seeing again.

Sienna stands there, gaping at us with a hand over her mouth. She looks a little fatigued, but otherwise fine. My pulse races at the sight of her, some part of me wanting to rush over there immediately to protect her.

Before I can blink, the man Dominic has pinned gets up and runs off. Dominic and I exchange glances, unsure of what to do.

I can't believe she's here. Did she see what happened? Did she watch as Dominic twisted the guy's arm until it cracked?

Is she freaked out now? Is she disgusted by us? I can't just stand here anymore.

"I'll talk to her," I tell Dominic. "See if Delilah is alright, and make sure that goon ain't coming back."

"No worries, I've got it." Dominic nods and heads into the shop while I jog over to Sienna, who's still staring at us, but her eyes soften on my arrival. I hate how relieved I feel to see her. I've spent so long trying to ignore any lingering feelings I might have had for her, but it's hard to admit that they haven't gone away.

"You alright?" I ask. "You came at a bad time." I approach her cautiously, some part of me worried she might bolt.

"I'm fine," she says, waving me off. "I saw what happened. Are you okay? It looked kind of intense."

I shrug. "No big deal. I've had worse."

She seems to be taking things in stride, which baffles me. Sienna gives off an innocent schoolteacher vibe, but there's something tough lurking under the surface.

"What did that guy do?" Her eyes take in my disheveled appearance.

"So that guy's with the Serpent Syndicate," I say. "They're bad news, major scumbags. They got kicked out of town ages ago, but now they're trying to sneak back in. The Serpents, they're no joke. They'll mess with anyone, innocent folks included. And that dude? He's the one who took out Beau's dad a while back."

Sienna gasps, glancing in the direction that he came from. "I can't believe he's walking around free. Why can't you guys go to the police?"

I shake my head. "It's not that simple. The Serpents, they got this thing. When they want to muscle into new turf, they start buttering up the local cops. Bribery, threats, you name it. Pretty sure they got some of the boys in blue on their payroll already."

The problem is, it's expensive as hell to bribe a bunch of cops, and I can't figure out where this influx of money might be coming from. There's more at stake than just their slimy presence—I worry that they're extorting members of the community behind our backs too.

"I see," Sienna says, offering a tight smile, her lips pressed into a thin line. "Sounds like they're a pretty big threat then. I was wrong for judging you. I didn't know that you were just trying to protect the town from them."

Relief floods through me, but it's quickly replaced by a surge of anxiety, along with regret. I shouldn't have pushed her away. Kicking her out was the worst move I could have made. I just couldn't deal with the old wounds she wanted to open up.

"We didn't want you getting mixed up," I tell her. "We thought we could just keep you from that stuff and it would keep you safe."

Sienna looks down at the ground for a moment before turning back up to look at me. "You know, I didn't think you cared."

"Well, we can't let our little pet get hurt, can we?" I ask, trying to be casual.

Her eyes dim and I curse myself for not being better at this. I'm no good with emotional shit, I can't even figure out myself most of the time. Trying to correct myself, I add, "I mean you were ours, you were ours to protect and take care of. That was the agreement, right?"

"I guess," Sienna says, her gaze flickering away before returning to mine, a hesitant smile playing on her lips. "You know I'm not as weak as I look, right? I grew up in a place like this, with bullies like that hanging around making life difficult. I know how to avoid provoking those kind of idiots into targeting me. In case you didn't notice, I'm plus-size, which puts a target on my back for bullies."

"People are shit," I tell her, irritation crawling over my skin. "Your size ain't got nothing to do with your worth as a person. It's bull crap that other people don't get that shit."

"Yeah, well. What are you going to do? Fight every person who calls me fat?"

"Maybe!" I shoot back, making her eyes widen. "I'm no pussy, and the Blades stand up for what's right," I add. "If it means getting my hands dirty, then so be it."

"What if you get hurt though?" Sienna asks, staring at me with a mixture of concern, and frustration.

"I'm tough," I tell her. "I can handle myself. But if I get hurt, it's not the end of the world. Ain't the first time."

"You've fought before?"

"Yeah. We went up against some of the Serpents about a year ago. Gave them a clear warning to stay out of town. Got my ribs busted in for my trouble."

Sienna's hand reaches out, almost instinctively, before dropping back down. "Oh God."

"I'm fine now," I reassure her. "It took me a while to heal but I'm all better." It's cute that she's concerned about me; I find myself smirking at that.

"I'm sorry I got you all wrong," Sienna apologizes. "I just assumed you were the same as the people I grew up around. That you were just thugs and bullies looking to cause trouble."

"I mean, we're not that different from them," I say, a bitter edge to my voice. "We're still bullies and thugs, just ones that also try to help the good guys once in a while."

Sienna shakes her head. "I think you're too hard on yourself. You never dealt with losing ... that person," she says, sidestepping the name. "And then you took the weight of keeping the peace in Caspian Springs too. It makes sense why you guys have hardened over the years."

"Maybe you're right," I say, taking a deep breath. "I should apologize. I was completely out of line with yelling at you for bringing up Emily. I've been keeping you on a tight leash the entire time and even though you agreed to it, I could have been nicer to you."

"Thank you," Sienna says, her voice hoarse. "You don't know what that means to hear."

"I'm sorry that you had to go through all that growing up too," I add. "You should have had someone to look out for you."

Sienna offers a small smile, but her eyes betray a hint of unease. "Yeah, but I made it through," she says, her voice carrying a hint of vulnerability. It makes my heart clench.

One quick glance around tells me that there's no one lingering nearby, but I still don't want to stand around in the open like this all afternoon. Some Serpents might come back to finish what they started.

"Hey, we shouldn't hang around here all day. Do you want a ride back to the house?" I ask. "We can get your car later."

"A ride?" she quirks her eyebrow.

"Yeah. I'm assuming you were looking for us so you could come home."

Sienna looks confused. "I don't know what you thought, but I came back to Caspian Springs to do my research. Not to come home."

"What?" I feel my heart jump into my throat. "I thought we were past all this bullshit now."

"I came here for a job," Sienna explains. "And I've let myself get distracted. I have work to do and I need to focus on that. If I go back with you, we'll end up in another fight within a few days."

"It won't be like that," I assure her. "I won't throw you out again."

Sienna scoffs. "Trust isn't something you earn back with a half-assed apology, Bastian. And right now, I'm not sure I can trust you." Her words are laced with disappointment as she steps away from me.

"Sienna, don't act like you didn't know what you were getting into. You agreed to our terms, remember?" My voice is edged with frustration.

Sienna's shoulders tense up as she turns to face me again. "I know what I agreed to, Bastian. But I never signed up to be treated like some pawn in your game." She meets my gaze with defiance, her tone sharp and unwavering.

"You gotta be kidding me. I apologized, Sienna. You knew what you signed up for, and now you're just bailing?" My voice cracks, frustration mounting.

I'm not backing down, Bastian. I won't let you force my submission like this anymore."

My jaw clenches. "Fine. Do whatever the hell you want. I'm done wasting my time." I turn on my heel and stomp off.

Things have gotten so damned complicated now. What good is apologizing if it doesn't even change anything?

As I round the corner, the image of Sienna's face refuses to leave my mind, the image of her standing there, arms wrapped protectively around herself.

Her words weigh heavy on me, especially the part about trust. I haven't always been reliable, but I did apologize. Admitting fault isn't my strong suit. It took a lot from me to stand there and admit I was wrong. Why isn't that enough for her?

Tightening my grip on my bike, I push the pedal down harder and pick up speed.

I don't need her anyway. It doesn't matter if I was starting to feel things for her. Like I told Dominic—she's an outsider and she doesn't belong here. It was the right decision to walk away.

I'm not here to get attached, I'm here to keep the town safe from Serpent scum. Sienna is just a distraction, I don't need her.

No matter what my heart feels.

21

SIENNA

As I watch Bastian storm off, my heart aches in my chest. Seeing him and Dominic again has brought up so much inside me. I didn't know that being around them again would leave me with such a lingering ache.

Our brief time together had opened my eyes, letting me catch a glimpse of a different life, one I didn't know I wanted.

But longing to go back is pointless. I'm not willing to bow and scrape at their feet for whatever small moments of kindness they deign to give me.

I may miss some of the small moments we've shared, like being the taste-tester for Dominic when he cooks, or playing *The Sims* with Caleb for hours, but it's for the best to separate from them and get some space.

I pull out my phone and send a text to Rich. I'm heading to campus to do some research in the library. Do you want to get lunch together?

His text comes in as I'm getting back into my car.

I'm about to go into a meeting with the department head. You can use the books in my office if you want, then I'll meet you there.

I smile, sending off my agreement, and then head out.

As I drive, the weight of my confrontation with Bastian hangs over me. From the start, I knew they were on the opposite side of the law, but I had unfairly assumed they were the ones causing problems. Finding out they're more like vigilantes has me reeling. How much else have I gotten wrong about them?

I've kept a distance between us because I thought it was the right thing to do—that I was protecting myself. Now I'm not sure if I was just trying to keep myself from getting too close to them.

There are so many thoughts going on inside my head that by the time I arrive at Rich's office, I'm not even paying attention when I slip inside and drop my bag on his couch. I blink, realizing I'm standing in front of his bookcase, staring blankly at the titles.

Running my hands along the worn spines, I try to decide which of the books here might help me understand some of the data I've collected. I don't need to do this, but I want to show that I'm interested in furthering my career in academia.

Nothing jumps out at me, so I shuffle over to the other bookcase, the one behind his desk. I'm perusing the titles when my eye lands on a half-open drawer with something shiny glinting up at me from the shadows.

Curiosity grabs hold of me as I lean down to see what it is, and I realize it's some kind of jewelry. I pull the drawer open a little more to take a better look, eyes scanning past the trinkets and office supplies. The object is some kind of necklace, delicate and ornate. It catches the light, glinting softly in the dim office. I lift it out of the drawer. It's a gold necklace with a pendant hanging from a thin chain.

The pendant itself is small and intricately designed with delicate patterns etched into the metal. It's beautiful, in a nostalgic sort of way. As I run my fingers over the surface, I notice a name engraved on the back in an elegant script. It's a simple name, but it sends a shiver down my spine.

Emily.

I recognize the name. How odd. What is this necklace doing in Dr. Thornton's drawer? Did it belong to her, or was it merely a coincidence?

It's probably just a coincidence. I mean, why would Dr. Thornton have something like this? It seems out of place amongst the assortment of pens and notepads and scattered paperclips. Is it hers? Was there more to the relationship between them than he led me to believe?

I stare at it for a moment longer, deciding I'm being paranoid. It's probably nothing. Maybe it belonged to his relative or a former student. I drop the necklace back in the drawer before closing it and turning my attention to the books on his shelf.

At that moment, I hear the sounds of footsteps outside Dr. Thornton's office, and his voice echoes in the hallway.

"I'm about to go to lunch but I'll meet with you later," he says to whoever is outside, then slips into his office. He sees me standing next to his bookcase.

"What are you doing over there?" he asks.

I wave. "Hey, I was just looking for a book that could help me better understand the data I've collected. I can't find anything that jumps out at me though. Maybe I could pick your brain about the book you wrote."

"What did you want to know?" Rich asks. "Was there any part of the book in particular that you wanted to know more about?"

Trying to think, I cast my eyes about, landing on a framed photograph on his desk—a group of smiling children standing with him in front of the community center. "I'm curious about the Haven Center," I tell him. "You talked about it in the book a little but I'd love to know more."

"Oh right. The Haven Center. Lemme think. Well, I met so many kids there, and they all grew to mean so much to me," he begins, his voice filled with nostalgia. "I'll tell you what though, it wasn't always easy. I worked with a lot of troubled kids but there were a few who stood out. They came from broken homes and saw way more adversity in their lives than most adults will ever see."

"Sounds tough," I tell him, sitting down on the worn sofa. "How did you handle it?"

He gives a chuckle, a shadow crossing his features briefly as he speaks. "Honestly? It was an uphill battle. Plenty of times I wondered if I was doing the right thing, if I was making a difference. But I think that kind of thing always plagues us in this line of work. Are we researchers or are we saviors? What is our role in these kinds of situations?"

As he continues to speak, my mind circles back to the necklace in the drawer. Something about it gnaws at me. I can't put my finger on what about it seems so odd, but there's something that has me unsettled.

"We also opened a counseling center, and I was one of the first class of interns there," he continues.

"I didn't know that," I admit, forcing myself to push away thoughts of the mystery necklace and focus on his words instead.

"I helped establish the center, as part of my doctoral thesis. My supervisor took the credit, but I brought the idea up during a meeting with her," Rich tells me, a tightness around his smile. "Being there for the kids was the most important thing anyway," he adds.

"How did your work with the kids influence your research?" I ask, genuinely curious.

"I never drew directly from individual counseling sessions," he says, eyes drifting to the window as if lost in thought. "But the challenges those kids faced were always at the forefront of my mind. I pushed for the committee to use my interviews, but they were worried about the ethical implications, so we tried to use the broader insights and challenges instead."

I stare down at the book in his hands, wondering about the ethical implications of using the private sessions of these children for research fodder. It seems almost exploitative in some way.

As though sensing my thoughts, Rich speaks up, drawing my gaze. "I want to assure you, that we took every precaution to uphold ethical standards in my research. An ethics committee meticulously reviewed every aspect of my work to ensure confidentiality and integrity were maintained.

I try to shake away the lingering doubt, reminding myself that Dr. Thornton's research was invaluable in improving the health services offered to communities across the country. "Right," I say. "Of course. Your research is amazing. I was really impressed when I read the book. It felt like for the first time, someone out there was seeing me and sharing my experience."

"That's what I wanted to do," Rich says. "You don't get to know those kids like I did and not have a soft spot for them. They deserve to have their stories told."

I try to push aside these suspicions, reminding myself of his invaluable contributions to research and the positive impact he's had on countless lives. Yet, there's something that nags in the back of my mind, questions that remain unanswered. The necklace's presence, the lingering concerns about his research ...

Despite my doubts, I do appreciate that he was willing to share this with me and offer guidance on my own research. Maybe I'm just overthinking things, letting my insecurities get the best of me. After all, Dr. Thornton has always been nothing but supportive and encouraging.

Are you ready to go grab lunch?" he asks. "I'm starving."

"Sure," I say, grabbing for my bag. "I appreciate you telling me more about your work."

"Anytime," he says. He stops, walking over to his desk to grab some papers. "Did you read *Family and Poverty* by Dr. Eric Clifton?" he asks, stopping by his desk to grab something.

"It's on my to-read list," I tell him. "I started it in undergrad, but I never got around to finishing."

He looks down for a moment, a frown on his face, then glances back at me. "We can talk about it over lunch," he says, giving me a broad smile. "It had a strong influence on my own work so it might be helpful for you too."

"Yeah, sounds good," I mumble, forcing a smile as we step out into the bright sunlight. My stomach is suddenly in knots and I don't know why. The image of the necklace in that drawer still tugs at the back of my mind.

"Sure, sounds good," I mumble, trying to mask the turmoil churning inside me. But as we walk down the corridor, a sudden thought strikes me like a bolt of lightning. Did he realize that I was the one who closed the drawer?

The realization sends a shiver down my spine, but I push it aside, unwilling to confront the possibility head-on. But as we head out to get something to eat, unease grows inside. For the first time since I met him, I start wondering about the true nature of Dr. Thornton's intentions.

22

CALEB

The days crawl by as I try to move past Sienna's disappearance.

The place feels emptier without her presence. I miss the easy banter between us, the way she could lighten the mood with a clever quip or that sweet smile. But now the mood just feels suffocating.

I'm sitting in the living room now, staring at the blank TV screen, lost in thought when Dominic enters.

"Do you have info on the updated signage?" His voice startles me and I jump a little, glancing up at him.

"Sorry," he adds. "Just wanted to check."

"Oh yeah I've got an ETA for us that the new signage will be in by Thursday," I tell him. I glance back at the TV, heaving a sigh.

"You have to get over it," Dominic says, voice low. "She's not coming back."

"I know," I turn, eyes narrowing as I snap at him. "Just miss the way things used to be, you know? Maybe we were trying to make up for all the shit with ..."

"Don't," Dominic warns, eyes flashing.

"Whatever," I say, pushing off the couch. "I'm just trying to get through the day."

"Fine. I'm heading to the shop," Dominic says, grabbing his keys from the hook. "I can't take any more of your morose attitude."

I flop back down onto the couch and glare at the blank screen as Dominic takes off. It's not like I'm going through some kind of emo phase. I'm not lying on my bed listening to angsty music while wearing seventeen layers of eyeliner. It's just been tough to lose someone I was starting to care about, that's all.

Picking up a comic book off the coffee table, I begin to flick through with listless energy. The doorbell rings, bringing me out of my funk for a moment, curiosity catching hold.

Walking over to the door, I crack it open and spot Sienna standing there on the front porch, arms wrapped around herself.

"Sienna," I say, my heart leaping into my throat. "What's up?" I push the door open and step outside onto the porch with her. My eyes widen upon seeing her standing there.

"I need to talk to you," she says softly. "All three of you." Hope blooms inside my chest, along with a dose of apprehension.

"Oh, uh. Okay. They're both at the shop right now. Can it wait until the end of the day, or do you need to talk to them now?"

Sienna chews her lip. "I guess it can wait."

"Wait, it's not like we're busy today. I'll call Dom and Bastian and have them come home right now. I feel like it's something important, right?"

Sienna nods and I pick up the phone, dialing Bastian's number.

"Hey," he says, picking up right away.

"Sienna's here," I say, forgoing a greeting. "She wants to talk to us."

"Shit." Bastian drops something and it clatters, echoing. "Okay, be there in a few, just … don't let her go anywhere."

"Wouldn't dream of it," I tell him. "See you soon."

He hangs up and I push the door open again. "You wanna come inside to wait?"

"Sure," Sienna nods, following me inside with hesitant steps. "I don't know why I'm here, but ... I had to come."

She sits down on the couch and I sit near her, not so close as to scare her away. "So how have you been?" I ask, trying to keep things light.

She gives me a tentative smile. "Good. Been busy working on stuff with the research project. We're almost at phase two."

"That's good," I respond, wondering what it is she might be here to talk about.

The front door squeaks open and we both jump, a little jittery.

"We're home!" Bastian calls. The two of them amble into the living room and they both catch sight of Sienna, sharing a look.

"What's up?" Bastian asks, opting for a casual tone as he drops himself into a recliner. I see the tension in his shoulders though, and I know he's just as curious. Dominic keeps his gaze trained on Sienna as he sits down on the other side of the couch.

"First of all, I know we had an arrangement, and I haven't been holding up my end," Sienna admits, fiddling with the strap of her bag as she avoids eye contact.

I suck in a breath, not sure where this is going. "I thought getting away was what I wanted. I thought it was better for everyone if I just left and didn't come back." Her voice wavers as she speaks. "But I don't know where I belong anymore. I don't know who I am without you guys."

Dominic's voice cracks as he speaks. "It's my fault. I let things get way out of hand." His shoulders slump with the weight of his remorse. "I shouldn't have let it escalate."

"It's not on you," Bastian protests. "I screwed up, okay? I know that."

"It's everyone's fault," I speak up. "We all played a part. We all acted shitty, everyone but Sienna. We put her in this position and she couldn't handle it anymore."

"Guys," Sienna says, closing her eyes for a moment. "This is the problem right here. You can't treat me like I'm just a toy you can pull out and play with when you feel like, then put me away when you're done."

We go silent, exchanging glances. Bastian bites his lip and Dominic curls his fingers into his palms. They both want to speak but they're trying to let Sienna talk.

"So, I'd appreciate it if you let me get out what I wanna say," Sienna continues. "You know, I was surprised as anyone that I like the stuff we do together. I liked spending time with you, even if it kind of ... scared me a little. And now I'm not sure where I belong anymore. So, I want to try again, but only if things are different this time."

The weight of her words settles over me, hardly daring to hope.

"What are you asking?" Bastian says, asking the question that's on the tip of all our tongues.

Sienna's eyes fill with an earnest determination and she takes a deep breath. "Can we try again? I wanna move back in here and be with you guys, but I want to do it on my own terms."

I suck in a breath. Could we do it? Could we try again with her? What if it doesn't work out this time? Could I let myself get hurt like this again?

"What are the terms?" Dominic asks.

Sienna goes quiet for a moment. "You want me, you can have me. I'll still do anything you ask but I want more trust. You have to let me leave when I want and go where I want when I want. No more following me around, no more making me stay locked up in Caleb's room."

The idea of letting her walk around freely when the Serpents are still such a looming presence admittedly scares me, but I know that she deserves to be allowed autonomy. Still, I can't quiet the voice in the back of my head. I need to see what the others are thinking.

I turn towards Bastian, trying to get a read on where his head is at. Dominic is facing him as well. Bastian's jaw is clenched, his expression tense with indecision as he weighs the options.

"Give us five minutes," Bastian says, standing up. "We're going to go to the kitchen and talk in private."

I follow, shooting a glance at Sienna as I leave. It feels like a dream, having her back here.

"What do you think?" Dominic asks. "Can we really trust her?"

"I want to trust her," I tell them. "I think she's tried to prove herself trustworthy."

"Can we deal with this whole 'independence' thing?" Bastian asks.

I nod. "Yeah, I think we need to. We let shit from the past haunt us for too long. I want to treat Sienna like her own person, not like the ghost of ... someone else."

"I agree," Dominic adds. "Sienna is willing to give us a fresh start. I say we take it."

"Alright," Bastian nods. We all head back into the living room, where Sienna is still sitting, her knee bouncing with nervous energy.

"Okay," Bastian says. "We agree to your terms. Where do you want to go from here?"

"I'm willing to move back into Caleb's room," Sienna says, giving me a soft smile. "Is that okay?"

"Fine with me," I answer, voice almost cracking from how quickly I respond. "I can help you get your stuff."

"There's not much," she says, a little giggle in her words. "I didn't take anything with me when I left."

I chuckle as well. "Right." We head out to her car, and I pick up her bag and a box of books that she's using for the research project and head back inside.

"Thanks for letting me stay in your room again," Sienna says as we walk up the stairs. "I missed sleeping next to someone."

"Yeah, me too," I admit. "It got lonely without you around." Relief is overriding the anxiety from earlier, and excitement courses through me. "Wanna play *The Sims* later?"

"Sure," she drops her bag onto the nightstand. "I should shower and change first. I've been wearing the same clothes every day since I left all the rest of mine here."

"Where were you staying?" I ask, curious.

"With Rich," she answers, rifling through the drawer with her clothes. My heart feels as though it's being squeezed into a vise. "He's got a huge place he inherited, I was staying in one of his guest rooms. I know that you guys might worry, but I assure you that it was completely innocent, I don't even think of him in that way."

She turns to face me and I move forward, needing to claim her for myself again. My lips meet hers and our bodies meld together, the longing finally being replaced by burning desire.

I move my hands over her body, cupping her ass through her leggings. She grinds into me and I let out a moan, slipping my tongue inside her mouth as we fall onto the bed together, limbs tangling up.

Our kisses turn more heated and soon I'm tugging at her clothing, trying to rip them off her. She sits up and shucks off each item of clothing in rapid succession, laying herself bare for me.

In a hurry, I shed my own clothes and line myself up at her entrance, easily gliding through the wet folds as I drive myself home. "God Sienna, I missed this. Missed you."

"Me too," she says, nearly breathless. "I dreamed about you, about this. You have no idea how badly I've been wanting you."

"Can imagine," I tell her, whispering it in her ear just to watch her shiver. "Cuz I've been wanting you too, just as badly. Wanting to fuck this perfect little body for so long. Wanting to show you just who you belonged to."

Dominic knocks and Sienna stiffens for a moment, but I call out for him. "Come on in," I say. "Join the party."

He strides in and grins, undoing the buttons on his flannel shirt. "Look at our sexy little princess," he rumbles. "Gonna keep you chained to this bed until you forget why you left it in the first place."

"Sounds good to me," Sienna giggles, holding her arms out for Dominic.

Dominic joins in and soon the room is filled with a symphony of moans and the rattle of the bed frame.

"Yes!" Sienna cries out, meeting my thrusts with her hips as Dominic teases her back entrance. "God! Yes!"

I'm glad she's back, even if I still have some lingering doubts. I hope she never leaves again.

23

DOMINIC

I awake to morning light filtering through the curtains, warming the room. Sienna's body is pressed against mine, memories of the night before flooding back. Something shifted between us last night, giving me a newfound appreciation for her presence in our lives.

I gaze at her sleeping form, marveling at her beauty.

"You awake?" I murmur, brushing a stray lock of hair away from Sienna's face.

Sienna stirs, her eyes fluttering open as she meets my gaze with a sleepy smile. "Morning," she replies, her voice husky with sleep.

Reaching out, I brush a strand of hair from her face, then hesitate. I don't want to ruin the moment, but the events of yesterday still weigh on me.

"I was thinking," I begin, my voice quiet in deferment to the early hour. "About what you said last night. About how we treated you like a doll we could play with and put away when we were bored. It bothered me because I ... I don't want you to feel that way. You mean something to me, more than I honestly expected."

Sienna's eyes soften, her fingers tracing lazy circles on my chest.

"You know, I was thinking last night about the first time I ever tried spicy food."

I lean over, capturing her hands in mine. "Oh?" I ask, bringing her hands up to kiss them.

"Yeah. The first time I ever tried spicy food I was a teenager. I didn't think I liked it. It was too much for me. I coughed a lot, my nose ran, it was way out of my comfort zone."

I'm not sure where she's going with this, but I stay silent, letting her speak.

"I ended up kind of craving another taste of it," she continues. "I don't know why, but I couldn't get the sensation out of my head. I had to try it again, to see if I liked it or I was just imagining it."

She runs her fingers over the stubble on my cheeks, sending tingles down my back. "It was still overwhelming the next time I tried it, but I started to like it, in a way. And then I seemed to enjoy the burn. I think maybe, sometimes, I don't mind being treated like a doll, or a toy."

My lips curl into a grin. "Noted."

"And when I don't want to be treated like a doll, I'll just tell you 'No spicy food today.'"

"So you want us to still treat you like before, unless you specify otherwise?"

She nods, rubbing her head against my chest. "Are you coming with me to campus today?"

"I thought you didn't want us following you around anymore?" I ask, trying to understand her better.

"I don't want you guys forcing your presence on me at all times," Sienna explains. "Doesn't mean I don't want your company though."

I reach down and pull her in for a gentle kiss, a flutter in my chest. She kisses me back, tentatively at first, but then becomes more bold and opens her mouth to me, letting my tongue enter and twine with hers.

Our bodies press together as we kiss, close enough to feel her heartbeat, and the two of us linger there for a few more moments before Sienna pulls away, a reluctant look in her eyes.

"We should get dressed," she says. "I need to get to campus soon."

"Yeah," I agree, mind still reeling from our kissing.

She disappears down the hall to Caleb's room, leaving me alone to get dressed. I pull on a pair of dark wash jeans and a short-sleeved hoodie. I slip my feet into a pair of Cole Haans and clasp my favorite silver chain around my neck.

Once I'm done, I take the stairs two at a time and jog into the kitchen to wait for Sienna. She shows up within a few minutes in a tight-fitting black top and a green pencil skirt. I whistle, appreciating that she's incorporating some of the clothes we picked out for her into her wardrobe now.

"You look good, Princess," I say, leaning down to give her a peck. "Ready to go?"

"Just let me get my bookbag," she says, skirting past me to bend down and grab the bag next to the coffee table. I reach out and smack her on the ass and she lets out a little squeak, turning to face me with a blush.

I grab her hand and we hop into the Firebird, heading out for the university. "I hope I can keep working with Dr. Thornton," Sienna says. "I hope it's not a problem for you."

"It's fine," I say, gripping the steering wheel tightly under my fingers. "I know he's your boss."

"He's been helpful with my research," Sienna confesses. "But it's been strictly professional between us. I don't know if that helps but ... I don't have any feelings for him outside of seeing him as a mentor figure."

"It's helpful," I tell her. "Thanks for reassuring me."

We stop at the Psych building and she gets out, leaning over the seat to kiss me. "I'll text you when I'm done. What are you going to do?"

"Probably just hang out," I tell her. "I have a notebook I keep with me, sometimes I write down random song lyrics I come up with. My brothers tease me about it, so I only do it when they're not around."

"Aw," Sienna makes a noise of sympathy. "Maybe I can see your songs sometime?"

"Maybe," I say, shrugging. "Anyway, go ahead and get out of here. I'll be fine hanging out alone."

She waves and heads off, leaving me to pull out my mini notebook. But before I can start jotting down lines, a message from Caleb pops up.

Serpents tossed Park Dry Cleaners. They're still there, place is a mess. We need backup.

I'm on my way, I quickly reply, then text Sienna. ***Got to go. Trouble with the Serpents. We'll pick you up later.***

Taking off, I glance in the rearview mirror and watch the campus fade into the distance. A sense of foreboding gnaws at me, as if this is the calm before the storm.

The front windows of the dry cleaners are busted in and glass is all over the pavement. There are clothes strewn about, spilling out the front door. As I approach the building, the inside is even more of a mess.

Hangers litter the floor, some bent or broken. Piles of garments are scattered everywhere, their fabrics stained with dirt and grime from being thrown around. The counter is overturned, shattered glass glittering on the carpeted floor, amidst the wreckage.

The acrid smell of chemicals stings my nose as I crunch through the broken glass. My heart pounds in my chest as I take in the extent of the damage, a cold fury burning in my veins. I clench my jaw, my mind racing towards revenge. These assholes have crossed a line, thinking they can just waltz in and wreck everything; not on my watch.

I curse, spotting Caleb and Bastian amidst the wreckage.

"Mr. Park was at the dentist," Bastian says, grim-faced. "He wasn't here."

"Oh, thank God," I exhale. "Anyone else around?"

"Not that we can find," Caleb says tersely. "But we think the Serpents are nearby."

"Time to show them how the Blades take care of things," I say, cracking my knuckles. "I'm not in the mood for negotiations anymore, what about you, Bastian?"

"Hell no, let's go fuck shit up," Bastian agrees, a grin on his face.

Three Serpents are hanging around the alley out back, kicking over trash bins.

"Why are you doing this?" Bastian demands as we approach. "Why the dry cleaners? Who's ordering these attacks?"

"Gabriel Diego's the one in charge," the pudgy one nearest him says. "Diego wants control of this sector of town. Park refused to pay, so we made an example of him."

"Why now?" I ask.

"Diego has plans," Pudge drawls out. "He's been consolidating territory and now he's ready to take back this town."

They saunter towards us, without a care in the world. "Get the hint, bro?" Pudge asks, his lip curled into a sneer. "You don't surrender to us, we keep spreading the word. Those who don't pay, fall."

"How about you just fall?" I offer. "Right here, right now."

The other two flank Pudge, identical maniacal looks on their faces.

I glance over to my brother. "Your call," I tell Bastian.

"Let's take 'em down," Bastian commands, his voice cutting through the tension as we brace for a fight.

Pudge charges at me, probably aiming to take me out first since I pose the biggest threat in his mind. I keep my fists close to my face, popping a left hook at him right as he reaches me. He staggers backward, his lip split from where my fist landed.

Wiping the blood away, he charges forward again, aiming a blow at my chest, then at the last second feinting and making contact with my side. It catches me off guard but I ignore the pain and aim another punch at his face, making contact with his cheek.

He hollers and cups his cheek before kicking out at me. When I twist to avoid the kick, one of his goons clocks me in the back of the head.

I grunt, pain exploding at the base of my skull. Shit, these guys are damned good. They're better than we expected.

The pain radiates down my back as I stagger forward, trying to keep on my feet. Caleb is clutching a hand to his cheek, a bloody line slashed into it and Bastian is bleeding freely from a cut on his forehead.

"Fucking dicks!" Bastian curses, spitting blood onto the pavement of the dirty alley. He holds his fists up, bobbing and weaving the next attack from the goon on his left. Spotting an opening, he clocks the guy in the side of the head, making the man go down in a heap.

Pudge is still attacking me rapid-fire style, forcing me to expend energy to stave off his blows. I'm nearly backed into a corner when I manage to duck under his arm with the next punch and grab him from behind.

Putting him in a headlock, I squeeze hard, watching his face go from red to purple. "Pass out," I hiss at him. It takes a few more seconds but he finally goes limp and I drop him.

The last of the three thugs is still going up against Caleb, but once he realizes it's three to one, he backs up and starts running.

"Looks like they've had enough," Bastian remarks, a smirk playing on his lips as the last one takes off like a frightened mouse.

As soon as he's out of sight, Caleb turns to us. "Let's get outta here before these assholes wake up."

"Smart move," I agree. "We can take the Firebird."

As we pile into the car, I glance back, wondering why the Serpents have grown so much more aggressive lately. Why are they stirring shit up all the time now? What's changed?

24

SIENNA

As I walk into the building, I catch sight of a bulletin board. There's a colorful flyer for a rummage sale. The flyer itself isn't what catches my eye though, but a thumbnail on the flyer of a few pieces of jewelry. The trinkets remind me of the necklace I saw yesterday, the one from Dr. Thornton's drawer.

Realizing my brain won't let it go until I get some answers, I decide to just ask Dr. Thornton about it. It's probably nothing but my brain won't rest until it's satisfied.

Rich is in his office when I knock and as I walk in, he's compiling spreadsheets of data. "Hey," I call out. "I'm returning one of the books I borrowed."

"Finished already?"

"I pulled a few things that were helpful," I tell him. "I talked to the boys too," I add, gauging his reaction. "We made up and I moved back in with them."

He gives me a thumbs-up and looks up at me. Is it my imagination or does he look disappointed in that? "That's great. Hang on one sec, let me just text one of my project managers back."

Once he's done, he turns in his chair to face me. "I'm glad you've worked things out. It hurts my heart to see those boys in pain still."

"Yeah, I mean it must have been hard for them since losing Emily," I say, trying to maintain a casual tone. "What was she like?"

"A little like you, actually," Rich comments, folding his fingers together as he thinks over my question. "She was very passionate about her work and creating a better community."

"Sounds like the two of you worked closely together," I comment, subtly probing.

"Well, she and the boys were a package deal," Rich says with a shrug. "It's inevitable we spent time around each other."

I nod, biting my lip. "And there was the whole thing where she fell in love with you," I say. Rich's eyes widen.

"I never meant for that to happen," he says. "I was just as hurt by her betrayal as the boys were."

"I'm sorry," I say, feeling bad for bringing that up.

My thoughts race as I try to bring up the topic of the necklace without being accusatory. I don't want to point a finger over something silly. Rubbing a hand over the material of my skirt, I opt for nonchalance.

"So, I was going through some old boxes in the house and I saw a photo of Emily. She was wearing a beautiful necklace in the picture. Did she often wear jewelry like that?"

"Well, I guess Emily had a unique sense of style. She often wore gold jewelry. There was one necklace she had that she wore all the time."

"Oh, speaking of jewelry, I couldn't help but notice a necklace in your drawer the other day. Did it belong to her?"

"Oh, that," Dr. Thornton gives me a soft, sad smile. "She gifted it to me after her confession. When she died, I found it again and I guess I couldn't bear to part with it. She was like a daughter to me."

Something inside of me tingles, like a warning. "But I thought you weren't that close to her?" I ask.

"We were brought together by circumstance," he says. "But we spent a lot of time together. She was with the boys for a year before her passing."

He grows serious, brows drawn. "Look, Emily also didn't come from the most stable home life. I gave her the same listening ear that I did for the boys. You know that it's common in that sort of situation to experience transference, and that's all that happened. She confused romantic feelings with the safety and security I offered. That's all."

It makes sense, I guess. It answers my questions. But something still feels missing, like there's a puzzle piece I'm not seeing. "I get it," I say. "I can understand. The necklace must give you a sense of comfort."

"It does," Rich says, nodding. "Emily was a remarkable young woman, much like yourself, Sienna. She held a special place in my heart, and her loss weighs heavily on me to this day."

"I'm sorry I brought up painful memories," I apologize. I feel like I've pried into Dr. Thornton's personal life and guilt gnaws at me. "I'm just here to drop off this book and turn in more data. I'll be out of your hair soon."

"I understand why you might have been curious," Dr. Thornton says, reaching out to grab my wrist. "But please don't go through my personal things. If you have any more questions about the past, you can just ask."

I nod, feeling sick to my stomach. I hate making people upset with me. "Here's the data," I say, handing him the folder. "I'll be back doing fieldwork. Probably won't see you for a few days."

"Have a nice day, Sienna," Dr. Thornton gives me a curt smile and I walk away, feeling like a fool.

As I head back outside, tears sting my eyes. It was so stupid of me to get into Dr. Thornton's personal business. I hope he doesn't fire me for snooping around. I shouldn't have pried. I always get ahead of myself and read too much into things.

A wave of guilt washes over me. I can't shake the feeling that I completely overstepped by prying into his personal life. I know it isn't my place to dig into his past, but my curiosity got the better of me once again.

Before I can spiral any further, my phone pings, alerting me to a text I missed from Dominic, saying he had to go take care of Serpent business. I look around, trying to decide if I want to go to the library to wait.

A car starts up and I jump, feeling on alert for some reason. Glancing over, I notice it's a black SUV and when I turn towards the library, it backs out and starts to circle the parking lot.

Feeling as though it's following me, I decide to double back. The SUV swings back around, cuts across, pulls in front of me, and stops short, one of the back doors opening.

Maybe they were just dropping someone off and I'm being paranoid again.

I turn to go around the car and suddenly there are three men on top of me. As duct tape is shoved against my lips, and my wrists are tightly bound, a surge of panic threatens to overwhelm me.

Shit! I think I'm being kidnapped! Tears well up and I struggle to breathe around the duct tape, feeling my lungs constrict.

Panic claws at my chest as I struggle against the restraints, my mind racing with questions. Who are these men? Where are they taking me? Will I ever see Dominic and the others again?

I need to think! I can't let them take me somewhere without trying to get help. My phone is in my bra, and I reach in with my bound wrists, pulling it out. It's hard to see the screen and I'm worried that the men who took me will notice I've got it so I fumble, trying to figure out who I could message.

My hands tremble as I fumble for my phone, the duct tape cutting into my skin. I have to send a message, I have to let the Ravenwoods know I'm in danger. Every second feels like an eternity as I struggle to send a text. I pray that it goes through and that someone gets my message.

"Diego says to bring her to the warehouse location," one of the men says to the driver in a low voice. I try to pay attention to what they're saying but it's hard to do while I'm being shaken about. The man in the seat next to me cranes his neck and I catch a glimpse of a winding tattoo of a snake.

In the dim light of the SUV, I catch glimpses of my captors' faces. Their hardened expressions send a chill down my spine. Who are these men, and what did they want with me? Snake-Tattoo catches sight of me staring.

"She sees us, she might make trouble if she knows anything," he says, voice deep and rumbling.

"Then knock her out," the man up front hisses. Panic grips me and I try to fling myself backward as he reaches down and punches me hard on the side of my head.

Pain eclipses me and darkness creeps into the edges of my vision. I struggle to remain alert but everything is growing dim. Finally, the world goes dark and I find myself falling into unconsciousness.

I wake with a gasp, searing pain throbbing inside my head. I feel cold and my vision is blurry.

Blinking several times, my vision clears and I realize where I am. I'm in the middle of a large, empty warehouse and when I try to move, I realize I'm tied up, sitting on the floor with my back against a metal support column.

The warehouse is dimly lit, with cracks in the concrete floor visible like jagged scars. Piles of cardboard boxes are stacked haphazardly against the walls, covered in layers of grime and cobwebs. Rusty metal beams crisscross the ceiling, and the air is heavy with the scent of mildew and decay, tinged with the metallic tang of rust.

The concrete floor is cold and unforgiving beneath me, sending a shiver up my spine. Nausea rises as I realize with growing horror that I have no idea where I am, no idea who took me, and no idea if I managed to send a message to anyone who can help me.

Oh fuck. I'm in so deep right now.

25

CALEB

"You okay?" Bastian asks as we haul ourselves out of the car and head into the house. "You got the worst of it."

My pants are torn, cheek stinging from a fresh cut, and I feel like I'll be sore tomorrow. But it could have been worse, and I'm glad that we all escaped relatively unscathed.

"Honestly, I'm just grateful we kicked their asses so they don't dare come back and hurt Mr. Park," I tell them.

"Me too," Dominic says, wincing as he walks up the steps. "Wish it was faster. Asshole got me straight in the gut."

"Did they get you anywhere else?" Bastian asks.

"Nah. They knew they were no match for me," Dominic brags. "That's why they were all trying to get in hits and that one slimer wanted to wear me down."

"They got me good in the face," Bastian admits. "I think I'll have a black eye tomorrow."

"Let me bandage that cut on your forehead," I tell Bastian.

"I'll clean up in the upstairs bathroom," Dominic offers. "I need a shower."

My phone buzzes as I'm taking off my jacket.

"Hey, check if Sienna texted back yet," Dom calls out as he heads up the stairs. "I texted her that one of us would go get her. She might be ready to go."

"Checking now," I say as I open her message. I laugh. "Looks like a butt-text," I tell Bastian as he takes off his shirt to examine a bruise on his ribcage.

"Call and see if she's ready to be picked up," Bastian suggests. I put the phone to my ear and it rings once before going to voicemail.

That's weird. I try again but this time it goes straight to voicemail. I shrug and pull my own shirt off, trying to see if I have any other cuts or bruises.

"Maybe she's at the library," Bastian says, grabbing a washcloth from the drawer. "Text her, ask her when she wants to get picked up."

Typing out the text, I hit send and lay my phone down on the counter while I help Bastian clean the cut on his forehead. Pulling a first aid kit out of the drawer, I dab on some antiseptic gel and bandage up the cut. "Looking good," I tease as I push the bandage down.

Bastian's eyebrows raise. "Okay, let's patch up that cut on your cheek, kid," he says as soon as I'm done. With a laugh, I hop up on the bathroom counter and he wipes the blood away, the smell of antiseptic wafting through the air.

"What did those guys say again?" I ask, hissing lightly at the stinging sensation. "They said someone named Diego is in charge, right?"

"Yeah, Gabriel Diego," Bastian confirms. "Has to be related to Jorge Diego, the former leader of the Serpent Syndicate."

"Maybe a son or a nephew," I offer. "What plans do you think Diego has?"

"The one with the neck rolls said he wants to take over that area of town," Bastian says, putting a butterfly bandage over the cut. "They have to be hitting up all the businesses in the southern sector then. The dry cleaners can't be the only place they've gone."

"Right," I agree. "There has to be at least six or seven businesses on that street alone."

Bastian counts out on his fingers. "There's the machine shop, that clothing boutique, and a couple of retail places. We ought to pay them all a visit, see who's been hit up and who might have gotten scared and added someone to the payroll."

"After we go get Sienna," I agree.

"Has she texted yet?" Bastian asks, wrapping his hand with an ace wrap.

I pick up my phone. "Nope."

"Try calling her again. We just need an ETA on when to go over there."

The phone goes straight to voicemail again and I hang up, glancing back at Bastian. "I can't get her."

"The princess wanted more freedom, but she knows she still needs to check in with us," Bastian grumbles.

"Yeah," I say, though there's a strange, unsettled feeling running down my back. "It's weird. I figured Sienna would've texted by now, even just to let us know where she's headed."

Bastian drops the trash into the can. "What did the message say?"

I hold out the phone, showing him the garbled string of letters.

Heiopwje

"Try texting her one more time, just tell her that if she doesn't text us in the next few minutes we're going to head to campus to get her." Bastian's frustration is palpable.

"We promised her space, remember?" I pause, weighing our options. "Let's wait a little bit longer."

"Whatever," Bastian says, voice gruff. "I'm going to grab something to eat."

I text Sienna again, telling her to call as soon as she's free, and then head into the kitchen to join Bastian. Dominic is making a sandwich and Bastian tells him what's been going on.

"She's fine," Dominic says, not even looking up from the food in front of him. "I dropped her off this morning in front of the Psych building."

"All the more reason to worry," Bastian mutters. "I just don't like her hanging around *him*."

Dominic shakes his head. "Take it easy, Bas. Grab a bite. It'll help calm your nerves."

"What time did you drop her off?" I ask, looking at the text again.

"Like eight," Dominic says. He picks up his sandwich and takes a bite.

"It's almost eleven," I tell him. "Are you sure she wouldn't have texted to get picked up by now?" A knot tightens in my stomach, hoping that she's just distracted.

Dominic pauses and checks his phone. "Yeah, that's odd. She was going to do some interviews later today too."

Bastian runs a hand through his dark brown hair. "We should just go over there," he says.

"Let's just wait," I tell him. "She'll text back soon, I'm sure. Maybe she got caught up reading one of her research books."

Bastian's hands shake as he slaps together a sandwich, his muttered curses barely audible over the pounding of my heart.

A knot tightens in my stomach, a silent warning that we're hurtling towards disaster with each passing moment. After making up with her yesterday, it feels out of character for her to go radio silent now. Her things are all still here, even her car. If she wanted to escape, she couldn't have gotten very far.

The time ticks by and the longer we don't hear from her, the more agitated Bastian gets. He barely eats his sandwich and by the half-hour mark, he's actively pacing, his boots echoing across the hardwood with each step.

"Calm the hell down," Dominic says, ever the reasonable one. "Sienna said herself that she's not going anywhere. There's no reason to worry she ran off. Her car is still here for Pete's sake, Bastian."

I shift on the couch, fiddling with my phone. Even if Dominic's words are meant to soothe our fears, there's part of me that can't stop stressing, feeling like something is wrong.

"I'm going to call her again," I say, standing up. I can't sit still anymore. My hands tremble slightly as I dial her number again, heart pounding in my chest at yet another unanswered call.

"Something is wrong," Bastian argues, a tic in his jaw from where he's clenching it. His pacing grows more frantic. "What the hell's taking her so long to reply?"

"Maybe I can just check her location," I offer, worry mounting. "If she's on campus, we'll see and then we can find her and ask her why she's got her phone off."

"You can do that?" Dominic asks, raising an eyebrow.

"Yeah, I put a tracking app on her phone," I tell them. "Thought it would be smart and look, now we can check."

"Just go get your laptop, nerd brain," Bastian grumbles. I jog up the stairs and grab my laptop, bringing it down to set it on the coffee table. The keys clatter under my fingers as I type in the website, the bright light of the screen casting a glow across my face.

Pulling up my tracker app, I ping her phone, squinting at the coordinates. "Where is that?" I ask. "That doesn't look like anywhere near Watford."

Bastian kneels down, pulling the computer roughly towards himself.

"Hey, careful," I warn him.

"Does that look familiar to you?" He looks up at Dominic and jabs the screen. "Right there. What does that look like?"

Dominic inhales sharply, breath catching in his throat, then curses. "That location's near Serpent turf. Why would Sienna be anywhere near there?"

I feel nauseous. "You think Sienna's working with the Serpents?"

"No way," Bastian says, shaking his head. "She didn't even know what the Serpents were until the other day."

"So, either she's in with them or they've ... they've taken her?" I ask, feeling bile rising inside me.

Dominic clenches his fists, conflict in his eyes as he struggles to rein in his emotions. "That fight," he growls. "That shit was a distraction. Why else would the Serpents hang around after tossing the dry cleaners? If they wanted to send a message, they didn't need to stick around to do it."

"They've got her," I whisper, voice hoarse. "They distracted us and took her when we weren't paying attention."

"Fuck!" Bastian swears. "I'm going to *kill* those bastards. They lay a hand on her and they're all dead, every last one of them!"

"We need to go, now," Dominic orders, steely determination in his voice. "The longer we take getting to her ... who knows what those vipers will do to her."

My jaw clenches, entire body tense. "Let's go."

We mount our bikes, engines roaring, echoing the way my heart pounds in my chest. "Hold on, Sienna," I whisper. "We're on our way."

The acrid stench of exhaust chokes the air as we push our bikes to their limits, the roar of the engines drowning out the frantic beating of my heart. Determination to find her and bring her home grows inside, eclipsing my fear and filling me with righteous rage.

26

BASTIAN

Fury radiates through me as I realize that we've been set up. The fight was a damned distraction, their real target was Sienna this whole time.

The question lingers in my mind even as we race to find her. Why did they take her? Why are they after her? What is she to them?

I told Caleb I didn't think she was working with the Serpents, but I can't be sure. Is it possible she's been playing us this whole time?

As we ride, my mind returns to the last time I was with Sienna before the blow-up. I kept pushing her away every time we'd get closer, so if she did betray us, I could understand why. She gave me so many chances and I screwed up every time.

Not this time. I vow that no matter what it takes, I'm going to treat Sienna the way she deserves once we get her back.

We pull into a parking lot so Caleb can check the GPS tracking app. He's got her location but if they move her, we want to be prepared.

"I can't believe they had the nerve to take Sienna," Dominic says, a tick in his jaw. "Those snakes haven't been in Caspian Springs in more than ten years. They just started showing up last year again, and all of a sudden they've ramped things up? It doesn't make sense."

"It's like they feel bold now that a lot of the old guard has died off or left Caspian Springs," I comment. "They started popping back up after the Haven Center closed but they weren't making as much trouble until now."

I breathe out, trying to control my frustration. Why here? Why now? That's the question we keep circling back to, over and over. There's something we're missing but I can't put my finger on what it is.

"They didn't have the numbers before," Caleb says, sitting up straighter. "Think about it. When the Crimson Blades drove them out of town all those years ago, a lot of the Serpents were killed or jailed. So they didn't have the resources to come back, or even to try."

"But now they've boosted membership," Dominic adds, a puzzled look on his face. "They're getting cocky because they think they have the backing to take over again."

"We can't let that happen," I say, voice grim. "If they take over, they'll do worse than what they did today, and they'll run this place into the ground."

"I got a lock on her location," Caleb says, balancing his laptop on his bike. "I don't know if she has her phone still, or if they took it but it's just here," he points to the screen. "They might have moved her, but we should be able to get there within the next ten minutes."

"We need a plan," I say. "Before we go in there, guns metaphorically blazing, we need to figure out how to get her out without bringing their full wrath down on us. It won't help Sienna if we all get taken out."

The sun is low in the sky, casting long shadows over the abandoned parking lot. I cup my hand over my eyes and squint as I face my brothers. "Sienna needs us right now, so we need to be smart about this. Caleb, what's our best approach?"

"We could use a distraction to draw them out while one of us sneaks in," he suggests.

"I can handle the distraction. You two focus on finding Sienna." Dominic says.

The rage inside me is on a simmer, replaced with a tightness in my chest. I hope Sienna is alright, I hope they haven't hurt her yet. I feel responsible because it was my deal that Sienna agreed to in the first place. I've already hurt her, and I won't be the reason she gets hurt again.

"What building is that?" I ask, pointing to the spot where the phone signal is blinking.

"That's the old tire factory," Caleb says. "It's been abandoned for a long time. That's probably why they have her held there."

I get an idea. "If we take this street here," I say, pointing at the map. "We can hide our bikes behind this building. We should have a decent vantage point from there, so we can figure out what's going on and where they're keeping her. It means we have an advantage because they won't know we're there."

Dominic nods. "Good idea. Maybe we should have equipped ourselves first."

"Probably, but it's too late now," I say with a shrug. "We'll just have to do this old-school."

"Let's go get our princess back," Dominic says, a fierceness in his eyes that shows how much he's grown to care for Sienna.

I stick my fist out and my brothers tap theirs against it and we head out again. Every second we delay is another second for them to hurt Sienna.

As we approach her location, we veer left into an empty office park. We don't want the Serpents to notice our bikes in the area, so we park two blocks over before killing the engine.

Dominic and Caleb do the same and we get off and check the tracking signal once more, just to be sure.

"She's still here, or her phone is," Caleb says. "No way to know which until we check."

"One of us needs to go over and spy on them. If all three of us go, we'll draw too much attention," Dominic points out.

"I'll do it," I volunteer. "Dom, no offense but your size means that they'd notice you instantly. And Caleb needs to stay here to track her signal."

"Be safe," Dominic says, clapping a hand on my shoulder. I nod and creep along the wall, keeping an eye out for any stray Serpents as I go.

Rounding the corner of the building, I keep low and run across to hide behind a dumpster on the next block. A few Serpents are patrolling this block, no doubt keeping an eye out for us.

I wait until they pass before taking off again, running to hide behind a stack of old pallets near the loading dock of the factory. The building is large, a looming presence in this part of town. Graffiti is painted across the walls and many of the windows are broken or boarded up.

It's far from the main drag here, with traffic only a low hum in the distance. The parking lot has seen better days, with weeds pushing up through the gravel.

There's two Serpents guarding the loading dock entrance, standing with guns strapped to their chests like they're in some kind of freaking war. Rolling my eyes, I creep closer, getting behind another dumpster. It's hard to be quiet, but I can't afford for them to see me. Not yet. Not until we've figured out where they're keeping Sienna.

The doors are flung wide open, enough to see what's happening inside. With the amount of Serpents standing watch, I have a feeling she has to be nearby. I watch a few Serpents load crates and roll them down the dock, then shove the crates into a truck.

What are they doing? Are they transporting something? It has to be weapons, with the size of those crates. Or it could be drugs. I'm not sure.

For the millionth time, I wonder where the Serpents got the resources to start running an operation of this size. They were barely hanging on by a thread the last time we saw them around town. Now they're smuggling guns or running drugs and causing all kinds of chaos in my town.

The rage boils back up inside me. If they think they can turn Caspian Springs into their Mad Max wasteland, they have another thing coming.

I keep as low to the ground as I can and slip closer to the loading dock doors. The musty odor of decay fills my nostrils and I step on something sticky. Trying to free my foot, it catches the side of the dumpster and makes a rattling bang.

Panicking, I fling myself to the ground and roll under a bush on the other side of the dumpster.

"What was that?" one of the Serpent guards calls out.

"Go check!" the other admonishes.

The guard starts walking closer and I suck in a breath, holding it. His footsteps crunch ominously over the gravel floor, drawing nearer to my hiding spot. I squeeze my eyes shut, praying that they won't look too closely at the bush.

"I don't see anything," the Serpent calls to his friend. He steps closer to the bush and I freeze, blood pounding in my ears.

"It was probably just a wild animal," the other Serpent calls. "Get back over here. Stop messing around. The boss said we have to make sure no one comes for that chick."

"Why are we guarding her again?" Goon number one grouses out.

"Because she's got some ties to the Blades," he hisses. "I don't know what, but Diego says he got an order to take her out."

My breath comes out in a whoosh as he walks back over to join his buddy, fear stabbing me in the heart. Who's ordering the Serpents to take out Sienna?

Getting to my knees, I crawl closer again, avoiding the dumpster, and peer into the warehouse. Several Serpents are standing guard over another door inside, which leads to the far side of the factory.

That must be where they're keeping Sienna. It has to be.

Resolve fills me up and I start creeping backward, trying to be careful. I start running once I'm past the dumpster but my foot hits it again, letting out another echoing bang.

"Someone's over there!" the Serpent guard yells. The two of them race towards me, but I duck in between the office buildings to the left, weaving my way through the alley until I disappear from their view.

I'm panting by the time I make it back, but I feel triumphant, having gotten away. "I know where they're holding her," I tell them.

"There's got to be a dozen or more Serpents hanging around though, so we have to be careful."

Keep hanging on, Sienna, I think. *We're going to get you out of there.*

27

DOMINIC

My heart is in my throat when Bastian comes racing around the corner. "I know where they're holding her."

Adrenaline courses through me at his words. That means she's here.

"There's got to be a dozen or more Serpents hanging around though, so we have to be careful," Bastian warns, taking a few panting breaths. "They're keeping her in the far side of the warehouse, there are at least three guards on her and more probably inside. I can't tell because I couldn't get that close," Bastian explains. "We have one shot at this but to better gauge the situation we need to get closer."

"We should go to the far side and try to look in through the windows over there," Caleb suggests.

"Good idea. Dominic, you still down to be a distraction?" Bastian asks.

"Roger," I say, tipping two fingers towards him. "You and Caleb focus on getting the info that you need."

We move out, keeping to the sides of the buildings and creeping across the narrow alley, trying to remain out of sight. Cutting through the empty field at the back of the warehouse, we circle the building until we're on the far side, where Bastian thinks they're keeping Sienna.

There are only a couple Serpents on this side and they're near an entrance, about two hundred feet away. We're far enough away that they can't see us, but I know I still need to distract them.

There's a bunch of rusted-out cars in the parking lot on this side so I dart forward and bang on one of the cars, then move around to bang on another.

The Serpents are instantly alerted and start running after me, but I continue to dart from car to car while my brothers rush over to the windows to peer inside.

A whistle catches my attention and I bang on another car before taking off running, doubling back to meet my brothers by one of the entrances around back.

"What's the news?" I ask.

"You don't want to know," Caleb says, face pale. Bastian looks sick, and his hands are shaking.

"They've got her tied up," he says through gritted teeth. "She's tied up and one of them, Diego I'm assuming, is standing over her with a knife. They're threatening to ..." He swallows hard. "They're saying that if she doesn't give in, they'll take her anyway."

My jaw clenches so tightly that my muscles ache, hands curling into fists as my knuckles turn white. I feel my pulse pounding in my ears like a war drum, drowning out all other sound. My chest heaves with the effort to contain the storm raging inside me and my vision blurs with white-hot anger.

Every fiber of my being thrums with a primal instinct to unleash my wrath on those slimy bastards who dare threaten someone I care about.

"Let's go," I order, voice deepened from the effort to contain my fury. "We need to get in there right *now*. She's in danger!"

"We can't storm in!" Caleb bursts out. He's shaking with his own barely concealed rage. "If the three of us go storming in there, without backup or without a plan, Sienna's going to be in even more danger. There's so many Serpents in there, they'll wipe us out before we even have a chance to get to her."

"She's already in danger!" I hiss. "Every second we waste arguing is another second with her in the hands of those bastards."

"We need a plan," Bastian says firmly, blue eyes steely with determination. "If we make a plan, we're going to give ourselves and Sienna a greater chance at getting out of this place alive."

With great effort, I take a deep, steadying breath. "Fine," I say, knowing he's right. We can't just go charging in. Sienna's safety is paramount. "What's the plan?"

"I saw some gas cans near the loading dock," Caleb says quickly. "They have to be using those gas cans for all their bikes. If we set their bikes on fire, they'll be forced to come investigate. I bet you most of them will come out and we can take on the ones who stay behind."

Bastian grins. "Smart move, nerd brain. Let's roll with that. You go watch the Serpents while Dom and I gas the bikes. Dom, come with me."

I follow Bastian, the two of us moving like panthers through the jungle as we stalk towards the bikes parked near the loading bay. Caleb keeps lookout for us as we open the cans and shake them over as many bikes as we can.

"Here, use my lighter," Bastian says, tossing it towards me. I think he knows how ready I am to burn these motherfuckers to the ground.

I take pleasure in flipping open the Zippo and setting the bikes ablaze. It takes less than a minute for the line of bikes to light up and we rush to the side of the building, watching the blaze consume everything in its path.

Within minutes, there's a few Serpents rushing out to see what's going on and they start yelling, summoning more in their wake.

Dozens of Serpents are in the parking lot now, trying to stop the blaze or attempt to keep it under control. While everyone is distracted, the three of us fly into the building.

There's only a few Serpents lingering inside, panic evident on their faces.

"Hey!" One spots us. "You can't be in here!"

"Fuck off," I growl before walloping him square in the solar plexus. He doubles over and I kick him as he goes down, laying him out.

Bastian and Caleb take the other guard, double-teaming him and taking him down as well. We head through the double doors, into the room where they're keeping Sienna.

It's dark in here, dimly lit with only the faintest rays of sun penetrating the grimy, busted windows, casting eerie shadows across the walls.

Fury erupts inside me as I realize that Sienna has been tied to a pole, wearing only her underwear. She's been gagged, and her face is streaked with tears. Someone, I'm assuming Diego, caresses the blade of his knife against her cheek.

Diego's smirk sends a chill down my spine as I step forward, my fists clenched at my sides. Sienna's muffled sobs echo in the dimly lit room, reminding us of the danger she's still facing.

"Drop the knife," I growl, my voice low and menacing. My heart pounds in my chest, adrenaline coursing through my veins as I lock eyes with Diego. His expression remains defiant, the glint of the blade casting sinister shadows across his face.

"I don't think I will," Diego retorts, his voice dripping with malice. "If you don't want me to slice her up, I'd turn around and leave."

"Not a chance," Bastian interjects, his jaw clenched with determination. "In case you didn't know, the princess belongs to us."

Diego's laughter echoes through the room. "I've been ordered to eliminate her," he says, his tone chillingly casual. "Orders are orders."

The weight of his words hangs heavy in the air, the gravity of the situation sinking in with each passing second. Sienna's muffled cries grow louder, and she rails against her restraints, trying to get free.

"Who's orders?" Caleb demands, his voice laced with barely contained rage. "What's the point of targeting her?"

"I'm afraid I don't have any answers for you," Diego drawls, a cruel smile playing on his lips. "I'm done talking now. Take them out."

The remaining Serpents spring into action, their movements fluid and coordinated. I steel myself for the onslaught, adrenaline surging through my veins as I brace for the fight ahead.

With a primal roar, I launch myself into the fray, fists flying as I clash with the Serpents. Each blow is met with fierce resistance, the sound of grunts and curses filling the air as the room devolves into chaos. I need to keep them distracted so Bastian and Caleb can take Diego down and get to Sienna.

The Serpents left are brutal, fast, and tough fighters. These are Diego's top lieutenants, the ones he keeps around to protect him when he's most vulnerable.

My only chance is to take them out one by one. If I can lay them out, they can't go after the others. Shooting out my arm, I land a hit on one, then whirl around to kick out at another one. "Come get me," I say, waving my hand towards a third.

He comes at me, managing to land a few blows to my neck and face, forcing me backward. I shake my head to clear my vision, seeing spots from the force of the blows. It's hard to keep on my feet but I can't let them hurt Sienna. I have to keep her safe. That's what I tell myself as I continue to trade blows with the Serpents.

Another Serpent punches me in the back, forcing me to my knees. As I fall, someone else drives a blade into my arm. I cry out in pain but yank the knife out of my arm, letting it clatter to the ground as I stagger to my feet. If they want to play dirty, I can play dirty!

Letting out a roar, I lurch forward and drive my fist into the nose of the Serpent who stabbed me, hearing a satisfying crunch as it breaks.

The Serpents around me start falling left and right as I unleash the rage inside me, desperate to keep Sienna from Diego's claws.

"Surrender!" Bastian yells, knife to Diego's throat. He must have gotten the drop on him while I fought my way through his lieutenants. "Let her go!"

Diego gives a jerking nod and Caleb rushes to Sienna's side, hastily untying her.

"Have fun explaining this to your boss," Bastian says as he moves away, hurrying over to help Caleb keep Sienna propped up.

Diego lets out a yell, but I've already taken out his men and the others are still busy with the fire outside.

"Give her to me!" I yell, running up to them. I scoop Sienna into my arms and we race outside, taking off for the business park where we left the bikes.

Sienna clings to me as we escape. "I'm sorry!" she sobs, fat tears rolling down her cheeks. "I should have listened. I'm sorry!"

"Shh," I say. "You're safe now. You're safe. We're here. We've got you. You're safe."

Once we arrive at the bikes, I help her on mine and we take off for home, exhaust fumes trailing behind us.

One question still lingers on everyone's mind as we leave though. Who is giving the Serpents orders and why did they want Sienna eliminated?

28

SIENNA

Once we arrive back at the house, Bastian slings an arm over my shoulder, helping me inside while Caleb assists Dominic. He'd been injured trying to save me, blood running down his arm where he was stabbed.

My wrists are bruised from where they bound me and I feel sore all over from being manhandled, but I'm mostly fine, so I beeline over to Dominic.

"Let me," I say, gently pushing Caleb away. "I had an alcoholic mom, so I know how to help tend to injuries." Guilt washes over me as I clean him up, every touch a reminder of my recklessness. His stoic facade cracks, betraying his fear and anger. His gaze softens as I examine the knife wound though, showing his relief that I'm safe at last.

It looks bad but the knife didn't go too deep, thankfully. Caleb brings me the first aid kit and I start bandaging him up. "You guys saved me. I didn't think anyone was coming."

"We got your text," Caleb says. "I kept thinking something was wrong because you didn't answer your phone."

"It rang when you called and they found it and took it away from me," I admit. "They smashed it up."

"I'm sorry we left you alone," Bastian says, pacing the room. "I know you don't want us following you around everywhere but ..."

"No," I cut him off. "I understand now. The Serpents are dangerous. I'd prefer if, at least for now, I don't go anywhere by myself."

The metallic tang of blood hangs in the air, a stark reminder of how close my brush with disaster really was. The entire ordeal left me shattered, desperate to be with the Ravenwoods again. Every thought was about getting back to them and being in their arms once more. I don't understand how, but in the short time I've known them, I feel so safe with them, so protected.

And I think I might be falling in love with them. Despite the darkness, they make me feel safe and secure. I don't think I've felt that around another person since I was a kid.

"One of us will be happy to stay with you from now on," Bastian agrees. As soon as I'm finished fixing up Dominic's arm, he pulls me away, holding me tightly to his chest. "I was so worried about you, Princess. Don't ever scare us like that again."

"I won't," I murmur into his chest. He kisses the top of my head and I wrap my arms around him and rest against his chest for a moment, breathing in his warm, campfire scent.

As soon as I break away, Caleb hugs me from behind, wrapping his arms around me and pulling me towards him. "We'll have to teach you some basic self-defense," he whispers. "You shouldn't ever worry about being taken by surprise again."

"I wish I knew why they targeted me," I say, turning to face him. His brown eyes look worried, so I pull him in for a kiss, heart racing with our closeness.

"How do you feel?" I ask Dominic, turning to check on him again.

"Better, now that you're here," he says. "I was so angry that they took you and I just went into a blind rage when I saw what they were trying to do to you. I think if I hadn't been so angry it might have been worse for me, but I was fueled by my adrenaline."

"I'm so glad you're okay," I say, crawling into his lap. He wraps his arms around me and I snuggle against him. "You guys were amazing back there. I can't believe you took them out. Lucky there was a fire distracting the other Serpents."

"That was us," Caleb admits with a nervous laugh. "We started the fire to distract them."

"Then it was very clever of you," I say, reaching out to pull Caleb towards us. "You guys deserve a reward."

My thoughts race, desire swirling in my mind. Do they feel the same pull, or am I alone in this newfound connection?

Bastian's fingers reach out, cupping my cheek. A jolt of electricity passes through me, leaving me breathless in anticipation of what's to come.

"Are you sure about this?" Bastian whispers, leaning in to look into my eyes with his penetrating icy blue gaze. "You were just kidnapped."

"I think I need it," I admit, my outward bravado hiding the vulnerability I feel inside, masking the fear that still threatens to consume me. "I want to feel connected to you."

"We can take care of you," Bastian says.

As he joins us on the couch, the space between us seems to shrink, the magnetic pull drawing us closer with each heartbeat. Hands trembling, I reach out, my fingers tangling in Bastian's hair as our lips meet in a desperate kiss. At that moment, all my worries and fears melt away, leaving only the intoxicating rush of desire.

With careful movements, Bastian pulls me towards him, giving me plenty of warning if to pull away. When I don't stop him, he pulls me fully onto his lap, kissing me feverishly, tongue licking the seam of my mouth for entrance.

My hips grind against his, something blossoming inside me. For the first time, I feel like I'm in complete control. It doesn't feel like they're using me, but like we're all a part of something bigger.

I moan and reach out to pull Caleb in, kissing him hard as Bastian moves to press wet kisses along my neck. Dominic's hands reach out, moving down to cup my ass and kneading it with a gentleness that takes my breath away.

"Yes," I whisper. "Please, I need you. All of you."

"How do you want us?" Bastian asks, nipping my ear and sending shivers down my spine. "Tell me what we can do to make you feel good."

His words shoot straight to my core, pulling a breathless moan from my throat. Feeling emboldened, I lay it out for them, "I want you inside me. I want Caleb to touch me, and I want Dominic in my mouth."

"Good girl, Princess," Bastian murmurs. "Your wish is our command."

They pull me along, taking me up to Bastian's room since he has the biggest bed. The California King dominates the space, with plenty of room for all four of us. Dominic shoves the pillows out of the way and Bastian pulls the covers back.

I'm still in my underwear from my kidnapping so the boys make short work of stripping me down. Feeling self-conscious of the bruised and battered state of my body, I go to hide myself, but Caleb and Dominic draw my wrists away and pin them with their hands.

"Your body is ours to worship, Princess," Bastian says as he strokes his thumb over my rapidly hardening nipple. "Don't hide it from us. Let us cherish you."

Tender caresses have me melting into the sheets as Dominic's large hands part my thighs, his fingers teasing my entrance.

"Please," I whimper, squirming under his touch.

"Shh," Dominic soothes me again with soft kisses along my inner thighs. "We want to take our time today. Just relax and let us show you how much we care."

Closing my eyes, I give up the last remnants of control as they begin to take me apart piece by piece. Caleb's kisses leave me feeling drunk as his mouth moves against mine, tongue twirling with my own before nipping at my lower lip.

Bastian's hands are everywhere, on my breasts, down at my waist, curving over my ass, then moving back up to pinch my nipples. It makes my head spin, unable to keep up with the sensations as they come.

Dominic's mouth descends down, lavishing attention over my clit.

I'm already wet but once his tongue flicks over the spot, it's as though the floodgates have opened.

"Yes," I whisper, fisting my hands in his hair. "God, yes Dominic."

"Say my name again," Dominic growls as he pulls away.

"Please Dominic, please keep going!"

Spurred on by my pleas, he dives back down and runs his tongue over me again, dipping into my hole before sliding back up to flick over my throbbing clit once more.

"Yes!" I arch my back but Caleb's hands move, pushing me back down as he continues to mark me up with his mouth and teeth.

Dominic's tongue continues its relentless teasing and I start to move my hips, body aching for more. "I think you're ready for us," his voice rumbles above me. I mourn the loss of him pulling away but then he's shifting and Bastian moves to take his place, rubbing the thick head of his cock through my wet folds. Every brush sends a jolt along my spine.

"Bastian, please, inside!" I cry out, frantic to feel him. He chuckles but lines himself up properly before sinking in, going slow as my body adjusts.

"Feel so good, so full," I whisper, breathless as he finally takes me to the hilt, hips flush against mine.

Bastian smiles before brushing the hair out of my face and leaning down to kiss me. He starts rocking his hips, thrusting slowly in and out.

Dominic has moved next to me, so when I turn my head I see his thick, veiny member. My mouth waters as I run gentle fingers over it. It pulses under my hand and I pull him into my mouth, nearly choking on the size. I adjust and swallow around it, enjoying the salty, musky taste of his precum on my tongue.

As Bastian works his hips in and out of me, Caleb's mouth and fingers are still moving over me. He trails one hand down the length of my body, teasing at my clit while he gently bites down on the nipple he has between his teeth.

There's so much going on that it's hard to focus. As Bastian's thrusts grow faster, I moan around Dominic's length and he begins to roll his hips, cock slipping deeper into my throat.

Caleb continues toying with my clit, rubbing circles into it as Bastian thrusts deep inside me, bringing me closer and closer to the edge.

I feel so close to them now, so connected. I want to stay with them and be by their side through thick and thin. I want to be Dominic's food tester, and I want to cuddle with Bastian on the couch while we listen to old country songs, and I want to play computer games with Caleb every night until the wee hours.

The clarity of my feelings shocks me, and I find myself coming apart at the seams underneath them with a long, drawn-out moan. As I do, Dominic thrusts deep into my mouth, and then stills, his seed spilling down my throat.

Breathing hard, I cling to Bastian as he picks up the pace of his thrusts. I can feel that he's close. Above me, Caleb moves his hand away from my clit to fist himself, frantically racing towards the finish line. As Bastian comes inside of me, Caleb paints a stripe of white over my belly.

The boys collapse on the bed next to me as we all come down from our collective high. Caleb pulls me against him and Bastian tucks himself on the other side of me, with Dominic on the other side of him.

"Thank you," I whisper. My heart is full to bursting and as I think back over my revelation, I realize I'm not as scared of the truth as I thought I'd be.

I'm definitely falling in love with them.

29

SIENNA

In the days following the incident, the tension that once hung heavy in the air between us gradually dissipates, replaced by a tangible sense of calm and security within the walls of the house.

As I sit nestled in between Caleb and Bastian on the worn sofa, my feet on Bastian's lap, I inhale deeply, savoring the comforting smell of campfire and cedarwood that surrounds me. The fireplace casts flickering shadows as I open up to them about my past.

"My mom never took me to do anything," I tell them. "She was always busy working or when I was a teenager, deep in her alcohol addiction. This is the furthest away from home I've ever traveled."

Bastian inhales sharply, reaching out to touch my hand. I don't flinch away like I used to. Instead, I let his warmth seep through my fingers, a small crack forming in the walls I've built.

The next day, he brings me to the bike shop with him as well, letting me watch him work.

"May not be the Taj Mahal but at least you're gettin' out of the house," he says, the smile he gives me utterly distracting. It doesn't help that he's parading around in a tight tank and low-slung work jeans, with a smear of motor oil on his cheek. We end up having a quickie on his workbench.

The next day, Dominic asks to spend the day with me. He brings me to an empty parking lot. "I'm going to teach you how to ride a bike today," he says. My eyes widen and I shake my head. "I couldn't. I'm sure I'd totally fail."

"You can do it, Princess," he encourages, showing me where the throttle and the brake are located.

Terror races through my heart over the entire short ride, but by the time I'm done, that fear is replaced with adrenaline and exhilaration.

"I can't believe I rode a motorcycle!" I say, flinging myself into Dominic's waiting arms. "I did that!"

"Amazing job, Princess," he says, pulling me in for a quick kiss. "Sometimes fear can be thrilling, under the right circumstances. I don't want you feeling like everything we do is so big and scary."

His words pierce me inside, making me realize that I've let fear hold me back for too long. "I get it. But I'm not sure I'm ready to do it again any time soon."

"Fair," he teases, ruffling my curls.

Despite the newfound peace, I still feel the lingering effects of being kidnapped. At dinner one night, Dominic drops a plate. The sound makes me jump, my heart racing as I struggle to catch my breath. Bastian's hand on my shoulder grounds me, but the fear lingers long after the noise fades.

Nightmares plague my sleep, dreams of Diego still holding me captive while his hot breath ghosts over my neck, the cool blade of the knife running along my cheek.

Those nightmares leave me restless and exhausted, often waking up in a cold sweat. Luckily for me, whenever that happens, one of the boys is there to offer comfort and respite from the storm inside my mind.

Nearly a week after the incident, I'm finally ready to venture back to the place where it all went down. "I need to go back to campus," I tell Caleb. "Can you come with me?"

His dimpled smile is instant and disarming. "Sure," he says. "Do you want me to come into the building with you?"

"Maybe you could hang around in the hall while I talk to Dr. Thornton," I suggest.

"Anything you wish, Princess," Caleb says. We head out to the Firebird and I load my files in the back before climbing into the passenger seat next to him.

The nickname sends warmth through my chest and I nod, linking his free hand with mine. "Thank you for coming with me," I tell him. "I know it's silly to be scared."

"You went through something difficult," Caleb says, stroking his thumb over my hand. "It's natural that you might still be spooked. You're not weak for struggling. Talking to us about it helps, right?"

I nod.

He squeezes my hand. "You can talk to me anytime. Even if you think it will upset me. I can handle the dark stuff."

We arrive at campus and walk into the Psych building together. "I won't be long," I tell Caleb, giving him another quick kiss. "See you soon."

I knock on Dr. Thornton's door and he calls me inside. When I step in though, his demeanor instantly shifts. His brows furrow and he stiffens, narrowing his eyes for a brief moment before giving me a tight smile.

"Sienna, what a surprise," he says. "I didn't know you'd be here today."

"I just came to drop off some more files," I tell him, showing him the stack I brought. "Is that okay? Are you busy?"

"I am," he says. "I can't chat, I'm afraid. I've got a meeting in a few minutes. Just drop the files off and you can leave."

"Is everything going alright with the project?" I ask, a chill of worry coursing through me. Is that why he's upset? Has something happened with his research?

"It's fine," he says, waving a hand. "You know how research projects can be. You don't need to drop off the files in person all the time," he adds. "Just give them to your supervisor. I'll look them over when I have the time."

A pit forms in my stomach. As Dr. Thornton's gaze flickers over me. His furrowed brow sends a ripple of unease through me, and I find myself fidgeting with the edge of my sleeve, unsure of what to say.

"Sorry," I apologize, setting the folders down on the corner of his desk. "I didn't mean to bother you so much."

Dr. Thornton sighs and pinches the bridge of his nose. "It's not you, Sienna. It's just that ... something that I was expecting to get done, ended up not being done. I'm just now finding out about it."

His tone lacks the edge I anticipated and I swallow, a small smile tugging at the corners of my lips. "I get it. I'm sorry it didn't work out. I hope it can get done soon. Is there anything I can do to help?"

Dr. Thornton shakes his head. "You have no idea how much I wish that were true but there's nothing you can do," he says.

Internally, I wrestle with the instinct to push him about his mood. I could be risking our professional relationship if I try to probe into the cause of his apparent distress.

Deciding to leave it for now, I tell him, "Alright, well, let me know if that changes. I'll just be going."

My mind races, replaying our last conversation. When I asked him about the necklace, he seemed almost agitated with me for bringing it up. I feel like I'm only getting half the information when it comes to his past with the boys and his relationship with Emily. Maybe I should dig a little, just to see if I can find more information.

Walking up to Caleb in the hallway, I ask if we can go over to the library to use the computer. He tilts his head at me quizzically.

"I need to do some research on something Dr. Thornton recommended," I lie. "Do you mind waiting in the car while I'm in the library? I'll be fine inside alone."

"If you're sure," Caleb says. "Then yeah. I'll meet you at the car when you're done?"

"It won't take long," I tell him. "I just need to look something up really quick."

We head outside and he walks me to the library before giving me a quick hug. "I'll see you soon."

I head inside and go over to one of the computers. I want to do this without the boys around because I don't want to bring up any bad memories, but I need to know more about the whole thing with Emily. It feels like there's more to the story than what I've been getting, and since I can't ask any of the involved parties, I'll have to do it myself.

Typing in her full name, I scan the results. There are a few things about her death, but then I notice an article about her and the boys. Clicking on the link brings me to a local news site.

As I read, a growing sense of unease fills my stomach. Emily and the Ravenwoods were planning on reopening the Haven Center together. The article detailed the plans they made, and the vision they had for the Haven Center. They'd gotten funding from a few large organizations and even had a whole timeline for their re-opening.

It makes sense that after her death, they couldn't continue with their plans. I wouldn't be able to either, everything would feel tainted. I stare at the screen, feeling like I've just found another piece of the puzzle that I didn't know I was missing.

The boys must have been devastated, not only to lose her the way they did, but it meant putting their dreams on hold.

When I head out to meet with Caleb, my head is still reeling. Why didn't they tell me about this? I wish I'd have known. For that matter, why didn't Dr. Thornton tell me about it when I asked him about the Haven Center?

I still feel like there's so much missing. I'm torn over asking them about it, but at the same time, everything has gotten to a better place since the fight and I don't want to shatter our peace by bringing up Emily again.

"Did you find what you were looking for?" Caleb asks as I slide into the passenger seat.

"Um, yeah," I stammer out. "Yeah, I think so. I'm not sure."

As I settle into the passenger seat next to Caleb, a whirlwind of thoughts consumes me. Should I reveal what I found out? Caleb's inquisitive gaze lingers on mine, but I offer a tight-lipped smile. With a click of my seatbelt, I push the nagging questions aside for now.

Once we arrive, Caleb follows me in the house and I go upstairs with him so we can watch the new *Sims* pack trailer together. I think he can sense the change in my mood, but he doesn't bring it up and I decide not to ask about the information I found.

"Thanks for going with me today," I tell him instead. "I can't wait for this new pack to come out."

"Me too," he says. "It looks fun. I love pirates and treasure hunting and stuff."

We chat about the new pack, speculating on what things might be coming with it and I try to ignore the lingering questions from my brief research.

If I ask about Emily, I might just upset them and we've spent so long getting to this place of calm, I don't want to bring it crashing down around us.

30

BASTIAN

Sienna has been quiet since she came home from the library with Caleb. Between that and the nightmares she's been having since the incident, I worry she's not doing well. Since it's a Friday night, I decide that the best thing to do to get her mind off things is take her out for a nice date.

"Hey," I say, peeking into Caleb's room. Sienna looks up at me from where she and Caleb are cuddled together, playing *The Sims*. "Get dressed. Something nice. Wear one of those outfits we picked out for you."

"Where are we going?" Sienna asks, shoulders tensing.

"Gonna take you out on a date. Just you and me, Princess. How does that sound?"

Her shoulders relax and the smile she gives me punches me in the gut with its brightness. "It sounds great," she says, hopping off the bed.

What about me?" Caleb whines, waving his hands around.

"You've got work to do for old man Buford, remember?" I chuckle, tossing a pillow at him.

"Yeah, but what if I want to go out and look pretty?" he counters, flashing a mischievous grin. Sienna laughs and slips past us to get ready.

I head into my room, trying to decide how I want to dress for our date. Picking out a deep tan button-up, I pair it with black jeans, a belt, and black boots. I throw my black moto jacket on top, knowing Sienna likes how I look in it.

I'm really trying here, for her, so I hope she appreciates the effort.

Stepping out of the bedroom, I'm shocked into silence when I see what Sienna has picked out. She's wearing a deep blue bodycon dress, with thin straps. The material is kind of velvety and it hugs her curves, stopping just above her knees. On her feet are strappy silver sandals with short heels. Her hair is pinned back away from her face and she's got dark makeup on around her eyes and a thin, gold chain on her neck. Her lips are painted bright red.

"Is this okay?" she asks, tugging on the hem of the dress. "You didn't say where we were going, so I wasn't sure."

"It's perfect," I say, pulling her towards me and crushing my lips against hers. "You look damned hot in that, Princess. I'm going to have a hard time keeping my hands off you."

Sienna blushes as we pull apart and I reach for her hand. "C'mon. Dominic is at the shop tonight and Caleb is doing some work for the old guy who runs the hardware store. It's just you and me."

"Where are we going?" Sienna asks, following along as I pull her towards the door. She grabs her purse from the hook as we step outside.

"Going to take you to dinner someplace nice, then we're going dancing," I tell her. "You down?"

"I've never done anything like that before," she admits. "I was pretty studious in college."

"Well good, I get to show you how we have fun around here," I say, opening the door for her. "You deserve a nice night out."

She gets in and we take off for Rosewood Grille, one of the nicer restaurants in town. Once we arrive, I step out of the car and walk around to open Sienna's door for her. She takes my offered hand and we head inside.

The restaurant is high on a hill, overlooking a wooded area. The outside is rustic, with wooden siding and a stone foundation. Inside, it's dimly lit, with flickering candles on each table.

The large space is dominated by the open kitchen in the center, with the smell of sizzling steaks wafting through the place as the hostess leads us past it, and up a set of stairs.

"What's the occasion?" Sienna asks as we're seated. A warm fire crackles in the large metal fireplace nearby and the floor-to-ceiling screened windows give an amazing view of the forest beyond.

"You've seemed kinda quiet lately," I tell her. "Thought you could stand to have some fun with us once in a while."

"It's sweet of you," Sienna says, reaching out to hold my hands. "I've never experienced this kind of attention from a guy before, let alone three. I guess I never understood why you guys wanted me in the first place."

My brow furrows at that. I can sense the unease in her gaze, the hesitation that hangs in the air. It tugs at something inside me, stirring a protective instinct.

I run my thumb over her hand, expression softening. "Sienna," I begin, my voice gentle. "It's not about what we want from you. It's more like ... what you bring into our lives. You were a breath of fresh air, or a light in the darkness."

I smile, bringing her hand up to kiss it. "Being with you, it just feels right."

She inhales, breath caught in her throat. Sienna's gaze intensifies at my words, expression growing heated. "You have no idea how much your words mean to me," she whispers. Her leg moves out, hooking around mine as she rubs her calf over me. The brush of her leg sends a thrill down my spine.

"Do you want to get out of here?" I ask, leaning closer to her. She nods eagerly, her eyes locking with mine. "Let's go," I say, taking her hand.

We rush out of the restaurant together, Sienna flying along beside me, the two of us eager to continue our evening together.

Our mouths fuse as soon as we exit the car and only part long enough for me to unlock the door. We start undressing as soon as we get inside, shedding jackets and shoes quickly, clothes strewn on the stairs as we head up.

Once in my bedroom, I hastily unbutton my shirt, shrugging out of the sleeves as Sienna hikes up her dress, revealing that she isn't wearing any underwear.

I growl and yank her towards me, kissing her hard. "You little minx," I say between bruising kisses. "You wanted to tease me, didn't you?"

"I thought maybe we could try that stuff again," she whispers in my ear. The scent of her perfume is intoxicating—something deep and citrusy with notes of vanilla and sage. It's making my head spin.

"What stuff?" I ask, kissing along her neck.

"That stuff with the safe word," she admits. I pull back, staring into her green eyes for a long moment.

"Are you sure?" I ask. "Things got rough back then."

"I trust you," Sienna says. Her words pierce my heart. "I want to try it again. It was fun at first, and hot, giving up control."

"Why don't we try something fun, but maybe a little less intense," I suggest. "Ease our way into this better?"

Sienna nods and I pull up my desk chair, pushing her to sit down on it. "I'd like to blindfold you and do a little sensation play, run a few things across your skin like feathers and silk scarves and tease you with them. Would you like that?"

She nods, eyes lighting up in enthusiasm.

"What's your color, baby?" I ask, reaching out to pull open the desk drawer and retrieve the blindfold I keep there.

"Green," she says, tilting her chin up to stare at me. "Green, for you, only you, Bastian."

Fuck.

I swallow hard and cup her chin, kissing her hard. "Good girl," I say. She whimpers and I place the blindfold over her head, adjusting it so it settles into place.

I kneel under my desk and pull out a shoebox, opening it up to reveal an assortment of toys. Selecting a few items, I walk back over to Sienna.

"I want you to keep still," I order her. "Don't move, or I'll have to tie you up."

"Yes, sir," she whispers breathlessly.

"Spread your legs for me," I tell her, nudging her thigh with a small riding crop. She obeys instantly, spreading them obscenely wide. Her beautiful, chubby pussy glistens, the evidence of her arousal on full display.

I start with the feather, running it along her bare arms and thighs, then up to brush over her clit. She lets out a squeak and jumps.

"Oops, that's your only warning, baby," I lean down and whisper in her ear. "You move again and you'll get one strike."

Sienna instantly goes still, thighs trembling lightly with the effort. "Yes sir," she says, voice soft.

"Color?" I ask, checking in.

"Green."

"Good girl," I praise, moving the feather across her pebbled nipples. She shivers but doesn't move and I test her further, running it back down over her thighs again. I can see her muscles strain with the effort of holding still but she restrains herself, hands by her sides.

"I'm going to try something new," I tell her, exchanging the feather for a length of silk. I let it drape over her thigh and drag it down, situating it so it sits between her legs and begin to tease it across her clit. She moans loudly but doesn't move.

"You're doing so well," I tell her, continuing to tease her. "You're such a good girl."

"Bastian," she whines. I know she's not used to being teased like this and I'm enjoying giving her this new experience.

I run the silk between her thighs once more before discarding it, choosing a small item, similar to a paint roller. This one is spiked though, with needle-like tips all over the applicator part.

Rolling it along her thigh, I watch in pleasure as she gasps out. The tips are too close together to be painful unless I press harder. She moans again and tips her head back, trying to hold still.

"Please," she whispers as I begin to roll it up and down her thighs. "Please, sir. Please, I need you. Please!"

She's got tears rolling down her cheeks from behind the blindfold now. I run it up her thighs again and between her legs, over her sex. She arches her back and lets out a high-pitched keen but stays still.

"You're doing so well. I'm going to reward you now," I tell her, discarding the roller so I can kneel and spread her legs. My mouth descends on her clit and she cries out, wrapping her arms around me. She tastes so sweet, so wet.

Stroking my tongue over her bud in repeated motions, I feel her throb under me, pressing her cunt against my face, desperate for more.

"Oh God! Bastian!" she screams.

The door opens and Caleb walks in, eyes widening. "What are you doing?" he says, voice deep. Sienna pulls off the blindfold and stares up at him.

He frowns and she shrinks back.

31

CALEB

Bastian's bedroom is dark when I walk in, the only source of light is his bedside lamp.

As I enter, Sienna bites her lip, averting her gaze.

"What are you doing?" I demand, a mischievous glint in my eye. Her lower lip quivers and she tenses. "Looks like our little princess is being naughty, fooling around with one brother without the rest of us here."

"I'm sorry!" The desk chair squeaks as Sienna jumps up, wrapping her arm around herself. "I thought it was okay, I'm so sorry I should have checked ..." I press a finger to her soft lips, silencing her babbling.

"Relax, love. You know you belong to all of us, so there's nothing wrong with you spending some one-on-one time with any of the three of us alone. I just thought we could continue the fun, hmm?"

I stroke my finger along her cheek, expressing my affection. "So let's see, how long were you alone in here with Bastian before I walked in?"

Bastian's smirk deepens as he casually interjects, "About twenty minutes." He leans back, folding his hands behind his head.

"So let's say twenty spankings, hmm?" I offer. Sienna's arms uncurl and she gives me a small smile before turning it into an exaggerated pout.

"No, please don't spank me sir!" she protests, waving her arms. "Please, I'll be good!"

"Too late," I say, crossing my arms. "Bend over the bed."

Sienna shuffles forward, tossing a glance at me. She sinks onto her elbows, the lingering smell of her perfume filling my senses as she passes by. The citrus scent is intoxicating and I reach out to stroke over her behind.

"Color, love?" I ask, checking in first.

"Green, sir," she says, voice muffled against the cotton duvet.

Raising my hand, I bring it down on her backside and Sienna inhales a sharp breath. "Count for me," I order her. "If you miss a count, I add another spanking."

I raise my hand again, enjoying the noisy slap of skin-on-skin and the way her ass jiggles when I make contact. With each progressive stroke, the flesh there heats up, turning a beautiful shade of cherry red.

Bastian sits on the desk chair, crossing his leg over his knee as he watches us. Sienna cries out a muffled "Ten!" and I bring my hand back again.

"Ten more," I tell her. "Can you take it?"

"Yes, sir!" she sobs out, squirming under me. "Please, spank me," she begs. "I've been so naughty."

I give her five strikes in quick succession and she raises her ass higher and higher, knees practically underneath her.

"God, you're such a weak-willed little slut, aren't you?" I ask, connecting with her ass once more.

"Sixteen!" she yells. "Yes, I'm a naughty, weak slut who needs you to punish me!"

I give her another three hard slaps and then rub my hand over her ass, reveling in how warm her backside has gotten.

"One more," I tell her. "I'm going to give you one more and then I'm going to tie your hands to the bedpost and fuck your brains out."

Sienna moans long and loud, her thighs rubbing together at my words. "Please, please give it to me, sir!"

Reaching my hand back, I slap her ass with as much momentum as I can, bringing it down hard enough to sting my palm.

"Twenty!" Sienna cries out, then goes limp from exhaustion.

Bastian jumps up and the two of us maneuver Sienna onto his bed, laying her out over the duvet and placing an overstuffed pillow under her backside. We use his silk ties to bind her wrists to the headboard.

"Color?" I ask, checking to ensure that the restraints aren't too tight.

"Green," she says, squeezing her thighs together again as she writhes about, seeking friction.

"Hold still," I tell her. "Bastian is going to prep you while I undress."

The metal of my belt jingles as I unbuckle it and shed my pants. I watch Bastian stroke over Sienna's dripping wet pussy, stuffing two fingers inside her while I unbutton my shirt.

Bastian thrusts his fingers in and out of Sienna's fluttering hole, playing her body like a violin as I strip off my underwear and socks. Tears track down her cheeks and I give my aching cock a few strokes. It's hard to hold back with Sienna.

I don't want to hold back any longer, so I surge forward, Bastian moving out of the way as I shift onto the bed, rolling over Sienna and trapping her hips beneath me.

Lining myself up at her entrance, I push inside, gliding through her velvety walls. It feels indescribable inside of her, she's so soft and warm and wet that I can't get enough. The scent of her arousal fills me and I bite back a groan, pulling her hips towards me so I can begin to pound into her, giving her the fucking I promised.

Our hips move together rhythmically, setting a frantic pace. The sheets rustle as Bastian moves onto the bed as well, using his fingers and mouth to lavish attention on her bouncing tits. He takes the nipple between his teeth, gently pressing down before using his tongue to suck, creating a feedback loop of mild pain and pleasure.

My hips move faster, cock stretching her walls as I thrust deeper. "You feel so good, Princess," I growl into her ear.

Sienna's cries get louder as she moves closer and closer to the edge. "Fuck!" she curses, arms tugging hard at the restraints. "Caleb!"

My hips snap forward, burying myself deep inside as we come at the same time. Sienna's eyes practically roll back in her head and I kiss her hard, biting her lower lip.

"How was that?" I ask as I pull out and lay next to her. Bastian moves so he's above her now, slipping inside with zero resistance.

"Felt good," Sienna says, panting as she tries to catch her breath. Her hips make little circles as Bastian begins to roll himself in and out. It doesn't take her long to tense up again, slick dribbling down her thighs and glistening in the dim light of the room as she comes a second time.

"Shit, Bastian!" she calls out, throwing her head back. She wriggles, shying away as he continues to pump himself in and out of her wet cunt. "Too much, too much!"

Bastian's smirk grows and he leans down. "I think you can handle it, Princess."

Sienna's eyes fill with tears and she bites her lip, rocking her hips to meet his. "I feel so sensitive," she whines. "So full."

"Can you come for us one more time?" I ask, turning to face her. She turns her head to mine and I reach out, brushing my hand over her cheek softly. "I want you to come one more time for us, okay?"

She nods, her hips still moving as she chases release. I bring my hand down, helping her along by stroking my fingers over her clit. She's so wet that my index finger glides right over the hood, catching on the bud. I flip between rubbing tiny circles into it and scissoring it between the first and middle fingers, testing to see which way she seems to like more.

Her hips buck up into Bastian's more frantically now and Bastian moves quicker to keep up. His shoulders are tensed, his eyes closed. He's been trying to hold off, but I can tell he's not going to last much longer and with a deep thrust, he comes inside Sienna with a grunt.

Sienna arches her back and lets out a wordless cry as she comes again, laying back against the pillows with a sheen of sweat over her body.

"You did so good," I praise her, kissing her lips as I untie the restraints and massage her wrists. "You took us so well."

Bastian slips out of her and off the bed. "I'll be right back," he says. He leaves to get stuff to clean up with and I pull Sienna into my arms, kissing her softly.

"Wow," she whispers, a playful smile on her lips. "I don't think I've ever felt so good."

"Glad we could be the ones to bring you there," I say, chest aching from how amazing I feel right now. "You deserve to feel good."

She nods, rubbing her face against my chest. "Thank you," she says. "I feel so safe with you guys."

A surge of warmth blooms in my chest. "Good. You're safe with us, Sienna. Always. We care about you more than you know."

Sienna places her head on my chest and I stroke a hand over her curls, reveling in how soft and silky they feel under my fingertips. Being around Sienna has shown me just how bitter and closed off I'd been for so long.

Ever since we lost Emily, I was scared to trust anyone, scared to let myself feel something. But Sienna's presence has made me want to try again, to give her my heart even if it means getting hurt.

It's simultaneously thrilling and terrifying. If I let myself fall for her, what does this mean for us? The arrangement had an unspoken timeline—things would end once Sienna's job was done here in Caspian Springs.

But now that everything is different, does that change things? Would Sienna stay with us once she's done with her research? Could we ask that of her?

Bastian comes back with a wet cloth and some ointment. He starts helping Sienna clean up, wiping the slick from her thighs before having her turn over to apply some cream to the marks on her backside.

She's delightfully red now, with some of the spots turning a nice bruise color. They'll last a few days probably. I love seeing her skin marked up from my hands.

My chest feels hollow as I think about her leaving us, the deadline looming on the horizon. I don't even know how she feels, so there's no way I can ask her to stay on our behalf. She deserves her freedom if that's what she wants.

I stay silent, only giving her a quiet smile when she turns to nestle against me once more. No matter what happens in the future, I'm just glad to have the time with her that we've gotten.

32

DOMINIC

"Okay, lunch is over. Back to work," Sienna says, poking me in the side as soon as she's done eating. "You promised."

"I should have never made that promise," I grumble. "You tricked me." I can't believe I fell for that pretty face. She's a master manipulator.

"I made an offer you couldn't refuse," she corrects, winking as she gets up to clean the dishes. I made stuffed salmon and rice for the two of us.

Bastian and Caleb are out all day, since Bastian is working on a bike at the shop and Caleb is fixing an issue with our website.

So Sienna had cornered me this morning, asking me to go with her for her morning interviews. Once that was done, she asked if I would like to have some fun with her after lunch, making it sound like she had something irresistible planned. The look she gave me had me instantly agreeing.

Now she pulls me into the living room, where she has a variety of nail polishes picked out so we could paint each other's toenails. My brothers are never going to let me live this down. It's my own fault for agreeing without finding out what she wanted to do first.

"Pick a color," Sienna says, showing off the dozen or so bottles she's placed on the coffee table. I shake my head and bend down, examining the bottles. If it were anyone else, I would never do this but Sienna has me wrapped around her finger, even if she doesn't know it.

Selecting a pale pink that I hope matches my own nail color closely enough not to be noticeable at the gym, I hand it to Sienna. She plucks up a bottle of shimmery blue and hands it to me.

"I've never really had friends to do stuff like this before," she confesses as she shakes the bottle.

I raise an eyebrow. "Not even in college?"

"Not really. I kept to myself a lot. I was shy, plus I couldn't afford to live on campus so I ended up missing the party years."

I clear my throat. "Well, are you going to paint them or not?" I ask. She smiles and sits down next to me as I lift my feet up on the couch for her.

"Do you want me to trim the nails too?" she asks.

"Whatever you want to do to torture me, Princess," I say with a playful wink. Sienna giggles and starts fussing over my feet.

Sunlight streams into the living room as we sit cross-legged on the couch, our identical grins reflecting the joy in this shared moment.

The doorbell rings just as she's applying the first coat of lacquer, and she jumps up to answer it. "I ordered something online," she calls out as she prances over to the door. "I wonder if it's already arrived."

When she opens the door though, she gasps and screams my name. I'm up in a flash, rushing to see what's got her so upset.

The tension crackles in the air as I square my shoulders, jaw clenched, while Sienna's breath catches in her throat.

It's one of the Serpents.

He's wearing a patched-up leather jacket, and a worn bandana wrapped around his head. His posture is slightly hunched, hands tucked into his pockets. A Serpent pendant dangles around his scrawny neck and he reeks of cigarettes.

"The fuck are you here for?" I ask, pulling Sienna behind me, fury radiating through me that they would come to our door. I keep one hand on Sienna, needing to know she's safe. Fear courses through me, wondering how they found us.

"Just came with a warning message from Diego," the man says, giving me a lazy smirk. "You've woken the beast with that little stunt. Thought you should know that if you don't back down, more of your precious people will suffer the consequences."

"Get the fuck off my property before I grab my gun and shoot you," I hiss at him, seething. He holds his hands up, sauntering away to his bike with a relaxed gait, as if unbothered by my threat.

I turn to Sienna, push her into the house, and lock the door behind us. "You're not going anywhere without us ever again," I mutter.

"I agree," Sienna says, putting her hand on my arm. "Until this is resolved, I don't relish the idea of becoming another walking target for those scumbags."

I pull her close to me and wrap my arms around her. "I'm sorry you got dragged into this mess. If we could stash you away somewhere safe until it all blows over, we would."

"I'm more worried about you," she confesses, tracing a light pattern on my chest. "You and Bastian and Caleb. There's only three of you guys and there seem to be so many Serpents."

Leading her over to the couch, I sit us down and grab the bottle of polish that she picked out for herself. "You don't need to worry about us. We can take care of things."

Sienna's eyes still hold anxiety. "But how will you guys defend yourselves if it comes down to a full-scale fight?"

"It wasn't always like this," I explain. "The Serpents didn't have the numbers they do now."

"What happened?"

"Once upon a time, the Serpents were just a small, petty gang of criminals. They made things rough for people in the neighborhood, but they weren't a big threat. I was just a baby when this was going on. After Caleb was born, things started to get worse." I explain, my mouth tightening.

She looks down at her hands. "That sounds terrible."

"It was pretty bad," I agree. "I have no real memories of it, but this place was turning into something out of an apocalypse movie. Criminals roamed the streets freely, busting up businesses and forcing them to pay for 'protection.' They harassed everyone and would make examples out of anyone who tried to stand up to them."

Sienna goes silent as she takes in my words.

"We were lucky though, because a group of men stepped up to protect the members of the community. They fought back and ran the Serpents out of town." My hands tremble as I continue.

"The original men called themselves the Crimson Blades, defenders of Caspian Springs. It was made up of the fathers, the uncles, and the grandfathers of the community. Some of those men died trying to protect us all."

Sienna's eyes narrow. "I can't believe they had the nerve to just waltz back in all these years later."

"We think Diego is related to the original leader of the Serpents," I tell her. "A son or nephew, so he wasn't around back then and doesn't take our threats seriously. He doesn't know how hard the Blades fought back in the day." I pause, trying to hold back the emotion that threatens to erupt inside me.

My voice trembles as I continue, reliving the painful memories. "My parents got caught up in everything …" I trail off, unable to hide the anguish in my eyes. "Dad was part of the Blades back then and they targeted my mother. Planted a bomb in her car that went off when she was on her way home from the store one day."

"Oh my God, I'm so sorry," Sienna says, reaching out. "That's awful. What did your dad do?"

"The Blades knew that things were getting out of hand. But they couldn't just fight the Serpents, they knew they had to take them down. So he and a few others managed to get their hands on Diego Sr.'s black book, all his associates, and how they got their funding.

Turned it over to the police. They came after Diego Sr. but the other Serpents attacked."

My hands turn to fists. "The Blades fought back but my dad died in the fight. When it was over, they ran the Serpents out of town for good, or so they thought."

"I understand why you guys are so intent on keeping them away from this town," Sienna says. "You must be furious to see them try to undo all the work your folks did to protect the community."

"I am," I tell her. "My grandfather was injured in the fight too. He never fully recovered the use of his leg. We thought they were gone but now they're back, with even more members. We don't know how they've managed it."

Sienna hums thoughtfully. "Maybe someone wanted revenge and is funding it," she suggests.

"We thought that too, but we don't know who would have that kind of money." I shrug and start on a second coat. "I don't know. It's useless to speculate. All we can do is try to keep them at bay until we can figure out a more permanent solution."

"I'm sorry you're going through this," Sienna murmurs, her voice laced with empathy. "It must bring up old wounds."

I soften my gaze as I meet her eyes. "Thank you," I whisper. "For being here, for understanding. I've never talked about this with anyone," I admit, my voice raw with emotion. "But with you, it feels different."

Sienna wraps her arms around me, holding me close as though she can shield me from the pain of the past. "You're not alone, Dominic. I'm here for you." She leans in, hugging me tightly.

"Thanks," I say. "I don't know what else to do right now, but I know things can't keep going like they are. We don't want to get others involved if we can help it, but it's starting to look like we may not have a choice."

"I get it," Sienna says. "I'm sorry."

She leans back and I finish painting her nails, the silence stretching between us.

As I work, my mind plays over our conversation and I realize that she's right. There are only three of us and dozens of Serpents. If we want a shot at taking them down, we might need to consider our options.

It might be time to recruit new members of the Crimson Blades.

Grim determination settles over me and I vow to talk to Bastian and Caleb as soon as possible.

33

BASTIAN

As I finish up for the day, I notice the vibrant colors of the sunset painting the sky above the shop in vivid hues. The fading light casts long shadows across the pavement, and the distant hum of traffic and the chirp of crickets relax me.

"Ready to go?" I ask, wiping my hands on a rag. The bike repair is done, and the customer will be picking it up first thing tomorrow morning.

"Yeah, let me just shut down," Caleb calls back, beginning to pack his things.

"I hope Dom had a good day with Sienna," I mention, putting away my tools.

"Seems like we successfully lifted her mood the other night," Caleb teases.

"Yeah, she's been a bit happier since then," I agree.

We head out to the Firebird and I climb into the driver's seat.

"I'm so hungry I could eat a whale," Caleb comments. "I skipped lunch to deal with the server issue on our site."

"Text Dom and find out if he wants us to pick anything up," I tell him. Caleb sends the text, then flips on the radio.

"He says that he and Sienna made chicken and dumplings," Caleb says a few moments later when his phone buzzes.

"Awesome," I say, turning left. We arrive home a few minutes later and head inside as the sun starts fading over the horizon.

As soon as we enter the house, Sienna rushes forward in a blur of motion and throws herself at me, her arms enveloping me in a tight embrace.

"Geez, I missed you too, Princess," I say, pulling away to check on her. She looks upset. "You okay?"

"We had a visitor today," Dominic tells us, expression dark. "One of the Serpent Syndicate came by the house."

My brows furrow. "You're shitting me. Did he do anything?" I glance back down at Sienna, ascertaining that she hasn't been hurt.

"I'm fine," Sienna says. "Dominic protected me. He never even got close."

Dominic's fists clench at his sides, his jaw tight with suppressed anger. "He left after I threatened him," he grits out, his voice laced with fury. "But it's not over. Diego wants us eliminated for what we did at the tire factory. He's willing to hurt innocent people just to get to us."

My heart races, a mix of anger and concern making me clench my fists as a surge of adrenaline courses through my veins. How dare they show up at our doorstep and threaten us. My gaze flickers to Sienna, protective instincts kicking in.

Caleb runs his thumb over his lower lip, shaking his head as he stares off for a moment. "These guys are going to make things hell for our town again. We can't let them get away with this shit."

"We won't," Bastian tells him, confidence in his gaze. "I won't let those motherfuckers walk all over us. They won't get a foothold in this place again."

"Dominic was telling me about the last time they were here in Caspian Springs," Sienna interjects. "And how your parents helped drive them away, but it cost them. I'm so sorry that happened. I wish I'd known."

"We didn't tell you," I reassure her, sitting down at the table for dinner. Caleb passes out plates while Sienna and Dominic bring the food over. "It was our shit to deal with."

"What happened after they drove out the Serpent Syndicate?" Sienna asks as she sits down. "Did you guys live with your grandfather?"

"Nah, Grandpa was too old to take us in," I tell her, reaching for the mashed potatoes. "He wanted to, but with his fucked-up knee and his health, he didn't want us to have to take care of him. So we went into a foster group home for boys."

Sienna's eyes meet mine. "That's tough. At least you guys got to stay together."

"Once the Serpents were gone, things got better though," I say.

"Yeah, and the community really pitched in to help. Some of the more active members did a whole thing and got the state to invest in opening the Haven Center. They wanted to give the next generation a better life and stuff."

"That's amazing," Sienna breathes out. "They truly rallied behind you guys."

"Yep," I nod.

"We met Rich there," Caleb says, his eyes growing distant as he gets lost in thought. "He was just a college kid when we first met him, but he helped tutor us in school and took us out places on the weekends."

Memories flood my mind as Dominic begins to speak. "We got close to him," he begins, a wistful smile tugging at his lips. "He was more than just a mentor. Rich felt like family. When he graduated, we thought he'd leave, but he stayed. He sacrificed so much just to be with us. He even got a research grant to continue his work at the Haven Center."

Caleb stares down at his plate. "We wanted him to adopt us. He wanted to adopt us too, but he couldn't afford it since he was living on student loans. But he did as much as he could for us, even after the Haven Center closed down."

Sienna's eyes widen with realization, her voice softening. "I had no idea you guys were so close," she murmurs.

"He took us to ball games, taught us how to ride bikes, how to drive a car … and he helped us with our homework and our essays all through school," I tell her, my voice soft as I reminisce.

"He was really like a dad to us in so many ways," Dominic adds, a pained smile on his face. "One time I came to him when a bully at school was making fun of me for my parents being gone. He taught me how to stand up for myself and I made that kid eat his words."

Sienna reaches out to grasp his hand, offering herself as comfort. "Wow. I wish I knew that before. What happened when your grandpa died?"

"He came to the funeral with us," I say. "He was always there, always. He wanted to adopt us at that point, but Caleb was almost an adult and we thought it didn't matter what our relationship was anymore, he was our dad in everything but name."

Sienna's eyes glisten, fingers twisting in her lap as she speaks. "You've been through so much," she murmurs.

I take a deep breath. "It was hard but we still had Rich. We thought everything would be okay."

Silence hangs over the table as we start eating, everyone lost in their own thoughts. Dominic is squeezing his hand rhythmically under the table and Caleb takes a few bites, then stops to sniffle.

Just a few years ago, the three of us sat at this very table with Rich and Emily, discussing our plans for the future. Now she's gone, and he's further away than ever before. I don't know if I can bring myself to admit how much I miss them both.

The mood has grown heavy, so Sienna clears her throat, trying to shift the conversation to a lighter topic. "You know," she says. "You never told me about what you liked to do as kids."

"I played soccer," I tell her. "Caleb was into those anime shows."

"And I did martial arts," Dominic adds. "Rich got me into it, after the bullying in middle school."

"I was in marching band," Sienna confesses. "I played the clarinet."

"I can see that," I tease. "You look like a band geek."

"Yeah?" Sienna playfully narrows her eyes. "Well, I was getting laid in marching band. Were you getting laid playing soccer?"

Dominic and Caleb both let out a whoop and Dom points at me from across the table. "She's got you there, bro," he teases.

"I hope he wasn't getting laid by the soccer boys," Caleb adds.

"I'll have you know I was the stud of the team," I brag, flexing an arm. "All the soccer groupies were after me."

"You mean all the soccer girls were after you because you broke their hearts," Caleb accuses. "I heard the stories."

"I was always a gentleman," I insist, sniffing and turning up my nose. "If anyone was a heartbreaker, it was Caleb," I shoot back. "He had that whole sensitive nerd thing going on. Girls flocked to him."

"If I was such a heartbreaker, how come I didn't get laid until senior year?"

"You know that has nothing to do with it," I protest. "You had a new girlfriend every week."

"If by girlfriend you mean girl who was a friend," Caleb said, ears turning red. I smirk and bump his shoulder.

"You have the Ravenwood genes," I tell him. "Means you're irresistible to the ladies."

"I dunno about that," Dominic protests. "I had one steady girlfriend through most of high school." He turns to Sienna. "She was nice, but she went away to school and we broke up."

"You said you guys broke up because she didn't like the Ramones," Caleb says, pointing an accusing finger at Dom.

"That's not a reason to break up with someone," Sienna protests.

"The Ramones are his favorite band," I say, chuckling. "Grace never liked Dom's music taste. I think that her leaving for college was the excuse he used to break up with her."

Laughter erupts around the table as we continue to share memories of our time in high school with Rich and the things we got up to, including the time we snuck out to see an R-rated horror movie.

"Rich was so mad," I say with a laugh. "But he said that we wouldn't get in trouble if we wrote an essay explaining the poor psychology behind the film's premise!"

Sienna laughs so hard she's got tears in her eyes. "Did you do it?"

"Dominic did," I confess. "And Caleb started but got distracted. I ended up being grounded for a whole month. I was so mad that I threatened to sign up for the military."

"Dang, that sucks," Sienna says. "Did you sign up?"

"Nope," I shake my head. "We ended up with different plans."

"Is that when you met Emily?" Sienna asks, her smile suddenly turning sober. "Oh God, I'm so sorry. I didn't mean to bring it up."

Dominic glances at me and the three of us exchange looks, a silent understanding passing between us. It feels like it's time to talk about her, to finally tell Sienna the story about her, and her place in our lives.

My gaze drifts to the empty chair where Rich used to sit, a pang of loss echoing in my heart. "No, it's fine," I say, my voice tinged with melancholy. "We're ready to talk about her."

34

SIENNA

"We're ready to talk about her," Bastian says.

Silence hangs in the air for a moment as I process his words. They're going to tell me about Emily?

I nod slowly, then take a bite of my dinner. I'm almost worried that if I say something, I might scare them off.

"When we were in high school, Rich was trying to get us to think about our futures," he starts. "We all had this burning desire to make our community a safer place, especially after the Haven Center was closed. It wasn't very long after that things started to go downhill and the last of the Serpents started poking around."

"We didn't know how we wanted to change things," Dominic adds. "Just that we wanted to protect our town. We came up with the idea of going to the police academy together and becoming cops."

"I wanted to be a detective," Caleb interjects. "But yeah, we were going to 'save' Caspian Springs and drive all the bad guys away."

"What happened?" I ask curiosity aroused. I can't imagine the guys as cops, it just seems so weird.

"The county tried to cut funding for school lunches," Caleb says, a distant smile on his face. "Rich was pretty upset about it, so we went downtown and joined a big protest. That's where we met Emily. I had just graduated."

"She was at the protest?" I ask.

"She was leading the protest," Bastian corrects me. "She was really into community activism and stuff, and she had this charisma that got everyone fired up. When we went to sign her petition, she managed to get us to sign up for a bunch of volunteer shit. One thing led to another, and she started coming here to the house to hang out."

"Oh, when did you get the house?" I ask.

"We bought it with the life insurance money from Grandpa's will after Dom graduated," Bastian explains. "Emily hung out here all the time and we told her about our plans to join the academy, but she convinced us that we could do better for the community by doing activism with her. We told her about the Haven Center, and she wanted to help us get it started back up again."

"She pushed us, made us see that we could do a lot of good with the Haven Center. We had so many big plans," Dominic reminisces. "Emily was like a breath of fresh air to us, someone from outside the community who saw the potential of it."

"Did you guys get funding?"

They nod. "We secured a grant from some interested organizations. It was hard but Emily studied stuff about non-profits when she was at school, so she helped us," Caleb says.

They tell me more about the plans they made for the center, and how she helped them along.

"We started getting feelings for her," Dominic confesses. "All three of us. It was easy to fall for someone like her."

I feel like I should be jealous, but it just makes me sad that they lost someone like her. "So what did you do?" I ask.

"We decided that it wouldn't be fair for all three of us to compete for her, so we figured if she was down for it, we could all share," Bastian says. "So we talked to her about it and surprisingly, she was fine with the idea of sharing. It worked out great. There was no jealousy, no competition, just us all growing closer."

I feel a profound sense of sadness well up inside me. "It sounds like you really loved her."

"We did," Caleb says, twisting his fingers together under the table. "We thought everything was perfect. Plans for the center were coming along and we got a timeline together for reopening it."

"But then we noticed for some reason Emily was spending a lot of one-on-one time with Rich," Bastian says, expression darkening. "She was avoiding us, growing distant. When we confronted her, she didn't want to talk about it."

"I didn't understand," Caleb admits. "I pushed her to tell me what was going on, but she just said that she couldn't tell us yet."

"That's when Rich came to us," Dominic says, expression haunted. "He told us that he and Emily had been out talking about plans for the center and drinking wine; they got drunk. She seduced him, and they slept together."

I gasp. The man who was like a father to them their whole lives slept with their girlfriend? My hand flies to my mouth. "No."

"He said it was a mistake, that he was so sorry," Bastian says, voice thick. "He kept apologizing. Told us that he let her down gently, but she didn't take it well. She screamed at him for using her and stormed off. He didn't know where she went and her phone was off."

I feel tears sting at my eyes. This must have been so devastating for everyone involved.

"Two days later, her landlord found her body," Dominic says, voice hollow. "She hung herself. Left behind a note that he gave to us."

Caleb squeezes his eyes shut and wipes the tears away furiously. "She said she'd fallen in love with Rich after all the time they spent together. That she ... she felt too guilty about her affair and couldn't live with herself, or without being able to be with Rich."

Tears stream down my face. This explains so much. I can't believe that I thought the boys were just mad at Rich for something petty. The truth was so much worse.

"We could never forgive ourselves and we blamed it on him,"

Caleb says. "I can't look at him the same way after what happened. I feel sick."

"I understand," I say, reaching my hand out to grasp his like a lifeline. "You felt betrayed by the very person who was supposed to always have your back."

"Now you know why we were so eager to push you away when you came to Caspian Springs," Bastian says, his voice sounding raw. "You reminded us so much of her, you two have the same kindness and the same passion inside you. We didn't want to get close, but you drew us in like moths to a flame."

I feel my heart clench. "Was I just a substitute for Emily then?" I ask, insecurity rearing its ugly head.

"No," Dominic says quickly, grabbing my free hand. "Never. You may be similar, but you guys are different too. In many ways, you're stronger than Emily was. She didn't have the same background as us growing up, or as you, so she didn't understand what the world was like. She wanted to believe in an ideal that wasn't always possible."

"You're stronger than she was," Caleb tells me. "She struggled when things didn't go her way, but you persevere and keep trying."

"I appreciate you telling me all this," I say with a sniffle. "It can't have been easy. It must have been painful when Dr. Thornton told you what he'd done."

"Felt like my heart had been ripped out," Dominic admits. "That's why we had such a hard time seeing you defend him. Our view of him was tainted that day. Even though he apologized, the fact that he did it was such a betrayal."

"I don't know how he can live with himself," I murmur. "He seems like he regrets it though."

"We just can't go back to the relationship we once had," Caleb says. "Some wounds can't be healed."

"Maybe in time," I tell them. "But I get why you're not ready to mend bridges with him just yet."

They must have had so much mistrust in Rich after that, wondering if he led her on, or if he deliberately got her drunk and seduced her.

I just wish I knew why he lied about it. Why did he tell me they only kissed? I get that he wanted to save face, but if he'd been honest from the get-go, maybe I could have helped fixed their relationship.

It gnaws at me, so I tuck the information away for later, when I have the bandwidth to confront him. Right now, I just want to be here for the three of them.

They deserve to feel loved wholly and completely. They gave up their original dreams for Emily, and she betrayed them in the worst way possible. I don't understand how she could take their love and throw it away like that.

"Let's watch a movie tonight," I offer. "Something action-y like *The Fast and the Furious*. Something to take our minds off things."

"Yeah," Bastian agrees. "That sounds like a good idea." Though he never cried when discussing Emily, I can see the pain in his eyes, and in the way he holds himself. He's fidgeting with the ring on his pinky, and he runs his hands through his hair repeatedly.

"Bastian was really torn up," Caleb confesses as we begin the dinner dishes together. "He took it hardest because he's the one who introduced us to Emily in the first place. He brought her around and he feels responsible for what she did."

"But it wasn't his fault," I whisper back, drying the plate in my hands. "Emily was the one who chose to betray your relationship."

"He's always been like that though. You know the story about us sneaking out? The reason he was the only one who got grounded was because he took the fall and said it was his idea," Caleb reveals. "Rich let me and Dom off with a warning."

I lean into him and wrap my arms around his waist. "I can't believe how much weight Bastian carries on his shoulders."

"You've been good for him," Caleb says. "You've helped him see he doesn't have to carry so much around on his own."

"I hope I can be good for all of you," I say as we finish the washing up. "You and Dominic and Bastian all mean the world to me."

"You mean the world to us too," Caleb says, bending down to kiss me. "Now let's go watch a movie about men stealing cars and driving them very fast."

He takes my hand in his and leads me into the living room where the other two are already set up. Bastian pats his lap and I go sit on it, next to Caleb. Dominic takes the recliner nearby.

As we watch the film, my mind drifts back to wondering again why Dr. Thornton lied to me. I don't know what his goal was with lying but I intend to find out.

He can't treat my boys like this and act like it's not a big deal, or act like they overreacted. It's not right.

35

BASTIAN

A weight feels like it's been lifted off my chest now that we've finally shared the story with Sienna. I didn't realize how much I'd carried around, holding so much back.

"Wait, did that guy steal that other guy's car?" Sienna whispers, attempting to keep up with the plot of the film.

"Yeah, but the other guy stole it from the first guy to begin with so he's just taking it back," I whisper back, my arm around her shoulder.

"I see." She nuzzles into me. "I think."

We finish the movie and head to bed, Sienna following me up the stairs. "Do you mind if I sleep with you tonight?" she asks, fiddling with the ring on her index finger.

I nod and she follows me into the bedroom, starting to undress. "I was hoping that tomorrow you and Caleb could spend the morning with me while Dominic is at the shop," she says. "I have some interviews and then I want to go to Walmart."

"We can do that," I tell her, stripping down to my boxers and throwing my clothes into the hamper. "What time do you need to be up in the morning?"

"Early," she grumbles. "Miss Antoinette wouldn't grant me an interview unless I came before she had to leave for work in the morning and since she's on first shift at the hospital, I have to be there by five thirty."

"AM?" I ask, incredulous. She nods.

"Yup."

"Good luck getting Caleb up that early," I joke.

"Oh my God, yes. He's a total night owl," Sienna agrees. "He doesn't get into bed some nights before two in the morning."

"He was worse in high school," I tell her as I climb into bed. "He would stay up all night playing video games some nights. We had to bribe him to go to sleep sometimes."

"I can't stay up all night anymore," Sienna says, shaking her head. "I get so tired by like, midnight."

She slips into bed next to me and we turn to face each other. "I hope he's not like that when we have kids," she jokes.

My eyes widen for a moment, heart racing. Is she serious or is she just joking around? Having a future with Sienna seems way too good to be true, and I don't want to get my hopes up so I try to play it cool.

"He'll be the fun dad, teaching them how to play video games until the wee hours of the morning," I joke back. "Dom will be the one to give the kids adventures. I'll probably be the boring dad who helps with homework."

"You're not boring," Sienna protests, punctuated with a yawn. "You'd be a good dad. You'd probably teach them how to sneak out, but you'd also make sure they were loved and cared for."

My heart is pounding in my ears now, and I open my mouth to say something but before I can, I realize Sienna has fallen asleep.

I shake my head and close my eyes.

The next morning, when I wake up, Sienna is already awake. I hear her downstairs making coffee, so I head down into the kitchen and wrap my arms around her from behind, pulling her to my chest. "Morning, Princess." She looks adorable wearing one of my T-shirts and a pair of pajama shorts. The aroma of coffee fills the kitchen and I inhale deeply.

"Good morning," she says, a cheerful lilt to her voice.

"You should have woken me," I chide.

"We had a long day yesterday," she says. "I didn't want to wake you or Caleb. I ended up interviewing Miss Antoinette by myself and came straight home."

"Still. I don't like you out there by yourself. We have to figure out what to do about the Serpents, so until they've been dealt with, just let us go with you next time."

"Fine," Sienna says, turning to face me. "You're ridiculous you know that?"

Just as I lean down to kiss her, Caleb comes into the kitchen looking bleary-eyed and sleep-tousled. "Morning," he says, squinting at us. "I smelled coffee."

"I was going to ask you and Bas to come with me to an interview this morning, but I decided not to wake you," Sienna explains. "I made coffee when I came back."

"Aw, you should have woken me up," Caleb protests with a yawn, rubbing his eyes. "I like helping you with your work," he adds, casting a sleepy grin at Sienna.

"Next time," Sienna promises, standing on her tiptoes to cup his cheeks and give him a soft kiss. "I'll take my big, scary guard dogs with me next time."

"Woof," I bark, earning a laugh from Sienna. She pats the top of my head.

"Good boy," she says. I chuckle and pretend to scratch my ear while shaking my leg, and soon all three of us are laughing.

Dominic eyes us as he comes down the stairs and shakes his head.

"Don't ask," I tell him.

"Wasn't going to," he shoots back, pouring himself a cup of coffee. "Have fun with these two mutts while I'm at work, Princess," he adds, coming over to plant a kiss on her forehead. Sienna lights up and hugs him.

"You have a good day too," she says. My heart clenches as I take in this scene of domestic bliss. I wish it could be like this always, but I know that her research is coming to an end.

On top of that, we have the looming Serpent threat hanging over us. If we don't get it taken care of once and for all, we're risking Sienna's life by staying with her.

Either way, we have to make a decision soon.

Feeling the weight of responsibility settle on my shoulders, I decide it's time to take action. As we wander the aisles of Walmart on our impromptu outing, the urgency of our situation weighs heavily on my mind.

"What do you need?" I ask, watching Caleb as he checks out a new video game and Sienna scans the books on the opposite side of the aisle.

"I need to pick up makeup remover wipes, a new paddle brush, and some pretzel sticks. I got a craving," she adds. "Also, sometimes I like to wander around and have Walmart tell me what I want, you know?"

I shake my head but Caleb wanders back over, nodding. "I get it," he says. "Sometimes you just gotta let go and let the universe tell you what it is you need."

"Exactly," Sienna agrees. I don't know that I get it but since Caleb seems to, I follow along behind the two of them as they wander the aisles, the scent of freshly baked goods wafting from the bakery and the squeaking of nearby carts accompanying us like a noisy symphony.

The last time we were this relaxed feels like it was years ago. I don't think I've seen Caleb smile this much since the early days with Emily. But it feels different this time too, because the relationship with Sienna feels like it was built on a more solid foundation.

Before, we were young, idealistic kids but Sienna keeps us grounded. I just want things to stay this way, but how can I ask that of Sienna when she was already attacked once? After what happened to our mom, the idea of a repeat with Sienna leaves me feeling nauseous.

"Hey, do you guys want pizza for dinner?" Sienna turns to me and holds up a frozen Margherita pizza, pulling me out of my head. "We can watch another movie tonight. Maybe something with fewer car races."

"Sounds good," I say, giving her a thumbs up. Caleb leans over her while they pick out a few more pizzas. I grin as they argue over toppings and brands and realize that I love this and I never want it to end.

My gaze lingers on Sienna as we move through the aisles, a surge of protectiveness welling within me. I want her to stay with us, to be ours forever. But the looming threat of the Serpents reminds me of how fragile this happiness is and I realize I need to make a decision here, I need to take action to keep her safe.

Fuck.

I don't know how I'll bring it up to her, but I know I can't ask her to stay as long as the Serpents are still a threat. If I want to ask her to stay, I have to get rid of them. Determination settles within me.

Pulling out my phone, I dial a number I haven't called in years.

"Hey, Dorian?" I ask. "This is Bastian Ravenwood. I have a question for you."

He sounds surprised to hear from me but when I explain what it is I need, he's more than happy to help. I hang up a few minutes later, feeling more confident.

This town is everything to me, it means just as much as Sienna does. If I have to get my hands dirty to keep it—and her—safe, I will.

As we stroll down the grocery aisles, Sienna grabs a bag of chips off the shelf, inspecting it with a critical eye. "Do we want these?" she asks, turning to Caleb and me.

Caleb shrugs. "A snack attack can strike any time, you gotta be prepared," he says with a mischievous grin, grabbing the chips and tossing them into the cart.

I chuckle, reaching for some cheese dip. "Yeah, and you know how cranky you get when you're hungry, Sienna. We can't have that," I tease, winking at her.

Sienna rolls her eyes, but there's a playful glint in them. "Just don't hog the chips, Caleb," she jokes.

Caleb feigns offense, clutching his chest dramatically. "Hey now, I'll have you know I have impeccable self-control when it comes to snacks," he declares, earning a snort of laughter from Sienna.

I raise an eyebrow. "Sure, Caleb. That's why we always find empty chip bags hidden under your bed," I tease, nudging him with my elbow.

He ducks his head, but he's still grinning. "A man needs fuel to please a lover," he says, winking at Sienna as he grabs another bag of chips.

Sienna shakes her head, amused. Once we're done, we head up to the register with our cart and I nudge Sienna out of the way, flashing my card. "I've got this," I tell her. Caleb eyes me, a silent question in his gaze but I wave him off. "It's fine," I tell him. "Don't worry about it."

Caleb nods and they bag everything while I pay. Once we're done, Caleb takes the cart, running forward and coasting through the parking lot.

"Let's go home," I tell them. "I need to go out for a while, but I'll be back before dinner. You two have fun with Dominic when he gets done at the shop."

"Everything okay?" Sienna asks. I nod and grab her hand with mine.

"Everything is perfect, Princess," I tell her.

With determination burning in my chest, I resolve to rid our town of the Serpent threat once and for all. As I glance at Sienna beside me, I know that I'll stop at nothing to ensure her safety and our future together.

36

DOMINIC

The afternoon sun filters through the curtains, casting a warm glow across the room. The faint hum of cicadas drifts in through the open window, mingling with the soft click-clack of Sienna's keyboard as she works diligently at her laptop.

Standing in the doorway, I watch her for a moment, admiring the way the sunlight dances in her hair, casting golden highlights against the copper waves.

Bastian's been making mysterious phone calls lately, tension from the Serpent threat lingering in the air. He's off doing an errand with Caleb, leaving me alone in the house with Sienna. With no repairs on the duty roster, I have an unexpected day off, a rare luxury in our hectic lives.

Leaning against the door frame of Caleb and Sienna's room, I clear my throat to announce my presence. Sienna glances up from her work, a warm smile lighting up her features as I enter the room.

"Hey, Princess," I say, crossing the room to sit beside her on the bed.

Her smile widens at my approach. "Hey," she replies, setting aside her laptop to give me her full attention.

"I thought you and I might do something together," I begin,

feeling a spark of excitement ignite within me at the prospect. "Maybe have a little fun?"

Sienna's gaze locks on mine. "What did you have in mind?" she asks, her voice taking on a playful lilt.

"If you're not busy, I thought maybe I could show you some new experiences," I offer. "I know Bas and Caleb gave you an intro into the kink scene, but I have some stuff I could show you too."

The chair creaks as Sienna stands up, moving to straddle my lap. "Oh?" she says, running her hands through my hair. "What kind of stuff do you want to try?"

I grasp her by the hips, pulling her into me. "I was thinking maybe you and I could experiment with role-playing. What do you think?"

"I've never done anything like that," she admits. "What did you have in mind?"

"This might seem odd but what do you say if we pretend to be an FBI agent and the mob boss's daughter, and we meet at a party and only have one night to be together?"

"I say ... fancy meeting you here, Agent Smith," Sienna says in a deep purr. "I wasn't expecting to see you after the incident in Venezuela," she stands up, body moving lithely as she walks over to the desk again and picks up her cup of water.

Holding it like a wine glass, she turns and gives me a sultry look. "What do you think you're doing?" she asks. "You know we can't be seen in public like this."

"Miss Winterthorpe, if you'd look around you'd notice we're entirely alone," I say, slipping into the role. "Why do you think I cornered you in your father's library tonight, on the night of his annual birthday gala?"

Sienna giggles and then turns her expression more serious. "It's dangerous to show up here at my father's manor, Agent. You don't think that some of his guests will recognize you?"

I surge forward, pulling her into a passionate embrace before leaning down to murmur in her ear, "I don't care. For you, it's worth getting caught if all we can have is tonight, Miss Winterthorpe."

"Agent Smith," Sienna sighs, leaning into me and kissing me. "You promised last time you saw me that you would teach me how to behave myself. Do you intend to keep that promise?"

I run my hands along her back, tilt her head back, and kiss her fiercely, nipping her bottom lip with my teeth before devouring her mouth, leaving us both dizzy and breathless by the time we break apart. "I always keep the promises I make," I say, voice deep.

She stares up at me with doe eyes and I push her up against the wall, pinning her in place. "Are you going to be good for me, or do I have to show you why they call me the best agent in the business?"

Sienna lets out a tiny mewl and spreads her legs, giving me a lascivious look. "I'll cooperate, but only for you, Agent Smith."

"Good," I tell her. "Then get on your knees."

She blinks at me and I snarl, grabbing her by the hair. "I said get on your knees, Miss Winterthorpe."

Sienna squeaks and falls to her knees, a thud echoing through the room.

"Color?" I whisper, leaning in close.

"Green," she whispers back. I smirk and undo the fly of my jeans.

"Go on then," I order. She reaches out and takes me in her mouth and I let out a sharp hiss. Sienna's mouth is one of my favorite parts of her, after her smile and her mind.

Pressing her deeper on my cock, I rasp out, "Take it all down, Miss Winterthorpe. Show me how you can use that nasty mouth of yours for other things besides ordering the deaths of innocent men."

Sienna swallows around me, saliva dripping from the corners of her mouth. She's struggling to breathe around my girth, and I enjoy watching her face as I start moving her head back and forth. "That's right, use your tongue," I tell her. "Scrape your teeth gently over the head."

As she moves to obey, I tighten my grip on her hair. She's forced to yank her own hair, bringing tears to her eyes as she continues. Her lips wrap around the tip and she grazes it lightly with her teeth, eliciting a deep moan from the depths of my throat.

"That's right, baby, just like that," I encourage. She chokes as I push deeper into her throat, coughing and pulling off a little before she readjusts.

"That's it, take it all," I say, stroking a hand over her hair as I push her back down.

Her tongue moves along the veiny underside and she hollows her cheeks and sucks hard, head bobbing back and forth. My eyes roll back in my head and I feel myself getting close to the edge. I don't want to come just yet though.

"Okay," I pull her off of me with a wet pop. "I want to see how good you can be for me. Take off your clothes and get on the bed. Touch yourself, but don't come until I've given you permission."

She stands on wobbly legs, starting to strip down.

"Slower," I say, crossing my arms. "Put on a show for me, darling."

Sienna smiles and I watch as she begins to tease me by lifting her shirt up inch by inch, then drops it back down before it reaches her bra.

Rain begins to patter on the window outside as she wiggles her hips side to side, creating a soundtrack as she then does a couple of body rolls, showing off her beautiful curves. I flip on some lo-fi, letting her dance for me.

"That's it, baby," I tell her. "Show me how sexy you can be."

My encouragement spurs her on, and she turns and shakes her ass before hooking her thumbs in her shorts and pulling them down, along with her panties. She drops them, kicking them out of the way before turning back to face me. Shimmying backward, she crosses her arms and lifts her shirt over her head.

I clap as she shakes her chest, reaching behind herself to undo the hooks, then lets it fall into her hands before twirling and taking it off with a flourish.

"Fuck. Go ahead and get on the bed now," I say, my voice husky with lust.

She struts over to the bed, lying on it before spreading her legs. Her teeth catch her lower lip and she bites down as she strokes a hand down her body and slips a finger between her folds. She lets out a shudder and starts playing with herself, stroking over her clit in slow swirls.

"Keep going," I say, bringing my hand down to squeeze my dick to keep myself from coming too quickly. "That's good, now slip one finger into your hole."

I watch her obey and she lets out a low moan as she continues to toy with herself. "Feels so good," she gasps out. "Feels like I could come like this."

"You may not come until I give you permission," I remind her. "I want you to keep yourself right on the edge, see how long you can hold off."

Sienna arches her back, picking up the pace of her strokes, pushing a second finger in next to the first. "Oh God, Agent Smith, please, I'm so close. Please let me come."

"Not yet," I tell her. "Keep yourself right there on the edge. Can you edge yourself for five minutes? I'm going to start a timer." I show her my phone and she nods, biting her lip as she moves her fingers over herself.

Wet squelching noises fill the room, a beautiful accompaniment to the sound of rain and the low music I put on.

I start stroking my cock, wanting to touch myself at the same time. It feels so good watching her open herself up to us, to the new experiences we've given her. I remember how shy and hesitant she was at first, and how scared she was about anything to do with this side of bedroom pleasure.

Now here she is, looking so confident and sexy as she obeys me, giving herself over freely. It's a heady rush and my hand moves faster, the edge coming quicker than before.

Her moans get louder, crying out as she keeps herself right on the edge, just as I ordered. My hand is now covered in precum drooling from the tip of my cock as I watch her touch herself. I can't hold back any longer, letting myself release.

I come in spurts that arch out and cover Sienna's soft tummy. She's got tears in her eyes and as the timer goes off, she lets out a long, low moan.

"Come for me," I tell her. Instantly she's coming undone, screaming out my name as her body tenses up.

"Fuck!" She curses and goes limp, little aftershocks catching hold.

I glance down at my phone and my lips curl into a grin. "Do you trust me?" I ask.

Sienna nods and I grab a box from under Caleb's bed, pulling it out. "Sit up," I tell her.

She obeys, a quizzical look in her eyes. Using a length of rope, I tie her arms behind her back and then tie her feet together. Adding a gag as a finishing touch, I stroke her cheek, lean down, and kiss her.

"Enjoy," I tell her, before slipping out of the room.

37

CALEB

A text alert pings from my phone and I check, it's from Dominic. I told him I was coming home and asked if I needed to stop to get anything, so I read the text and grin.

Heading inside, I take the stairs two at a time and push open my bedroom door to find Sienna sitting in the middle of the bed, all tied up nicely like a present.

She's naked, ropes crisscrossing around her body so her hands are tied behind her back and her ankles are crossed and tied together. Panic is replaced by reassurance in her eyes when she spots me. Her curls are messed up and she's got tear tracks on her cheeks—a sight for sore eyes.

"Hello Miss Winterthorpe," I say, strolling into the room. "Agent Smith tells me he finally caught you. It's time for you to be interrogated now."

Sienna's green eyes light up in understanding before she narrows her eyes at me. I sit in front of her and reach out, pulling the gag from her mouth.

"Here's how this is going to work, Miss Winterthorpe. I'm going to do whatever I want to you until you give up your secrets." I run my hand up her thigh and she trembles, letting out a whimper. "When you've had enough of my torment, tell me the code word, which as you know will end all of this, do you understand?"

"How ..."

"When you're ready to stop, say the safe word," I say, dropping character for a moment to explain. Sienna nods, understanding the game now. "What is it again?" I want to make sure she remembers.

"Rutabaga," she whispers. I reach out and stroke her cheek.

"Good job. Just say Rutabaga when you're ready for the game to be done," I say, then slip back into character. "Now tell me everything, Miss Winterthorpe."

She juts out her chin. "No. I don't have to tell you anything, Agent Lothario."

I grin at the name, then school my features. "Very well then. Perhaps some pain will jog your memory." I reach out for the box Dominic left out and pick up the leather and fur flogger. It's about twenty inches, with rabbit fur falls and a leather handle. I run it over the skin of her thighs before bringing it down, letting it tickle her skin.

"Are you ready to talk?" I demand.

"You have to do better than that," Sienna says, setting her shoulders high despite the restraints. I bring the flogger down on her thighs a little harder.

She winces and jumps, jutting out her chin. "I'm not talking, Agent Lothario."

I bring the flogger down over her skin a few more times, waiting to see if she can handle the pain. She hisses as the falls strike her skin, but her pupils are still blown wide with her arousal.

"You'll never hear me talk," Sienna hisses. "I'm immune to your torture."

"We'll see about that," I say, bringing the flogger around to land a few lashes on her back and down over her ass. She sucks in a breath then lets out a moan, clearly enjoying the pain.

I'm impressed by how much she can take, but I check in just to be sure. When I get a green light, I keep going, raining harder blows all over her body.

Sienna's moans get louder as I continue and I decide to try a different tactic, pushing her down so she's laying on her back with her limbs still tied together. I start raining blows over her pussy, reveling in the animalistic noises she makes.

"You like that, you little slut?" I ask. "Or are you ready to talk? I won't stop until you give me the code!"

"Never!" she cries out. "I will never betray my family like that."

"Clearly torture doesn't work on you then," I say, discarding the flogger. "I'm going to have to pleasure it out of you."

I lean down and lick a wet stripe up her pussy, enjoying the sweet, musky taste. "How about this, Miss Winterthorpe? You may not come until you give up the code."

"You won't tempt me," she spits out.

I move my face down and bury it in her wet cunt, nosing over her clit as she writhes against me. I'm enjoying getting into character and playing around with her way too much. Whatever Dominic set up between them, we'll have to revisit again with all three of us.

Sienna's arching off the bed now, squirming to get away from my relentless pleasuring. I reach out and grip her by the hips to hold her in place, driving my tongue into her hole, flattening it out and angling for that spot inside her that will drive her over the edge.

"Oh God!" she cries out. "Don't stop!"

Hands around her hips, I wriggle my tongue in and out of her hole, then lick up to her clit again, then take it between my lips and suck. She shrieks, thrashing against the restraints.

"Caleb!" she cries out, unable to get away from me. "Please, please, I want to come!"

"Give me the code," I tell her.

She rolls her head from side to side and wails, refusing even as I bring my fingers down to add to the mix.

"The code, Miss Winterthorpe."

She tries to hold out, but her resolve is wavering and finally, after another firm stroke of my tongue, she breaks down, stuttering out, "Rutabaga!"

Immediately springing to action, I undo the restraints with one swift pull, yanking them away and unbending her limbs, massaging the feeling back into them.

"I've got you," I tell her, kissing away the tears. I pull away to strip off my clothes quickly, then come back and line myself up at her entrance, pushing inside.

Sienna whimpers, grabbing at me with her fingers as I start to work myself in and out. "You're such a tease," she whines.

"You love it," I tell her. She blushes and nods. "Then fuck me properly, Princess," I tell her. Her hips start moving in time with mine, the sound of our bodies rocking together filling the room. There's some lo-fi on the stereo, something Dominic must have put on earlier and it reverberates a haunting melody through the room.

"Oh God!" Sienna cries out, raking her nails down my back. I mash our lips together, kissing her frantically as we continue to pound into each other. "Deeper, harder," she urges. I snap my hips faster, driving as deep as I can inside of her as we move together.

"I'm gonna come!" she cries out, digging her fingers into my back. I continue the same pace, then move my fingers down to twist over her clit and she lets out a scream before tensing up as she releases.

My own cock throbs inside of her, her inner walls milking me as I slam my hips against hers, then spasm as I come.

"Fuck," I whisper, collapsing beside her breathlessly. "You did so good, baby. You're a natural at role-playing. We should do it again sometime."

"I had fun," she admits. "I would love to try something like that again. It was kind of hot being tied up like a present for you."

"We can revisit that too," I assure her. I pull her close to me and kiss her forehead. "Thanks for the welcome home."

"How was your day?" she asks, stroking a hand over my chest.

"I mostly spent the morning working but Bastian's got something going on that he's not talking much about yet. I think it has to do with the Serpents. He sent me to deliver a package to Joe at the hardware store."

"Should we ask him about it?"

"Nah, it's probably best to let him tell us when he's ready," I say. "You know how he can be about that kind of thing."

"Oh yeah, I do," she agrees, nodding her head so her hair rubs against my skin. It feels so soft and silky and I reach down to run my fingers through a curl, rubbing it between my thumb and forefinger.

"Oh, I meant to ask you about something," Sienna says, tracing her fingers through the sprinkle of chest hair on my sternum.

"Hmm?" I ask, closing my eyes as I get lost in the sensation.

"The stuff you told me about what happened with Rich and Emily. It wasn't the same story he told me."

I sigh, looking down at her. "What story did he tell you?"

"He said that she kissed him and he turned her down. He didn't say anything about sleeping with her or having an affair."

I feel my hands clench. "Well, he's an asshole. No wonder he tried to save face with you by lying about it. He probably thought that saying it was just a one-time kiss made it sound less terrible than it was."

"Are you sure there wasn't something more going on between them then?" she asks. "If he lied to me about it ..."

"I don't think he was trying to lie to cover up anything more sinister," I tell her. "He had no reason to lie to us and every reason to come clean with the truth. I think he just didn't want you to think badly of him after you found out what he did, especially since it was a catalyst for everything else."

"Maybe," Sienna says, biting her lip. "Why did the Haven Center even close down in the first place, by the way? You guys never said what happened there."

"It was some funding issue," I tell her. "I don't really know, that's what we were told. They ran out of funding and the grants stopped coming through I guess." I hadn't even really thought about it at the time, just accepted that those sorts of things happen in a place like Caspian Springs.

"I see," Sienna says, licking her bottom lip as she takes it in. "Makes sense. It just sucks that it had to shut down."

"Yeah," I agree. "But I don't wanna dwell on old stuff like that anymore. I want to cuddle you and then beat you at *Halo* later."

Sienna narrows her eyes. "Oh, you're so on."

I pull her in for a kiss, her question lingering in my mind. Would we have been able to get the center back up and running if not for what happened with Emily? It feels too painful to speculate on the what-ifs, so I just try to let it go and focus on spending time with the woman I love.

Even if it means leaving some questions unanswered.

38

SIENNA

A gnawing sense of unease has been growing inside me ever since I found out the truth about Emily and Dr. Thornton, but it still feels as though there are missing pieces to the puzzle.

"I need to go turn some work into Dr. Thornton, can you take me there?" I ask Caleb after dinner. I need to talk to Dr. Thornton if I want answers.

Caleb nods. "Yeah, I can go with you," he agrees. "Dom and Bastian are going to be tied up with some repairs at the shop. But I've got a feeling it's actually got something to do with the Serpents though."

My anxiety spikes at the mention of the Serpents and their constant looming presence in our lives. "You think they're going to go up against them?" I ask, my voice tinged with concern. The thought of the two of them in such danger without backup sends a shiver down my spine.

"No, I don't think they'd do something reckless like that," Caleb reassures me, though he rubs his hands over his arms, uncertainty evident. "You'll know when we're ready to make a move."

I nod, hoping he's right. As we head upstairs, the weight of impending confrontation hangs heavy in the air. Despite Caleb's reassurances, my mind races with worry, unable to shake the sense of impending danger that lurks just beyond our reach.

With everything going on with the Serpents, part of me wonders if I should be so worried about this situation with Dr. Thornton. It seems almost trivial to be so concerned about the boys' past relationship when their very future hangs in the balance.

On the other hand, I do feel like I need closure on this situation. It's affected them so deeply that it almost feels like we can't move forward until we can all move past it.

I fall into an uneasy sleep that night, spending the whole night tossing and turning. I wake up sweaty, haunted by the lingering image of Emily's face as she accuses me of stealing the Ravenwoods from her.

Exhausted, I make myself a cup of coffee and try not to be consumed by the overwhelming urge to run away from it all. It won't help anyway since the Serpents are still lurking around.

"Are you okay?" Caleb asks, coming into the kitchen to wrap an arm around my shoulder.

"Fine," I tell him. "It's just work stuff." It's not exactly a lie but I feel uneasy concealing the truth from him. He nods and squeezes my hand, a comforting lifeline in this sea of turmoil.

I'm doing this for them, I tell myself as we make our way to campus. I need to help them resolve things once and for all. Still, the idea of confronting Dr. Thornton leaves a bad taste in my mouth, since I don't know how he'll react. Will he finally tell me the truth this time?

As I push open the unlocked door to Dr. Thornton's office, a chill rushes over me, the temperature inside significantly colder than the hallway. The faint scent of old books mingles with the mustiness of the room, and I find myself enveloped in a cocoon of academia.

Since he's not back from class yet, I decide to look at the necklace again to appease my curiosity. I want to look at it more closely and see if I missed anything.

Opening the drawer, I push aside pens and old papers to find it but it's not there. Digging through the scattered office supplies, I realize with growing concern that the necklace is gone.

Carefully moving things back to their original places, I push the drawer closed and exit his office, electing to pretend I was waiting for him in the hallway. I have more questions now than ever, so I brace myself for the inevitable confrontation.

When Dr. Thornton finally appears, I offer him a forced smile, masking the turmoil raging within me. He eyes me up and down as he approaches, lingering on the files in my arms. Something about the way he looks at me sends a shiver down my spine.

"What can I do for you today, Sienna?" he asks, his tone clipped.

"I came by to drop off these," I hold them up, summoning my inner strength. "Also, I had more questions about the Haven Center. Can I come in?"

Dr. Thornton opens his door and silently waits while I step inside.

"What do you want to know?" he asks, leaning back in his chair. He has an aura of indifference, but his hands grip the pencil he's holding so hard his knuckles are turning white.

I drop the files on his desk and sink into the worn sofa as I try to figure out where to start. "I guess I just wonder what happened to make it shut down? I've been getting vague answers from everyone about funding. I don't understand how a place like that could stop getting funding."

He stares at me for a long moment. The stubble on his cheeks has grown since the last time I saw him, and he's got dark circles under his eyes.

Finally, he speaks. "I really don't know. I was away when it closed down. I was told that there was some mismanagement of funds or something along those lines. It was terrible for the community, but I didn't want to let it get in the way of my research or my commitment to the boys, so I stayed."

I nod, chewing my lip. "I know, it's just such a shame. Do you think maybe it would be worth trying to reopen it again?"

Dr. Thornton pinches the bridge of his nose. "I'm not sure,

Sienna. I know they've tried to open the Haven Center before, but it was unsuccessful."

"Bastian and his brothers told me about that," I say, trying to seem casual. "They said they had worked with Emily to reopen it but when she died, they just gave up on the dream."

"Yes. It was all very tragic," he agrees, sounding impatient. "I'm afraid that's all I know though. Is there anything else I can help you with?"

"They also told me what happened with you and Emily," I say, slowly standing up. "I don't understand why you didn't just tell me the truth."

Dr. Thornton flinches, hands shaking as he speaks. "Is that why you came here?" His eyes bore into mine, turning watery. "You think I don't regret the things I've done? I didn't want you to judge me before you knew the story. It was a mistake and I live every day knowing I was the reason that Emily ... took her life. Nothing can fix that."

"Are you sure about that?" I press, my voice tinged with desperation. "I know you miss them, and they miss you too. I can help you." I don't know why I'm pushing so hard to fix this, but I know I can't leave here until I try.

"I'm sorry, but there are some mistakes that can't be taken back," Dr. Thornton insists. He sighs and scrubs his face with his hand. "Sienna, you're a kind, compassionate girl but as psychologists, we know that seeing something like that changes a person inside."

"Sir, those boys are hurting more without you. They need their father back!" I don't understand why he can't see how much more he's hurting them by staying away. If he would just talk to them ...

Dr. Thornton's voice cracks as he wipes his eyes with a tissue, his words heavy with resignation. "There's nothing that can be done," he murmurs, the weight of his sorrow palpable in the air between us.

Frustration boils over. "Don't you care about them at all?" I ask, all but shouting now. Does he not want to fix things?

"Enough!" Dr. Thornton thunders. "You've overstepped. Please leave my office. I can't bear to talk about this any longer."

I grab my bag and flee, his words burrowing under my skin. My heart is heavy and my eyes start to sting. I know I'm about to cry, so I duck into the bathroom and let out a muffled sob into my fist.

"Fuck," I curse, my voice coming out ragged. A surge of frustration and helplessness washes over me, threatening to drown out my resolve. I've always been the fixer, the one who tries to mend broken things, but now I feel utterly powerless. How can I help when everything I do seems to make things worse?

Why does everything have to be so complicated? All I want to do is help my boys. They deserve to have their father back in their lives, but Dr. Thornton is so sure that there's nothing that can be done.

I don't understand what's changed. The first time we met, I remember him telling me how he'd do anything to fix what happened. Now he seems to think it's beyond fixing.

I sniffle and wipe my eyes, cleaning myself up so Caleb won't be suspicious when I come out. Dr. Thornton's story doesn't add up and I'm starting to think I need to do some more digging. Any father worth their salt would only care about seeing their children happy, and he knows it would make them happier to have him around.

If this situation was just about Emily, I would leave it alone, but I think there's something else going on. Every time I bring up the Haven Center, Dr. Thornton seems like he's avoiding giving me real information. I think that it must be connected in some way. I just don't know how yet.

Walking back out to the car, I spot Caleb leaning against the side of the Firebird, texting on his phone.

"Hey," I say, trying to pretend I haven't been crying. "I'm ready to go."

"Everything go alright with him?" Caleb asks.

"Yeah, it was fine. I just asked him some questions about his time working at the center," I say as I get into the car. "Nothing big."

"Let's go home," Caleb says. "Do you want to stop somewhere for dinner first?"

"Sure," I say, giving him a small smile. "Maybe we can go eat at the diner."

Caleb nods, pulling out of the parking lot. I'm glad he didn't pick up on my turbulent emotional state. I just can't handle trying to explain what's going on right now. When I brought up my concerns before, he brushed it aside, but I think he's too close to the situation.

Something is going on with Dr. Thornton and I intend to find out what it is.

39

BASTIAN

When we arrive home, I spot Sienna sitting on the couch staring off into space, as though lost in thought. The house is silent, save for the ticking of the clock above the TV set.

Caleb has been pacing the room and he turns when we walk inside, rushing up to greet us.

"How did it go today?" he asks, shifting his weight from one foot to another. Sometimes I forget just how young he still is, despite everything we've been through.

"It was fine," I say, bringing my hand down with a clap on the shoulder. "We should talk in the living room."

My phone starts ringing so I grab it as I hang up my jacket, watching Dominic and Caleb sit down with Sienna.

"Bastian," I answer.

"It's Nathaniel." Joe from the hardware store says, forgoing a greeting. "They got him."

My face instantly falls, and I feel as though someone just sucker-punched me in the gut.

"What?"

"It just happened. They cornered him when he was getting out of his car," he explains. "Annabeth and Beau are absolutely in pieces." A muscle in my jaw ticks and I clear my throat.

"I'll call you back once I've figured out how we're going to handle this," I tell him. Joe hangs up and I run a hand through my hair, shoulders tensing up. How am I going to tell the others?

A growl erupts from my throat. I should have taken care of this sooner. They warned us this was going to happen.

Marching into the living room, I slam my phone down on the coffee table, making everybody jump.

"Joe just called. The Serpents killed Nathaniel Brant. Beau's grandfather," I add for Sienna's benefit.

Sienna gasps, hands flying to her mouth. Caleb turns pale, gripping the sleeves of his jacket as he processes the news.

Dominic's mouth sets in a thin line. "Nathaniel was one of the old guard, an original Crimson Blade," he spits out. "They were sending a message by targeting him." He clenches his hands into fists, shaking with unbridled rage. "Let's go, we're doing this now."

"We can't," I tell him. "We've only just started implementing the plan. It's going to take more than what we've got now to go up against them."

Dominic's eyes darken. "They're not getting away with this!" he hisses.

"And they won't," I assure him. "We were going to talk about it anyway, so you might as well know that I've been recruiting, talking to people all around town about this, and a lot of them agree that they want to help us take the Serpents down once and for all."

"What does that mean?" Sienna asks, chewing on her fingernail, revealing her anxiety about all this.

"It means that the Crimson Blades are getting new members," Dominic speaks up. "We've got half a dozen people or more who are willing to join up with the Blades to take the Serpents down."

"I called the bank," I add. "Took out an equity loan on the house. We've put plans into place to get some of the cops back on our side, so they'll look the other way if it comes down to a full-scale fight. We also started stockpiling weapons."

Sienna's voice trembles as she speaks, worry etched on her face, "This sounds dangerous." Her fingers twist together and her knee bounces with restless energy.

"If there is, we haven't found it yet," I say, voice grim. "You don't have to stay if this is too much for you. I know you never signed up for this."

"I'm not going anywhere," Sienna says, crossing her arms. "You guys are too important to me."

"We should go check on Annabeth and Beau," Caleb speaks up, his tone almost eerily calm. His eyes are staring off in the distance and his shoulders are by his ears. "They need to know that we're here for them."

"I'll go with you." Sienna stands up.

I turn, holding out a hand. "I need you to stay here," I say, my eyes betraying the vulnerability inside. "Please? I need to know you're safe."

She seems to understand so she nods. "Okay," she says. "But I want to help."

"When I figure out what you can do, I'll tell you," I reassure her, reaching out to pull her into my chest for a tight embrace. My heart is racing, my mind in turmoil as I realize how serious things have become now.

"Be good," I tell her, leaning in for a kiss. She hugs me back and kisses me, then gives Dominic and Caleb a kiss as well before we head off.

I can't shake the tightness in my chest as we take the Firebird over to the Brant's place.

We went to school with Annabeth. She was in Dominic's grade, and she used to invite us over to her apartment complex on hot summer days, where we'd play together in the pool.

I think back to the memories I have of Nathaniel, and how he used to give us popsicles all day while we swam. He was a kind man, but fiercely protective. And now he's gone, leaving behind his daughter and his grandson.

My jaw clenches so tightly that I fear it might crack. "We need to rally everyone together," I say. "Reinstate the Crimson Blades, but as protectors this time. We've acted little better than thugs ourselves, lording over the community. It's time we become the protectors that the Blades were meant to be."

"We will," Dominic vows, eyes never leaving the road as he drives. His hands are clutching the steering wheel with a death grip. "And when we take down the Serpents, we keep it running, to make sure nothing like this ever happens again."

The sky is dark as we get out of the car, clouds covering the sun. The complex is teeming with officers still, and paramedics are taking away Nathaniel's covered body. A chill runs down my spine at the sight of him there, lifeless.

We approach their door, avoiding the cops lingering and talking to witnesses.

"Hey," I call out. Beau runs up to us and throws his arms around Dominic's waist.

"They're taking my grandpa away," he sobs. Dominic lifts him effortlessly, tucking him against his shoulder as he begins to walk and rub circles into the boy's back.

"How are you holding up?" I ask, coming to sit next to Annabeth on the couch. She looks up at me, face red and swollen from crying.

"I want you guys to get them." Her voice is hoarse as she stares me down, clenching her hands into fists. "I don't care how. They deserve to pay."

"We're going to," I tell her, reaching out to grasp her hands. "Annabeth, look at me. We're going to get those bastards, and we're going to kill the man who did this. We'll make sure that they never do anything like this again."

Her grip on my hands tightens as her shoulders shake. Tears fall from her eyes as I pull her into a hug. "Thank you, Bastian. Knew you guys would have my back."

"Your dad was a great man," I tell her. "We're gonna avenge him."

I spend a few minutes just calming her down while Dominic walks around with Beau. The cocky little boy that we know is gone, replaced with someone more quiet and subdued. It feels unnatural.

Out of the corner of my eye, I watch while Caleb walks around and talks to some of the cops in a low murmur. A few shake their heads, but he talks to one officer for a while before coming back over to me.

"I got intel," he says quietly as he passes by. "Let's get out of here. We can reconvene at Dave's."

"We gotta go, Bethy," I tell her, pulling away. "But I promise you, we're gonna take care of this."

"Thank you," she says again. "I'll let you guys know when the funeral will be and stuff. Just ... be safe, okay?"

I nod and the three of us take off again while making phone call after phone call on our way to the bar.

As we step into the bar, the air feels heavy with tension, the usual buzz of activity replaced by a somber silence. The neon signs flicker weakly, casting eerie shadows across the dimly lit room. The smell of stale beer and cigarette smoke hangs in the air, mingling with the palpable sense of apprehension.

I realize with shock just how much the community has been affected by the Serpents' presence when I see more than two dozen men and women standing around when we walk in.

"We came," Lora says, stepping forward. She's been working at the Quik-Mart since her son died a few years ago. She looks better than she has in a while, a fire in her eyes as she stands in front of me.

"Are you sure about this?" I ask. She nods, along with some of the others.

"We grew up under the regime of the old Serpent Syndicate," she says. "Some of us were kids when they were here last, and we remember what they did to us."

"They attacked my father's store," Jin Park says, his voice laced with venom. "It was only by sheer luck he was at the dentist that day. I want them to pay for destroying our livelihood."

I stand in front of the crowd. "We know we're asking a lot of you. The cops think we're already a gang of hoodlums, and this ain't gonna help. You'll have targets on your back now. If any of you want to back out, feel free to leave."

No one moves.

"You're not in this alone," Joe calls out. "I may not be as young as I once was, but I'm a tough old bastard. Their reign of terror ends now. Whatever you need from us, we'll do it."

"The Blades aren't just a gang," I say. "We're a family. And as a family, we protect our own and keep them safe." I produce a red bandana, holding it out for Jin Park.

"Take it," I order. "But remember, now that you're part of this, there ain't no turning back.

Jin accepts it, his fingers trembling slightly as he takes it in his grasp. With a determined nod, he ties it around his wrist, the red fabric standing out starkly against his skin.

The rest of the men and women present come forward and swear their loyalty to the Blades, each one getting a red bandana as well.

"The first thing on the list now that you guys are part of the crew is that we're officially declaring war on the Serpent Syndicate," I tell them. "They're public enemy number one. Any Serpents you see, don't hesitate to eliminate them."

With that, the group slowly begins to disband. Some exchange solemn nods, while others linger, their expressions a mix of determination and apprehension. Outside, the distant wail of sirens serves as a grim reminder of the dangers that lie ahead for us all.

"There's no going back now," I say, my arms crossed tightly over my chest as I fix my brothers with a steely gaze. "We're ready for war."

40

SIENNA

As I watch the boys leave, a knot forms in my belly. I can't help the mounting anxiety at the thought of the three of them confronting the Serpents again.

The stories of the boys' time at the Haven Center come back to mind right now. That place was a beacon of hope for them at one point. The presence of the center made a difference in the lives of the members of the community too, rebuilding what was lost after the fight with the Serpents.

Pulling out my phone, I start looking up more info about the center. Dr. Thornton's vague answers left me with more questions, and I want to get to the bottom of it. It's not just about uncovering the truth; it's about seeking justice for those who depended on the center's services and were let down by its demise.

Why haven't I looked into this myself yet? I should have done that instead of talking to Dr. Thornton since he didn't seem to know either. An article catches my eye and I start reading, my eyes widening as I scan the page.

"Misappropriated funds cause youth center to close?" I read out loud to myself. The article mentions the director, Lorna Hull, so I switch tabs and look her up, trying to see if I could contact her. She lives just on the outskirts of town, not that far away from here. If I leave now, I could talk with her before the boys get back.

My heart is pounding in my chest as I grab my keys and jacket and head out the door. It's dark outside, the chirping of crickets and the faint smell of a nearby bonfire permeating the air around me.

A faint whisper at the back of my mind wonders if there's more to Dr. Thornton's involvement than meets the eye. He was there when the center was open and when it closed down, and then he was involved when the plans to reopen the center were developed.

The urge to dig deeper spurs me on and I drive as fast as I can, praying the boys don't come home before I get back.

When I arrive, I look at the address again to confirm. She lives in a tiny, run-down apartment building next to a Quik-Mart.

The parking lot is cracked, weeds poking through the pavement. Trash litters the ground and when I inhale, I can smell stale cigarettes and urine.

Wrapping my jacket more tightly around my shoulders, I walk up the concrete steps of the building and knock insistently.

Lorna opens the door, her weary eyes meeting mine. She's a tall, slender woman with dark eyes and curly hair she's wearing in a bun. She's got on a hotel maid's uniform and she glares at me. "I don't want any magazines," she says, ready to close it.

"Miss Hull, I'm not here soliciting," I interject, blocking the door. "My name is Sienna Bennett. I'm working on a research project for Caspian Springs and I need to ask you some questions about the Haven Center."

"It's late," Lorna says, hand on her hip. "You need to talk to me right now?"

"It's kinda urgent," I insist. "I just need to ask you a few questions."

She relents, leaving the door open as she heads back inside. I follow, my heart pounding with anticipation. The spicy scent of curry permeates the air and my stomach growls, reminding me I skipped dinner to come here.

Jazz plays quietly in the background as she gestures for me to sit on her threadbare sofa.

"What do you want to know, Miss Bennett?" Lorna asks, her tone impatient.

"I read an article about the Haven Center's closure," I begin, the words tumbling out. "I couldn't help but wonder what really happened."

A shadow passes over her face. "It was a difficult time for all of us," she admits, her voice barely above a whisper. "We poured our hearts and souls into that place, only to have it torn away from us. Six months before we closed, grant money started going missing."

"Did the police investigate?" I ask.

She crosses one leg over another and leans forward. "The police don't usually care what happens in a town like Caspian Springs, but the whole thing became a federal issue when the board of directors discovered that millions of dollars disappeared into thin air."

I gasp and cover my mouth. "I can't imagine how hard it must have been for you," I say softly.

Lorna's gaze softens at the gesture, a faint smile tugging at the corners of her lips. "Thank you, Sienna," she says, her voice choked with emotion.

She stares at her lap. "I never got over it. When the police investigated, the money trail was hard to follow. It went in and out of the accounts of several of the staff members, including myself and the assistant director, but the money was never touched, so even though it looked like several of us were embezzling, they couldn't point the finger at any one of us."

I stare at her. "What? That's crazy. And they couldn't find where the money led?"

She shakes her head. "Nope. They closed the investigation at that point but the damage was done. The board of directors voted to shut everything down and I was fired for letting it happen."

"That's crazy! They blamed you even though you didn't touch the money?" I ask, my voice high with emotion.

"None of us did," Lorna says, voice rising as she squeezes her hands in her lap. "I trusted my staff. They would have *never* stolen that money."

"Who do you think stole it?" I ask. "Or what do you think happened?"

"I'm not sure, but I know that it wasn't any of the people who worked for the center."

I sit back, trying to wrap my mind around this. "So I told you I was doing a research project and that's true," I say. "I'm working for Dr. Richard Thornton," I tell her. "He worked at the Haven Center back in the day as well. Did you know him?"

Lorna's expression darkens. "Rich? Oh, I knew him," she says with a bitter laugh. "I never liked him. I can't believe he's still using the people of the community for his research. Or maybe I can."

"You didn't like him?" I ask, shocked. I wouldn't have thought he was the kind of person to rub anyone the wrong way. I guess I'm learning all kinds of new things about him.

"Nope," she says with a pop on the P. "He was way too eager to get involved in those kids' lives. I thought it crossed the line sometimes. We were supposed to be there for them, but there were boundaries in place and rules to follow. He thought that since he was a volunteer, the rules didn't apply to him."

"What do you mean?" I ask.

Lorna scoffs. "Well, he gave the kids money all the time. And he had his favorites. Everyone could see he preferred these three brothers the most and he spent all his free time with them."

"You don't think he was just trying to be there for them?"

"I think he picked the kids who were the most vulnerable. I never liked him using kids in his research. Never sat right with me. It felt exploitative, not helpful. He wasn't there to change those kids' lives, he was there to use them to make a name for himself."

I blink, taking it all in. "So you think he wasn't there to give back then? You don't think he made a difference in their lives with his research?"

"He certainly thinks he made a difference," Lorna says with a scoff. "He had an ego the size of a planet, even when he was just an undergrad volunteer. It got worse when he became a counseling intern. I think he thought of himself as some kind of savior to the kids."

Hearing her opinion of Dr. Thornton feels like it's starting to fill in the missing pieces of the puzzle. "What about the funding issue? Was he ever a suspect in the whole thing?"

Lorna sighs and shakes her head. "As much as I'd love to blame him, he wasn't even around when it was happening. He had to leave for a while to take care of his uncle who got sick. When the police were investigating, his uncle had just died so they ruled him out."

I nod and tap my fingers against my knee, ruminating on this information. I can't believe I was naive enough to think that Dr. Thornton was innocent. Now I'm convinced he's involved in the center closing.

Something occurs to me and I look up. "Where did his uncle live?"

"Few hours away. Why?"

"No reason," I say, waving a hand.

Something about all this isn't adding up. Dr. Thornton mentioned he inherited the manor home from a relative, but if his uncle lived hours away, why would he have a home here?

"Thank you for your time," I add, realizing I've gone quiet for too long. "I'm going to go now. You answered all my questions."

"I hope you find what you're looking for," Lorna says, standing up to walk me to the door. "Can I ask what you're trying to find out?"

"I'm not sure yet," I tell her. "But I'll let you know when I do."

Taking off, I drive back home, hoping the boys haven't come back yet. The Firebird isn't there when I pull up, so I breathe a sigh of relief.

Lorna's words replay in my mind, casting a shadow of doubt over everything I thought I knew. The pieces of the puzzle are starting to fit together, but one crucial piece remains elusive: Dr. Thornton's true involvement.

The more I learn, the more questions arise, and a sinking feeling settles in my chest. What if Dr. Thornton isn't who he claims to be?

What if his connection to the Haven Center's closure runs deeper than anyone suspects?

As I pull into the driveway, I'm torn between confronting Dr. Thornton or sharing what I've learned with the boys. The thought of shattering their illusion even further brings an ache to my chest. I can't do that to them, can I?

41

DOMINIC

I wake to the suffocating weight of bodies pressing against me. Sienna insisted I join her and Bastian in his bed last night. Now, as I blink away sleep, it feels too crowded, too much. I have to get up.

Sienna stirs beside me, her breathing shallow and uneven. She slept poorly, tossing and turning all night, clearly struggling with the looming presence of the upcoming conflict. She's trying to be strong, but her fear is palpable, the anxiety radiating off of her even in her sleep.

Checking my phone, I see a text from Caleb. He's gone for a morning run, promising to be back soon. His absence is keenly felt, a silent reminder of the impending storm gathering on the horizon.

Bastian's voice breaks the uneasy silence, his words carrying the weight of our shared burden. "We need to figure out who's going to stay with Sienna," he says, his tone clipped.

My chest tightens with a surge of protectiveness. "What do you mean?" I ask softly, trying to keep my voice low to avoid waking Sienna.

"When the fight happens, one of us needs to stay behind with her," he says, staring at the blankets. "They already tried to use her against us once before. If we leave her here alone during the fight, we leave her vulnerable."

"I'll stay," I offer. "Sienna will be safe with me."

"You can't," Bastian says, frowning as he looks up at me. "You're too important. I think me or Caleb should stay."

"Bas, you're the leader here. You can't stay behind," I point out.

"If it means protecting her, then I'll stay," he insists. "She means everything to me, to us. I can't let her be here alone."

"We can't afford to lose you from this fight," I tell him, slipping out of the bed. If this is going to turn into an argument, I don't want to wake Sienna. "You're too valuable as our leader."

Bastian follows me, stuffing his feet into slippers. "Maybe Caleb should stay behind then," he suggests. "He'd be the best one to leave with her. He's smart and quick-thinking. He knows how to get out of tough situations. If we leave him with Sienna, he can protect her more than just physically."

"That's a good point," I say as we head down the stairs. I walk over to the coffee maker and turn it on, needing the ritual to soothe my agitation. "But just so you're aware, it won't be an easy sell. Caleb won't want to be left behind."

"We'll have to talk to him when he returns," Bastian says, shrugging. Sitting down at the table, he sighs. "I gotta call Sal soon. He and Tommy are on patrol right now, keeping an eye out for the Serpents."

A beam of sunlight streams through the kitchen window, casting shadows across Bastian as he checks his phone. I can't help but notice the worry lines on his face, the tension in his shoulders. He's been trying to hold everything at bay for so long by himself, but we're not alone anymore.

"It's been a lot easier since we let other people join in," I say, handing him a cup of coffee. "I know you were against it before, but it feels like it was the right call to make."

Bastian takes it, inhaling the rich aroma of the dark roast I'd selected. "I only said that because I didn't want things to be like they were when we were little. I thought that if the Crimson Blades were big again, we'd just attract trouble. But I was wrong, I shouldn't have fought so hard to keep it to just the three of us." He rolls his shoulders back, as though preparing himself for the coming conflict.

"I wish you'd let us help you carry some of that weight," I tell him, reaching out and laying a hand on his shoulder. He's always tried so hard to be the leader, even as kids. I felt like it was my job to roll with his decisions just so I could protect him from the consequences.

"You're one to talk," Bastian says, scoffing. "You put yourself in the role of our protector a long time ago and you've let it define you ever since. Like the bike shop," he points out. "You never wanted it. That was just a backup plan after the plans for the center fell through."

"You put the dream on hold too," I point out, putting it back on him. "Whether you admit it or not, the center was just as much your dream."

"Maybe we should think about revisiting that dream then," Bastian says, looking out the window as Caleb comes jogging back up the steps. "We can talk about it later though. Right now we need to convince Caleb to stay behind with Sienna."

"Absolutely not," Caleb says as soon as we tell him what we came up with. "I'm not staying here to look after Sienna. She will be fine in the house, but I can't watch your backs from here."

"I don't want Sienna left alone," Bastian argues. "If we leave her alone, she's vulnerable." His face is growing red, a sure sign that he's growing impatient with Caleb's defiance.

"But you guys are vulnerable without me there to fight alongside you," Caleb says, clenching his hands into fists. "You can't deny that we work better as a team when it's all three of us."

"Be that as it may, you're staying here and that's final," Bastian snaps.

"Bas, you know you can't order him around like that," I tell him, playing peacemaker once again. "I know you want him to stay behind to protect him, but this is as much his fight as it is any of ours. I'll stay behind if it means that much to you."

Bastian looks thunderous. "No! You're our best fighter. I'm sorry that we need you, but we do. We haven't got half a shot without you there."

"Then what are we going to do?" I ask, feeling as though we're out of options. "We're at an impasse. Do we stay behind to protect Sienna or not?"

"Maybe we can draw straws," Caleb suggests. "If we leave it to chance, then it's equally fair."

"I don't like this," Bastian grumbles. "If we don't figure this out soon, we're liable to argue about this all day." He looks down at his phone, cursing. "Shit. It's Sal. He's calling me, which means that something is going down."

"Bastian," he says, putting Sal on speakerphone so we can all hear.

"Boss, they're coming," Sal's voice echoes through the speaker. "The Serpent Syndicate are about to march on the town unless we agree to meet with them and settle this once and for all. Joe heard from Lin Park that the Serpents know we've declared war on them, and they're coming to face us."

The three of us stare at each other for a moment, the dawning realization that the fight is inevitable now, that it's happening and there's nothing we can do to stop it.

"What are their numbers?" I ask, leaning in. "We need to know what we're up against."

"Lin Park thinks he saw between thirty and forty," Sal says. "That's more than we've got."

"We can take them." I clench my fists. "There's enough of us now. And we have what we need."

"Are you sure we have enough?" Caleb asks, chewing his lip as he glances around the room.

I take a deep breath and nod. "We have more than enough. We're ready."

"Who's going to stay with Sienna then?" Bastian demands, standing up. "One of us has to stay behind."

"It's too late now," Caleb insists. "They're here. There's no more time to argue. All of us go or none of us go. Sienna will be safe here, I promise."

"Fine." Bastian runs a hand through his hair, a nervous tick when he's stressed. "We can't spend all day arguing, let's just fucking go then."

"How do you want to do this?" I ask.

"Sal, you still there?" Bastian calls.

"Here, boss," Sal says.

"Send a messenger to the Serpents. We're meeting them at the old auto plant on the edge of town. Tell 'em one hour. Then get everyone there."

"On it," Sal says, before hanging up.

Bastian turns to face us. "It's now or never," he says. "Let's go get the weapons. We'll load 'em up in the Firebird's trunk and head out."

We follow Bastian out the door, too focused on the mission to say goodbye to Sienna. I think none of us want to say goodbye anyway, for fear of the goodbye being permanent.

The bike shop's air is thick with dust and the faint smell of motor oil. Sunlight filters through grimy windows, contrasting with the somber mood inside. Bastian, Caleb, and I move quickly as we start loading the weapons into the Firebird.

"Pass me that crate, Dom," Caleb grunts, wiping sweat from his brow.

I nod, grabbing a heavy wooden crate. The rough texture of the wooden handles grounds me amidst the chaos. With a heave, I carry it towards the Firebird.

Metal clangs against metal as we load the crates into the trunk, punctuating the tense silence between us. Outside, traffic hums in the distance, contrasting with the quiet intensity inside. The sunlight streams through the windows, casting eerie shadows.

"We're gonna need more ammo," Bastian mutters, his jaw set in determination.

"Yeah, we can't risk running out," Caleb agrees, his expression grim.

"We have a stash of weapons in the office," I say, boots making soft thuds on the shop floor as I head inside the tiny room, reaching under the rickety metal desk to pull out a box of street weapons.

Lugging it back out, I show it to Bastian. "Had some of the neighborhood kids bring me their baseball bats and shit, stuff that we can use as makeshift weapons. Hell, I think there's a Skip-it in here somewhere."

"That thing will clock someone in the face nicely," Bastian agrees, sticking the box in the backseat.

As we close the trunk, the weight of responsibility settles on my shoulders. With a final glance around the shop, we prepare for the battle ahead, knowing our town's fate hangs in the balance.

"Let's go kick some Serpent ass," Bastian says, narrowing his eyes and squaring his jaw. We take off, heading into the unknown.

42

SIENNA

I wake in an empty bed, the chill enveloping me as I come to. The boys are downstairs and I hear them arguing about something. Creeping to the edge of the staircase, I move as quietly as I can to hear what they're saying.

The conversation gets louder when Bastian takes a call and I hear someone on the other end, telling them that the Serpents are on their way into town, spoiling for a fight. Anxiety spikes inside me, realizing that the storm that's been brewing has finally come.

"Who's going to stay with Sienna then?" Bastian yells. "One of us has to stay behind."

My hand flies to my mouth, trying to contain my gasp. They're arguing about who has to stay with me. I don't know if I should say something, but I realize that even if I did, it would be useless. I can't stop them from going, and I can't change their minds.

The only thing I can do is protect them in the only way I know how. I have to confront Dr. Thornton and find out the truth, once and for all. I know he was involved with the closing of the Haven Center, I just can't figure out how, or why.

But those boys suffered enough losing Emily, I won't have them longing for what could have been with a man who might have done something terrible.

Now is the best time to go talk to him. The boys are busy with their fight and talking to Dr. Thornton would keep my mind off of worrying about them. I should go now, while they're distracted from arguing over who's going to stay with me.

I quickly get dressed and sneak down the stairs again, holding my breath as I pass the kitchen. They don't notice me, too busy discussing the situation.

Grabbing my keys from the holder by the front door, I slip out and race over to my car, taking off before they can notice I'm gone.

I leave my phone on silent, praying that the boys won't know I'm gone. I just need to talk to Dr. Thornton and get some answers, if not for my own curiosity, then for the sake of Bastian, Dominic, and Caleb.

It's too early for him to be at the school so I decide to go to his house, hoping to catch him before he can leave. When I pull up, I notice his car is still in the driveway.

Steeling myself, I head up to his house. The porch is cast in shadows and I raise my hand, ringing the bell with a shaking finger.

Dr. Thornton answers the door, confusion on his face. "What are you doing here, Sienna?" he asks.

"I need to talk to you," I say, fidgeting with my fingers. "Can I come in?"

Dr. Thornton glances around then pushes the door open and waves a hand for me to enter. "Fine, but make it quick. I've got class soon."

"I'll be brief," I tell him. "I just needed to ask you some questions. I went and talked to Lorna Hull yesterday, the former director of the Haven Center. She told me some things about you."

Dr. Thornton lets out a barking laugh. "Lorna?" he asks. "She never liked me. She was strongly opposed to using psychology to help the children heal from their trauma. I think she had it out for me because I was young and I had big ideas for how to help the kids."

"That's not exactly the story she told me," I say, crossing my arms.

"She said you were exploiting the kids in your research. That you used them to make a name for yourself. I don't understand why you'd do that. Your work could have stood on its own."

"Sienna, I don't know what you've gotten yourself mixed up in, but I can help you. I think you've spent too much time with the Ravenwood boys. Your view of me is colored by their experience. I know you want to protect them from what I did, but the best way to protect them is to leave the past in the past."

Doubt gnaws at the edges of my mind. Have I been too hasty in judging him? But then I remember what Lorna said about him being so self-important. Is he manipulating me like he did the boys?

"You know, I used to think you were completely brilliant," I tell him, staring at him with a mix of pity and disdain. "I looked up to you and after I read your book in high school, all I wanted was to study under you."

"That's very flattering but I don't ..."

"And now I think that you should have told me from the start that you slept with Emily," I say, my voice steady but firm. "Because now I don't trust you. And now I think that maybe there's more you aren't telling me."

I raise my eyebrows. "Like how the grant money went missing around the same time you left to care for your dying uncle. But then you showed back up with this house."

"I told you it was an inheritance," Dr. Thornton says, jutting his chin out. "I never lied about that."

"Funny," I say, stepping forward. "Lorna said your uncle lived hours away from here. So why would your uncle have a house conveniently located so close to the university?"

"It wasn't directly inherited. I used the money from my inheritance to purchase the house," Dr. Thornton says, stepping backward. "You can understand why I wouldn't go around telling people all the details."

"I think that you always have an answer for every question I throw at you," I tell him. "Like the necklace. If you rejected Emily, why would she give you her necklace?"

"Sienna, please, you have to understand that Emily was in a very fragile state of mind when she gave it to me," he says, his tone pleading.

I take a step forward, invading his personal space. "Then why didn't you give it to the boys? They would have cherished a keepsake from her like that. You could have reached out and given it to them, but you didn't. You never wanted to mend the relationship with them, even when I threw you a lifeline."

"How could I forgive myself for what I did to them?" he cries out, raising his hands in frustration. "You're accusing an old man of doing something sinister, but you have no proof, only speculation."

"I wonder what would happen if I look into *your* financial records," I say. "Maybe the police would be interested to know you bought this place shortly after the center closed."

"Sienna, I'm warning you. Leave this alone," he says, eyes full of tears. "You don't know what you're talking about."

"I think you're full of it," I spit out. "You've lied to me from day one."

"Sienna," Dr. Thornton says, a warning note in his voice. "Stop now."

"I'm not leaving until you tell me the truth!"

Dr. Thornton's expression darkens, and in a swift motion, he lunges towards me. I scream, throwing my hands up but his hands wrap around my throat.

Pain hits immediately, followed by panic as I grab for his hands, and pull, trying to get him off of me. When that doesn't work, I throw my body weight forward.

If I was ever grateful for being plus-sized, it's now, as I shove him backward into a nearby wall, knocking off several pictures with a loud bang.

Spots start popping up at the edges of my vision as we wrestle for control and I push him into the wall as hard as I can, knocking his head against a framed photo. Glass shatters and sprays around us and he shrieks, dropping his hands from my neck to check on his head.

I pivot to flee, but before I can escape, his hand snatches my ankle, sending me crashing to the ground. I scramble for purchase on the oriental rug in front of me, desperate to get away.

My heart pounds in my chest like a drum as I grapple with Dr. Thornton in the middle of the living room. The rough texture of the rug scrapes against my skin as I thrash beneath him, my breath coming in ragged gasps. I can taste the metallic tang of fear on my tongue, the adrenaline coursing through my veins as I fight for my life.

He's stronger than he looks, hauling me backward by my foot and pinning me underneath him. I stare into his eyes, the mask finally slipping away as he stares back. He looks deranged, face red, eyes manic.

Kicking out, I knock him backward into a side table, knickknacks tumbling down around us. I roll out of the way, but he manages to lurch forward and pins me in place with his body.

"You're not going anywhere," he snarls. I throw my hands up but the last thing I see is a heavy, marble statuette coming towards me.

Pain explodes behind my skull and the world goes black.

I come awake in stages.

Head throbbing with pain, I blink awake, reaching up to touch it.

But as I reach out, I find my hands bound together with thick duct tape. Panic surges through me as I realize I can't move a muscle. My heart races as I frantically search around me to figure out where I am.

The darkness is suffocating, pressing in on me from all sides. I can barely see my own hand in front of my face, and the silence is deafening.

But the muffled roar of an engine interrupts the silence and my stomach lurches with dread as I realize where I am. Memories flood back in a rush—Dr. Thornton's house, the confrontation, the struggle. He attacked me, tried to kill me, and now I'm tied up in a dark place.

I strain against my bindings, desperate to escape, but it's futile. The tape holds firm, cutting into my skin with every attempt to free myself. Fear grips me as I think about what Dr. Thornton might do to me, and where he might be taking me.

Without warning, the car slows to a stop, the engine's noises fading into silence.

My breath catches in my throat as I hear the faint sound of footsteps approaching from outside. Dread washes over me in waves as I realize with chilling clarity where I am and what awaits me.

Dr. Thornton is going to kill me, and no one can save me.

43

CALEB

As we approach the abandoned auto plant, my heart races with anticipation and fear. The sun beats down relentlessly, casting harsh shadows on the gravel beneath our feet.

"We brought weapons," Bastian reveals to the assembled Blades. "Guns, ammo, knives, anything you could want. Take your pick."

"We need to get a move on," Dominic urges. "The Serpents are already on their way. We need to get to the warehouse so we have the advantage. There's plenty of places to use as cover in there, and the Serpents are going to fight vicious, and fight dirty."

"Let's go," I say, walking back to the car and popping the trunk. Gleaming metal winks up at us and I reach in and grab a gun. It's going to be a rough day and I'm starting to realize that I might not survive.

Just as the fear rises, so does a sense of resolve. This is bigger than me now, this is not just about the Serpents versus the Blades. This is about how we've been screwed out of so much in our lives, and the Serpents aren't going to take anything else away from us.

"Whatever happens, I'm glad to have fought beside you," Bastian says quietly to me and Dominic. "Now let's go show them what the Blades are made of."

Bastian's determination is palpable as he addresses the group, rallying us for the fight ahead. But amidst his words of encouragement, I can't shake the knot of fear tightening in my chest. This isn't just another skirmish; it's a battle for our lives and our freedom.

Memories of past struggles flood my mind. But amidst the turmoil, a sense of determination takes hold. This fight is bigger than us—it's about justice, retribution, reclaiming what's rightfully ours.

Dozens of engines roar at once, and tires squeal on the gravel, announcing the Serpents' arrival.

Each Blade stands together in a line, making a tight formation as we face off against the people who have made our lives hell for too long.

"Last chance to back down!" Diego calls as he gets off his bike. He pulls off his helmet and his wide smirk is visible from where I'm standing.

With a nod to my brothers, I steel myself for the battle ahead. The weight of the gun in my hand is a reminder of the stakes, but I refuse to cower to these bastards. We've come too far to let the Serpents win now.

"Crimson Blades never back down," Bastian hisses through clenched teeth, hands balled into fists.

"If it's a war you want, it's a war you've got," Diego says with a shrug. "Kill them all," he orders.

The world erupts into chaos as I scramble, rushing to duck behind a stack of pallets with my gun, peeking out and taking aim at the first Serpent I see.

He goes down with a scream, but I spot another pointing their gun at me and I have to duck to avoid being blasted.

Gunshots whizz through the air around me as people start fighting. Serpents clash with Blades, some going hand-to-hand while others choose to position themselves strategically and hunt down the enemy as they come.

I'm running on pure adrenaline now, trying to keep myself alive while showing the Serpent Syndicate that the Crimson Blades won't go quietly into that good night.

A Serpent comes at me, running as they fire shots, forcing me to retreat into the warehouse. Inside it's dimly lit, the only light streaming in through cracks in the grimy, boarded-up windows. The dirty concrete floor is covered in a layer of dust, making me cough as I push a stack of tires over in my wake.

The man following me trips and stumbles over the tires, crashing to the ground. I throw myself at him, wrestling for control of his gun and when I get it, I smack him in the face with it before doubling back around to the pallets outside again.

He doesn't follow me, so I consider that a win. I need to be strategic about this, and smart. I'm not as good a fighter as Dominic, and I don't have the gun skills that Bastian has. If I'm going to fight, I'm going to have to play dirty.

"You can't hide forever, little boy!" A crowing voice taunts as they take aim at my head. I barely duck behind the wooden stack in time as a bullet goes flying past me, burying itself into the brick wall of the plant's warehouse.

"Listen," I call out. "You need to aim a little to the left next time. You'll get there!" I'm taunting him, psychologically playing with him to keep him off-balance.

"Shut up!" he screams, shooting again. This time I'm prepared so when I tuck and roll, I'm out of the way of the bullet that lands right where I was hiding.

Serpents and Blades alike are falling left and right around us as we continue the fight. I run low to the ground towards an abandoned half-finished car as more bullets spray the air above my head, the acrid scent of gunsmoke hanging heavy in the air.

Someone screeches out, "I'll kill you!" and when I whirl around, Sal and I come face to face, guns pointed at each other. We lower our weapons immediately.

"Serpent to your four o'clock," Sal hisses. I duck as he fires off a shot, taking the approaching Serpent out at the knee.

"Good shot," I compliment him, feeling sweat trickle down my back in the sun. He nods and we turn back-to-back, an unspoken agreement to watch out for each other as we use the same hiding place for leverage.

"How do they have so many members now?" Sal yells over the noise of the fight. "They were run out of town when I was a teenager, they had nothing left!"

"I have no idea!" I yell back. "We've been wondering the same thing!"

I shoot at another approaching Serpent, missing him by a few inches. He continues approaching and I know I'm going to run out of ammo if I don't reload soon so I shove the gun in my waistband, pulling out a set of brass knuckles from my pocket and slipping them on. My heart pounds, adrenaline fueling it as I stand up.

"I've gotta go," I tell Sal. "I need more ammo."

"Be safe out there," he says, giving me a curt nod as I start making my way through the makeshift battlefield.

Racing past rows of half-finished cars, I weave between stacks of wooden pallets as I try to get back to the Firebird, screams of the dead and dying echoing around me.

Dom is currently wrestling with a Serpent on the ground as I fly past, beating the man's face with the butt of his gun. I push my anxieties to the side, reminding myself that Dominic is a great fighter and that I don't need to worry about him.

A Serpent flies out from around the side of the building, smacking me in the side with a baseball bat. I let out a grunt of pain and double over. He tries to attack me again but this time I grab the top of the bat as he swings and wrench it away. He goes running and I throw the bat to the side, continuing on towards the car.

Finally, I reach the Firebird but a Serpent pops out from behind a nearby bike, making me jump. He screeches and rushes at me but I throw a punch, landing it straight in his face. The brass knuckles make a crunch as they connect, the man falling down as blood begins to pour from his nose.

He screams and thrashes and I fall on top of him, beating him until he goes limp. Pulling back, I wipe my face, smearing blood across it as I stagger off of him and limp towards the car. I need a second to breathe after that hit to my ribcage.

Panting hard, I load more bullets into my gun and turn around, ready to fight some more when I realize that Bastian and Diego are grappling together nearby, Diego trying to pull the trigger on his gun to shoot Bastian in the stomach.

Blood pounds in my ears as I rush over and stand above them, aiming my gun at Diego's head.

"You move and I shoot!" I tell him. Dominic races over with his own gun and joins us.

"It's over, Diego!" he yells.

Diego throws another punch at Bastian, who blocks it, twisting his arm behind his back. He forces Diego to his knees, and Dom and I keep our guns trained on the Serpent's leader.

"Drop the weapon!" Dominic thunders. Diego holds his hand out, letting the gun dangle from his grip before it clatters to the ground.

All around us, the fighting starts to slow to a stop as the Serpents realize their leader is on his knees in front of us.

"Kill him," Bastian says, spitting out a mouthful of blood. He wipes his brow, a sneer on his face. "Go ahead, Dom. Shoot the bastard."

"Wait!" Diego yells. "I have information!"

"We're not interested," I scoff.

"You'll want to know this," he insists, looking at Dominic. "It's about Dr. Richard Thornton."

"Rich?" I raise an eyebrow. "How do you even know him?"

"I know you guys were close to him," he says, a smile curling on his lips. "Let me go and I'll tell you what you want to know."

"How about you tell us first, then we'll decide if the info is worth sparing your pathetic life?" Bastian says, eyes flashing dangerously.

"Fuck you," Diego curses.

I cock my gun and Diego yells out again, "Wait! Fine. Dr. Thornton was paying us!"

The three of us freeze, looking at each other as Diego continues. "He paid us a lot of money to cover up a crime about two years ago. That's how we had the resources to go after this territory again. He's been giving us money. If you want to go after anyone, go after him. We're just his pawns."

"Nice try," Bastian says. "You're lying."

"I ain't lying, bro," Diego insists. "Ask him yourselves. He came to me two years ago or so, looking for help. Said he did something, and he needed our help to get away with it. Told me he'd pay me enough money to do whatever I wanted if we helped him."

As Diego's revelation about Dr. Thornton sinks in, a whirlwind of emotions overtakes me. Disbelief, anger, and profound sorrow collide within me, threatening to consume me from the inside out.

The image of Emily's face flashes before my eyes, her laughter echoing in my mind. She died two years ago.

Rich came to them two years ago to cover up a crime.

Bastian's cry of denial echoes in the air, mirroring the turmoil raging within me.

As the reality of Dr. Thornton's betrayal settles in, I feel a profound sense of loss wash over me. The foundation of trust that we built our lives on has crumbled, leaving behind a gaping void of betrayal and heartache.

"Rich killed Emily ..." I say, the pieces finally falling into place. "He killed her and covered it up!"

Dominic's brow furrows, his eyes flickering with conflicted emotions. I can see the internal struggle etched on his face, torn between his sense of justice and the desire for retribution. His clenched fists betray the intensity of his emotions, the decision weighing heavily upon him.

My heart aches with grief for Emily, but a voice reminds me she wouldn't have wanted this, she wouldn't have wanted the bloodshed. Before I can voice my concerns, the decision is made for me.

"Kill him," Bastian says, cold fury radiating from every pore.

Dominic and I raise our guns and pull the triggers, emptying them into the filthy bastard until he flops over, blood pooling beneath him.

"It's over," Bastian says, turning to face the remaining Serpents. "Your leader is dead. Surrender now or face the same fate."

The Serpents slowly raise their hands in surrender one by one. I breathe hard, feeling the sting of tears in my eyes as I come to grips with what I've just found out.

The woman we loved is dead, at the hands of the man we once considered a father.

44

SIENNA

The trunk pops open and sunlight temporarily blinds me. The figure in front of me is lit from behind, casting an eerie glow and obscuring their features until Dr. Thornton's face gets closer, revealing himself as he bends down and yanks me up by my wrists.

"Come on," he growls, pulling me to my feet. I try to struggle but he pulls out a gun from behind his back, pointing it straight at me.

Fear and adrenaline course through me as I walk, unsteady from our fight and the blow to the head I received, but he nudges me forward with the barrel of the gun to my back as I walk over overgrown grass and leaves.

The building we're at is some kind of old fire station, converted into an apartment. The place looks abandoned though, devoid of any of the usual signs of life, and the garden is overrun with weeds.

My face is wet with tears and snot as I put one foot in front of the other, trying my best to keep my wits about me as Dr. Thornton shoves me through the creaking front door.

Once inside, he keeps making me walk until we head up the steps and into a rundown loft apartment. It looks as though the owner abandoned it in a hurry, leaving everything behind.

A photo on the console table by the front door catches my eye and I let out a muffled scream when I realize it's a picture of Emily with the Ravenwood boys.

Turning back to Dr. Thornton, I stare at him and he nods. "This is Emily's old place," he confirms.

There's no light in here, and no heat so it's cold and a shiver shoots down my spine. The place looks eerie, like Emily left for a while but she's still coming back. A cozy blanket is still draped over the back of a gray chenille couch. A stack of books is still on the black wood and glass coffee table.

Dawning horror washes over me as I realize that Dr. Thornton is completely and totally insane. This man is nothing like the person I thought he was.

He forces me to sit down in a striped, overstuffed armchair and pulls the gag down, the musty smell of the place overpowering me.

"I suppose you want to know why I brought you here?" he asks, pushing his glasses up on his nose. He steps back, gun pointing towards me as he walks over to the TV stand, picking up another photo. This one is Dr. Thornton with younger versions of Bastian, Dominic, and Caleb.

"I thought it fitting for you to find out my story in the same place that Emily found out," he says, setting the photo back down. "After all, she's the center of it all, isn't she? That's why you kept digging."

I stay silent, staring at him with wide eyes.

"Emily never fully trusted me," he says, floorboards creaking under his feet as he paces. "She asked me all kinds of questions about my time with the boys and started digging around in my past. She looked into the financial records of the Haven Center like you did, but she didn't stop there. She played detective and looked into my own financial records, realizing that I had bought the house at the same time that the Haven Center's funding went missing."

My heart races, breath hitching as I realize I was right. Dr. Thornton did have something to do with the missing money.

"Why?" I ask, my voice hoarse.

"She wanted to know the same thing," Dr. Thornton says, scratching the back of his head with the gun. "So I told her the truth."

He sighs and shakes his head, a bitter tinge to his voice as he continues, "The committee funding my research at the Haven Center had decided to pull my funding. They claimed my work was exploitative instead of helping the children."

He clenches his hands into fists for a moment, then relaxes them. "My knowledge in psychology came in very helpful at that point," he says, reaching down to bring my chin up with a finger. I jerk my head away and he chuckles. "I manipulated the senior staff at the center into giving me the information I needed to access the finances."

He's insane, I think to myself.

"It was surprisingly easy to get them to reveal enough about themselves to hack into the accounts. Over the course of six months, I funneled money from the Center to my own account, but I was very careful not to leave a trail pointing directly to me."

"How could you?" I spit out. "How could you take money away from those kids?"

"How could they shut down my funding!" Dr. Thornton roars. "Years of research, down the tubes. All that time I spent working with those kids, gaining their trust to use for my research, it wasn't fair! I deserved that money."

Lorna was wrong about Rich. He didn't fancy himself a savior to those kids, he thought of them as nothing more than lab rats. I curl my lip, my stomach churning in fear and disgust.

"Just before the police started investigating, I left, claiming that my uncle was sick. It wasn't long before the police came but they ruled me out as a suspect since I wasn't there."

"The police couldn't track the money trail?" I ask. "How?"

"I had the senior staff's personal information. I used the things I knew about them to hack their own accounts and transferred the money to a shell corporation. The trail ended there because the shell corporation wasn't connected to me in any way. They couldn't figure out who it led to."

"I just don't understand why you went through all that trouble to steal money," I say, my voice wavering. "You had everything. You had a family who cared about you. Don't you care about those boys at all?"

Dr. Thornton sits across from me on the couch and clicks his tongue. For a fleeting moment, I catch a glimpse of something behind Dr. Thornton's eyes—a hint of insecurity, a shadow of doubt. It's gone in an instant, masked by his facade of control, but it lingers in the air like a ghost of his true self. "Oh, probably not," he admits. "I don't really feel anything for anybody, to be frank. You could probably diagnose me with psychopathy."

The fact that he could so casually sit there and reveal that to me is bone-chilling. Anger floods me. All that time with the Ravenwood boys and they meant nothing to him? They thought of him as family, and he threw it all away for his own selfish gain?

I have to choke back the bile that rises in my throat.

"When Emily discovered the truth," he continues. "I knew she had to go. There was no way I could let her take everything away after I worked so hard to get it. So, I came here and I killed her. Made it look like a suicide."

Even though I'd already guessed the truth, my blood runs cold. How could I have been so blind? Anger simmers beneath the surface, but it's overshadowed by a profound sense of betrayal.

"And I'm going to do the same to you, sweetheart," he adds, standing up and walking over to caress my cheek with the barrel of the gun. I yank my head away but he presses it to my cheek. "Won't it be a poetic touch? Having you kill yourself in the same place that Emily did?"

"How are you going to make the boys believe that I killed myself?" I ask, adrenaline pumping through me as I try to keep him talking. I have to do whatever it takes to keep him talking. "They'd never believe that I wanted to die."

"You're surprisingly hard to kill," he admits. "I believe the Ravenwoods might love you more than they loved Emily. I tried to get that local gang to take you out, but they seem to have rescued you."

I gasp, the revelation sending shivers down my spine. "You sent the Serpents after me?" I ask, voice high. The fact that the betrayal goes back that far shouldn't surprise me, but it does.

"Who do you think helped me cover up Emily's death?" he asks, a smirk on his face. "For the right price, they made it look like a suicide and I was off the hook."

Tears sting my cheeks and I grip the arms of the chair so tightly, my knuckles are white. Nausea rises at his utter callousness. The man before me is nothing but a monster, capable of unspeakable cruelty without a shred of remorse.

"Now," he whispers menacingly, ripping the duct tape from my wrists and pushing the gun into my hands. "You're going to take this and you're going to put it here," he moves my hand up so the gun is now pressed into my temple.

My hands tremble uncontrollably, each heartbeat echoing in my ears like a drumbeat of impending doom. Nausea churns in the pit of my stomach, threatening to overwhelm me.

"That's a good girl," he coos, bastardizing the Ravenwoods' praise. "You're going to pull the trigger on my signal."

"What if I don't?" I demand, trying to pull my hand away. "What if I stop you?"

"You could try," he says, tone far too calm. "But if you don't cooperate, I'll call up the Serpents and give them the orders to kill each of your precious Ravenwood boys, one by one in front of you."

He puts my finger on the trigger, the metallic click of the hammer as he pulls it back echoing through the silent space.

My throat tightens in despair at the thought of letting anything happen to my boys. I have the strength to go through with this. I can't let him hurt them. The thought of losing them ignites a fierce determination within me.

Memories of the Ravenwood boys flood my mind. Heated gasps in the darkness, warm hands on cold days, sharing meals, sharing our lives, the laughter and the joy ... I love them.

I have to protect them. Even if it means my own death.

My entire body trembles as I try to calm myself down.

"Do it," he hisses. "Pull the trigger."
He steps back, waiting.

45

BASTIAN

A bitter taste fills my mouth as I grapple with the weight of Rich's treachery. The familial relationship we shared with him now feels like a cruel mockery, a joke played at our expense. How long has he been like this? A man who wouldn't hesitate to kill someone doesn't become that way overnight.

I clench my fists, struggling to come to terms with all of this. How could someone we opened our lives to harbor such darkness? Has he always been this way?

Memories flood back, every moment tainted with the knowledge that all of that was a charade, a facade he'd carefully constructed to conceal his true intentions.

Even if Diego wasn't the culprit, he couldn't be allowed to live after this. He was complicit in letting Rich get away with murder.

Vision blurring, I watch as my brothers follow my orders, gunning down Diego in cold blood. Disgust twists inside of me, settling heavy in my stomach as I turn away, walking towards the car.

The sound of my brothers' footsteps echoes behind me, their presence a silent reassurance in the midst of a storm.

Dominic's jaw is set in a firm line, eyes reflecting the same determination and sorrow I feel inside. Caleb's normal jovial nature is replaced with steely resolve, gaze fixed ahead as he tries to hold back the tears in his eyes.

My hand pauses on the car door handle as I turn to face my brothers. The weight of recent events hangs in the air. "We did what we had to do," I say quietly, my voice barely above a whisper. "Diego left us no choice."

Silence hangs over us like a heavy shroud as the gravity of the situation settles in. Then, without a word, Caleb steps forward and clasps my shoulder in a silent gesture of solidarity. Dominic follows suit, his face grim but determined.

"We did what we had to do," Dominic echoes. "Now we need to confront Rich."

"Let's go home first. We need to check on Sienna," I say, my thoughts racing with concern for her. We left her alone without even saying goodbye and urgency gnaws at my insides. Her presence is a warm balm on my mind, and I need to know that she's survived the storm unscathed.

With a determined yank, I pull open the door and slip into the driver's seat, turning the key in the ignition with a click, the engine roaring to life. Caleb gets into the back seat while Dominic steps aside to talk to a few of the Blades, ordering them to clean up the mess and make sure the remaining Serpents leave without fuss.

As we head home, my heart pounds in anticipation, every moment stretching out like an eternity. The only thing I want right now is to fall into Sienna's arms and hold her close until the storm inside me subsides. Being around her soothes my soul and I'll feel at ease when she's in my arms.

I bring the car to a halt in the driveway, breath catching in my throat at the familiar sight of home. The three of us get out and file in the house, no words spoken as our minds churn with the newfound knowledge of our paternal betrayal.

Heading up the stairs, I grip the banister, each step weighing on me as I head to my room, where we'd left her this morning.

"Sienna?" I call out, stepping inside. The bed is empty, sheets rumpled. It's quiet in here, my voice echoing.

I call her name again, poking my head into Caleb and Dominic's rooms in turn, but she's not there either.

Dominic calls her name from the stairs, turning to face Caleb who is in the kitchen grabbing ice for the nasty bruise on his side.

"Is she down there?" he asks.

Caleb looks around, concern etched in his features as he realizes he doesn't see her. He puts the ice back in the freezer and walks over to the bathroom door, rapping on it with his knuckles. The door creaks as it swings open, revealing an empty bathroom.

"She's not here," Caleb says, panic in his voice.

"Where is she then?" I demand, rushing down the stairs. "Where would she even go?"

He whips out his phone and calls Sienna immediately, but the phone goes straight to voicemail.

Dominic moves around, searching the closets and the other bathroom. "Sienna!" he yells.

"I don't think she's here," I say, a grip of terror seizing my heart. "Guys, where would she go?"

Caleb's voice is hoarse as he speaks, "She was trying to ask me about Rich. She thought that he was hiding something, and I brushed her off. You don't think she went to confront him, do you?"

My mouth sets in a thin line. "That's exactly what she would do," I say, clenching my fists. "Caleb, do you still have the tracker in her phone?"

"Of course I do," he snaps. He sprints upstairs and grabs his laptop, the noisy clatter of keys filling the room as he begins to search for her. "Shit, her freaking phone is broken or something because the tracker can't get her signal."

"What are we going to do?" I ask, gripping my hair with my hands. "If she's gone to confront Rich, there's no way he's going to just let her go. We have to find her, dammit!"

"I have a confession," Caleb says, twisting his fingers as he looks down at his lap. "I implanted a tracker into Sienna after her kidnapping. I just couldn't stomach the idea of something going wrong where she doesn't have her phone."

"Fuck, you're a genius, nerd brain!" I say, grabbing him and kissing his forehead. "Find her!"

Caleb immediately gets straight to it, pulling up another site and searching for her.

"She's ..." He stares at the screen, voice fading out.

"Where?" I demand. "Where is she?"

"Emily's apartment," he whispers, pointing at the screen with a shaking finger.

"What's she doing there?" Dominic asks, crowding around the computer to look, brows furrowed in concern.

"I don't know but I have a bad feeling about it," I say. My insides feel like ice, and bile rises in my throat. "We have to go, *now*."

Dominic and Caleb nod, silent communication passing through, drawing strength from each other, bound by the unshakable bond we share. In unison, we head out to the car and Dominic gets into the driver's seat this time, putting it into gear even before we've gotten our seatbelts on.

Caleb sits in the front seat, using his phone to track Sienna's location. All his attention is focused on directing Dominic as he races us through the darkened streets.

"Do you think he has her?" Caleb asks as we careen around a corner, the tires screeching on the pavement. Exhaust fumes perfume the air, leaving a cloud of smoke in our wake.

"I don't know," I say, my jaw set in a hard line. "If he does, there will be hell to pay for him."

"Nothing would surprise me at this point," Dominic admits. "Rich isn't the person we thought we knew. That man is gone, if he ever existed. All that matters right now is finding Sienna. We can't let him hurt her."

"I'm going to kill the bastard myself," I mutter, muscles aching with the tension in my neck and shoulders. "If he lays a hand on her, he's dead."

"We have to get to her," Caleb says, clutching his phone with a death grip. "Maybe she's just there to find out more information."

"Do you still have Rich's phone number?" I ask, urgency in my tone. "We should call him. If he answers, he doesn't have her."

"I deleted him from my phone," Caleb admits, voice cracking. "I couldn't bear to see his contact information."

Dominic clears his throat, eyes never leaving the road. "I still have his number." Caleb immediately grabs his phone from the center console and unlocks the screen, scrolling through the contacts.

Putting the phone up to his ear, he listens intently as it goes straight to voicemail. "His phone is off," he says, cupping a hand over the receiver.

"Leave him a message," I whisper in a hiss.

"Rich, this is Caleb Ravenwood on Dominic's phone. I know we haven't talked in a while, but I was just reaching out to ..." Caleb falters, trying to think of an excuse. "To ask you a question about something. Call me back." He hangs up and places the phone in his lap.

"Maybe he's in class," Dominic says, though I don't think any of us believe that. I think we're all thinking the same thing—that whatever Sienna is doing at Emily's apartment, Rich is involved.

The loft apartment, a renovated fire station, sits on the northern edge of town, just on the outskirts. We had always joked about Emily living so far away and now it feels further away than ever as we race towards it.

My heart is in my throat as we approach the building, panic gripping me as I realize there are lights on inside.

The three of us tumble out of the car and push inside the building, the door letting out an ominous creak. I hear voices from her apartment, and we take the stairs two at a time, racing inside.

Our worst fears are confirmed when we come face-to-face with the sight in front of us. Sienna is kneeling on the floor, Rich's hand over hers as they press a gun against her temple.

"Do it!" Rich yells at her. "Pull the trigger already, or you'll never see your precious Ravenwoods again!"

"No!" I scream, feeling paralyzed. Time seems to slow down and my legs feel like anchors as I try to move before it's too late.

46

DOMINIC

My heart shatters like broken glass.

Rich is holding his hand over Sienna's, a gun pointed at her head.

Time seems to slow to a crawl as I race against the inevitable. Horror consumes me as I wonder if I'll get there in time.

And then, like a whirlwind, memories come flooding in.

Fragments of memories assail me—the blur of movement as Sienna jumps on me for a hug, the warmth of her touch, the taste of her kisses, fleeting glimpses of the moments we've shared.

Then, amidst the flickering images, one memory surfaces with the crystalline clarity of a chilly morning, the breeze rustling through the leaves as the sun crests over the horizon in the tiny park. Sienna and I are seated on a weathered bench, our breath forming wispy clouds in the chilly air.

"I can't believe you made me get up this early," I complain, *blowing on my hands and rubbing them together.*

Sienna's tongue pokes out between her teeth as she smiles, reaching for my hand to entwine with hers.

"You didn't have to come with me," she teases, *rubbing her thumb over the back of my hand. "You could have let Caleb come. He offered."*

"Yeah well, I haven't seen you in a few days," I say, kissing her on the nose. "I missed you."

"We had sex like, all night last night," she says with a giggle, eyes shining as she looks up at me.

"It's not the same," I whisper, leaning down to press our foreheads together. "I like spending time with you."

"You're not the scary monster I thought you were," she admits, her voice soft. "You're more like a big, cuddly teddy bear."

"I'm not a teddy bear," I complain. "More like a grizzly bear."

"You're a grizzly bear who is a teddy bear on the inside," she amends.

"Only for you," I say quietly. "And only on certain days. Like today."

Sienna and I sit there for a few minutes longer, drinking our thermoses of coffee as we wait for her first interview of the day to arrive. In that moment, surrounded by the calm stillness of the morning and the comfort of her presence, I felt a sense of peace wash over me—a feeling I never wanted to let go of.

I can't let Rich hurt Sienna. Not after she's brought so much into our lives. She's changed us, changed me for the better. I was bitter and jaded before she sashayed into Caspian Springs in her Mary-Janes and schoolgirl skirts.

Now I feel like I can see a future for myself, I feel like I can dream again.

And nothing will stop me from protecting Sienna from danger.

Time speeds up again as I finally reach Rich, knocking the gun out of his hands. Rich dives for the it as I pull Sienna up and shove her behind me, towards Caleb.

She stumbles into him and he grabs her, protecting her while I face Rich, who holds the gun up.

"Don't move!" he yells. I freeze in place, holding my hands up. Taking a careful step forward, I try to placate him.

"Rich, it's me. It's Dominic. You've known me almost my whole life. Put the gun down and we can talk, Rich," I say.

"I said don't move!" Rich repeats, pulling back the hammer with a loud click. My heart is pounding so hard in my chest that I feel like everyone can hear it. Blood pumps in my veins and I feel the adrenaline surge inside me as I take one more cautious step forward.

"I warned you!" Rich shouts, pulling the trigger.

The gun goes off in a flash of smoke.

Time slows down once again, the bullet almost frozen in the air as I stare at it.

Memories surface again, this time of when we first met Sienna.

"She's dangerous," I say, watching her from the window for a moment before we go inside. "She doesn't belong here."

She glances up and I catch sight of her face. It's round, like a cherub, with an oval shape and soft, glossy red curls frame green eyes and full lips. The breath feels stolen from my lungs as I stare at her, wondering how someone who looks like an angel could be such a devil.

Time speeds up again as the bullet pierces me in the leg.

I scream in pain, going down on one knee as blood begins to pour from the wound, dripping onto the floor.

After the gunshot, Caleb lets out a strangled gasp, his eyes darting between Rich and Sienna, his expression torn between fear and determination. Rich then turns the gun on Sienna, intent on finishing what he started.

I can't let that happen, so summoning all my strength, I continue lurching forward, refusing to let him gain the upper hand.

Before he can pull the trigger again, I shove him into the wall, his head bouncing off with a loud bang. His eyes are wild, darting around the room.

He grabs my shoulders and wrests them off of him. "You have no idea what you're doing, Dominic. Sienna isn't who she says she is. She's a dangerous con artist. I was trying to save you from her!"

"You're a liar," I growl out, grabbing his wrist as I try to wrestle the gun away. Pain radiates outward from my leg wound like fire spreading through a forest. It consumes everything in its wake, leaving me feeling dizzy and cold. I keep fighting though, bending his wrist back as I try to remove the gun from his grip.

Sienna is screaming in the background as Caleb unties her, pleading for Rich to let us go.

Bastian takes a step forward, as if to intervene, but hesitates, unable to go up against the man he once considered like a father.

"Please, just listen to me," Rich pleads as we fight for control. "Sienna came to me with a story about how she thinks I was responsible for the center closing. I told her it wasn't true, but she threatened to kill me unless I came with her. She brought me here to Emily's place to guilt trip me into confessing. She was the one who had the gun!"

Bastian's eyes narrow with anger and disbelief as Rich's true intentions become clear. "You're lying," he screams, throwing himself into the fray. "You're just trying to manipulate us, why else would you shoot Dominic?"

He almost manages to get the gun from Rich but Rich twists his arm, dropping him to the ground. "Enough!" Rich yells. "I'm cleaning up your messes once again."

"How could you do it?" I ask, feeling clammy, sweat beading on my forehead. "How could you kill Emily?"

"You know she killed herself," Rich argues, desperation in his voice. I move forward, leg almost numb from the pain now. "Don't forget who cared for you all those years ..."

"And now you're trying to kill someone we care about," I say, taking another painful step forward. Fury burns cold in my chest, ice in my veins. "How long have you been lying to us? How long have you been manipulating us?" I demand, wanting answers.

"You have to believe me, I only ever wanted what was best for you," Rich says, holding his hands up. "You're delirious from the pain, Dominic. You need to stop before you hurt yourself worse."

"Shut up!" I spit out. "Just stop talking!" I can't take it anymore, so I tackle him to the ground, needing to finally get the gun away from him.

Items start falling around us as we tangle on the floor, bumping into chairs and tables, knocking over framed photos and knick-knacks, leaving a trail of destruction in our wake. We roll through glass shards that slice up my skin and as I wince, Rich takes the opportunity to smack me in the face with the butt of the weapon.

"Dammit, Dominic, do something!" Bastian barks, frustration seeping into his voice as he watches the chaos unfold. He scans back and forth between us and Sienna, torn between the desire to protect her and the dangers of escalating the situation.

Rich raises the gun again and Bastian moves, lunging for him. Rich snarls, his grip tightening on the weapon as he struggles to maintain control, the three of us locked in a deadly dance of wills. Each moment feels like an eternity as it ticks past, the room echoing with grunts and strained breaths.

There's a deafening bang as the gun goes off, the sound reverberating through the room like a thunderclap. Time seems to stand still as everyone in the room freezes in shock and horror.

Rich slumps over, clutching his chest. Blood seeps out between his fingers and he looks up at us, helplessness in his eyes. The mask seems to slip away, anger and frustration flickering on his face for a moment before he seems to give up, resigning himself to his fate.

"I'm sorry," he murmurs before the light goes out of his eyes.

"No!" I rush forward, bile in my throat as I scramble to reach him before it's too late. For everything that happened between us, Rich was our father for most of our lives. I can't let this happen!

I grab at him, shaking him. "Wake up! Dammit, wake up Rich!"

Tears sting my cheeks as the reality of what has just happened sinks in like a stone in the pit of my stomach.

Everything seems to happen at once. Sienna screams out, slumping into Caleb's arms. Bastian chokes, vomiting onto the floor as he takes in the sight before him. Caleb looks pale, swaying on his feet.

"We have to get out of here," I say, taking charge and hurrying over to Caleb to put my arms around both him and Sienna to keep them from falling over. "We need to leave like, *now*."

Bastian wipes his mouth with the back of his hand and rushes over, scooping Sienna into his arms. Caleb seems to come back to himself, shaking out of his shock. He throws an arm around me, helping me limp out to the car.

Throwing one last look at Emily's apartment, I sprawl into the backseat of the car, my mind racing. Sienna is safe now, but at what cost?

47

SIENNA

I lurch awake and for a moment I think I'm still stuck in the trunk of Dr. Thornton's car, whizzing along as he takes me somewhere secluded to kill me.

Then I realize I'm in the backseat of the Firebird next to Dominic, and Dr. Thornton is dead.

"She's awake," Caleb calls out, half-turned in his seat to face me. He's pale but otherwise looks unharmed.

"What happened?"

"You passed out after the gun went off and killed Rich," Caleb explains in a shaky voice. "We carried you out to the car. Dominic is losing a lot of blood, so we need to get him looked at as soon as possible."

I turn to face him and Dominic's face is drawn, his skin ashy. He looks like he's on the verge of passing out himself.

"Stay with me," I whisper urgently, reaching out to grab his hands in mine. His skin feels clammy and icy beneath my fingertips. "C'mon, stay with me," I urge.

"We can't take him to a hospital, they'll ask too many questions," Bastian says, glancing at us in the rearview mirror. "We need to take him home."

"I can clean up the wound and sew it up if it's not too bad," I tell them. "But we have to hurry."

"I'm going as fast as I can," Bastian snaps. He tenses, then forces himself to breathe out. "I'm sorry. I'm just completely fucking shaken up after you got kidnapped for the second time. Why did you go and confront him?"

"I'm sorry," I say, remorse filling me now that I'm safe. "I should never have done that. I was just trying to protect you guys."

"You could have gotten killed," Caleb says, eyes red-rimmed and voice hoarse. "How could you do that to us?"

"I needed to know the truth," I say, clenching my jaw. "Rich was hiding something and I needed to find out what."

"We know he killed Emily," Bastian says, pain in his voice as he speaks. "Diego told us Rich paid the Serpents to cover it up."

"It's because she found out what was going on," I tell them. "Emily looked into the same things I did and found out that the story about the center's closure didn't add up. She confronted him and he killed her. She was never having an affair with him, he used that as an excuse to hide his misdeeds."

Caleb scrubs a hand over his face, looking so much older for a moment, a noise of anguish escaping him. "She never slept with him?"

"No," I say, reaching out one hand to take his, squeezing it tightly. "She never betrayed you guys. Rich wanted you to think that so you wouldn't discover that it was actually him who embezzled millions from the Haven Center, forcing it to close. He did it because the committee reviewing his research pulled his funding."

"I can't believe he'd do that to us," Caleb says, sniffling. The weight of Dr. Thornton's betrayal hangs heavy over us in the car, a reminder that no matter how well we think we know someone, we never really do.

I decide not to tell them what he told me about being a likely diagnosed psychopath. I can't bring myself to ruin the only happy memories they have left with the awful truth. "He wanted you guys to stay a part of his life," I say instead. "He thought that this was the way to do it."

"I don't know if that's true, but thank you for saying so," Bastian says, voice soft. We're almost home now and Dominic is fading in and out of consciousness from the amount of blood loss. He lets out a moan and I pull off my cardigan, using it to wipe his brow.

"We're nearly there," I say, stroking his cheek. "Stay with us. What day is it?"

"The day you tell us you're never leaving again," Dominic mumbles.

"I'm not going anywhere," I assure him. "Let's just get you home and cleaned up first."

Once we arrive back at the house, Bastian and Caleb support Dominic and I rush to the door to unlock it so they can carry him inside. They deposit him on the couch and Caleb runs to grab the first aid kit.

Standing over Dominic, I examine the bullet wound. It looks nasty, blood everywhere, his skin gaping open around the hole where the bullet entered. The scent of burned flesh is pungent. Bile rises in my throat as I realize that if it weren't for my recklessness, he wouldn't have been shot.

I swallow my nausea and start stripping Dominic's clothes from his lower half, leaving him in his boxer briefs as I examine the wound. It's deep but didn't go all the way down to the bone and I breathe a sigh of relief, though it's mixed with remorse for my impulsive actions.

"Get me like, all the sterile bandages you can find," I tell Bastian, who is fidgeting as he watches us. "And Caleb, I need you to get me something for him to bite down on, a belt for the wound, and a knife. Sterilize it first. That bullet needs to come out as soon as possible."

"Can you even do that?" Caleb demands, glancing back and forth between me and Dominic as he writhes in pain on the couch. "I thought it was bad to take the bullet out."

"We can't go to the hospital so we're going to have to make do," I say, impatience rising. "You guys may call me *Princess*, but I grew up in a neighborhood just like this one."

"I didn't think you had experience removing bullets though," Caleb mutters.

"Don't question my knowledge," I say, refusing to tell him I learned how to do this from watching medical TV shows.

Caleb rushes to follow my orders and gathers the supplies, leaving them within arm's reach on the coffee table. The sky is nearly dark now, the sun casting long shadows through the slats in the blinds.

"Now go get towels. Lots of towels," I say, voice firm. "Like, all the towels. He's going to bleed everywhere."

Bastian returns with a bag of sterile bandages and some needle-nose pliers. "I figured you'd need it," he says gruffly, tossing them on top of the stack of supplies.

"Good thinking," I say as I start cleaning the wound as best I can while Dominic moans and thrashes around. "Hold him down," I add.

Bastian steps in, pinning his brother down by the shoulders from behind the couch as I continue cleaning the wound out with alcohol. The tang of iron in the air dissipates as I wipe the blood away.

Dominic is sweating and swearing now, but when Caleb comes back with a wooden spoon and shoves it between his teeth, he bites down on it and stops thrashing so much.

I take the belt, wrapping it tightly around his thigh and buckling it so it can stop the bleeding while I work on his lower leg. Once I get the wound clean enough, I grab the knife Caleb brought, keeping my hands steady as I press it into the hole so I can gauge how deep the bullet is.

Caleb rushes to grab towels, bringing down a huge stack just as I hear the tinny cling of metal on metal. "Found it," I say, gritting my teeth as I take the knife out of the wound. "I'm ready to take it out now."

Dominic braces himself as I push the needle-nose pliers inside, gripping the bullet between the metal nose and slowly, carefully extracting it. The bullet comes out relatively easily and I plop it into the glass cup that Caleb brings over.

"Done," I say. "Now I need to sew him up." Caleb hands me dental floss and a needle and I thread it before cleaning the wound again, then I start sewing up his leg.

"Fuck!" Dominic curses, but he's starting to regain color. "I can't believe that asshole shot me."

We all chuckle weakly at his joke, trying to appreciate the humor in a situation like this. "At least you didn't get shot in the butt," I offer.

"Yeah, no offense, but I don't think I would have been able to help her sew up your ass," Caleb adds.

"How did the fight go with the Serpents?" I ask as I finish sewing his wound closed. "You're still alive, so I'm guessing it went well?"

Bastian's voice brims with a mix of pride and defiance. "We kicked their asses," he declares, jutting his chin. "Diego surrendered. He told us what happened with Rich to spare his life, but we took him out anyway."

"I know you did what you had to do," I say as I bandage Dominic's wound with fresh gauze. "He helped Rich get away with murder, and he killed one of your own people."

"We did what we had to do to keep you safe," he tells me, a scowl on his face.

"I know you're mad at me for leaving without saying anything," I say, my voice wavering.

Bastian's voice is gruff when he responds, "You're safe now, that's all that matters. Just make sure Dominic lives and we'll be even."

I know that they were mad at me for leaving without saying anything, but I didn't think we were back to square one. My heart sinks in my chest and I focus on finish bandaging up Dominic before stepping back to check on him.

I turn and ask Dominic, "How are you feeling?" He gives me a thumbs down.

I nod. "We need to get some painkillers into him. And he needs antibiotics so the wound doesn't get infected."

"We know this clinic we can take him to later tonight," Bastian tells me. "They won't ask questions, but they aren't open during the day. The doctor there will give us whatever we need."

"Right," I say, heading into the kitchen to get Dominic some analgesics and a glass of water. While I'm in there, I take a moment to gather myself, leaning on the counter with my palms.

After everything we've been through, I would understand if they decide they don't want to be with me anymore. I've proven to be nothing but trouble in their lives. Besides that, I've done nothing but judge them since I arrived, blaming them for things that were entirely the fault of Dr. Thornton.

Nothing I thought was true is actually true. In reality, the man I'd idolized since I was a teenager was a cold-blooded psychopath, and the thugs I thought were street trash turned out to be the heroes.

I wish I could explain to them how I feel, but I don't know where we stand anymore. Bastian seems so upset with me and it's got my stomach in knots. Guilt washes over me, gnawing at me from the inside. I'm the reason their father figure is dead.

"Are you bringing the painkillers?" Caleb calls out. I straighten up and grab them from the drawer before taking a cup out of the cupboard and filling it under the fridge dispenser.

"Be right there!" I call back.

My heart aches in my chest as I walk back into the living room, wondering where we can possibly go from here.

48

BASTIAN

Once the adrenaline has worn off, I feel a weight lift from my shoulders. All the tension I'd been carrying for the past two and a half years feels like it's suddenly gone.

Learning that Rich was the one who betrayed us and not Emily still has me reeling inside. I blamed Emily for so long and it wasn't her fault. My heart lies heavy in my chest at the knowledge that she died an innocent woman.

As angry as I am at learning that the person who we trusted more than life itself was a con man, I'm grateful to Emily and Sienna for pursuing the truth, even if it came at great cost.

Emily's memory will be honored, but first I need to apologize to Sienna. I can tell that she's been avoiding me, and she's got a haunted look in her eyes whenever I see her.

I wander downstairs where Dominic is dozing, leg propped up on a pillow on the couch. Sienna is in the kitchen, sitting at the table and staring at her phone. She's been sleeping on the recliner so she can keep an eye on Dominic as he recovers.

Cornering her, I hold out a stuffed dragon, a peace offering. She looks up at it and smiles, my heart racing with a tumult of conflicting emotions—guilt for how I've treated her, longing for us to reconcile, and a lingering fear that she might still reject me.

"Hey," I say, waggling the toy in front of her.

"Hi," she says, reaching out to take the dragon, her hand warm against mine as they brush. She runs her fingers through silky soft fur, petting the blue and green toy with a fond smile.

The hum of the fridge is the only noise in the room for a beat, besides the sound of our breathing. I struggle to find the right words, my throat tightening with unspoken apologies.

"I need to apologize," I tell her. "I was an asshole."

"No," she shakes her head, sorrow in her eyes as she sets the dragon aside. "I should be the one to apologize. I made a snap judgment when I first met you, deciding that you guys were losers and thugs." She closes her eyes and presses her hands together, resting them against her forehead.

"I let it cloud my view of you, even after everything you did for me. I should have told you guys where I was going, I shouldn't have gone without you. I wanted to protect you, but it wasn't my place. I put you guys in danger." Sienna opens her eyes and I sigh, reaching out to tuck a strand of hair behind her ear.

"We didn't make it easy for you to get close to us," I admit. "It's not your fault that you held back. We kept you at arm's length. I know it's no excuse, but when I saw you there at Emily's apartment, it all came flooding back, and I thought for a moment that you betrayed us too. I lashed out unfairly."

"You only lashed out because I was rude to you in the first place," she protests, letting me lean into her space.

"I guess we were both in the wrong," I say, a wry smile on my lips. "Can you ever forgive me?"

Sienna pulls me close, pressing her lips to mine with a featherlight brush. "As long as you forgive me too."

"I know you wanted to protect us but from now on, talk to us. If you think something is going on, let us help you. You don't have to do everything alone anymore."

"The same goes for you," she tells me, poking me in the side. "You and Caleb and Dominic are so insular, you never tell me what's going on."

"I know it was frustrating. We thought we were protecting you by keeping you in the dark, but I guess we just all need to be more honest with each other."

"Agreed," Sienna says with a firm nod. As I look at her, our eyes lock in a silent exchange of unspoken words and unbridled desire. Her green eyes sparkle as I pull her up from the chair and kiss her, gently at first but with a growing sense of urgency.

"I need you," I whisper, cradling her face between my palms. "Right now. I need to make you mine again."

"Take me upstairs," she whispers back. A glance back at Dominic confirms that he's still sleeping soundly, so I take her by the hand and lead her up the stairs.

Caleb is in my bedroom when we walk in. He's been on edge lately and has slept in my room since Sienna's been sleeping downstairs.

"Hey," he calls, putting his laptop away. "What's up?"

"We made up," I say, bringing Sienna's hand up to kiss it. "And now we're going to do the fun part of making up. Wanna join?"

Caleb grins. "Count me in." He slips off the bed to stand behind Sienna, the two of us closing her in like a Ravenwood sandwich. Lifting her hair from her neck, he leans down and kisses it tenderly, peppering little kisses here and there while I bend down and kiss her lips once more.

Sienna lets out a breathy moan, leaning into Caleb as he runs his hands down her sides and slips them under her shirt. His fingers caress her soft skin, leaving goosebumps in his wake. She shivers and parts her lips, letting my tongue invade her mouth.

My tongue swirls around hers in a heated dance and I pull back, biting down gently on her lower lip. Caleb brings his hands up and unhooks her bra, sliding his fingers around her front to cup each breast in hand, squeezing and kneading as she ruts up against me.

I feel the strain in my jeans as she grinds her body on me, cock filling out until it's throbbing with how badly I want her. Her hands reach out, pulling me against her as the three of us sink onto the bed together.

Hands grapple with clothing as we undress, raging desire coursing through us. Sienna's breathy moans fill the room and Caleb slips a finger in between her wet folds, teasing her as I pull Sienna down to kiss her more passionately.

My leg hooks around her hip, the two of us grinding into each other like horny teenagers. Caleb's fingers thrust in and out, adding wet, squelching noises to the symphony.

Sienna pulls away, panting hard. Her eyes are bright with lust. "Do you think you and Caleb could take me at the same time?"

The question catches me off guard and I glance up to look at Caleb, who stares blankly back at me. I don't think in our wildest dreams we would have imagined Sienna wanting both of us at the same time.

"How do you want us?" I ask, reaching out to stroke her cheek.

"Both of you inside me, together," she says, biting her lip. "Is that okay? Or is it too much."

I run a hand through my hair, needing a moment, and look up at Caleb, who nods.

"We can do that for you, baby," I tell her. "Want us to stuff you so full that you can't take anymore? Want to feel us both claiming you at once?"

"Yes," she breathes out, fingers digging into my shoulders as she rolls her hips into mine once more.

"It's gonna take a little extra prep," Caleb whispers into her ear, before biting gently on the lobe. She lets out another breathless moan and throws her head back to look at him.

"I want you. Both of you," she says in a deep, sultry voice.

I smile. "Anything you wish, Princess."

Shifting so I'm on top, I push her down onto the bed and we begin prepping her hole to take us both, my fingers joining Caleb's as we tease and stretch her.

Her eyes are watery as she watches us work. "You both mean so much to me. I can't believe I get to be with you."

"You mean the world to us too," I say, Caleb nodding along. "You came into our lives like a whirlwind and upended everything we thought we knew. It scared us, but you're worth it."

"I never thought I'd feel anything for anyone again, not after what happened to Emily," Caleb confesses, a softness in his eyes that I haven't seen in ages. "But here we are and we're so grateful to be with you. I know Dominic is too."

Sienna's hips are moving continuously now as we increase to three fingers each, and she throws her head back. "I'm so close!" she cries out.

"Come for us," I tell her. "C'mon baby, let it go."

Sienna goes tense and her body shakes as she comes, liquid squirting onto our fingers. I lick it off with a devilish grin and wink. "You're ready for us," I say, pulling away.

Before she can mourn the loss of our fingers, I flip her so she's on top of me once again. "I'm going to slip inside of you and Caleb will go in from behind," I explain. "I need you to breathe in and out slowly as we do this, and stop us if it starts to hurt."

Sienna nods, closing her eyes as she breathes for me. I slide inside, her walls feeling looser and fluttery after her orgasm. Caleb positions himself behind her, sliding his cock in next.

"It's a tight fit," he grunts as he starts to push inside. Sienna tenses for a moment and we all stop, waiting for her to adjust.

"You okay?" I ask.

"Keep going," she orders, fingers leaving bruises on my arms. We resume our movements until Caleb has bottomed out inside her. She feels incredibly full, and it feels so good. I don't think I'm going to be able to last like this.

"Ready?" Caleb asks, voice husky with desire.

"Fuck me," Sienna demands, rolling her hips. The sensation is almost too much, and I have to try hard not to come immediately.

We start a slow push and pull, finding a rhythm that works for us as we both take her at the same time. It doesn't last long though because within a few thrusts, my orgasm is ripped from me with a strangled cry.

"Fuck!" I curse, legs shaking as I come inside her. Caleb pulls out just in time and comes all over her, then collapses on the bed, spent.

My forehead is dotted with sweat as I lay next to the two of them, coming down from the blissful high I just experienced.

"I love you," Sienna says, reaching out to grab both our hands in hers. "I love all of you so much."

"We love you too, Princess," I say, heart feeling full enough to burst.

"And Dominic does too, but he'll tell you that when he's all better," Caleb adds, giving her hand a gentle squeeze.

"I don't want to leave you," Sienna says, her voice growing soft. "I know that this thing between us was sort of on a deadline with my work but when I'm done, I don't want to leave."

My heart clenches as I turn to face her, reaching out to cup her cheek. Caleb moves so he's spooning her from behind, hands around her middle.

"We don't want you to leave either," I confess. "You're ours, now and forever."

49

DOMINIC

I wriggle my leg, stretching it out in front of me as our friend Puck looks it over. "I think it's healed up nicely," he announces, Stan the cat giving his meow of approval next to him.

Puck is a vet, the only person we know in the tri-state area who could take care of my injury "off the books" and wouldn't ask questions.

"So, I'm good to get back to working at the shop then?" I ask, giving him a wry smile.

"I'd take it easy for a few more weeks with operating heavy machinery but otherwise you're good to go," Puck says, reaching down to pet Stan's head.

"Thanks for looking me over," I say as I hop off the exam table. My leg feels completely fine, with only the occasional twinge in my shin here and there. I've got a sick-looking scar now too, which is a bonus.

Plus, I've had Sienna all to myself for the past few days, since she's been monitoring me to make sure I'm totally healed. I don't mind sharing her with my brothers but it's also nice to have that one-on-one time too.

She's waiting for me in the brightly lit lobby when I exit the room, giving me a hopeful smile. I give her a thumbs up and she squeals, rushing forward to hug me tightly. As she hugs me, I can't help melting into the comfort of her embrace, reassurance coursing through me.

"I'm so glad you're all better," she says as she pulls me down to kiss me. Mrs. Barnabas and her old pug give us nasty looks for the PDA, but I don't care. I've missed being close to her physically.

She's been afraid to touch me ever since she bandaged me up, worried she might hurt me if she did. I've tried to reassure her that I'm fine, but she wouldn't so much as hug me without a clean bill of health.

I think she was just scared after she saw me bleeding out from the gunshot wound and had to be the one to patch me up. I lean in to kiss her back, senses overwhelmed by the sweet scent of her hair and the softness of her lips against mine.

Breaking apart, we link hands as we exit the vet's office. Caleb is waiting in the car and I wave, pointing to my leg. He gives an excited honk of the horn and we get inside.

"So, you got the all-clear from Puck?" Caleb asks.

I grin and nod. "Yup, I'm totally healed. Puck told me Sienna's clean-up job was damned near perfect, by the way," I tell her. She beams and we take off for home.

Once we're home, Caleb makes himself scarce, claiming that he's got to go to the library for some reason. Since Bastian's been taking care of business at the shop because of my injury, he's not home either, leaving Sienna and me at home.

"I just wanted to say thanks again, for saving me," Sienna says as we sit down on the couch together. "You risked your life for me. If you hadn't gotten the gun away from him, I wouldn't be here."

"When I saw you there, I didn't even think," I admit, reaching out to cup her cheek in my palm. "Seeing you in danger ... everything else blurred. It was like instinct took over. I couldn't bear the thought of losing you, Sienna."

Her skin feels soft and smooth under my touch, sending a jolt of electricity down my spine that I haven't felt in a few weeks.

"You and Bas and Caleb put your lives on the line for me. I feel like I don't know what I did to deserve that."

"It's because you're you," I say, rubbing her cheek with my thumb to chase the spark. "You're Sienna Bennet, you're special and beautiful and amazing and smart and you challenge us to be the best versions of ourselves."

"Is that so?" Sienna asks, raising an eyebrow with a mirthful smile.

"Yup, it's just that simple," I tell her. I move my hands so both of them are cupping her cheeks and she and I can look into each other's eyes as I lay my heart on the line for her.

"I love you, Sienna. I know you and Bastian and Caleb talked about it already, but I wanted to make sure you know that I love you as well."

"I love you too, Dominic," Sienna says, eyes bright and shiny. "Being around you just makes me feel so safe and protected. You're brave and kind, and you inspire me to want to try new things."

She pauses, shifting closer to me on the couch. "And actually, now that you're better, there's something new I want to try with you," she says, leaning forward to whisper in my ear.

Sienna's whispered words send a shiver down my spine, igniting a fire of anticipation inside of me. "What is it you want to try?" I ask, reaching out to trace the soft shell of her ear with a lone finger.

"Do you trust me?" Sienna asks, her voice going straight through me.

I lean forward and bend down, looking her straight in the eye. "Of course I trust you."

"Enough to let me tie you up?" she asks, a nervous look in her eyes.

Curious about where this is going, I nod and she stands up, taking me by the hand to lead me upstairs. Once we're in my room, she pushes me down onto my desk chair and pulls out a familiar box from under my bed.

I raise an eyebrow but stay silent, wanting to see what she's got up her sleeve. She pulls out some bondage rope and begins tying my hands and feet to the chair before stepping back to admire her handiwork. I test it out, the silk bonds tight on my skin but comfortable.

"Now, Agent Smith. You thought you could get away with tying me up and leaving me for the feds to find, but you'll find I'm more clever than you anticipated," she says, leaning into my space. A shaft of sunlight hits her and she looks every inch the seductress she's playing.

My lips quirk upward before I manage to school my features. "How did you get away?" I ask.

"I seduced your partner into letting me go and have returned to punish you for your little stunt."

"You have a lot of nerve showing up here again, Miss Winterthorpe. I demand you untie me at once."

"You'll be singing a different tune soon," she warns, dropping to her knees in front of me. I let out a stifled groan, the anticipation making my dick throb. She unbuckles my belt and unzips my jeans, pulling out my hard cock, running teasing fingers along the length.

My hands move, trying to reach out for her but they stop short, bound to the chair. She's got me at her mercy as she leans down and licks a wet stripe from the tip to the base before swallowing me down inside her mouth.

I let out a soft curse, struggling against the bonds.

"Color?" Sienna asks, worry lines creasing her brow. Warmth spreads through my chest, touched that she wants to check in with me.

"Green, baby. You can keep going," I encourage, lifting my hips as much as I'm able. She dives back down immediately, hollowing out her cheeks as she begins to suck. Her mouth is so warm and wet, tongue silky soft against my heated flesh.

I throw my head back, loving the helplessness I'm experiencing at her hands. She's come such a long way, from a timid and shy girl to this confident, sexy woman who isn't afraid to take charge. It makes my head spin and I feel myself getting close so fast.

She pulls off with a wet pop and looks up at me from between my legs, eyes round. The scent of her perfume clouds my senses and desperation rises. "Are you going to be good for me now?" she asks, using a finger to tease the crown as she speaks.

"What do you want from me, Miss Winterthorpe?" I demand, shifting my hips. "I'll give you whatever you want."

"Beg me," she says in a sultry voice, leaning down to give me a kitten lick. "Beg me to let you come."

"Please, please let me come," I beg, a note of whining in my tone. "Anything you want is yours if you let me come."

"Good boy," she says, leaning back down to continue, moving her mouth up and down the shaft quickly as her tongue teases me. I want to fist my hands in her hair, but I'm forced to remain still.

I feel myself growing tense, falling over the edge and Sienna takes me down her throat, swallowing every last drop.

"Fuck!" I curse, letting my head loll backward. She continues to lick me clean until I feel oversensitive. "Okay, yellow," I tell her. She stops and looks up at me, frowning.

"I'm fine, but I'm ready to be released. I want to be able to touch you now."

She grins and undoes the restraints quickly, letting me free. I scoop her up and lay her on the bed before climbing on top of her. "You're so beautiful," I whisper in between heated kisses. "So perfect. I just wanna keep you here with us forever. Keep you safe and love you. See you grow round with our babies."

Sienna freezes and pushes me away gently, sitting up in shock. "You what?"

"I'm sorry. Is that okay?" I ask, leaning back so I'm sitting on my knees, guilt washing over me. "I know that's a big ask, but it's been on my mind lately. I want us to be a family with you, and have kids."

Her eyes light up. "I think I want that too," she says, pulling me towards her. "I want to be with you guys forever, and I want to have a family with you."

The door opens and Bastian and Caleb come in, smirking at the sight of us on the bed together. "Looks like you guys are having fun without us," Caleb complains.

"We were just getting started," I tell them. "You're free to join in."

Bastian shrugs out of his jacket and Caleb crawls onto the bed with us. "I'm so glad you're with us, Sienna," he says, coming up behind her. "You complete us."

"You complete me too," she admits. He kisses her fingers and I go back to kissing her lips while Bastian comes up on the bed and begins tugging off her pants.

Afterward, the four of us lay together in the bed cuddling and I lean back, hands behind my head.

Everything is just about perfect.

50

SIENNA

Bright sunlight hits my face as I step out of the doctor's office, fresh air replacing the smell of antiseptic. I breathe it in and close my eyes for a moment, grateful for how far things have come for us since that fateful evening at Emily's apartment.

The new Crimson Blades had stepped up that day, not only protecting the town from the Serpent threat but also by doing what needed to be done. When the police found Rich's body, in his own home, they'd ruled his death a suicide.

There'd been a note left, confessing to his guilt over embezzling the money from the Haven Center, and his role in Emily's death. The police were far too happy to close two cases at once to look much deeper into things.

"Hey, are you daydreamin' again?"

Bastian's voice pulls me from my thoughts and I look up to see him leaning against the car, looking way too cool in a leather jacket and sunglasses. I walk over to him and reach up to give him a kiss. He bends down, our lips meeting for a brief moment, but it's enough to send a flutter to my belly.

"I was just thinking about everything that happened and how

lucky we are," I tell him. He reaches out and rests a hand on my belly, rubbing little circles into it, a smile on his face.

"Thornton may have been a bastard, but he brought us to you, and now we have this little one," Bastian agrees. "So he did one thing right in his miserable life."

"I don't want to think about him today," I say. "I have news about the baby that I want to share, but I want to wait and tell everyone at the same time."

"Oh man, is everything alright in there?" he asks, concern etched on his brow.

"Everything is fine," I tell him. "It's exciting news."

"Is the due date sooner than we thought?" Bastian asks, opening the car door for me.

"No, and don't speculate," I say, slapping his hand away as he tries to pinch my butt as I get inside.

"Fine, I can wait," he says, crossing over to his side of the car to get in. After we found out I was pregnant, they traded in the bikes for an SUV, so now we have three cars.

Bastian reaches out and grabs my hand, squeezing it as we take off to pick up Caleb. He's started his first semester at Watford, studying computer science. He's become obsessed with cybersecurity since my second kidnapping, and we nudged him towards that field.

"How's our little peanut?" Caleb asks as he gets into the car, reaching up to give me a quick kiss on the cheek.

"She has some kinda news about it, but she won't say until we're all together," Bastian grumbles. "Dom won't be home until five."

"He's been so busy at work lately," I complain, rubbing a hand over my belly. It's still quite small since I'm only fifteen weeks along but it will be growing quickly.

"Yeah, but that's to be expected. They just reopened the Haven Center a couple of months ago," Caleb says.

After the scandal with Rich came to light, the former board of directors of the center was suddenly clamoring to get it back up and running. The optics of having someone like Dr. Thornton get away with criminal activity because of an inefficient investigation didn't look so good.

The news of Lorna Hull's reinstatement as Director of the newly established Haven Center had brought the community a sense of relief. Her compassionate leadership had been a guiding light for the community at one time, and her reinstatement promised new stability on the horizon.

It wasn't just her return that filled us with hope though. An unexpected will was discovered among Rich's things, stating that he was leaving behind a sum of money equal to what he'd stolen, along with quite a large sum to the Ravenwood boys, who "he considered his own children." Dominic had been given a position on the board of directors for the center, to help run things with fresh eyes.

We arrive home and the boys help me inside, despite my protests. They've become a little overprotective after everything that happened, and I can hardly blame them.

"How is Dr. Gavin?" Caleb asks as we settle onto the couch to relax. Bastian clamors around in the kitchen, trying a new cooking experiment. They closed the bike shop since it never brought in much money, and he decided to take up all the household duties for now.

"She's good," I say, resting a hand on my bump. "She says that next semester I can start lecturing."

Dr. Jordan Gavin is the head of the Psychology Department and my academic advisor and boss. I got a job working for her after Rich's death. She was impressed by my research and my depth of knowledge and admitted me into the graduate program as well as offering me a job as her assistant.

Things are going pretty well for us right now, and when I get to share the news, I know that it will be even better.

At five thirty on the dot, Dominic arrives home, pulling off his tie and discarding it immediately.

"He's here!" Caleb calls.

Bastian appears from the kitchen, wearing an apron with "Kiss the Cook" written across the chest, the tantalizing aroma of barbecue filling the air, making my stomach rumble in anticipation.

"That means we get to hear the news about the baby now, right?" he asks, excitement in his tone.

"There's news about the baby?" Dominic asks, brow raised as he leans down to kiss me.

We pull apart and I pat the couch next to me. "Good news," I tell him, standing up to go grab my purse. I rifle inside, bringing the ultrasound to show them. "It's not just one baby. We're having twins!"

Laughter and excited chatter fill the room as Caleb and Bastian exchange high-fives over my head, their voices blending in a symphony of joy. As they pull me in for a group hug, I can feel the warmth and strength of Dominic's arms around me, his touch a tangible expression of his love and excitement, eyes filling with tears. "Two babies," he exclaims. "Two!"

Caleb grins. "Hell yeah. Twice the amount of love to share."

"This calls for a celebration," Bastian says, a gleam in his eye. "You've been feelin' under the weather for so long and we missed being with you. Do you think you might want to spend the night with all three of us again?"

The flutter of happiness in my belly turns to desire with little warning. Now that I'm out of the first trimester, I've started missing the feel of their bodies against mine. I've been waking up to my hands between my thighs with flashes of memories of dreams where their hands are all over my body, touching and kissing me everywhere.

"Yes," I whisper, leaning into Bastian as Dominic caresses my belly. "I've missed it being the three of us. We're all so busy lately."

"Tonight is just for us," Dominic rumbles, bringing his hands up to cup my larger breasts. "You have any special requests?"

"Only that I want you to take me from behind while Bastian fucks me senseless, and Caleb fucks my throat," I tell them, the flames of desire licking through me at rapid speed.

The three of them give each other identical grins before they drag me up the stairs and pull me into Bastian's bedroom. After I got pregnant, Caleb and I moved into his room. Caleb's room will be the nursery, and Dominic elected to keep his room since he runs hot at night.

"Let's get those clothes off you," Bastian says, pulling at my cardigan. I feel a little self-conscious as they strip off my sweater and shirt, exposing my belly. I'm a big girl to begin with, but now I feel like my stomach looks larger than ever.

"God, you're so gorgeous," Caleb says, voice breathless and husky. "You look like an absolute goddess, Princess."

Their words wash over me, soothing me like a balm to the heart. Dominic lifts me as if I weigh nothing, setting me on the bed on my hands and knees, eyes dark with lust.

The three of them descend, running hands all over my body to touch me, drawing little gasps of pleasure and moans of delight from my lips.

After what feels like an eternity of teasing strokes and careful prep, I find myself riding high while Bastian pumps into me from below and Dominic takes me from behind. Caleb plays with my nipples while I suck his cock, his favorite place to be.

I feel so full, the wall between my entrances stretched thin as they rock into me. My body sings in pleasure as they move, the sensations almost too much.

"Fuck!" I curse around Caleb's cock, sucking hard.

"Oh God, Sienna!" Caleb cries out, shoving himself down my throat as he releases. I swallow every drop just as my body starts to crest over the edge.

Screaming out their names, my thighs quiver as I come, only able to stay upright because of Dominic's hold on me. Bastian pulls out so he can shoot his load all over my tits as Dominic rams into me from behind, hard enough that I know I'll walk funny tomorrow. I don't care because he feels so good inside me right now.

Dominic's body tenses up as he releases deep inside me, cum dripping down my thigh when he pulls out. The three of us collapse together, slowly recovering from the intensity of our coupling.

"I love you, all of you," I say as we lay together. "I am so glad we found each other."

"We love you too, Princess," Bastian says, curled up with his head on my chest. "You belong with us and we belong with you."

"Yeah, you're ours," Caleb agrees, a yawn punctuating his words. "And those babies are ours too."

"How do you guys feel about using the name Emily if one of them is a girl?" I ask, nervous about their reaction.

"Are you sure?" Dominic asks gently.

"Yeah, it would be a lovely way to honor her memory and the significance she had in your lives. If there's a boy, I want to name him after your grandfather."

"Jack and Emily," Caleb tests out. "I like the sound of those names together."

"Me too," I agree.

As I relax with the three loves of my life, I can't help basking in the warmth that surrounds me, the feeling that I've finally found where I belong. It took us a while to get here, but I wouldn't change a thing.

READY FOR NEXT *book in the series?* **Get your copy here.**

THIN ICE (PREVIEW)

DESCRIPTION

1 hookup 5 years ago + 1 daughter of the coach + 3 star hockey players = happy ending?

A one night stand five years ago changed my life forever. My sweet daughter Abigail is my life and the reason I advocate for women's rights in the male dominated world of sports.

But when I become the physiotherapist for my dad's hockey team, I don't expect to run into my daughter's baby daddy... and two of his hunky best friends.

Zachary, the goalie, is irresistibly handsome and definitely off-limits.

Lennox is calm and relaxed off the ice, and a menace with skates on his feet.

Justin is the passionate, Casanova playboy of the team.

Only one of them is my baby girl's father...

But all *three* of them want me.

1

LUCY

Thank God. I eased my head left and then right. Muscles that had been bunched and tight for the last hour finally released, and I groaned while massaging the nape of my neck. Daylight forced me to blink when I pushed open the door, and I felt like a zombie waking from the dead until my vision cleared.

The walk from the clinic to my car was a few dozen feet, but it felt like forever before I slid behind the wheel. "If I never have to do a clinical rotation again, it will be too soon." I knew clinicals would be a bitch, but I still wasn't prepared for the sheer number of hours I'd spend locked inside a tiny room listing injuries.

My phone shrilled my dad's tone from my purse, and I fished it out before it rolled over to voicemail. "Hey, Dad."

"Dinner's ready. You want to come over and eat with us?" His smooth voice held out hope I'd say yes.

I nodded and cranked the car. "Let me pick up Abigail. I'll see you in an hour."

"Okay. I'll tell your mom to hold dinner for you." He signed off without a goodbye, but I didn't expect one. Dad's great, but he wasn't the warm and fuzzy type.

I spent the whole drive to Abigail's day care drumming up names for my future physiotherapy clinic. Nothing sounded right. I wanted to convey healing with strength but with that undertone of softness. Pulling up at the day care, I smiled at Abigail's teachers and stepped out to help my daughter into the backseat.

"Hi, Mama." She bounced over to me, her sunshine smile plumping her cheeks.

I scooped her into a hug and tugged off her backpack. "Hey, sweetheart. Did you have a good day?"

"Uh-huh." Abigail's blonde ponytail draped down the back of her neck. "Did you?"

I waited until she'd strapped herself in and I'd gotten behind the wheel again to answer. "It was a good day." I pulled out on the highway and eased toward Dad's. "Listen, sweetie, we're going to stop by Gram and Gramps for dinner, okay?"

"Okay." She played with the straps on her seat and kicked her feet back and forth. "I have homework."

"Really?" I switched between watching her in the mirror and keeping an eye on the road. "What kind of homework?"

Her toes caught on the passenger seat and she pulled them back while humming her favorite song. "It's due tomorrow. It's about my family. Who's my daddy?"

Whoa. My entire body spasmed at the question, and I tightened my grip on the wheel to keep the car on the road. How was I supposed to tell my daughter that I didn't know her daddy? She was the result of a one-night stand in college. A night I don't remember except for a bright red strawberry birthmark on the right side of a muscular neck.

Thankfully, we pulled into my parents' driveway and Abigail forgot all about her assignment. How could I help her finish it without telling her the truth?

"Gramps!" Abigail wiggled in her seat and yanked off the straps holding her in place.

My dad—the head coach of the next up-and-coming professional American Hockey League team—grinned playfully at Abigail and cupped his hands around his eyes while pressing his nose to the glass. He might be a bit short-tempered with his team, and with me, but he loved his granddaughter with every cell in his body. "Abby, are you in there?" He knocked on the glass. "Hello?"

"Gramps, I'm here." My daughter popped up from her seat and pecked on the glass with her little fingers. "I'm right here."

He opened the door and wrapped her up in a bear hug. "Hiya, kiddo." He gave me a quick nod of welcome and turned for the house. "Got something I need to talk to you about, Lucy."

I stiffened automatically and had to force my jaw not to clench. The last time he said those words to me was right after I told him I was pregnant with Abigail. A conversation that had gone over like a blowtorch on ice. We'd put that behind us, but I never quite got over the disappointment I saw on his face that night.

Mom met us at the front door and ushered us all into the kitchen and straight to the old, scratched-up kitchen table I'd done homework on for as long as I could remember.

"How were your clinicals?" Mom wasted no time in passing around plates already filled with food and helping Abigail over to her seat.

I broke open my dinner roll and slathered it with butter. "Not bad. Glad they're over."

"What happens now?" Dad asked while adding salt to his potatoes. "You're still helping out at the women's and teen's advocacy center?"

"Yeah." I shook my head. "It's so sad. Over forty percent of teen girls stop sports because of self-esteem and body image issues." I forced myself to stop there before I delved into the harsh reality of it all. I'd stopped playing hockey at sixteen for those very reasons. It took years for me to understand that my body shape had nothing to do with my ability to play. I was a devil on the ice. Always had been. But I'd quit because of my size and suffered for years before I finally found peace with myself and a body shape that I loved. But I really didn't want to go into all that with my dad. "I found a building that's available for rent. Now that I'm fully licensed, I can open my own clinic."

A look passed between Mom and Dad, the two of them having a whole conversation with a single look. Man, they were good at that.

Dad set his fork aside and dropped his hands to the table. "About that." He gave me a small smile. "I have an offer for you." His smile widened. "I'd like you to consider becoming the team's physiotherapist."

I choked on the bite of roll and slapped a hand over my mouth to keep bits from flying across the table.

Dad waited for me to recover, watching me with that look I'd seen all through my childhood.

"You want me to work with you?" I almost couldn't believe it, but now that we were sitting here, I remembered all the times he'd asked me about my hopes for a future clinic. He knew I was worried that I'd never make it out on my own. Most businesses failed, even those with a degree behind them.

He leaned over the table and laced his fingers together. "It's been on my mind for a while. We could use someone who can check out the guys between games. Makes sense to have someone on staff."

"And if I think they need to be pulled from a game?" I couldn't help asking. "Will you trust me to have both their best interest and the game's outcome as a priority?" I'd never worked with my dad before, but he'd been at enough of my games as a kid and I'd seen enough of his coaching through the years to know he had a *no-holds-barred* mentality. He didn't believe in holding back.

Well, neither did I, especially when it might mean a player's career.

His jaw ticked a couple times, but he nodded slowly. "I'll have questions, and you have to take the player's choices into consideration." He held up one finger. "But if you tell me they need to be pulled from a game, I'll listen."

I took another bite of my roll to give myself time to think.

Dad's grin fell and he turned serious. "Of course, there's no fraternizing with the team members. You'll be considered part of the team. No relationships among team members." He attempted to make it sound like a joke. "Never had a woman on the team before, but I'm trusting you to keep it professional. Especially since you're all the same age."

I laughed at the thought of hooking up with one of his players. "Don't worry, Dad. That won't be a problem." Not only did I have a strict policy about not dating my clients, but I had no interest in dating period. Not when I was on the cusp of a new career and had a daughter to raise. My days were full enough. I didn't need a guy to fulfill any lingering desires.

He nodded and resumed eating. "Good. Meet me at the rink at eight tomorrow morning. I'll introduce you to the team and get things rolling."

~

I shouldn't be nervous. So why did I have to keep wiping my hands on my pants as I crossed the parking lot the next morning? A blast of cold air hit me square in the face when I pulled open the side door and stepped inside. I'd never quite gotten used to the cold that came with ice hockey. It settled in my bones and made me long for hot chocolate, thick gloves, and boots. I'd have to learn to deal with it if I wanted to keep this job. And I did. From the moment Dad mentioned coming here to work, I'd felt drawn to it. I missed hockey. I never felt cold once I stepped on the ice. It was the sitting and watching that put an ache in my joints.

Shaking off the thought of gliding across the ice, I turned toward Dad's office while tapping out a text to him that I was on my way inside.

Concrete walls and a low ceiling made me feel a bit claustrophobic, but I could deal with it.

Seconds later, he stuck his head out from a door down the hallway and waved me closer. "Right on time." He stepped out and closed the door behind him. "Come on. The guys will be on their way out onto the ice. We'll catch them there."

"Great." For some reason, my voice came out high and squeaky. Which was the opposite of great. I cleared my throat and focused. I couldn't let it get to me that I was about to be working with one of the world's leading hockey teams.

Dad led the way down a concrete-walled corridor with gray doors on either side. Man, someone either really loved the muted color or they'd just been too bored to bother choosing different ones. "Your office will be here." He pointed at an open door.

I spotted an examination table and a long row of shelves and cabinets as we hurried past. "Am I expected to be with you during games and practice or should I stay back here?"

"Whichever makes more sense to you." He increased his pace and held a hand overhead. "Lennox, hold up."

A man ahead of me lifted his mask and slapped a hand to the back of the man ahead of him. Brown hair curled around the edges of his helmet, and dark eyes found mine as he looked past my dad. "What's up, Coach?"

With thick pads and helmets, it was hard to get a good look at the team. They all turned to face Dad.

Another man paused. "Are we canceling practice?"

Dad motioned them all to step back into the hallway, and we stopped a few feet from my new office. "We'll start practice in a minute."

The two men ahead of Lennox removed their helmets and I stopped dead in my tracks, my heart kicking hard against my ribs. What the hell was that? The guys were gorgeous and as different as night and day. Though they were both tall and probably muscular—it was hard to tell with the padded uniforms—one had blond hair and light blue eyes while the other had short dark hair and eyes the color of coal.

"Guys, this is my daughter, Lucy. She's going to be your new physiotherapist. It will be her job to help make sure any injuries are treated right away and with the utmost attention to detail. Do not make her life difficult. We're all professionals here, and I expect you to act like it." Dad looked each man in the eye, and they all responded with straightened shoulders and nods of respect.

I'd dealt with a few men from professional teams of varying

sports during my clinicals. A few were assholes, but they'd generally been a good bunch. I expected the best from Dad's team because he demanded respect and gave it to his players in equal measure.

Dad introduced me to the entire team—all twenty players—but their names and faces blurred together after a while.

Except for three men. Lennox with the dark eyes. Justin with the blond hair and playful smile. And Zachary. Zachary in particular held my attention. Something about him struck me as familiar though I couldn't put my finger on which detail stood out to me. They were all gorgeous in their own way, and I found myself almost stuttering over my words when Dad introduced me.

Heat scorched my cheeks and I prayed they'd think it was cold from the ice rink and the frigid air shooting down on us turning my cheeks bright red. I brushed off the lingering attraction and focused. Of course I'd be drawn to the three hot guys in hockey gear. I hadn't had sex in five years. Being in close proximity with a gorgeous guy was bound to get any woman's libido going. I could manage this. No problem. I was here to work and nothing else.

"Thank you for taking time to meet me." I fisted my hands to keep from wiping the sweat on my pants and jerked my head over my shoulder. "I'll be setting up my office in there. Feel free to come by anytime. I'll also be attending all your games and practices. If you have anything you need checked out, don't hesitate to ask."

Some guys would take that as a free pass to make a crude joke, and while I saw a few guys make suggestive faces, they all remained quiet.

Dad clapped his hands. "Alright. Everyone onto the ice. Big game this weekend."

They all filed toward the end of the hallway where an open door gave me a view of the ice rink. The clatter of hockey sticks rang through the air to mix with the good-natured ribbing among the team.

I turned my back on the retreating team and stepped into my new office. It still smelled of paint and drywall dust, but I didn't care. I had my very own office. A squeal of excitement tightened in my throat.

Footsteps sounded behind me and I whirled around. Justin stopped in the open doorway and leaned his shoulder on the frame. His heavy pads made him look bulky, but the slight grin teasing his lips drew my attention.

I licked my lips and he followed the action with a smoldering look that caused heat to pool low in my belly. "Can I help you?"

"Oh, I hope so." He took a step into the room, coming close enough that I caught the flecks of gold in his blue eyes.

Holy hell the guy was hot enough to make me catch fire with nothing more than a look.

"Justin, right?" I forced my legs to move and walked over to the examination table. "What can I do for you?"

He followed behind me, his presence lifting the hairs on the back of my neck and sending jolts of awareness down my spine. "I think I pulled a muscle. Could you check it for me?"

2

LUCY

Bullshit. The word lingered on the edge of my tongue, and I bit my inner cheek to keep from saying it out loud. I couldn't risk making a fool of myself on the first day, but something about the guy's cocky smile told me that he had another muscle group in mind.

I was ninety percent certain he was full of shit, but I waved for him to come on in. "You're going to have to remove your pads."

He yanked off the outer layer of his uniform so fast he could have been a professional stripper. Oh, wait. They were all about the slow tease. So, what did that make this guy?

His blond hair stood up in short spikes that would be flattened once he wore his helmet for more than five minutes, but the jagged look suited him. As did the cocky demeanor radiating off him. He strolled over to the exam table, and I'll be damned if he didn't have a slight limp every time he moved his right leg.

"I need you to fill these out." I grabbed a stack of forms and shoved the clipboard at him.

He smirked while writing. "I was going to stop by your dad's office on my way out of practice and find out what I was supposed to do. Then he goes and brings you on board." He lifted his head and gave me a long once over that for some reason didn't feel as creepy as it should. If anything, it made my pulse beat faster. This one was trouble. "Must be my lucky day."

I crossed my arms and leaned a hip against the cold countertop. My new digs were brighter than the mundane gray outside, but the beige walls and white countertops could still use some color. I'd see what I could do about bringing in some paintings to liven up the place. He handed the clipboard back to me. "I think it's everyone's lucky day, Justin." I met his smirking grin with one of my own. I knew how to deal with guys like him. He'd flirt and maybe ask for my number. But he'd never take anything seriously. Guys like him never did.

I didn't like judging him after a two-minute interaction, but everything about this guy screamed *player*.

"What's the problem?" I rubbed my hands together to make sure they wouldn't shock him with cold and narrowed my focus on his leg.

His smirking grin fell and he stretched out his leg. "Most likely a hamstring strain." My eyebrows shot up and he laughed. "I've had them before, so I know what they feel like. There's a tight sensation here." He pinched the back of his leg, right over the hamstring.

"Scoot back onto the table and lift your leg." I didn't touch him yet. Wouldn't if I could keep from it, but I had to once it came time to perform the range of motion test and to be able to properly document my findings.

Damn. He had fine muscle tone.

"Need me to take my pants off?" The smirk returned.

I lifted his leg and tested his range of motion. "Do you want to stay on the team?"

"Yes. What does that have to do with it?" His hiss of pain sliced the air.

I winced for him. "Sorry. But you heard my dad. No fraternizing." I lowered his leg to the table and stepped back. "I'm happy to report you can keep your pants on."

"You're a smart ass." He propped up on his elbows. "I like it."

"Yeah, well, don't think it makes you special. I'm a smart ass to everyone." It wasn't a complete lie. I usually tried to be more professional, but Justin made it easy to loosen up. "And you're also right about the strain. You remember what to do?"

"RICE." Justin swung his legs over the edge of the table. "Rest. Ice. Compression. Elevation. Got it, doc."

"And come see me again if it gets worse. An MRI might be in order to make sure you haven't torn it." I scribbled the diagnosis on his paperwork and looked at him through lowered lashes. "You should probably take a few days off skating."

He started shaking his head before I even finished speaking. "No way. Big game this weekend. I can't miss it."

I'd expected that response. "You know what happens if you ignore an injury." I said it as more of a threat than anything. Hockey players were notorious for skating through injuries. I once played a whole game with a broken nose because I couldn't bear the idea of disappointing my teammates.

Justin slid from the table, the move bringing us face-to-face. And damn it all if I didn't want to kiss him right then. It made no sense, except that I hadn't gotten laid in almost six years and the raw masculinity mixed with Justin's devil-may-care attitude made him far too attractive. I wasn't about to break my dad's rules. Not even for what I was sure would be a scorching hot kiss that might have the potential for more.

The disappointment wouldn't be worth it. Before I could recover enough to step back, Zachary and Lennox slammed the door open and burst over the threshold.

"Geez, man, what's taking so long?" Lennox smacked his helmet against his palm. "We need to run drills." His long hair feathered around his face and he scraped it back with a frustrated huff.

Zachary scuffed his knuckles over his cheek after setting his helmet back on the crown of his head.

"Oh, you know." Justin winked at me and stretched one arm past me to grab his gear. His breath whispered over my cheek, eliciting a rush of goosebumps. "Just falling in love with the doc."

"Cut the shit." Zachary scowled and knocked on the doorframe.

"Stop hitting on Coach's daughter. We all know she's out of your league."

The compliment combined with his sour tone twisted my stomach and caused a sour taste in the back of my throat. I stepped back and to the side, opening up the space between me and Justin.

He made a noise in the back of his throat that might have been disappointment, but he pulled on his gear and stomped over to Zachary and Lennox.

The reality of Zachary's words punched straight to my heart. I wasn't looking for a relationship, but having the possibility ripped away from me hurt more than I anticipated. I pushed all the hurt away and focused. "He needs to watch that leg. Maybe let him take it easy out there today." I lifted my eyebrows and met all three men's gazes head-on. I would not allow my burst of attraction for them to impede my work. I couldn't risk losing what little ground I'd gained by taking on this position.

Besides, a relationship would interfere with my goals. I wasn't about to give up my hopes and dreams for a quick and dirty tumble.

Lennox hooked Justin's arm and hauled him toward the hallway. "We'll take care of him." His dark eyes blazed when he looked back at me over his shoulder. "Thanks for seeing him."

"It's what I'm here for." I shrugged like it didn't matter, even though it did. Very much. I needed these guys to trust me with their injuries. They didn't have to find me attractive. That would hurt more than it helped in this situation. But they did need to respect me as a medical professional and someone who could help them.

The three of them filed out of my office and thumped down the hall, the sound of their hockey sticks rattling along the way. I shook my head to clear it of any lingering hormones and wiped down the exam table with an antiseptic towel before pulling fresh paper over the edge and tucking it in.

My phone buzzed from my pocket and I pulled it out far enough to check the screen. The sight of Abigail's preschool number caused my heart to stampede and I answered with a breathless "Hello?"

"Miss Ashley, this is Mrs. Perkins. I'm calling to inform you that

Abigail took a little spill at school today." The woman's calm voice did nothing to ease my panic.

"What happened? Is she okay?" I glanced around the room to make sure I wasn't forgetting anything, then remembered all I'd brought in was my phone and keys.

Mrs. Perkins took a deep breath. "She seems fine, but we would like for her to see a doctor."

"What happened?" I repeated.

"It seems she fell off the swing while out on the playground. She's up and playing but has complained of a headache, and there is some swelling."

Oh God. My hand trembled on the phone. Not Abigail. Not my baby. I couldn't stand for anything to happen to her. She might have been unplanned and a complete shock, but I loved that girl with every bit of my heart. "I'll be right there."

"Thank you. We look forward to seeing you. I'll make sure Abigail is ready to go when you arrive."

I hung up the phone before I said something I'd regret. Abigail's school was fantastic. We hadn't had any problems all year. But I knew that if I kept listening to her talk then I'd go apeshit. It was better for both of us if I ended the call and used the drive over to calm down.

Sucking in a deep breath and closing my eyes while I let it out slowly, I lowered my shoulders. "She's okay. It's a minor bump. Outward swelling is good. It means the trauma hasn't gone inward." I imagined a lump and potential bruise on my baby girl's face and all the breathing in the world couldn't calm the storm spinning out of control. Stuffing my phone in my pocket, I rushed out of the office and hurried down the hallway.

Dad would be in his office for the first hour of practice. He always finished up business calls while the team warmed up. He'd join them on the ice later. I had to tell him that I was leaving early. Not my best moment on my first day, but it couldn't be helped. Thankfully, I knew he wouldn't mind. Dad might be a hard ass, but he would do anything for Abigail. I'd have to fight him to keep him from meeting me at the doctor's office. Hell, he'd be more upset about the fall than me. Nothing bothered him more than his granddaughter's tears.

My sneakers squeaked on the harsh concrete until I stopped outside Dad's door. His voice filtered out as I raised my fist to knock. "Listen, I know it's a rough start to the season, but this kid has promise."

My ears perked up at his serious voice. The one Abigail called his fussy man tone.

"I'm not saying I will trade him. I'm saying the option is on the table. Zachary has proven himself as a top-notch goalie. You won't be sorry to have him play for you."

This was the part of the business I didn't like, players getting traded around and talked about behind their backs. Zachary would get a say, of course, but he wouldn't know until the last minute that his name was getting thrown around.

I knocked and waited for Dad to call out before I twisted the knob and entered. His office was a shrine to his job. Posters of his best players lined the walls and trophies filled the shelves. He sat behind a cluttered desk with his phone to his ear and his feet propped up on top of a stack of folders. He ended the call and waved for me to come closer.

Poor Zachary. The guy deserved to know he was up on the chopping block, but I wasn't about to be the one to tell him.

End of preview. Get the full story here.

ABOUT THE AUTHOR

Check out my entire catalogue available on KindleUnlimited.

The Forbidden Reverse Harem Collection

Boss Daddies | Good Girl | A Nanny for Christmas | Brother's Best Friends for Christmas | Christmas with Daddy's Best Friends | Lie No More | Thin Ice

The Bratva

Season of Malice | Season of Desire | Season of Wrath

Sinister Alliances

Unlikely Protector | Unlikely Avenger

Printed in Great Britain
by Amazon